Finding Air

By K. D. Smith

Copyright © 2014 K. D. Smith

This is a work of fiction. Names, characters, businesses, places, events and incidents are either the products of the author's imagination or used in a fictitious manner. Any resemblance to actual persons, living or dead, or actual events is purely coincidental.

Published by K. D. Smith

Cover design by K. D. Smith

ISBN-13: 978-0692278895

ISBN-10: 0692278893

www.KDSmithAuthor.com

Chapter 1

Josie

I looked down at Freddy as we were running. He looked as miserable as I felt. Freddy is my German Shepherd. He isn't always thrilled about running either.

"Just a few more minutes buddy, then we can stop and get a drink," I promised him. His eyes shot to mine when he heard the word *drink*. He knew that meant we were close to the walking part of our morning routine.

We always run to the coffee shop a couple miles away from the house, get a drink and then walk back home. Like Freddy, the second part of the routine is my favorite. I look forward to sipping my coffee on the way home. Freddy looks forward to getting spoiled by Rick, the owner of *Cool Beans*.

Rick is one of my neighbors, and a good friend. I don't usually have male friends, but I figured out fairly quickly that Rick is harmless, he is also incredibly gay. He and his partner Eddie are two of the few people I truly enjoy spending time with. Freddy adores Rick, and the feeling is mutual. Rick was leery of my dog when we first met, but in true Freddy fashion, he won Rick over in no time. After several runs to the coffee shop with treats always on hand, Freddy and Rick became fast friends.

Rick always gives Freddy a big bowl of water and a couple of dog biscuits when we arrive. I think it's sweet, and once I even tried to pay Rick back for the treats he bought for Freddy, but he wouldn't hear of it. See? A nice guy. There really are some out there. They're probably all gay though.

As we rounded the corner leading to the coffee shop I looked down to make sure Freddy was hanging in there, and I ran straight into a hard flat chest that belonged to one really big man.

Oh shit.

I looked up at the man and took in his appearance quickly while he reached out to steady me. He had dark hair that was cut short, but looked as if it was growing out and needed to be cut again. His eyes were blue, but not just any blue, a deep blue, almost an indigo blue. Wow.

Freddy let out a low warning growl. The man removed his hands from my shoulders and looked at me with a gaze I didn't quite understand. It made me nervous and I automatically took a step back.

"I'm so sorry," I said sounding a little too out of breath. "I didn't see you there. It's okay Freddy," I said softly patting his head to let him see I wasn't in danger, although I felt the panic starting to rise, I was fairly certain that this was an accident and not a threat.

He kept giving me that look, whatever it was, and started to talk. I looked up at his lips and noticed how nice they were. Full and defined, surrounded by his five o'clock shadow. He had a very rugged look about him. He had to be over six feet tall. He wore gray cut off sweats that covered his thighs and a black sleeveless t-shirt that was stretched tight across his muscular arms and chest. I noticed he was also drenched in sweat. He must be a fellow runner.

"...can you hear me?" He said looking like he thought I might have some sort of disability.

Oh great. The first man I've found attractive in the last two and a half years and he thinks I can't hear.

"Yes, sorry, what did you say?" God. I'm such a nerd.

"I asked if you were okay." His eyes were still narrowed on me like he wasn't sure I understood.

"Yes, um, I'm okay. Sorry, I was just surprised and a little startled," I said as my cheeks started to burn. Go figure. I was blushing. Great.

As if it wasn't bad enough that I was sweating, and my hair was no doubt a frizzy mess even though it was tied back in a ponytail.

I had on my running shorts and an old t-shirt that said *chicks rule* across the chest with a picture of a little baby chick under it.

"Well, I'm just glad your dog didn't eat me for breakfast." He smiled. Oh my. He was ten times better looking when he smiled. Shit! I need to get out of here.

"Freddy wouldn't eat you unless you gave him good reason," I reassured, somehow feeling the need to make sure he didn't think my dog was the Cujo type.

I looked down at Freddy. He gave me an annoyed huff. He knew we were close to the coffee shop where his treats and water bowl were waiting. I kept patting his head. I think if it's possible for dogs to roll their eyes, he just did it at me. And here I was trying to defend him.

"Your dog's name is Freddy?" he asked looking a little amused.

Now this was hard to explain. There is a reason behind the name. I thought it was a great name, but it was too long of a story to tell while I was standing here sweating with a baby chick on my shirt, and it was personal. It's never good to share personal details.

"Yes," I said, knowing I looked even more uncomfortable than before.

He looked like he was waiting for me to explain but I wasn't about to do that because I would no doubt sound like an idiot.

"Um, we better go," I mumbled, trying to avoid his eyes. "Freddy needs a drink."

"I was just going to grab a coffee, would you and Freddy like to join me?" he asked.

Oh. My. God.

This is not happening. I have avoided men for so long that I didn't even know how to respond to that question. I stood there fidgeting with the leash trying to think of a polite but firm way to decline.

I avoid situations like this on purpose.

I considered it for a minute knowing I would never accept. This man seems nice, but they all do at first, don't they? They just don't stay that way, I reminded myself.

He's certainly a ten on the hotness scale, but that just made him more intimidating. His eyes were too intense. He was too large, and not just physically. He had a presence that was overpowering. He held himself in a way that exuded confidence, like he was completely comfortable with himself. It made me wonder what he did for a living.

I realized it didn't matter, and he was watching me waiting patiently for an answer. I decided to do what I normally did. Fake it.

I put on my best fake professional smile, the one that says *I am not afraid, I can handle this, I am a strong independent woman,* and said, "No thanks, we just have to stop in for a minute and then we have to get home. Sorry about running into you." With that, I turned, pulled Freddy's leash and quickly got inside the coffee shop.

Chapter 2

Gunner

As it turns out, it wasn't too much trouble to find Josephine Elizabeth Black. She obviously doesn't know who I am, but I remember her. She went to school with my little sister Summer.

I knew who she was as soon as I heard the name. She'd always been a pretty little thing, even if she was a little too shy and quiet. If I didn't already know who she was and where she went to school it would have taken me longer to find her.

It was as if she wanted to stay invisible. I hadn't been able to find an address for her or a listed telephone number. She also didn't have a bank account in her name.

I would have found her eventually though, that's what I do, and I'm good at it. Grand Rapids is a large city with a lot of rural area around it, sometimes people take a while to turn up. Luckily, all I had to do was make some phone calls to the right people and because we all went to the same high school nobody even asked why I was looking for her. Then again, most people don't question me.

I needed to get a read on what was going on with her. Unfortunately, Josie didn't leave much of a trail. People who are careful not to leave a trail usually have a reason they don't want to be found. In my experience, the reason is usually bad.

I know that Faith Snyder is her best friend and has been since childhood. Since Faith is well known and well-liked by almost everyone, I was willing to bet that Josie's reasons were not the usual type of bad. Maybe.

From what I learned, she moved to Detroit for a job 3 years ago after graduating college. It didn't last long. She's been back in the area for about two and a half years now. Nobody knew why she came back so hastily, and most people hadn't seen her around much, except to know that she and Faith were usually together.

I really wasn't planning on getting a coffee, but I was hoping she would take me up on my offer so I could try to figure some things out about her. I wanted to know why she left Detroit so quickly. Not to mention why she seemed to be hiding out.

I was surprised to get a call from a Detroit man two days ago named Brian Hanson. He was her former boss. Apparently he's been looking for Josie and figured she was back in this area. According to him, he wants to find her because she stole some money from him while on the job.

When I asked why he didn't involve the police, he said that he wanted to find her first so he could talk to her before turning her in. He said he would go easy on her if she admitted what she'd done. None of that made any sense to me. Something about the whole thing sounded off.

I agreed to look into it out of curiosity more than anything else. Red flags started going up when I couldn't find a bank account in her name, or any other information that was normally accessible if you knew where to look.

Today I decided to run into her and see if I could engage her. I can usually get a read on people by observing them. Definitely by having a conversation. Most people are sickeningly obvious.

It's clear she's hiding something, but she sure as hell doesn't look or act like a thief. If she is, she's a cute one. The way she blushed just talking to me made me think there was no way she could be capable of pulling off something like embezzlement. Then again, you'd be surprised what people are capable of. Most people will disappoint the hell out of you every time.

She appeared quiet and shy like I remembered, but now I picked up on something else. She's skittish for some reason, and what is up with the guard dog? Freddy. Who the hell names a big German Shepherd Freddy? I guess

Josie does, but hell if I know why she looked so serious when I asked her about it.

Just when I thought I had her pegged as the shy, quiet, good girl type, she pulled out the fake smile for me with a little attitude behind it. Maybe she's a bad girl with a really good act going. For some reason I felt compelled to find the truth.

I walk into the coffee shop and get in line behind her. There are several people separating us now because she took off so quickly, obviously uncomfortable enough to want to get away from me.

I take her in from behind, starting with her running shoes. They are well worn, she obviously runs frequently. She has slim ankles peeking out over her socks, and muscular calves and thighs. Not too muscular, but I can tell she tries to stay fit.

Damn, she has a nice ass. The spandex running shorts cling to her curves as I scan my eyes across the swell of her hips. I'd like to run behind her and watch that ass wiggle for a while, or I'd like to run in front of her so I could turn around and watch her from that angle too. No doubt it would be quite a show.

She may be wearing an old, ratty t-shirt, but what was underneath looked luscious. She was short, but she had great curves in all the right places.

Okay, I better quit thinking about her tits and ass before she turns around and sees me with a hard on. She'd probably sic that damn dog on me for being such a pervert.

Her long brown hair was pulled back into a ponytail with little wisps escaping at the sides of her face. While she was studying me on the street I noticed her face was free of make-up and she had a natural beauty. Her eyes were a mix of green and brown. Everything about her made me more interested.

The guy behind the counter looked up and saw her, he smiled in a happy, familiar way. For some reason that immediately put me on edge. Especially when she smiled back and blew him a kiss.

"JoJo! Freddy! I'll get his bowl and your coffee, be right out!" the dude yelled to her. He was practically hopping with excitement and waving a very loose hand at her. I smiled. Guess I didn't have competition after all.

I decided I was going to get to know Josie Black one way or another. She doesn't seem like the party girls I usually play with for fun. Christ knows I've had enough of them to last me a lifetime. Always the same games and manipulation when dealing with that type. The games became boring, not to mention annoying.

Josie seemed different, but for all I know she could be a thief and a naughty girl underneath her pretty blushing cheeks and shy behavior.

Somehow I doubted it, but one thing's for sure, she's a puzzle I'm going to enjoy solving.

Chapter 3

Josie

I turned to go out to the sidewalk sitting area and saw him waiting in line. He smiled like he was still amused which I found both annoying and sexy, so I pretended like I didn't see him and kept walking.

He made me extremely nervous and turned on at the same time. Not a good combination. I haven't been turned on in years. I don't want to be turned on. For crying out loud, he only touched my shoulders and I swear I can still feel his hands on me. I've never felt anything like it before.

It's not like I'm a total novice. I used to date. I've had boyfriends before. Granted, I don't have a lot of experience, but I've never had this kind of reaction to a man before. Everything about him makes me tense.

The way he watched me like he was trying to figure me out made me uneasy. I don't need any help being nervous, I'm nervous enough when everything is normal.

This guy would make a great fantasy, but in reality I know I should get away from him. I don't like anything that brings my anxiety level up. He certainly brings a lot of things up, I thought to myself as those blue eyes passed through my mind again. Damn.

I closed my eyes for a second trying to clear the vision from my head as I sat at one of the patio tables. Freddy flopped down at my feet panting, waiting for his water. I started to fidget, my foot bouncing up and down as I waited.

Get it together Josie, I told myself. He's just some guy you bumped into on the street, he only offered you a coffee because he felt bad. Nothing more. Nothing I can't handle. Right.

As I gave myself a pep talk Rick came out and gave Freddy his water and treats. He bent and rubbed his ears while talking to him like a baby. Freddy ate that shit up. Big, bad guard dog. Sure. He loved it when someone babied and pampered him.

I would probably love getting that much affection too, I thought, as If *that* would ever happen. A girl can dream, right? In my dreams I'm not a neurotic, damaged mess. In my dreams I can have someone that close, someone I feel safe with, someone I can trust. Dreams are sometimes dangerous things. I know that for a fact.

"So what's shakin' JoJolicious?" Rick asked in his usual carefree tone.

14

He comes up with all kinds of weird names for stuff. That's just his personality and he's one of the few people who can make me forget my troubles and laugh for a while. I love that about him.

I smiled at him, trying to forget my depressing thoughts of affection. "Nothing much, just out for our morning fix," I told him as I took a sip of the coffee he sat down in front of me. Delicious.

"Mmmhmmm, and who was Mr. Muscles in there checking out your ass?" he said as he crossed his arms over his chest and stuck his hip out.

Rick doesn't miss much, but surely he must be mistaken. There's no way Mr. Indigo was checking out my ass. Was he?

"If you're talking about the guy in the sweats, he's just someone I ran into, literally," I explained. "And I'm pretty sure he wasn't checking out my ass. He's way too hot for that, and there are way better asses to look at."

"Here we go with that again," he sighed. "I've told you a million times girl, you're *hawt*!" He made a little sizzle noise and stuck his finger out.

Yes, this happens frequently. Rick trying to convince me that I am too attractive to sit at home and not go on dates. Whatever.

I rolled my eyes. "Not quite. And you don't get to judge female hotness. Only male hotness," I shot back at him with a little bit of my fake attitude.

"Oh honey, I judge all hotness. I may prefer one over the other, but I can still judge."

"If you say so," I laughed. "Besides, he thinks I have a disability."

"What? Why on Earth would he think that?" Rick said as he looked at his skinny reflection in the front window. He smoothed his blond hair and fixed the collar of his polo shirt. It would have been a good look for him, but the pink shirt was paired with lime green pants. *Bright* lime green pants. I know better than to judge appearance, so I kept my mouth shut even though the pants were ridiculous.

Rick and his partner Eddie are complete opposites. Eddie is quiet and tough looking. He doesn't have a large, boisterous personality like Rick. Somehow they fit together perfectly.

I sighed, "Because he was trying to talk to me and I was so busy looking at his blue eyes and luscious lips that apparently I didn't hear a word he said." Geez, I felt myself blushing again just admitting it. *Such* a dork.

"Ohhh, now this is something new!" Rick clapped his hands together quickly a few times. "I've never seen you hot after a guy! You usually don't give anyone a second glance!"

He was saying all of this excitedly, like he just discovered the fountain of youth. It was over the top. It was Rick. I was used to it and somehow his crazy antics always made me feel more at ease.

"Yeah, well, I couldn't help it, he startled me when we ran into each other and I just kind of froze," I said with a bit of shame.

Truthfully, I hate that I had that reaction. I thought I had acquired better skills. I worked hard over the past couple of years to overcome my fears and ensure that I would never freeze in a dangerous situation again. I guess I still have more work to do.

I would like to think if it had been anyone else's body running into mine, I wouldn't have froze up that way. It's this guy, there's something about him that made my brain malfunction when he was too close.

Yes, it was definitely his fault. His eyes. His sweaty muscles. His lips. They're all at fault, I decided.

"Honey, who wouldn't freeze if they ran into that sexy beast?" Rick asked. "I mean, I might have pulled a Freddy and drooled on him if he ran into..." his eyes got big as he paused, "Oh shit, girl, brace yourself, here he comes." He whispered loudly enough for everyone at the nearby tables to hear.

Oh crap. I looked up to see Mr. Indigo heading our way. *Eeek!* He was so beautiful. I envied his confident stride. He didn't look like he would be scared of anything.

He locked those gorgeous eyes on me again like I was some kind of mystery. I wanted to say, *sorry pal, you aren't missing anything special here, just move along.* Of course I didn't, instead I stared at him like an idiot.

"Hey, are you sure you don't want to share a table while we drink our coffee?" He asked again. "It looks like you're going to stay a while after all." He gave me a smirk like he knew I was lying all along. Shit. My foot was bouncing. I knew I should have left sooner.

"Actually I'm on my way out," I said putting on my fake smile and hoping he wasn't going to push it. "I need to get some work done, but thanks anyway. Nice, um, running into you."

Oh god. I did *NOT* just say that.

"Work shmork," Rick waved his hand. "You set your own schedule, you have time to talk to this hunky man here." He said like he was someone's grandmother, then started to pull out a chair, but I shot him a glare. He would pay for that later.

I stood up quickly. This guy was making me crazier than my normal crazy. I didn't feel like I could catch my breath, it was coming too fast. I tried to calm it without making it noticeable.

In. Out. In. Out. I can handle this.

"I have a conference call this morning that I can't be late for," I lied while taking my slow purposeful breaths.

"I'll see you later, Rick." I said as loudly as I could, but it came out quiet and squeaky. Damn. I gathered my coffee with shaky fingers along with Freddy's leash and started to leave.

"Are you okay honey?" Rick asked me with a look of concern on his face.

He knew that I had panic attacks sometimes, although he had never pushed me on the issue. I looked at him and wanted to be angry at him for trying to instigate things with Mr. Indigo, but I couldn't be when I saw his worried face.

"Yes, fine," I nodded my head a little too quickly and tried to give a reassuring smile. "Just need to get going. Thanks."

Rick gave me a warm smile and said, "Anytime, JoJo."

I knew he meant it, just as he knew I meant my thanks to be for more than coffee.

I lifted my free hand in a small wave and turned leading Freddy towards home. I fought the urge to look back. I knew Mr. Indigo was watching me.

K. D. Smith

Chapter 4

Josie

By the time we arrived back home I was feeling better. I spent the walk back reminding myself of how far I've come. I may have had a minor freak out today, but considering all of the freaking out I had done in my life, that was mild. I handled it, walked away, and talked myself down. That was proof that I was doing well.

I was doing what I was supposed to do. I was putting one foot in front of the other and living my life. I may be a bit neurotic, I may never be able to have a normal relationship again, but I was alive. I was functioning, and most days, I was happy with that.

When I walked into the house, Faith was in her room getting ready for work. I walked in, sat down on her bed and watched her apply her mascara. She always looks so put together. She wore a flirty flared skirt with a sleeveless blouse. Her blonde hair curled around her face.

Faith worked as a secretary at one of the publishing companies downtown. She always wears the cutest outfits. I, on the other hand, work from home, and spend most of the year in yoga pants. That's fine by me. I prefer the solitude and anonymity of not dealing with a lot of people face to face.

Michigan can be a cold place. The weather is usually unpredictable. It's summer now, and even though the summers are short, they can get incredibly hot and humid. During the hot months I mostly wear shorts and tank tops. Every now and then I wear one of my sundresses to help stay cool, but nothing I wear ever looks as good as Faith.

I don't mind that. She's a beautiful person inside and out. She's been my best friend and soul sister for as long as I can remember. We met in grade school. I was a child with a doting father and a mother who hated that my father showed me any kind of attention or affection. I was shy and had a hard time making friends.

Faith, on the other hand, was talkative and bubbly. She drew me in. I was surprised to learn that Faith was in foster care at the time. I didn't even really understand what that meant back then, except I knew that she didn't live with her parents. It was a miracle to me that she never seemed to be down. She always had a smile for everybody.

"What's up?" she asked, giving me the eyebrow. "You look a little red. Did Freddy give you a run for your money this morning?"

"No, Freddy was as ambitious as always," I told her looking over at him while he was stretching out on the rug for a nap. "It was the man I ran into while we were running, and by that, I mean literally, ran *right* into him," I declared softly smacking my hands together as an illustration.

She was starting to get that concerned look on her face. I hate that look, so I keep talking. "It was just an accident, but he asked me to have coffee with him. Of course I said no, but there's just something about him. He kept looking at me in a strange way, and he was so gorgeous. I mean seriously, off the charts hot. He made me so nervous I forgot how to talk," I told her with no shame because she knew me well enough to understand.

"Wait, back up," she said. "So you ran into this guy who's so hot you can't talk, and he asks you to join him for coffee, and you say NO?" She's looking at me like I'm crazy. "Josie, this is the first guy I've heard you say anything like that about in over 2 years!"

"I know, I know," I sigh.

"Girl, it is about time! You know, your birthday is in a few days and we're going out. This is a breakthrough, we must celebrate. We'll take Rick and Eddie with us, maybe Justine too.

I'm not listening to any excuses this time. It's time for you to get out there."

"Ugh, Faith, I don't want to go out. I can't..." I start to explain why I can't possibly go, but she interrupts me by putting her mascara down, putting her hands up and saying, "No way Black, you are *not* getting out of this. We are celebrating your birthday. It is way past time for you to get in the game."

"Believe me *Snyder*," I say referring to her by her last name as well. "I would like to be in the game. I just haven't found the right person yet."

It's true. I would like to meet a man. Learn to have hot, passionate, satisfying sex. Forget all of my troubles, and just lose myself in a few wild moments. I just don't know if I can ever really do that. I'm pretty sure I will never have a normal relationship again. I still hope that I can at least have sex someday.

"Well, we're going to fix that. We're going out, and we're going to find you someone to play with," she smiles and wiggles her eyebrows at me. "It's like riding a horse Josie, I know it's scary as shit the first time you get back on, but once you do it, you'll see that it *is* possible for you to enjoy yourself and have a sex life again."

"I don't know if I'm ready for that," I tell her, "but okay, I'll go out with you. Just please promise me that you aren't going to push anything."

She looks offended, "You know I would never push anything that isn't good for you. If it doesn't feel right, then no big deal, at least let's go out and have some fun for once. You stay home so much that I worry about you."

"I know, but I'm really doing okay," I tell her. For some reason I feel the need to defend myself. "I was thinking on the way home about how far I've come. I mean, I'm working and I have some steady clients now, I'm training twice a week at the gym, I'm seeing Dr. Palmer every week. I have Freddy, and we run every morning. I know it doesn't seem like a lot, but I feel like I've worked really hard to get to this point."

"I know you have," she said sincerely, "You're doing great JoJo. It's just sometimes you're wound so tight, I'm afraid you're never going to relax and have fun again. You're so precise about everything. Everything is scheduled, planned, overthought to excess."

Well, just tell me how you really feel Faith, geez. I know she's saying these things because she truly cares, but I'm trying not to feel hurt by her words. "I know," I whisper. Because I do know. I know I'm different now. I think about how care-free I used to be and almost cringe at how naïve I was.

She might be right, but I'm not going to tell her that. I know she loves me and wants me to be happy. What she doesn't understand is that if I allow myself to unwind and let go, I might just never be able to get myself back together again. I'm afraid all the pieces will scatter away and I won't be able to get them back. I'll be lost again.

"Please don't think I'm criticizing you. I understand how hard it's been, and I know you've been working like crazy to get your life back." She paused like she wanted to say more, but couldn't figure out how to say it. I know her so well, I could almost see the wheels turning in there.

"Just spit it out," I said. "You've already told me that I walk around like there's a stick up my ass, how much worse can it be?" I joked.

"Well, okay...just promise you'll hear me out."

Oh hell. This didn't sound good. I nodded so she knew that I was agreeing even though I didn't want to.

"I know a big part of the reason you're always on edge is because you're worried that he's going to come after you. I think you should have him checked out. See what he's up to. I truly believe you're safe now, it's been over two years. I think if you have someone look into him, you will finally start to feel a little more at ease," she said gently.

The thought made my stomach turn. The truth is, I did have a reason to think he would come after me. Just thinking about this was making me sweat.

If he found out that I was messing with him from afar, then he would definitely come after me. He couldn't know though. I'd been so careful.

Maybe Faith's right. If I have someone look into him then maybe I'll know if he has anything figured out or if he's looking for me. Maybe I can relax a little.

I know I'm playing with fire, but damn it, that asshole deserved a little bit of retribution.

"You mean hire a private detective?" I asked still mulling it over.

"Yes. Do you remember Summer Layne? She was in our tenth grade English class. Anyway, she moved away, but one of her brothers is a P.I. He has an office downtown," she informed me.

"I remember her, but wait, wasn't her brother the one that you…"

"NO! Different brother. It doesn't have anything to do with him." She said and looked away quickly. There was something that happened between her and one of those Layne boys, but she didn't like to talk about it. From what I know I think she had feelings for him, and he didn't reciprocate.

"It's just someone local we know that could probably do the job and help you out. Here," she handed me a piece of paper. "I wrote down the number to his office. Just think about it, okay? I really have to get going or I'll be late for work."

I took the paper from her. "I'll think about it," I promised since she already put the idea in my head and I won't be able to help thinking about it anyway. "I'll see you tonight." I said giving her a hug and then heading to the shower.

Do I really want to do this? I don't even know how much something like this will cost. I made enough money to get by now that I had some steady clients. Nothing like before when I was head of the IT department for a motor company in Detroit, but I suppose I can set up a meeting and find out the expense. If I can't afford it, I just won't do it.

Then I wondered how much background I would have to explain to a P.I.

Bad idea.

I need to stop thinking about all of this. I haven't even started the work day and already I ran into the hot guy, freaked out because for the first time in two years I wanted to kiss someone, agreed to go out on my birthday, and possibly hire a private investigator.

Holy shit. I hope the rest of the day is normal and boring. I like normal and boring.

I'm accustomed to sticking to my typical routine. Not shaking things up too much. Not giving myself any reason to get more uncomfortable than necessary. I closed my eyes and prayed that I wasn't about to make a huge mistake.

K. D. Smith

Chapter 5

Gunner

Imagine my surprise when I open up my calendar on the computer for the next day and find an appointment with Josie Black. I pick up the phone and tell Marina, the receptionist, that I need to speak with her.

I wonder why Josie would have made an appointment. I was certain that she didn't know who I was yesterday when I ran into her. Now she's making an appointment at my office?

I briefly consider letting one of the other guys take the appointment so she won't put two and two together, but I decide against it. There is something strange going on with this case, I can feel it.

First, I felt an off vibe with Brian Hanson who wants me to locate her, then when I found her I sensed something strange from her. I am still willing to bet that she isn't a thief, but maybe that's why she's so nervous and why she seems to be hiding out.

I planned to find a way to talk to her again anyway, this is going to work out better than I thought. She's coming to me. I'm not sure what kind of work she needs done, but maybe it's something that will explain the embezzling claim.

Normally, I wouldn't go out of my way to try to figure something like this out. I get hired to do a job and I do it. I don't have time for getting overly involved in the bullshit of digging up more than is necessary to complete the job. If it were anyone but Josie, I wouldn't be going above and beyond. I would find her, turn her over, and collect the check. End of story. For some reason my gut was telling me not to jump the gun.

Marina opened the door and stuck her head in saying "What's up boss?"

Marina is great at her job and I appreciate the fact that she is comfortable being the only female I have on staff. She can handle the intensity that comes with the territory. She didn't even blink an eye when testosterone levels started going off like fireworks, which happens often.

She sure as hell didn't look like a guy, but she fit in like one of them. I don't know what I would do without her keeping track of everything for me. People can think what they want about her appearance, I don't give a shit.

"I noticed I have an appointment scheduled with Josie Black today," I say giving her a look that told her I wanted her to explain.

She didn't need me to say more, I loved that about her, she just picked up on it and said "Yep, she called yesterday afternoon. Said a friend gave her our name and number and she was interested in possibly hiring a Private Detective. Something about checking into someone. She seemed a little guarded about giving any information on the phone so I didn't ask a lot of questions. That's all I know, besides that the person she wants checked out isn't local."

Well, this just keeps getting better. I wonder if the person she wants checked out is the same person who happens to be looking for her. Now I'm even more suspicious. Maybe Josie and had a sexual relationship with her boss in the past. The thought makes my jaw clench.

That guy sounded like an arrogant asshole on the phone. I hope this isn't some kind of lover's quarrel I'm about to get involved in. That's the last fuckin' thing I need.

She doesn't seem the type to hook up with her employer. The guy has money though, sometimes that's all it takes. And on that thought, I decide to let it go because I don't like the idea that Josie is one of those women.

"Thanks Marina, make sure to let me know as soon as she comes in," I tell her still turning around the possible scenarios in my head.

"Sure thing," she winks at me and closes the door behind her.

I sit there for a few more minutes trying to figure out what might be going on, but decide there's nothing I can do at the moment. I have to wait until Josie comes in, then maybe I will finally figure out what's behind all of this.

My phone beeps with a text. I reach across my desk and grab my phone. It's from Walker, one of my brothers. Walker is a cop, just like I used to be before I left and started my business.

It's good to have someone to communicate with at the station, but I'm hoping he's going to quit and come work here with me. He's too good to be sitting around that den logging paperwork and tiptoeing around the red tape that comes with being a cop. I appreciate the boys in blue, especially since I know what it takes to be one, but it's definitely not for me.

> **Walker:** Looked into it. Can't find anything that stands out on JB. BH has some skeletons in his closet though.

> **Me:** What kind of skeletons we talking?

> **Walker:** Several assaults. Nothing stuck. Sounds like a mean SOB with rich boy complex.

> **Me:** That was my impression too.

> **Walker:** I'll have Jack check further, he's local.

Me: Thanks bro. Basketball later. Prepare to lose.

Walker: You're the loser, I'm gonna kick your ass.

I smile at that. We have a typical brother relationship. We fuck with each other constantly. If only the rest of my family relationships were that simple.

So, Brian Hanson has a temper. It doesn't tell me much except my gut reaction to him is spot on. That doesn't mean he's anything but an asshole though. I still don't know if there's more of a connection with Josie, other than being her employer. Whether she wants to or not, she's going to explain some things.

K. D. Smith

Chapter 6

Josie

Layne Investigations and Security. I read the sign on the door as I walk into the waiting room. I look around and notice that it's decorated in a sleek and stylish manner. It gives off a business vibe, but it's also very masculine. I guess that's what you'd expect from someone who does security and investigations. I'm not sure how many people work here, or if it's just one guy and his secretary.

As I walk closer to the reception desk I notice the woman I must have spoken to on the phone yesterday. Holy crap. She doesn't look anything like she sounds. She's wearing black pants, black boots, and a black vest with nothing underneath. It doesn't show anything it shouldn't, but it gives her almost a biker look, or maybe it's a punk look. I'm not really sure, but she looks like a badass.

Her hair is black and styled in a short spiky way that would look crazy on most women, but somehow it suits her. She has on dark lipstick and nail polish in the same dark wine color.

She has to be the coolest secretary I've ever seen. I picture her getting out of work and jumping on a Harley to head home to her biker husband and biker kids. They probably all wear only black and all have spiky hair.

"Josie Black. I have an appointment," I tell her when I get to the desk, trying not to stare. I give her a smile while I wish I could look as cool as she does. I bet nobody messes with this girl.

She smiles back at me and says "I'm Marina, have a seat, I'll tell the boss you're here. Would you like a drink or something while you wait?"

"No thanks," I say, then I realize how dry my throat is and how I need to try to keep my nerves in check. I change my mind and hope it doesn't piss her off. "Um, actually, if you don't mind, I'd like some water please." I know I sound hesitant, but she strikes me as the kind of person that you don't want to make mad.

"Sure thing," she says and turns away.

I walk across to a row of chairs and sit down right by where I can see two exit signs. Call me paranoid, but I watch for those exit signs whenever I'm in a public place. I feel better knowing that I can get out quickly if I need to. When the panic hits I start to feel the walls closing in on me and, sometimes a quick exit to a wide open space with fresh air is all I need. I've learned that the hard way.

I watch Marina as she heads into a small doorway and I can't help that my jaw drops a little when I see how tight her pants are. And they're leather! Wow, that can't be comfortable. Somehow she makes it look comfortable though. She even has a great ass.

I'm so jealous of her right now. I can't imagine ever being able to carry off a look like that. Why can't I be the kind of woman who rocks leather pants and makes it look good?

I try to tell myself I'm not so bad. I look down at myself and think I'm glad I didn't wear my yoga pants. For one thing, it's too hot, but Faith insisted that I couldn't have an appointment with a Layne brother looking like I was headed to the gym. Whatever.

I'd be the one paying him if he takes this job. I should be able to wear whatever I want. However, once I take in all that is Marina, I am so glad that I'm not wearing a hoodie.

Instead I picked one of my sundresses that I usually don't leave the house in. At least it's cool and comfortable, but I usually don't like showing this much skin in public.

I bet Marina doesn't mind showing skin. She's showing way more skin than anyone else I've ever seen working in an office. I bet outside of work she wears fishnet stockings and wields a whip. I look down at my navy colored sundress and try not to feel inadequate.

Faith put up a fuss over what I wore to this meeting because of the man who owns this place. I was more worried about looking like I knew what I was doing than impressing him. Unfortunately both scenarios left out yoga pants and running shorts.

I paired my dress with brown strappy sandals that laced around the ankles and tied in the front. Somehow I didn't think tennis shoes would look quite right, but damn if walking in these things weren't a pain in my ass.

Faith had finally approved of this outfit after several rejections, so I decided to go with it just so I didn't have to try on more clothes.

She also made me take out my ponytail. I rolled my eyes just thinking about it. My chestnut brown hair was hanging long and straight. She suggested I curl it but that was definitely going too far. At my glare she finally gave up. She knew she had gotten her way with everything else. I even wore make-up. When I'm at home I don't wear make-up. Running doesn't require make-up either. Freddy sure as hell doesn't care if I have mascara on. The only cosmetic item I use habitually is my peppermint lip gloss, which I can't live without.

I agreed to the make-up, but I kept it light and natural looking. Faith tried to come at me with an eye-liner pencil and I gave her the cross symbol with my fingers to keep her at bay. She was insisting on doing something *smoky* with my eyes. Whatever that meant. The last thing I needed was to look like a raccoon.

If she's giving me this much trouble about coming downtown to a meeting, I'm fairly certain she will drive me insane before we ever go out tomorrow night for my birthday.

Marina came back and handed me a bottle of water. She was even prettier than I thought when I first saw her. She had a little diamond in her nose. Normally I wouldn't think that was pretty, but on her it was. I was trying not to look too closely as I thanked her for the water, so I glanced down at my feet. My legs were crossed and one foot was bouncing nervously. I put my hand on my knee and tried to calm myself down.

I looked back up and Marina was staring at me with a smile. Almost as if she wanted to say something but decided against it. Instead she just said, "You can go on back. Just head down the hall. It's the door at the end." I tried to return her smile, but I'm pretty sure it came out as a face scrunch.

I stood and started walking deliberately down the hall. Taking a few deep breaths and letting them out slowly while trying not to fall off of my damn shoes.

There's nobody else in the hallway, just a few closed doors. I stop and take a second to lean my back up against the wall and gather myself. I'm not sure if I'm doing the right thing. The last thing I need is to set something in motion that will lead Brian Hanson straight to my doorstep. If that happens there is no doubt in my mind that he will kill me.

He already insured that I didn't go to the cops by threatening my life. He was dead serious when he said he would kill me if I turned him in. I saw it in his eyes. He would probably make it as painful as possible and enjoy every second. I shiver at the thought, I have never met anyone as evil as him.

I should probably drop this need for vengeance. I know it's unwise, but nobody has the right to do to a person what he did to me. I sure as hell can't pretend it never happened. Lord knows I've tried that.

Faith would kill me if she knew what I was doing. I just get so angry sometimes. He took away my power. There was no justice for him. After what he did to me I fled back to Grand Rapids, and although I'm living near where I grew up, I think I was careful enough that he can't find me even if he tries. If he ever does find me, I need to be prepared. I have to believe that I could handle him better this time.

The things I did for vengeance were small. Some may even say petty and childish. But you have your power taken away by some evil bastard and see how angry you get.

I'm tired of being scared all the time. I'm tired of dealing with the trauma that he put me through. I absolutely hate the idea that he got away with it. I hate it so much that it burns inside my gut. It fuels me.

It gives me a little satisfaction to know that I'm disrupting his tidy little operation. To know that I'm an anonymous pain in his ass. To know that he's probably aggravated and annoyed. Sue me, but I enjoy the hell out of that. He deserves all of it and more.

I did things smart. I thought things through before making any moves and I was very careful not to leave any trails. I'm sure Faith would disagree about the smart part. She would probably be right, but it's better than sitting around waiting to fall apart. It gives me purpose. It drives me.

When the idea first came to me, I just couldn't help myself. I planned and plotted, and planned some more. Before you know it, I was feeling better. I was feeling more in control. I was feeling justified. So I made my first move. I hacked into the company computers and wreaked a little havoc for him. Then I took several months planning and creating my next masterpiece.

A virus, made especially by me just for the evil bastard. I'm sure that he had fun fixing that mess. After all, it's not my fault that his computer security sucked even worse than before. It's also not my fault that he made it so easy for me. It's almost laughable when I think about it. And to be honest, if I weren't so scared all the time, I would laugh my ass off.

I'm not sorry one little bit either. The only thing I'll be sorry about is if I screw up and he finds me. I know I have to be careful with the next move I'm planning. That's why it would help to have someone check up on him so that I can determine what the danger is before I advance to the next phase. I just have to be sure he doesn't ever find out.

I also know I am causing myself undue stress by not dropping it and letting it go. But screw that. I'm not going to drop it. Somehow, to me, dropping it means that he wins. That what he did is okay. It was not in any way okay.

I've tried so hard to come out of that dark place. The place where I couldn't leave Faith's couch. The place where I could barely make myself shower. The place where I didn't function at all. Where I stared into space and rocked back and forth crying for days.

No, I can't go back to that place. I've come too far. I need to keep moving forward. And as crazy as it may be, taking down Brian Hanson is something that I can't stop myself from doing.

Revenge is a great motivator and serving justice, even if it's the vigilante kind, is one of the few pleasures I can enjoy since he ruined my life. The SOB was finally reaping what he sowed, even if only by a fraction, and that was because I was making sure of it.

After a few more deep breaths I walked to the door knocking lightly to announce my arrival.

I can do this.

I'm just going to treat this like a business meeting, nothing more.

Just then the door swung open and a large African-American man came barreling through. I jump a little and step back out of his way. He's a good looking man. He didn't look happy though. In fact he looked quite pissed. Yikes.

I blink and try to pretend that didn't happen. I walk back to the open door and as I glance inside and see the man behind the desk I stop short and stare.

Oh crap.

This is not good.

Double crap.

It's Mr. Indigo!

Chapter 7

Gunner

I watch Isaiah storm out of my office and shake my head. He'll cool down eventually. Telling a man like Isaiah bad news is like poking a sleeping bear. As I'm thinking maybe I should follow him, I see Josie standing in the door to my office staring at me in surprise.

Hot damn.

I knew she was pretty, but what the fuck has she done to herself? I take in her little dress and toned, tan legs. My eyes kept going south. God I would like to turn her over my desk and fuck her in nothing but those sexy as shit heels. As my eyes travel back up I take in her curves. I can tell she's nervous by the way her chest is rising and falling a little too fast. Her hair is down, falling over her shoulders, long and deep brown.

Beautiful.

The look on her face is showing shock at seeing me again. Oh yeah, she remembers me alright. There's something else, some other emotion that crosses her face, but I can't tell what it is before she hides it and puts on that damn fake smile for me.

Showtime.

"You? Are you Mr. Layne?" she asks me sounding a little confused. She's looking around like maybe she's in the wrong place.

I stand and go to urge her in. I smile like it's the biggest coincidence in the world. "That's me," I say walking towards her. "You can call me Gunner."

"Gunner? Oh...well I... Um, I mean, I'm Josie."

I grin at how she's fumbling for words but still trying to keep it together by holding her hand out for a handshake. This is a surprising move, but she's probably trying to keep it professional. I take her small hand in mine and give it a gentle shake. She stares at me for a few seconds and then quickly looks away. What is that about?

I try to lighten her mood a little and say, "If I knew you were coming to see me, we could have just had this meeting over at the coffee shop when you tried to run me over."

I watch as her face goes from surprise, to confusion, to embarrassment. Those pretty cheeks blush pink. Fuck, she's cute. I wonder again if there is a bad girl underneath. I'm not sure if I want the answer to be yes or no as she pulls her hand away.

Again I try to assess her, comparing her to other women I know. The ones that drink, spend, and fuck excessively. The kind that set their sights on you and it's like trying to escape missile lock when you want to get rid of them. I'm intrigued by the differences and cataloguing them in my head.

"Sorry about that," she says looking a little shy. "I mean about running into you, and about my dog growling at you. Freddy is a little over-protective."

"So I noticed. It's probably a good thing he's protective, you probably have assholes trailing you all over the place."

Instantly she stiffens and looks like she's seen a ghost. "Why do you say that?"

Is she serious? I'm saying that because she's hot. I'm not sure what's going on in that head of hers, but her reaction puts me on edge because I see fear in her eyes.

"Relax Josie. I just meant that you're a pretty woman. And you're out running around in those running shorts I saw you wearing the other day. I'm sure most men take notice. I know I did."

I give her a little grin and watch her already flushed cheeks get even brighter. Her mouth opens but then she clamps it shut and doesn't say anything. She can't be that unaware of the effect she has on men. I saw her turn more than one head as she was walking through the coffee shop.

"I'm sorry, don't look so offended. I'm just being honest. You have a great ass, and spandex does wonders for it. I won't apologize for noticing, but I will promise not to talk about it anymore."

Way to be professional Layne.

I feel the need to put her at ease.

"How about we forget that and talk about why you're here. Have a seat." I say, trying to get my mind off her ass and back to business.

Chapter 8

Josie

Oh.

My.

God.

Did he seriously just tell me he was checking out my ass the other day? Rick was right! The thought gives me a warm feeling low in my belly and I take notice of the slow somersault I feel taking place there.

Gunner. Mr. Indigo's name is Gunner. Gunner Layne. Even his name is sexy. Figures.

I don't know what it is about Gunner, but he does things to me that I can't explain. It's like my body physically reacts to him before my brain ever catches up. When he took my hand in his and held it a little too long it made my knees weak. His hand felt so strong and warm, it made me want to walk into him and wrap my arms around him.

I can't believe I'm even thinking this.

Pull it together Josie!

I'm trying not to fidget, and I know I'm blushing. Damn it! I close my eyes briefly trying to sort myself out. When I open them I see his amused eyes sparkling at me. He's wearing that sexy smirk on his face and I wonder if he's playing with me. Is he making fun of me?

To get some distance from him, I walk towards the chairs in front of his desk. I remind myself why I'm here. This may not be serious business to him, but it is to me so I need to stop acting like a swooning teenager.

"What can I do for you, Josie?" He asks as he walks around his desk and sits down in his chair crossing his arms over his chest. The black T-shirt he's wearing stretches across his biceps as he leans back and looks at me with his eyebrows drawn together. Suddenly he's all business, and I can see why he's a successful investigator. His eyes are sharp and intense and even though I've done nothing wrong I find myself wanting to squirm under his scrutiny.

I swallow, trying to process the change from grinning playboy to scary security man. Only a minute ago he essentially told me I have a great ass.

Really? I think again. Maybe I need to pay more attention to what's going on back there.

Okay, I decide I need to ignore the ass comment. I can't think about that right now. I don't know what to do with it.

I sit down and smooth the skirt of my dress down while crossing my legs. I look him square in the eye and say, "I'm curious about someone, and I want to have them investigated." There. I said it. It's out there.

Whew!

That wasn't so bad. I can totally handle this.

Then I quickly add, "But I don't really know what that entails."

He leans forward. "Well, I would need to ask some questions. Gather some information to get started. I would brief my team, and we would start looking into things for you. It's hard to tell how involved a case will become before we start digging. Is there something specific you're looking for? If we know that, we can narrow the investigation and save some time."

We? Team? He said team. So it wouldn't be just him doing the investigation. He would have to share the information with other people. I don't like the idea of a team. People talk. Even professionals who aren't supposed to. Someone could easily say something to someone and that would be the end of it. I'd either be on the run or dead.

I can't risk it.

"I didn't realize there would be a team working on it," I say softly while my foot is bouncing up and down radically. "I was hoping to only deal with one person."

He narrows a curious gaze on me. It's the same look he gave me at the coffee house. The one that feels like he's trying to read my mind. He almost looks frustrated or mad. Certainly I hadn't made him mad, had I? I shrank back in my seat a little at the thought.

"That's usually not how things work. We have quite a few open cases going at once. That means I need to spread the work around. My group of men is small, but they are the best at what they do. They are more than capable," he assures.

Uh-oh. Maybe I offended him by questioning his team, so I try to explain, "I understand, it's just that, well, this is really sensitive information. If something goes wrong... let's just say things won't end well."

That's the understatement of the year.

In fact, the more I think about it the more panicky I get. Maybe I could trust one lone detective, but not a whole group of people that I don't know, and who have no idea what damage they would cause if word got out to the wrong people.

I need to get out of here. I feel myself start to get clammy.

I shouldn't have come. This was all a very bad idea.

Air.

I need some air. This room feels like it's getting smaller by the minute.

I get out of my chair and see Gunner watching me. I'm not sure what he thinks of me, but it doesn't matter. I can't afford to mess up. I can't afford to trust anyone.

"I'm sorry," I whisper, "I can't do this." I try to take a deep breath knowing I need to speak louder. "I think this was a bad idea." I head for the door trying not to run. "Thank you for your time."

Chapter 9

Gunner

Shit. I'm losing her. Fuck if she's not jumpy as hell. I can't let her leave without finding some answers. I'm pretty sure this reaction of hers has nothing to do with guilt and has a lot to do with the fact that she's scared out of her mind.

"Josie, wait," I get up and follow her to the door.

She turns around and the look I see on her face takes me by surprise. She's pale and she looks like she's starting to shake and have trouble breathing. Not good.

I take another step towards her out of concern, but she backs away. I try again, but she backs away again and holds out a hand as if in warning, but I'm not sure what she's trying to say.

"Talk to me babe. You're starting to freak me out here. Are you okay?" I ask, but don't move towards her any further.

"I'm f-fine," she says and tries to put on that fake smile of hers. Damn if that smile isn't starting to piss me the fuck off.

"You don't look fine, you look like you need to sit down."

"I'm okay," she tries to re-assure me again. "Really. I'm sorry I wasted your time." And with that, she turns and walks quickly down the hall like the building is on fire.

I want to chase after her, but I really don't have a good excuse, other than I don't like seeing her so upset.

I watch as she turns the corner into the lobby. Another few seconds and she will be out the front door. I hear Marina say, "Have a nice day," and I know that's it, she's gone.

Shit! That didn't get me anywhere. If anything it will make it even harder to approach her again. Fuck! Why didn't I just tell her she could only deal with me?

I walk down the hall to Marina. She's usually good at reading people and I want her take on Josie. She looks up from her computer as I walk behind her desk and lean back on it.

"What's the vibe?" I ask without having to explain further.

"Scared shitless," Marina said scooting back her chair and looking up at me. "Nice, pretty, but nervous as hell. Thought she was going to jump out of her chair when I handed her a bottle of water."

"I'm getting that too," I mumble almost to myself. "I just can't figure out if she's scared because she did something she regrets, or if she's scared of someone or something else."

"She doesn't strike me as the type that would do something bad enough to warrant that kind of edginess, but then again, it takes all kinds," she says with a sigh and a wave of her hand.

I know exactly what she's saying. We encounter way too many whack jobs in this line of work. The bad guys will usually surprise the shit out of you. I've learned to expect the unexpected. "I just can't picture her as a thief, can you?" I ask.

Marina laughs. "If that girl is a thief, then I'm a virgin."

Now *that* makes me smile and say "keep dreamin', that ship has sailed *far* from the fuckin' shore."

She belts me in the arm, giving me a mock glare and then goes back to work. Damn, for a chick, she's got a good jab. Not that I would ever tell her that.

******

Joking with Marina reminds me of my sister. I remind myself I need to call her soon. I can't understand her staying away like she does, I know it hurts my parents. She's withdrawn and I know something's off.

I shake my head, no sense in worrying about that right now, I've got enough to figure out. Summer insists that she's fine, so I have to trust her to come to us when she's ready.

She's stubborn as hell just like the rest of us. In fact, she might be the worst of all.

No.

Hunter is definitely the worst, but she would come in second. Nobody is as hard headed as Hunter.

Hunter, I wonder about him too. He's the middle brother, and has always been a loner. I don't think any of us were too surprised when he up and joined the Army. He's moved up the ranks since then but doesn't go into detail about his missions when we speak.

I'm not surprised that he's involved in some covert stuff. That's the kind of shit that he would excel at. I'm hoping when he's discharged he will join the business and help me run it. I'd like him and Walker working with me full time. That's what I envisioned when I first started this company.

Back behind my desk I realize I need to get focused and figure out this situation with Josie. I have plenty of other cases on deck, but I just can't let this go until I know the truth. It's starting to piss me off how much of my time is spent wondering about her.

I know tomorrow is her birthday. Looks like I'm going to have to pay her another visit.

K. D. Smith

Chapter 10

Josie

"I can't believe I'm wearing this dress," I mumble to Justine who's sitting across the kitchen table from me.

"Girl, you look fine, stop fussing. If I could go out with you I'd be wearing something half that size," she says wiggling her eyebrows at me.

I laugh a little. She probably would too. Justine lives a couple houses down from us. She's absolutely gorgeous. Clear ebony skin, dark curly hair that she gets styled to perfection. It's hard to believe she's a single, working mom. I don't know how she has the time to look so good, but she does.

Her son Levi, who's two years old, is sitting on the kitchen floor banging a couple of cars together while he makes crash noises. I adore them both.

Sometimes I look after Levi if Justine gets in a jam. She always acts as if I'm doing her a huge favor, but I actually love it when she leaves Levi with me. Not to mention, Levi loves it here, but

I suspect that has more to do with Freddy than it does me.

I look over and see Freddy watching Levi crashing the cars together. His head is tilted to the side like he just doesn't get it, but still, he sits by Levi and keeps watching.

I have been so lucky to find these people. Living here with Faith, across the street from Rick and Eddie, Justine and Levi a few houses down and Mr. and Mrs. Williams a few houses down on the other side, who I have sort of adopted as my grandparents, it feels like I finally have a family. It's really all I've ever wanted since my Dad died.

My Dad was wonderful to me growing up. My mother was a different story. When my dad died I felt like part of me died with him. He was the one person in my life who I could always count on besides Faith. My mom never liked the closeness we shared. Even after he was gone she seemed to resent me for it.

It didn't take her long to use the life insurance money and relocate to Florida. I wasn't surprised, in fact, I felt relieved to get rid of her and the negativity that she brought into my life. No matter what I did it was never good enough for that woman.

Trying to shake those thoughts, my mind turns to what I keep trying *not* to think about. My meeting with Gunner yesterday. I feel like a fool for the way I ran out of his office, but there's nothing I can do about that now. There's no sense in stressing about it, I'll probably never see him again anyway.

For some reason that thought feels like a punch to the gut. I think of those indigo eyes, big strong hands, muscled chest... oh boy, here I go again.

Knock it off Josie!

So he's the first guy I have truly been attracted to in a long time. That doesn't mean he will be the last. I need to resign myself to the fact that Gunner Layne is a thing of the past. Maybe Faith is right. Maybe I need to get back on the horse, so to speak.

Faith couldn't believe it when I told her the guy I ran into at the coffee shop was Gunner Layne. She actually squealed and jumped up and down.

Until I explained that I wouldn't be seeing him again that is. Then we argued over whether or not I should hire him, but in the end it's my decision and I have to be comfortable with it, so she backed off.

Rick walks in with a balloon and a bottle of champagne then starts belting out the happy birthday song. I have to laugh, because seriously, Rick should *not* sing. Ever.

Levi looks up at him clapping his little hands and smiling. Freddy's head tilts further to the side like he's hearing a dog whistle, and Justine just shakes her head. She knows Rick is always over the top.

Sometimes Justine invites all of us over for mojitos during the week and it can get pretty loud. They are so crazy, and I love it.

I take the bottle from him, "Champagne? It's not like I'm retiring, it's just a birthday," I tell him with a stern look I can't quite commit to.

"Jojo, when was the last time you went out with us? What's that?" he said holding a hand up to his ear, "Oh that's right, the answer would be *never*!" He practically shouts.

"This is a night to celebrate! First you're flirting with a man, and I do mean a hunky, beefy, and seriously *hot* man. Now you're going out to the club with us. If this isn't a good excuse for champagne, then I don't know what is! Besides, it's your birthday!" He grabs me and hugs me. I can't help but laugh. He's right. I love mojitos at Justine's house, but I never go to the bars with them.

"Flirting? Beefy and hunky? You been holding out on me girl?" Justine asks with a raise of one inquisitive brow.

I quickly try to defuse this line of questioning. Justine can be like a dog with a bone. The last thing I need is to be thinking about Gunner. No, no, no. "It's no big deal," I tell her. "He was just someone I ran into on the street while jogging. I mean we literally ran into each other." At this juncture I stop to give my hand gesture of smacking them both into each other.

"He offered to buy me coffee, I declined even though he was quite hunky, I will admit. It wasn't a big deal." I give her an innocent smile hoping I am convincing.

"You're so crazy," she says shaking her head. "Turning down coffee with a hottie when you're *obviously* attracted to him. I guess I need to start running. Maybe I'll get lucky and run into a big beefy man," she sighs and looks away wistfully. "I'd give him coffee and soooo much more."

I believe her. She totally would.

"Happy birthday Jojo," Eddie says walking into the kitchen. He gives a low whistle. "Look at you! You clean up good. I see I'm going to be on guard duty tonight."

I give him a smile of appreciation, "Thanks Eddie," I say giving him a hug. He gives the best hugs. There are times I've gone over to their house under false pretenses just to get one of those hugs. I think he might suspect it, but he never says anything. He's just that nice.

"Faith Snyder, you better hurry it up or I am changing out of this dress!" I yell down the hall. I swear, that woman is probably trying on her millionth dress by now. She had a field day trying to get me ready this afternoon. The first dress she tried to put me in barely covered my ass, with a back so low I swear the top of my ass was showing. I refused to even think about it.

She kept showing me different options, until finally I picked the one that looked the least slutty but was still alluring and looked like it belonged at a party. It was a dark pink silky dress with spaghetti straps. The bodice was fitted to my body and then the skirt flared out and hit me about mid-thigh. I paired it with some silver, strappy heels.

The dress wasn't too revealing, at least not compared to the other options she gave me, so I went with it. It still seems a little over the top, I hope I don't look like a giant lollipop. Surely Justine or Rick would be glad to tell me if I looked ridiculous, and they hadn't, so I trusted that I looked okay.

I even put soft curls in my hair and left it all down around my shoulders. I did my make-up a little darker than I normally would. I hoped the look was club worthy.

Just as I start handing out glasses, I hear LMFAO start blaring over the sound system in the living room. I turn around and see Rick start dancing to *I'm Sexy and I Know It*. Justine got up, shimmying her way over to him and starts pretending to spank him. You see why I love these people? Constant entertainment.

I start getting into the party mood now that the music is pumping. Music always helps my mood. In fact, my music library is so eclectic that it probably looks as if it were created by someone with a personality disorder.

That thought gives me a private laugh, because hey, who knows, maybe I am a little bit mental, but tonight I'm going to live it up anyway. For once in my life I'm going to allow myself to forget and have fun. Just for one night.

Just then Faith walks in wearing a short silver dress, and I do mean *short*. I hope she doesn't plan on sitting or bending. I give a slight grimace at the thought. She puts her hands up in the air doing her *raise the roof* dance she's been perfecting for the last fifteen years, then she turns. Holy crap. There is no back to her dress. There's only enough material in the back to cover her ass. Barely.

I shake my head and remind myself to have a fun night. It's not going to be fun if I worry about Faith in that dress. I think to myself that my two drink limit isn't going to work for tonight. If I'm going to survive this I need a good buzz. "Bottoms up!" I whisper and chug my champagne.

K. D. Smith

Chapter 11

Josie

We've been at the club for about an hour and a half. I still haven't left the table, but I'm feeling extra happy. Drinks keep showing up and I keep drinking them. No wonder I'm not nervous about anything. I should totally do this more often!

When we came in I found a round booth near the back that's close to an exit, plopped myself down, and here I sit. Faith keeps begging me to dance with her, but so far I haven't given in, so I must not be that drunk.

I feel myself starting to wiggle to the music in the booth while I do a little seat dancing.

Rick and Faith are on the dance floor doing some serious booty shaking while Eddie and I are at the table. I watch them totally amazed at how easily they move.

I look over at Eddie and yell "Faith has on red underwear! I just saw them!"

He laughs at me like I'm joking, but I'm completely serious. He looks over and says "Oh shit!" He puts his head in his hand, "I should probably go warn her, Rick will just encourage her to show more."

That makes me laugh like a loon because Rick would *so* do that. I watch him get up and walk over to them and see Faith's mouth open in a big O then her eyes follow going into the same shape as she swings her eyes to me, then she runs over to the booth and sits down.

"Nice panties," I say, "Red is definitely your color." I give her a wink and a smirk that feels a little lopsided.

"Seeee!" she yells, "If you were out there dancing with me you could have warned me! It's all your fault!" Then she gives me a fake huff like she is seriously mad.

"Whatever! If you were worried about flashing your girly bits all over the place you should have worn a dress that covers your ass!"

She gives me a fake gasp, "Shut up or I will punch you in the face! My dress is awesome!"

This is nothing new. We may act totally immature around each other, but that's what best friends do. At least that's what we do. We've been doing this since we were kids.

"Go ahead and punch me in the face, because I'm going to kick you in the ass!"

"You can't kick that high, shorty!"

We both look at each other and start laughing hysterically.

Rick and Eddie join us and Rick says, "Hey JoJo, I saw you over here dancing in your seat. It's your turn, c'mon!"

I shake my shoulders to the music and say, "No thanks, I prefer dancing in my seat." I give him a little more to show him that I'm not kidding. I am a great seat dancer. I can't fall down if I'm sitting.

Faith keeps laughing at me and I hear Rick saying, "Holy shit, we've got to get her drunk more often."

I wag my finger at him to let him know that's a bad idea. "Only this once, it's a special occasion."

"Yeah," Faith yells, "we are going to get her back on the horse!"

"You did *not* just say that! I was talking about my birthday you hooker!" She must be even more drunk than I am because that makes her laugh too.

"Look around. Do you see anyone that you want to ride? I saw a super hot one over by the bar," she says pointing and squinting in that direction like she can't focus.

Eddie and Rick look at me like they don't know what to think. They've never seen me with a man. They are used to Justine dating often and Faith going on occasional dates, but not me, never me. Dang it, if I wouldn't really like to get back on the horse.

It's not like I've never had sex. When I was a senior in high school I dated my lab partner Shane. He was on the soccer team. He asked me out a few times. He was really nice to me and I was tired of being an 18 year old virgin, so I gave it up in the back seat of his Ford Taurus. Needless to say it was over quickly and it wasn't even pleasurable. He quit talking to me after that. Asshole.

My second experience with sex came a couple years later when I met an older guy named Jim. He was divorced with two young kids he had custody of every other weekend. Back then, he seemed perfect. He knew what he was doing in bed and I enjoyed learning exactly what he could do. He promised to teach me all kinds of things, but after a few months I caught him in bed with his ex-wife. Asshole.

My third experience was with Brian. Which brings me to the messed up state that is my life right now. For someone my age I'm not very experienced, but it's not like I've never had good sex. I know what I'm missing, but most of the time I don't let myself think about it.

Tonight I am thinking about it though. I'm feeling good. My dress looks sexy, and Faith keeps talking about riding the metaphorical horse, which is probably why I keep thinking about it.

As I sip on my cosmo, I look around the club. There are some good looking guys, but I haven't been approached, and I sure as heck am not doing the approaching.

"It might help if you leave your seat, ya know," Faith leans over and says in my ear. "Let's go to the ladies room. All these drinks are catching up with me. Time to break the seal."

I roll my eyes at her. "Nice," I say, "alright, let's go. We're going to the ladies room guys, be back in a few." Then it was Ricks turn to roll his eyes because he knew trips to the ladies room were never fast. I just gave them a little wave and started heading to the other end of the bar. I could feel Faith behind me holding on to the edge of my dress so we didn't get separated in the crowd. I tried not to think about how crowded it was and just kept my eyes on the door to the bathroom.

I notice plenty of girls giving Faith dirty looks as she walks in. This doesn't surprise me. It's typical girl behavior. It just means she looks hot and they don't like the competition. I may threaten to punch my best friend but that's just us joking around. Nobody else better say an unkind word to her, I would always have her back and she would always have mine.

Once we're done using the bathroom and checking our hair and make-up in the mirror. We are back out the door. "It's Bruno Mars!" Faith yells, "We *have* to dance, *please*!" She gives me the pouty face pulling on my arm.

I give her the hand gesture to go first and I'll follow. I'll dance this one but only because I love this song, *Locked Out Of Heaven*. Then I'm going back to seat dancing.

We're having a good time dancing together, while were moving around each other to the beat of the music, when I see a guy come up behind Faith and start trying to move with her. I see her expression turn into surprise and she turns to see that he's cute, so she starts dancing into him.

I decide that's my queue to leave when I feel a guy starting to dance behind me too. From the look on the guys face behind Faith I think they must be friends. I'm not sure what I should do, but Faith gives me an encouraging nod, so I slowly start dancing again. I try to have fun with it, but when I feel him grind his erection into my ass, I decide that it's time to head back to my seat. The song is over anyway.

Besides, who just does that to someone he's never talked to before? I'm not a prude or anything, but I don't find that very sexy. You could at least say hi and give me a name before you rub your junk on me.

Eww.

I turn and say, "Thanks for the dance," and quickly walk to the table where Rick is wiggling his eyebrows at me.

"Shut it," I say sitting down and taking a good swig of my drink.

"He was cute honey, maybe he can be your horse." He smiles and does more of that weird eyebrow thing.

"Nah," I say, "He was rubbing his stuff all over me and he didn't even bother to say hello first.   That's not normal is it?" I say as if I'm appalled at the thought.

Eddie laughs and says, "Normal is a broad term in a place like this JoJo, someone like Rick might like it, but it's definitely not for someone like you." Rick pretends to look offended until he smiles and shrugs his shoulders like it's true but he can't help it.

That's when I see him walking towards me. I feel the smile sliding off of my face and heat staring to creep up my neck. *Shit*! Gunner. He's wearing jeans and a button down black shirt that's untucked but fitted to him. His sleeves are rolled up slightly and I notice how muscular his forearms look. I swallow and blink and look back to his face. He's smiling. I think my cosmos might make him look even sexier, if that's possible.

Uh-oh.

K. D. Smith

Chapter 12

Gunner

I never pegged Josie for the clubbing type, but here she is, just as I was told. I watched her for a while before I approached. I saw her talking and laughing with Faith, the guy from the coffee shop, and some other guy. She looked like she was enjoying herself.

I had to adjust myself when I saw her moving in her seat and wiggling her bare shoulders to the music as if dancing without going on the dance floor. I thought she looked hot in my office the other day, but this was something else.

She looked like she dressed for a man's attention. Trying to be sexy. Fuck if it didn't work too. That little dress looked good on her. That hair, those heels, I wanted to wrap them both around me. Though the new look made me wonder if she was meeting someone.

I watched as she went to the bathroom and came out with her friend. I saw them dancing, and her friend dancing with the guy who approached. When the second guy came up behind Josie, she looked a little surprised and uncomfortable. Her movements weren't as easy as they were before. Her eyes more aware. I was a little surprised she didn't walk away.

If I was honest with myself I was hoping she would. I was afraid to find out she was just another party girl like the rest. Then again, even if it would be a disappointment I could work her more easily, in many ways.

When I saw her jaw drop I knew the asshole behind her had started making his move. She didn't turn around or reciprocate, I didn't know if it was because she wasn't that type of girl, or if was just because she wasn't interested in that type of guy.

I watched her face as I approached the table. She was smiling. Damn, she was beautiful when she smiled. I don't think I'd ever seen her with a real smile on her face before. As I walked toward her though, I saw it disappear.

Fuck.

What was that about? Then I saw her cheeks turn pink. Was she blushing before I even approached? When she looked up at me I could see something working behind those big hazel eyes of hers. Interest? Attraction? She picked up her drink and threw back what was left, taking a visible swallow.

"Hey Josie," I said sitting down next to her without giving her a chance to turn me away. I put my arm around the back of the booth behind her semi blocking her in and gave her a smile. Her eyes got bigger and she quickly looked away.

The guy from the coffee shop said, "So, we meet again, it must be fate," and gave me a wink. The guy next to him gave him an elbow in the ribs.

"What?" He whined with insolence. "I mean it must be fate for Josie not for me!"

That got a laugh out of me. The dude was definitely a little scary, but he seemed nice enough.

"This is Eddie, by the way. And I'm Rick, in case you've forgotten. I'd wait for Jojo to give introductions, but I think the horse has her tongue." He gave her a wicked smile and turned back to me.

"And you are?" he asked. From the corner of my eye I saw Josie put a hand to her forehead like she was embarrassed.

"Gunner Layne," I said sticking out my hand for a shake.

He took my hand. "Gunner. Sounds very *cowboyish*." He said with emphasis giving Josie big eyes. "Well, if you'll excuse us, the dance floor is begging me to come back," he tossed his head and walked off giving Josie some type of look I didn't quite understand.

"Soooo... Aren't you going to say hi?" I ask turning toward her.

"Um, hi... what are you doing here?" she asked so quietly I had to bend my ear down to her so that I could hear her but when I did it was hard not to be amused at her question. Straight and to the point. No muss, no fuss. I like that.

"I was here with a friend, but he took off a few minutes ago. I spotted you just as I was about to leave," I lie.

"Oh," she looked away like she didn't know what else to say, and then said, "We came here for my birthday."

"Happy birthday," I feign surprise. "How about a birthday dance? I promise not to step on your sexy shoes."

She blinked at me and opened her mouth and shut it again. Just then a waitress came with more drinks, as she sat the drinks down on the table she gave me a flirty smile and a wink, making sure to bend at the waist and give me a clear shot of her cleavage.

I wasn't interested, but I heard Josie make a little *hmph* sound beside me and I noticed her foot started bouncing, which I also noticed she did when she was nervous, only this time she seems annoyed.

Faith appeared at the table and sat down saying "Yeah, thanks for the drinks, but we can do without the show." Then she gave her a sweet smile like she didn't hold it against her.

Josie smiled at her friend and immediately picked up one of the drinks and drank the whole thing. Well, well, maybe she did like to get her party on.

"That guy was a douchebag. He asked to take a picture of my ass. Seriously? Who just asks someone that? I mean, I know it looks good, but have some manners for crying out loud," Faith huffed scooting into the booth so she was across from us.

She looks up and finally notices I'm sitting there with Josie. She looks surprised and then she grinned and then looked over at Josie and grinned even more. "Gunner Layne, long time no see."

I gave her a questioning look and said, "Faith?" She nodded at me. Of course I already knew it was her, but I couldn't say so. "I thought so. I remember you hanging with my sister sometimes."

"How is Summer? I haven't seen her in forever!" she made a wide move with her arm spilling some of her drink then looking briefly annoyed about it. My assessment was telling me that they were both buzzed, but Faith was heading quickly from being buzzed to just plain drunk.

"Good as far as I know. She moved and I don't get to talk to her as much as I'd like to."

"And Hunter?" She asks hesitantly.

Uh oh. I know that look. Please tell me she is not another one that Hunter fucked and left behind.

"Same. Gone. Not a lot of contact."

She nodded, and if I am reading her right she seems a little sad, or maybe resigned, either way I don't imagine this is a good thing.

Then I see her shake her head a little as if shaking off the mood and I notice her studying me, and looking back and forth between me and Josie.

"So what are the chances that you run into Josie here at the club, *and* while running, *then* she walks into your office, and now here you are *again*. That's pretty amazing."

Luckily I'm good at not giving anything away through my body language, because damn, she might be onto me.

"I know, it must be fate," I said giving her my best charming smile. "I was just asking her for a birthday dance."

"She'd love to!" Faith yelled. "Believe me, she could use a good birthday....dance." She giggled and gave Josie a little wave. "I gotta go make a call, have fun!"

Chapter 13

Josie

I looked at Faith who was standing behind Gunner pointing at him and mouthing the word *HORSE!* And then, in case I didn't get it, she did it *again* and starting making a motion like she was holding onto reigns and galloping! Yes, galloping! I'm going to kill her later.

I look away so I can't see her acting like an idiot. I take the rest of Faith's drink that was left on the table and drink it all. Thank goodness I have a good buzz going, or I would completely be freaking out.

I don't know what to say or do, so I decide to take him up on the dance. I mean, it has to be better than sitting here not saying anything or trying to avoid his annoyingly gorgeous eyes.

"How about that dance?" I said.

He smiled, stood up out of the booth and reached a hand to me. I put my hand in his and start to stand. There it is again. That same tingly awareness that zings through my body when my skin touches his.

Nice.

Just touching his hand does things to me I don't understand. I think I might be at my drink capacity, because I stumble a little as he leads me to the dance floor but he just puts an arm around my waist and keeps going.

God, he smells good. The music playing isn't slow, but he pulls me into his arms anyway and starts to move with me. I'm not sure what to do so I put my hands on his shoulders.

Oh dear God, now it's not just my hand, the whole front of my body is tingling where his body is touching mine. I am staring at his chest because I'm afraid to look up and see his eyes. The top few buttons on his shirt aren't buttoned and I can see a tattoo peeking out just where his buttons start. It looks to be on the right side of his chest, but I can't really tell anything about it, other than to know it's there. I'm dying to unbutton his shirt so I can see what it is.

He leans down and says, "Penny for your thoughts," in my ear and it makes me shiver.

"I was just thinking about unbuttoning this," I said touching the top button holding his shirt together. I see a surprised look on his face that changes into a grin. I realize what I said, I feel my cheeks turn red and I start stumbling for an explanation. "I mean... I meant... your tattoo, I was just wondering what it was."

Somebody shoot me!

Clearly, I should never drink my weight in cosmos ever again.

"You wanna take my shirt off and find out Josie?" he says as he pulls me closer into his body so that I can't stare at his chest anymore because my face is pressed up against it. I could say that I'm not affected by this, but it would be a lie.

The truth is I want to close my eyes and rub my cheek up against him like a cat. He's so big and warm, and his voice is so deep I can feel it rumbling in his chest when he talks. Just the thought of taking his shirt off is making my body hum.

"Yes," I whisper. Then say "No!" quickly pulling my head away, hoping like hell he didn't hear the first answer.

He gives a small laugh and I feel it in his chest. I don't know if he's laughing because he heard me, or because I'm acting like a lunatic. I feel like an idiot. I can't seem to think straight, and with him touching me it's even worse than before.

"You are a mystery, that's for damn sure," he says looking down into my eyes.

"Well, I guess it's a good thing you solve those for a living." Holy crap, why did I just sound like a sex phone operator when I said that?

Apparently he thinks so too, because his hands on my waist move. One drifts lower so that he's holding it at the top of my ass, the other goes higher up my back so he's pushing my breasts into his chest. My nipples are so hard I just know he can feel them rubbing up against him.

"You're right, and I'm extremely good at what I do." I feel his hand move further down on my behind. He gives me a smirk that's so damn sexy I'm pretty sure my panties got a little wet.

I try to remember that I should be careful with him, after all, he is a detective. It's hard to keep secrets from someone like him, but Lord help me, I just want to have this one worry free night with him.

I promised myself I would relax and have fun tonight, and here I am with Gunner's arms wrapped around me. I need to enjoy it, just for tonight. Everything will go back to normal tomorrow.

I look up into his eyes and then down to his sexy mouth. One night. No regrets. I'm going to feel like a normal woman tonight. A normal woman with a normal, healthy attraction to a man. Before I can overthink it and stop myself, I push up on my tiptoes and brush my lips against his. I close my eyes and feel his breath against my lips.

I hear him let out a low grunt and then he closes his mouth over mine. It's not a slow kiss. It's deep and needy. I feel his tongue push past my lips and start to explore my mouth. I'm pretty sure I made a whimpering noise because I feel my knees get weak.

He has me crushed to him and I hold on for dear life. I lock my arms around his neck and, start using my tongue to match his. He started to pull back and straighten himself, but I didn't let go. I could feel my feet leave the ground and I was hanging on him.

"Fuck," he ground out between gritted teeth and then put his mouth back to mine. It's the hottest kiss I've ever had in my life. I'm pretty sure I could burst into flames at any moment.

I can feel his erection pushing against my lower belly through my dress and I want it. Bad. I don't even think, I just lift one leg and try to wrap myself around him.

He pushes my knee back down and pulls his mouth away. I hear myself make a little whimper of protest, but he bends and puts me back on my feet, luckily I'm still holding on so I don't melt into a puddle on the floor.

"Not here," he says in my ear. I feel like I'm in a daze, I can't really talk, I'm just staring at his lips and holding on to him praying that he will give me more. "Jesus. Hold that thought and let's get out of here."

I nod my head and he turns me and starts leading me out of the club, still holding me around my middle. He stops for a second and I see him talking to Eddie. I'm not sure what he says, but Eddie looks to me with a question in his eyes and I grin at him dazedly. Eddie in turn grins and nods at Gunner.

When we push through the doors he backs me up against the building and starts kissing me again. I'm not sure how much more I can take. Every time my body starts to simmer down, he does something to set me on fire again.

He pulls his lips away a few inches. We are both breathing heavily and he says "God, please tell me that you aren't too drunk for this."

I shake my head and he slams his lips back over mine. I think I breathe his name a couple times but it comes out muffled because I can't quit devouring his lips with my own.

"Don't worry Josie, I got you." I'm not sure what he means by that, but I hope he means that he's going to put this fire out soon, because if he doesn't I don't think I can take it.

Every time he calls me baby it only gets worse. I don't know what to think of myself at this point, and I don't care. It's been a long time since a man has touched me, and never in my life has a man touched me like this.

This is painful and glorious at the same time. He picks me up and carries me in his arms into the parking lot still kissing me. I don't know if people are watching us, and I really do not care. I just need him to hurry. This is my night and I'm going to have it with Gunner Layne. On my birthday.

Happy Birthday to me!

When he sets me down I feel something cushioned between my legs and I gasp. Oh god, whatever it is feels good. I want to rub myself on it. In fact, I think I start to do just that when I hear him cursing and feel him putting something on my head. What the hell? I look down and see that I'm sitting on a motorcycle and he's putting a helmet on my head.

"I've never ridden a motorcycle before," I tell him as a little bit of sanity starts to come back. "And I'm wearing a dress. Can I ride on a motorcycle in a dress?" I blink up at him thinking, *oh God, please say yes*.

"Yes, just press yourself up against my back and tuck your dress in. I don't want anyone seeing up that dress but me."

"Oh..." I breathe. I really just want this dress off of me. If I don't rub myself up against something and find some friction soon I'm going to spontaneously combust. I rest my hands on the seat in front of me while he's buckling my helmet and squeeze my thighs together as much as possible. Maybe if he could just start it, maybe the vibration will take care of this ache.

"Please Gunner," I plead rocking on the seat a little bit. "Let's go."

He leans down and runs his tongue over my lips again making me take in a sharp breath. "Josie, you're killing me. Hold on." He says climbing on in front of me and pulling my arms around him. I scoot as close as possible and tuck my dress in while he starts the motorcycle. Oh my…. *Yes*!

I know I'm breathing hard and grasping onto him and he probably thinks I'm a sex starved hooker, but I can't help it. "If you come Josie, it better be on me and not on my bike."

Chapter 14

Gunner

I feel Josie behind me, pressed into me as close as she can possibly get. Fuck I feel her tits pushing into my back, and the heat of her pussy so close. This is not what I expected when I tracked her down. I mean, sure I wanted her and I had since the moment I saw her, but this is different than any other time I've found myself attracted to a woman.

She was on fire for me. The smallest touch had her responding to me in a way I never imagined. I've never had someone respond to my touch the way she does. It's almost as if it's instant, automatic, involuntary, like she can't stop herself even if she wants to.

The last thing I want is to take advantage of her. I don't know how much she drank, but God help me, I don't think I can back off now. I want her. *Bad*.

She looks so sexy in that dress. I don't know if I've ever seen anyone so sexy. Something about her just draws me in. Her face flushed with arousal, her hair wild, her lips swollen from my kisses.

Fuck if I didn't want to take her right in the damn parking lot. She looked so dazed, like she was in a haze of need. I definitely wanted to be the guy to take care of that need.

I thought for a minute she was going to come when I put her on my bike. God that was hot. The thought of how she had rocked her pussy against my seat was driving me crazy. I bet she's so wet right now. I wonder if she's leaving her juices on the back of my bike. Damn, just the thought is making my dick so hard I feel like it's going to bust out of my zipper.

I'm trying to concentrate on getting us safely to my place, but my mind isn't on the road. My mind is thinking how fucking good she feels behind me. I can't wait to get my hands on her. If I can get her that worked up in public, I'm dying to see what she's like in private.

I never imagined that if I got a chance to get my hands on her she would come apart at my touch the way she did. She was practically begging me to give her pleasure. I can't wait to see what she looks like when she comes, I bet it's fucking beautiful. I want to make her come over and over again until she's screaming my name.

If I would have expected this to happen I would have planned another place for us to go. I made it a point to never take women to my place. This would be the first time I broke that rule, and fuck if I cared. She's worth it. I would deal with any fallout later.

Looks like Josie Black is a party girl after all. I thought I was tired of those, but not this one. This is one party girl I'm dying to figure out. It's not even about the investigation. Technically I shouldn't be doing this. I mean, sure sometimes I use my way with women to get information, but not like this. I don't fuck them.

I sure as hell don't take them to my place. Right now my thoughts of Josie have nothing to do with the investigation. I don't even care what she did or didn't do.

I'm not turning her over to that asshole in Detroit either way. I've decided to tell him I can't find her. Whatever is going on with her will wait until tomorrow. Tonight I just want to get her in my bed. If I make it all the way to the bed. Highly doubtful.

K. D. Smith

Chapter 15

Josie

I'm pushed so close to the back of him, it's driving me crazy. My thighs are spread wide to accommodate him and I put my hands up under his shirt to hang on. God he feels so good. His abs are hard and muscled.

I'm so tempted to put my hands lower and feel him, but I decide that's probably not a good idea while he's driving. We pass other cars and normally I would be freaking out that my dress is hiked up to the top of my thighs, but right now none of that bothers me.

I can only think of Gunner and how he feels against my body. I close my eyes and enjoy the wind whipping around me cooling off my body that has been heated since the minute Gunner sat next to me in that booth.

I turn my head and lay it against his back. I never thought I would ride on a motorcycle, but I'm not scared. He looks like he's comfortable riding and his confident manner extinguishes my fears.

Before I know it, he stops the bike and I feel his hands reach back and rub up and down my outer thighs before he reaches up to yank off his helmet. "Can you climb off?" he asks me.

His voice sounds tight like he's trying to hold back or keep control. For once, I don't want a man to hold back. I want all of him. I want him to feel as wild as I do. I want him to ache as bad for me as I'm aching for him.

I put one heel down onto the pavement and hold onto him so I can lift my other leg over and stand beside the bike. He immediately follows and starts taking off my helmet. I see him put it away in a bag on the side of the bike and he takes my hand leading me towards a building. I'm trying to keep up with him the best I can, but it's hard in these shoes. I grab ahold of his forearm to try to get him to slow down for me, but then I get distracted by how good his forearm feels.

I can feel his strength in it and for once it doesn't scare me. I run my fingers along a vein I see running up his arm. He's looking down at me and stops to put his mouth on mine again. Then he's feeling my arms. I feel his big rough hands rubbing up and down my upper arms. I look at him and am totally mesmerized by this man.

He lets out a long breath and says in a low voice, "If you look at me like that when I'm only touching your arms I can just imagine what you are going to be like when I get my hands where I want them."

That just makes me stare at him even more. I swallow and look at his mouth again. The things he says are so hot, but I want him to kiss me again. He turns and starts walking again saying, "Let's get inside because if you keep looking at me like that I'm going to fuck you right here where anyone can see."

That gets me moving. We enter the building and he guides me to an elevator and pushes the button with an up arrow.

Oh no. *No, no, no.*

I hate elevators. Actually I hate any kind of closed, small spaces. Especially if they're dark.

"Can we take the stairs?" I ask looking up at him.

"Do you really want to walk up six flights of stairs in those shoes?" He looks confused. "This is faster and I need to get you inside my apartment."

I'm mentally battling myself. Is it worth ruining this moment over? I mean, I can handle an elevator for a few seconds right? I've done it before but only when it's necessary. I don't want to do it, but I feel like I need to.

I just want to get to his apartment quickly and forget about this. As I'm thinking, the elevator doors open and he looks at me. I try to steel myself and then I walk in. He's right behind me. Turning to the panel he pushes the number six. I close my eyes and hang onto the rail next to me willing myself to breath normally.

"Open your eyes, baby."

Baby, there it is again. It makes my stomach flutter and I feel warm inside, but I can't open my eyes yet. So I just shake my head no.

Hurry up!

"Josie, open your eyes," he commands.

I open them and see him right in front of me with questions in his eyes. I can't take the questions so I reach up and kiss him to put a stop to them.

It was a good decision, because his mouth distracts me from panicking about the small space. He has me pushed back against the wall with his tongue deep in my mouth when I hear the ding.

Thank God.

The doors open and my breath comes out in a whoosh. I quickly skirt around him and get out the doors.

He doesn't say anything, but I get the sense that he can tell I don't want to talk about it. When we get to a door he puts his key in and opens it wide pulling me inside.

Once we're in, he pushes it closed and locks it. Once he's done he turns to look at me and I can see the heat and desire in his eyes.

In one swift movement he picks me up in his arms and carries up some stairs as if I weigh nothing. His lips are on mine as he walks and then I feel myself being put down on something soft, which I assume is his bed, but my eyes are closed and I don't want to open them.

I'm in Gunner Layne's bed!

I don't want to think. I just want to feel. I put my hands in his hair and pull him as close as I can get him then I feel his weight settle into the bed covering me. His kiss is wild and hard and I love it. It gives me no time to think. All I'm worried about is this sensation that's building in my core. I know that my panties are drenched and I just want them to come off.

"God you feel so good," he groans. "I wanted to go slow and take my time with you, but I don't think I can right now. Tell me you want this, Josie. I need to know that you are clear about what we're doing here."

I wish he would quit talking. I just want him to keep going until he's buried deep inside me. I nod my head and quickly whisper, "Yes," and then I feel something inside me melt further. He wants to make sure that I want this. That makes me want him more.

He puts his face in the crook of my neck and starts kissing me there. It sends shivers straight through me. I feel his lips move around the front of my neck and then down to the top of my dress where he licks the swell of my breasts right above the fabric. His hands move underneath me and I hear the zipper go down and feel the freedom of the material loosening on me. This dress was so fitted it didn't need a bra so once the zipper is down he pulls the material free. My nipples are standing at attention begging for his touch. He immediately puts his mouth over my nipple and starts sucking on it.

"Mmmm" I practically purr. The sensation is wicked. It's sending jolts of pleasure right to my clit. I arch my back trying to get more. His mouth comes off of one nipple and heads straight to the other while his fingers are rubbing and pulling at the one that just came out of his mouth. I can't think or talk, I'm just breathing heavily and whimpering for more. I guess this is what happens when you go a long time without sex, without even being able to pleasure yourself, and then find an insane attraction to a sexy man.

"You have perfect tits," he says taking his mouth off of my nipple and bringing his lips back to mine. His lips are touching mine when he says "I could suck on them all night."

Dear Lord. I'm about to go crazy here. I thought I had good sex before, but this feels like electricity is coursing through my body. I just want to keep going. The more he talks dirty to me like that the more turned on I get. I can feel the slickness between my legs as I move.

I'm fumbling with his buttons trying to get access to his skin so he raises up and yanks it off. I can't see him clearly because it's dark, but there's enough light coming in the window that I can see the outline of his body, and it's beautiful.

He moves away from me and I feel him tug the hem of my dress so it's sliding down my body leaving me in only my pink lacy thong and heels. He bends and takes off my shoes dropping them to the floor and then his hands run up my legs, over my hips, to the waist of my panties and he pulls them off. He takes in a sharp breath when he sees my bare sex.

"Open for me Josie" I hear his deep voice rumble. He puts his hands on my knees and pulls them open and back so that I'm wide open for him to see. "Jesus, I can see how wet your pussy is for me baby, it's glistening in the moonlight. Fucking beautiful." With a groan he puts his head right between my thighs and runs his tongue over my clit. My hips jerk and he holds them down with his hands while he's using his tongue on me.

I hear myself begging him, saying the word please over and over again, but I'm not sure exactly what I'm asking for other than more, I just need more. When I think I'm going to die he pulls his hand from my hip and puts his finger inside of me and sucks my clit into his mouth.

Yes!

"Oh God!" I moan. "Gunner!" I feel my body shaking and stiffening, and I come. It seems to last forever. When it finally subsides, he takes time to keep giving me licks here and there, bringing me back down, but it's almost like my body knows there's more. Just as quickly as I come I feel it start to build again.

"Fuck," I hear him say and he takes me and turns me over on his bed. He pulls my hands up above my head and wraps my hands around the bars on his headboard. "Hold on to that, and don't let go."

Oh sweet mother, what is he doing to me? I feel him grip my hips and lift them so my ass is in the air. I feel his hands rubbing and squeezing my ass. I don't know what to do. I've never had sex this way before. So I just hang on like he told me to.

I can feel the pressure building again. It feels so good and I want to come more. My body is telling me that a bigger orgasm is on the way. I should be ashamed but I'm not. I arch my back and wiggle my ass back into his hands.

He reaches down underneath me and I feel him roll my nipples between his index fingers and his thumbs. Then he runs his hands back down my ribs to my ass again. I feel him lean down placing kisses on the small of my back and the cheeks of my ass. All I can do is moan and whimper for more.

I hear him pull down his zipper and I know it's finally going to happen. Gunner is finally going to give me what I need. I want so bad to turn around so I can see him and touch him, but I don't, I hold on like he asked. I hear him say "I've wanted to get my hands on your hot little ass since I saw you in those fuckin' running shorts."

Wow. Yes! I want to tell him to fuck me. I've never said anything like that before, but I'm sure as hell thinking it.

I feel him rubbing and squeezing my ass, pulling his fingers through my wetness, and then rubbing some more. Then that's when it happens.

Smack

What the hell? Did he just hit me?

Smack

He does it again, I feel his palm hit my ass. I freeze. I can't help it. The sound of someone slapping me triggers memories I don't want to face. I hate that sound. All of the excitement I was feeling halts and I am bracing to get another slap.

"Stop!" I beg.

I let go of the headboard and fumble my way off of the bed as quickly as I can to get away from him. I feel the panic quickly taking root.

Oh God, what the hell have I done? No, no, no, not again!

My mind is going over everything I've done wrong at warp speed.

I've been so stupid. Thinking I could let go for one night. I should have known. Now I've gotten myself in a really bad situation.

I drank too much.

I rode on the back of a man's motorcycle.

I'm alone with him in his house and I have no transportation to leave.

For shit sake, I think I even left my purse and my phone back at the club with Faith.

I'm naked!

Oh God, I've spent so much time being careful never to put myself in a situation like this again. Now here I am, back in the same situation I vowed I would never allow to happen.

I can't breathe.

My hands come up to my chest trying in vain to get myself to take in air. I don't even know where my clothes are! I don't know where the door is to leave. I'm looking around frantically and I can't make sense of anything. I grab a throw blanket off of the bed and wrap it around me. I need to get out of here.

Chapter 16

Gunner

What the fuck?

My mind tries to adjust to the quick change in situation. Luckily I'm trained for that, but my throbbing cock is slowing me down a little. I look at Josie and see her wrapping up in my blanket. She looks like she did in my office when she wasn't breathing right, only this is worse.

"Josie, talk to me baby, what just happened?" I ask sounding as confused as I feel.

I don't understand this. She was so hot for me. It had been insane since the minute we made it to my apartment. She responded to me just like she did in the club.

I even asked her to tell me she wanted this, so I could be sure she wasn't drunk or out of it. She hadn't said much, but she had made it clear she wanted to do this. In fact she was practically begging for it. She even came all over my face and it was the hottest fuckin' thing I'd ever experienced. I could still taste her.

I shouldn't have spanked her. Shit. I didn't really give it much thought except that I'd been dying to do that to her since seeing her sexy little ass in spandex. Most women loved that shit. In fact, I'd had women ask me for it. Not that I was going to share that.

I never considered that she wouldn't respond just the way she had been all night. Shit, I fucked up. I should have went slower. I must have scared her. I couldn't have physically hurt her. I knew that much.

She had been so responsive, it never occurred to me that something might freak her out.

"Josie, please, tell me what happened." I practically beg. "I'm sorry, I shouldn't have spanked you without knowing if you were okay with it, and I was so turned on I didn't think."

I start to walk towards her and she scrambles away.

Fuck!

Now what do I do? She's scaring the shit out of me. She's not breathing right and her face is pale all of the sudden. The desire I've seen all night in her eyes is gone. Her eyes are wide and when she glances at me all I see is distrust and fear.

She's looking around for something I'm not sure what. I can't tell what she needs. I want to go to her and comfort her and calm her down, but I don't want to make it worse.

I don't care, I can't stand seeing her like this. I go to her and take hold of her upper arms. She tries to pull away but I'm not letting her go. I need to help her calm down.

"Just breathe baby, you gotta calm down and breathe."

She just shakes her head and I can feel her whole body trembling. Her hands move up to her throat while she's still trying to hold onto the blanket.

"Air." I hear her wheeze.

I don't know what she means, there's air all around her all she needs to do is take it. I'm not sure what to do, so I pull her over to a window and open it. I see her put her face close to it, but it's not enough. Her fingers touch the screen like she needs it out of the way and she's shaking her head.

"Breathe baby, just breathe!" I almost yell at her. I see her flinch and try to pull away again. Shit. Okay, I need to stay calm, raising my voice is not helping.

I have an idea, remembering how she didn't want to ride in the elevator. Could she be claustrophobic? It doesn't really make sense because she's not in a small space, but it's the only thing I can think of. I hurriedly grab her and swing her up into my arms. I head down the stairs as quickly as I can. I head over to the balcony doors, open them and step out with her.

I hear her trying to breathe, but it's coming in irregular gasps and now there are tears running down her face. I put her down in a chair and kneel down in front of her.

"Look at me Josie." I say as calmly as I can but she continues to take in the harsh painful breathes that are not close enough together. I'm afraid she's going to pass out if she doesn't get her shit together. She doesn't look at me, instead turns away from me a little and she pulls her knees up and wraps her arms around them. She's almost in a fetal position rocking back and forth, still trying to breathe.

Fuck me.

"Look at me Josie!" I use the deepest, most commanding voice I can muster but keeping it calm and steady. It must work because she jumps but then she turns her head and looks at me. "Look in my eyes baby, breathe with me."

Then I start taking in long slow deep breathes hoping she will follow my lead. Finally, she starts to mimic what I'm doing. After a few minutes, she is breathing normally again, but she's still trembling. At least she has stopped with that rocking shit. Jesus, what the fuck is all of this about?

I have a suspicion, now that I've seen her panic attack, but I pray that I'm wrong. The thought of someone hurting her makes my blood boil.

"I'm not sure what happened in there, but I need you to explain it to me so that it doesn't happen again," I tell her. "You can trust me Josie. I want to help you. And I'm not sure what you think, but I would never hurt you, physically I mean, if that's what you thought I was going to do."

The pieces were starting to fit together now. I can't believe I didn't put it all together earlier. The way she was skittish on the sidewalk outside of the coffee shop. The guard dog. The way she ran off when I wanted to talk to her. The look on her face when she backed away from me in my office. She was scared. Not scared like a guilty person who didn't want to get caught. Scared like someone who had been hurt in a really bad way.

She stood wrapping herself further into the blanket and walked over to the railing of the balcony looking out. She was doing better, but she had a faraway look in her eyes. I hate that I did this to her. I want to fix it. I wanted to go back in time to when she was smiling at the bar and then writhing in my bed.

To be honest, I'm a little disturbed at how bad I want to take care of her. I've never felt this protective surge running through me as strong as it is right now. It's been my job to keep plenty of people safe, but this is different. The fact that she's this scared makes me want to kill someone.

She speaks so softly that I barely hear her, but she says, "I'm sorry, I don't like that s...sound, I wasn't expecting it." Then closes her eyes tightly like she's trying to block it out. Damn it. If only I could go back and change it.

"Let's go inside and talk," I say gently, hoping like hell she will open up with me this time.

Instead she shakes her head no and wraps herself up as tightly as she can. "I can't," but that's all she says. I figure maybe she needs more time outside to get herself together, so I just nod and stand there with her. We just look out into the darkness at the downtown lights for a while.

I think of the things I've learned about Josie tonight. There's no way she's a thief. She is definitely not a party girl. And most surprising, someone has hurt her, bad enough to give her panic attacks. I don't know who yet, but it's now my top priority to find out.

Chapter 17

Josie

The cool night air feels so good but I can barely appreciate it right now. I can't believe what a disaster this night has turned into. That smack on the ass triggered my panic attack and now that it's over he wants answers. I can't really blame him, but there is no way I can explain it to him. Just admitting to him that the smacking sound is what triggered it was mortifying.

He could have brought home any woman he wanted tonight, and he picked me. I was starting to feel guilt that his night was ruined because I was a basket case. God, he didn't even *finish*. At least I finished. Somehow that made it worse.

"I need to go home," I whisper.

"You're not going anywhere until we have a talk." I'm a little surprised at how stern his voice sounds. I feel my body shrink back from it, at the same time I find myself wanting to comply. It's not that I'm scared of Gunner, he's been more than understanding so far, without showing any anger towards me.

"Can we just forget this please, so I can go home?" The more I think about how I freaked out on him the more embarrassed I get.

Hell, most women would probably pay to have a man like Gunner giving them a slap on the ass. If it wouldn't have caught me so off guard maybe I would have enjoyed it too, but there's no going back now that he's seen how messed up I am.

"I'm not forgetting one moment of tonight, baby. Not the way you smell, the way you taste, the way you came for me, or the way you had a panic attack and almost passed out because you couldn't breathe." He says with such a serious look on his face I don't know what to do, so I just look back out at the night.

I can't believe he's saying these things. Doesn't he get it? I'm not the kind of girl who's going to be fun for him. He should know that after what he witnessed tonight.

"I...I'm not sure what kind of stuff you get off on Gunner, but I'm not your girl." I gave almost a bitter laugh. I want to be, I *so* want to be, but I just can't. He spanked me, what if he tied me up or something? If he thought this was bad, he would really love seeing the kind of meltdown that would cause.

"I shouldn't have done that, I can see that now. Fuck, I was so worked up and you were so responsive to me, I never gave it a second thought. Most women like that kind of shit. I should have seen that you are the kind of woman who needs things to move a little slower. All I can say is I'm sorry, but don't shut me out. We both got caught up, and baby, up until that spank, I don't regret a second of it. I would like to understand though, so I don't do anything to upset you again. Next time I want you to enjoy it, all of it, until we are both so spent that we can't move."

There are so many things that pop into my mind while he's speaking, but the part that's resonating with me the most is him saying *next time*. Is he serious? There isn't going to be a next time. I already feel like a fool. I thought I was ready but obviously I'm not.

"There isn't going to be a next time." I blurt. How do I explain any of this without saying too much? He smirks at me, oh great, he's back to smirking.

"There *will* be a next time, because I liked the taste I got, and I haven't had nearly enough."

I sigh at the same time I feel my cheeks heat. If only there could be a next time, but tonight proves that it's a disaster waiting to happen. Gunner is definitely not a man you can dismiss easily. I'm going to have to give him a little bit of the truth in hopes that it will be enough to make him see that I'm not what he wants.

I start to shiver a little bit as the breeze picks up. That's one thing about Michigan summers.

The days can be hot, but the nights can still be really cold. Gunner notices I'm getting cold and without asking me again, he puts his arm around my shoulders and steers me inside.

I notice we are in a living room that's decorated in all brown tones. He sits me on a large leather sectional sofa. I look around the room. This is the first time I'm actually seeing it. Just thinking about how I was so hot for him that I didn't even look at my surroundings makes me feel ashamed. I drop my head down into my blanket filled hands. I should have never went out tonight.

"I feel so stupid," I mumble into my hands. I know he's waiting for me to start explaining myself. I can feel his gaze piercing me. I guess I shouldn't put it off any longer. The sooner he understands that I'm not good for him, the faster I can get out of here.

"I shouldn't be here. I should have known better than to go out, and I definitely should have known not to come home with you, but if you want me to be honest, you're the first man I've been attracted to in a very long time. I got carried away." I pause letting that sink in. I look down at my bouncing foot hoping he will understand.

I'm not ready for him. He needs a woman who can meet his needs. I give my head a frustrated shake and say, "It's like I can't think straight around you, and for some reason my brain malfunctions. I just wanted to have one night. One night of not worrying and... What? Why are you smiling?" I ask exasperated when I see how happy he looks. Here I am spilling my guts and he thinks it's funny?

"Well, from what I've gathered, you're attracted to me, and I make your brain malfunction. Is that right, Josie?"

He's teasing me right now. I'm sitting here naked in his living room and I've just had a major freak out. I feel like a total fool and he wants to make fun of me?

"I'm trying to be serious here, Gunner!" I cry.

"I'm sorry," he says clearing his throat. "Keep going."

I don't keep going. He's not taking me seriously. I just shake my head.

"Okay then, answer some questions for me, you said you haven't been attracted to a man in a long time, why?"

Well, why doesn't he just jump right to the heart of the matter? "I don't want to talk about that," I say quietly, as I curl my legs under me on the couch so my foot will stop drawing attention to how nervous I am.

He scowls at me and says, "Tell me what you're comfortable with then, for now. Do you mean you haven't had a boyfriend in that long, or you haven't had sex in that long? Explain."

"Both." I whisper not looking at him, trying to avoid any complicated answers that will lead to more questions.

"I'm going to assume the panic attacks have something to do with that?"

I don't want to go into this. I don't want to tell him anymore. I don't say anything else, I just shrug and look away.

"Fine, I just have one more question. Is this the reason you want to hire a private investigator? Because if you need my help, all you have to do is ask."

I stare at him and then quickly look away again. This is all getting too complicated. If I tell him, he has to share the information with his team. I don't think I can trust that. Not with the plans I have. It's all too dangerous, and as much as I would like to have someone like Gunner in my corner. I just don't know what to do. This is all too much. I need to get away, I need time to think about all of this.

I stand up and head towards the stairs. I need to find my dress.

"Josie, where do you think you're going?" he growls at me. It makes me slow a little then speed back up. Uh-oh, I know I'm making him angry, but that's just more incentive for me to leave. If I can just use his phone to call a cab, I can go downstairs and wait by the door.

"I need my dress. I have to get home." I tell him.

"Babe, I get that you're freaked out, but like I said. You aren't going anywhere until we talk." He says stalking up the stairs behind me. He's still wearing only his jeans, that are unzipped by the way, not that I noticed. His chest and ab muscles move as he's walking up the stairs. His biceps rippling as his arms swing. I try not to notice that either. I tear my eyes away and I spot my dress at the foot of the bed on the floor. I go pick it up, still clutching the blanket around me with one hand and start to head into the bathroom.

"I wouldn't put that on if I were you, you'll be much more comfortable sleeping in one of my t-shirts." He says walking over to a dresser, opening a drawer and pulling one out.

"I have to go, I'm not sleeping here. If you can please just let me get dressed and call a cab, I'll be out of your hair."

"Clue in Josie, because this is the last time I'm saying it. You aren't going anywhere until we talk. I understand that you're not ready right now. So let's get some sleep, we'll worry about everything else in the morning. You are not getting dressed and going out in a cab in the middle of the night, and I'm not taking you home. Put on the t-shirt," he says throwing it across the room at me.

I'm in such shock from him just basically telling me he's not letting me leave that I drop the hold I have on the blanket and catch the t-shirt. Here I am standing naked with a dress in one hand and a t-shirt in the other looking at him in disbelief. I can practically feel my eyes bugging out of my head.

"You can't stop me from going home!" I practically yell and stomp my foot at him. "I'm not staying here, Gunner!"

I see that smirk spread across his face and I yank the dress and t-shirt in front of me to cover myself.

"Just making sure you're taken care of. After what happened earlier, I'm not letting you out of my sight until I'm sure you'll be okay. I'm the one that caused it, and I need to make sure you're good. The end."

I can see the sincerity in his eyes. He's feeling guilty when he shouldn't be. None of this is his fault. It's Brian Hanson's fault, and my fault for coming over here tonight without thinking.

I close my eyes and say softly, "Thank you for your concern, but I'll be fine. You aren't responsible for this. You may have triggered the panic attack because there are things you don't know, but you aren't the cause of them."

"Exactly. I triggered it because there are things I don't know, which is my point. That's why we need to talk. I don't ever want to do that shit again. I need to know what to avoid, and you need to tell me, because this a long way from over."

I shake my head. He isn't getting it. "Gunner, I can't stay here. There's nothing to talk about because this *has* to be over. Trust me when I tell you that you're better off this way."

He narrows those gorgeous eyes at me and I feel the intensity of his words when he says, "Trust you? Now there's a thought. Okay, Josie, I'll trust that you're right about this, *for now*. I'll give you some time without pushing you about anything, *for now*. In return, you and I are going to spend some time getting to know each other."

I try to process this, he's trying to make a deal? And I'm pretty sure he loaded that deal in his favor. Having Gunner in my space isn't going to help me. I can't think around him. He makes me crave things I shouldn't. Of course I can't tell him that, so if this is what I need to agree to in order to get out of here, then I'll do it. "Fine," I lie, "now please take me home."

He chuckles. "I told you I'm keeping an eye on you tonight and I meant it. I won't push for answers, and I won't touch you unless you want me to. Deal?"

He's infuriating! I turn on a huff, march into the bathroom and slam the door. I hear him laugh. Jerk. I don't even know how to explain to him that I can't sleep here. I don't have my sleeping pills and I can't sleep without them. If I do, I have nightmares and end up awake at all hours of the night.

I splash some cold water on my face. God, I'm just so worn out. This whole night is catching up with me. I dejectedly hang the dress on the end of the towel rack and put on the t-shirt.

I look at myself in the mirror and see that the t-shirt says in big letters, *Property of Layne Investigations and Security* on it.

Just wonderful.

It's huge on me, but I'm glad. I'm feeling way too exposed tonight. I wish I knew where my panties went. After tonight, they're probably beyond salvaging anyway, I think while shaking my head at myself.

What a freakin' disaster.

I pull open the door and see Gunner has removed his jeans and is wearing only his boxer briefs. I swallow. Can't he just quit being so sexy for once? Geez!

He smirks, like he knows my thoughts. "I'll take the couch," I say heading towards the door in a hurry to get out of the room and away from him in only his underwear.

"You're not sleeping on the couch, babe. We're both sleeping in the bed." He tells me.

When I start to protest he walks over to me and gets close to my face looking into my eyes. "I promised not to push, and I keep my promises. But baby, we are not sleeping in separate rooms. There's nothing to be shy about. You came all over my face tonight, remember?"

I think my jaw just hit the floor, *he did not just say that*! I mean, it is the truth, but he doesn't just have to say it out loud like that! I can feel my cheeks turning red just from remembering exactly how it felt to have his face down there. Damn it all to hell.

"Fine Mr. Bossy, but it's your loss. I can't sleep without my sleeping pills, and since you wouldn't let me go home, I don't have them. That means I'm probably going to keep you awake the rest of the night, and not in a good way either!" With that I walk over to the bed, yank back the covers and crawl in. And just to make my point, I slap them back over myself in a quick angry move.

"We'll survive, don't worry." He says like it's nothing, then walks into the bathroom and shuts the door. For the first time I look around taking in his bedroom. He has a big bed frame with long sleek, silver bars on the headboard. All of the accent furniture looks black and masculine. His walls are gray. Even his sheets and comforter are black and gray.

He comes out a minute later, turns out the light, and climbs into bed with me. He slides across the bed and presses his front into my back, puts one arm over me, kisses my cheek and settles in pulling me closer. "Night beautiful," he whispers.

I let out a loud sigh and try to scoot away but he instantly pulls me back against him. I hear him give a low chuckle, like he knows exactly how frustrating he is and he enjoys it. How can someone be so infuriating and so sexy at the same time? I squeeze my eyes shut. God please help me sleep without dreams. I need this night to be over and I need to forget about Gunner Layne, even if he did just call me beautiful.

Chapter 18

Gunner

I feel her breathing slow and evenly in my arms. She's not talking, but at least she's here. I don't know what it's going to take for her to trust me but I'm not giving up until she lets me in. I'm getting to her, even if she won't admit it. I smile thinking about how she called me *Mr. Bossy*. Little does she know, I'm going easy on her. This is nothin'.

I suddenly feel guilty for expecting her to share her secrets, when I'm holding onto my own. I already decided to send Brian Hanson packing, but I need to come clean with her about the reason we "ran" into each other. I can't do it yet though. I have a feeling once she knows, she will shut down on me completely. She's already so distrustful.

Fuck, just remembering how she couldn't breathe tonight makes me angry. I don't know if it has anything to do with her former boss, but I was willing to bet that whatever happened to her, happened while she was in Detroit.

I know one thing, nobody is going to lay a hand on Josie again. Nobody but me. She is now under my protection, she just doesn't know it yet.

I need to be around enough to get her comfortable with me. I'll have to take it slow and let her decide when she's ready to be physical with me. This is totally new territory for me. I can't even believe I'm thinking like this.

Something tells me Josie isn't accustomed to a man who's reliable being in her life. If she learns that I can give her that, maybe she will let me be with her. Lord knows I don't deserve a sweet girl like Josie, but I'm not giving her up now. I've had a glimpse of her, and it's enough to let me know that she's what I've been wanting all along. Not only is she beautiful, she's sexy, smart, and funny when she forgets to be nervous.

I think about the way she slammed the bathroom door, and I like that too. She's spirited underneath all of that apprehension.

Having her lying in my arms, in my bed is killing me, but I like having her close. I like the feel of her, and the smell of her, and seeing her brown hair spread out all over my pillow. But fuck if I don't have a hard on again. It seems to be a constant problem with her around.

I promised her that I wouldn't push, but damn it. Just thinking of her in my *Property of Layne* t-shirt with nothing underneath was enough to raise my blood pressure.

I didn't miss the fact that her panties are still on the floor where I threw them and she hadn't had a bra on with that dress, which meant there was nothing between my hand and Josie except that t-shirt. All I had to do was pull it up a little... Fuck!

Quit being an asshole Layne!

Time to think about baseball. I close my eyes and try not to think of her naked. The all-star game is coming up. I wonder who's going to be picked. I run through some players in my head. Trying to decide who would be the best choices. Who the hell am I kidding?

I open my eyes and see that she's breathing heavier. I wonder what happened to her that requires her to medicate herself in order to sleep. What makes her stay awake all night keeping watch while everyone else is asleep? What or who is she so afraid of?

Slowly and steadily I pan to find the answers. I know that right now more than anything, I just want her to feel safe enough to sleep with me and not be afraid. She looks peaceful while sleeping. I look down under the covers, and even her little foot is still for the moment. That's a good sign.

****

When I wake in the morning, it's still early. I notice that sometime during the night I rolled onto my back, and surprisingly enough Josie has turned over and is sleeping with her head on my chest. It makes something deep inside me feel content for the first time in a long time.

I take in her beauty. Her hair drifting over my arm. Her long lashes resting against her cheeks. Her lips slightly parted.

Shit, if I don't get out of this bed I'm going to break my promise. Her hand is splayed across my stomach, if she moves it down much farther she's going to get one hell of a wakeup call. With a sigh of regret I scoot out of bed as carefully as possible. She stirs a little, and gives a small sleepy sound, but then settles.

I brush my teeth and take care of business, throwing on some pajama pants. I head to the kitchen to start the coffee and make us some breakfast. She doesn't realize it, but today is the beginning of *Operation Win Josie.* She may think she's going to push me away and stay hidden behind those walls of hers, but she better think again. There is way too much sweetness, and life, and passion in that little woman to have it hidden away. She should not live in fear. She deserves better, and I'm going to make sure she gets it.

Chapter 19

Josie

I wake up feeling so comfortable that I debate falling back asleep for a minute before I decide to open my eyes and see what time it is. As I take in my surroundings, I remember what happened the night before.

Shit!

I slide out of bed noticing that Gunner is nowhere to be seen, so I head to the bathroom to take care of myself. I spot a spare toothbrush and make use of it. One thing's for sure, cosmos do not taste good the day after.

I hope Gunner will let me wear a pair of shorts or something. I really don't want to put that dress back on and do the walk of shame. I think back to how caring he was with me last night. Then I remember how bossy he was. Better to focus on that.

I square my shoulders and decide to go find him. It doesn't matter whether he's wonderful, or bossy, or both, he's not for me.

I follow my nose to the kitchen. I see him cooking scrambled eggs and toast. I realize how hungry I am. It smells so good. I had every intention of getting out of here fast, but the smell of breakfast, and coffee, and the sight of Gunner in his PJ pants have me re-thinking my plan. I try not to stare at the tattoo on his chest. I notice it's some kind of tribal design around the letter L.

Hot!

When he looks up and sees me standing there in his shirt he comes over and takes my hand leading me to little table for two by the window. He pulls out the chair without a word, waits for me to sit, and then scoots my chair in, all the while still holding a spatula in one hand.

Next thing I know he bends down, kisses my forehead and says, "Mornin' baby." Just like that. No awkwardness. No anger. Nothing but good morning. I'm not sure what to do with this.

"I take it you slept well?" he asks.

I think about it for the first time. I did sleep well. In fact, that's the first time I remember sleeping without a sleeping pill and not having nightmares. Usually I have to take them just to make sure that I'm so out of it I can't even dream.

I'm pretty sure I shouldn't tell him that, so I just nod my head. I cross my legs and he gives me a look when he notices my foot start bouncing.

"Um, thanks for last night," I tell him, feeling strange and not really knowing how to address it. "I mean, for helping me, you know...and I'm sorry."

"I hope you're hungry," he says plating up the eggs. Before I know it there is coffee, eggs and toast in front of me. It looks delicious. Evidently he has decided to keep his word about not pushing me for explanations. Thank goodness. I relax sitting back to enjoy the food.

"This is really good, thanks," I say eating another forkful of eggs. "You don't really strike me as the cooking type."

"Eggs and toast are about the extent of my culinary skills," he laughs. "Well, unless you count heating up canned soup, or making a frozen pizza. How about you, do you cook?" He asks sitting down to join me.

"Sometimes. I like to cook if there are other people around," I tell him. It's true. I usually don't do it just for myself, but I cook often if Faith is going to be home. Sometimes I make stuff and take it to Rick and Eddie, or Justine. They all force me to make my cucumber dip for every single mojito night, and most of the time they talk me into making my Kahlua trifle too.

Most recently I made a lasagna and took it over to Mrs. Williams because I knew she could use the help. It worked out better for me if I kept the carbs in other people's homes.

"Maybe you can repay the favor later and cook me dinner," he says looking at me with a raised eyebrow.

"I, um, don't think I can. I have to get home and do some work, and Freddy and I still need to go for our run."

"I need to get in a run too, how about if I tag along with you and Freddy?"

I didn't have a good enough excuse on the tip of my tongue so I just give him a shrug.

"I doubt Freddy and I will be able to keep your pace," I say, "but I guess we can give it a try."

"It's time Freddy and I have some quality time together anyway, he should get used to me." He states this like he's planning on moving in or something. I don't know what he's thinking, but if he wants a run, fine, we can go for a run, but then he is going home and I'm doing my best to forget about this disaster.

"So why did you name him Freddy?" he asks again.

I take a breath. I suppose it's a safe enough topic. So I tell him, "I'm named after Josephine March, from the book *Little Women*. It's one of the few good things my mom ever did for me. I like the name, because she was my favorite character." I'm a little embarrassed to explain it so I just say, "Anyway, Friedrich was Jo's professor. He was nice to her and he looked out for her, so I named my dog Freddy after Friedrich Bhaer, one of the other characters."

I pick up my coffee and start drinking, hoping to avoid any more questions. Most people don't question why my dog has a name like Freddy, but this guy doesn't miss much. I guess that's why he makes a good investigator. I need to be careful with him. He could push his way past my defenses and figure out what I'm up to before I realize it.

"So you don't have a good relationship with your mom?" he asks. I set myself up for that one. I suppose talking about my crazy mother is a fairly safe subject.

"No. She moved to Florida when my dad died. We've never been close," I tell him. "I only hear from her if she runs out of money from gambling too much." I don't know why I say that. I notice him scowling and wonder what's caused that face again. He seems to do that often, especially if he doesn't like something. I'm not sure why he would care that my mother is a bitch. It's not his problem.

"Does she do that often? Contact you asking for money, I mean?"

"Not too often anymore. She blew the life insurance money pretty fast, and I tried to help her a few times, but when it got to be a habit, I just couldn't keep up. I don't make enough to keep doing it." He continues to scowl, so I think I better change the subject.

"Would it be okay for me to use your phone and call a cab?" I ask. "I might need to borrow a pair of shorts, if you don't mind. I can return them later if you decide to run with us."

"Finish up, then I'll get you some shorts and take you home myself," he says.

"You don't have to..."

"Nope, don't have to, but I'm going to anyway, because I want to," he says like it's the most logical thing in the world.

"Fine." I sigh, I'm not about to sit here and argue with him. The man is like a pit bull when he has his mind set on something. He can drive me home, go for a run later, then things can return to normal.

I can't handle these emotional highs and lows that come from being around him. "You're very bossy, you know that right?" I say finishing off my toast.

He laughs, "I suppose I am, I'm the youngest son, but my mom says I was born telling everybody what to do."

That makes me smile. I can picture little bossy Gunner issuing orders to his family. "How many siblings do you have?"

"Three. Summer, who's the youngest and the only girl, and then me, Hunter, who is in the Army, and Walker, a cop."

"Poor Summer," I say shaking my head. I can't imagine having three brothers, especially if they are all like Gunner.

He smirks. "Yeah. No wonder she left, she was probably afraid she'd never meet anyone with the guts to ask her out. How about you? Any siblings?"

I shake my head no. I always wished I had siblings.

"So," I say, "What made you decide to be a detective?"

"I was a cop, like Walker, but it wasn't for me. So I opened my office, and I'm hoping my brothers will join me in the future. Right now I have a few good men, but I would love to have my brothers around now that business has picked up. They're good at what they do."

"Why didn't you like being a cop?" I wonder aloud. I get caught up in him and the way he talks so freely about family. It makes me wish I had a big family who I fit in with.

"Three reasons." He says, always straight to the point. It seems abrasive and rude sometimes, but there are other times I like how decisive and clear he is on everything. "One, I don't like rules and red tape, I'd rather get shit done. Two, I don't like seeing people using a badge to get away with shit they couldn't normally get away with. And three, I like to make good money."

I don't really have anything to say to that, it all makes perfect sense when he puts it like that. I stand up to take care of the dishes, he just sits back and watches me take our dishes to the sink and rinse them off. I also turn and rinse out the pans he used on the stove, then I put them in the dishwasher. It's not full so I just close it and wipe down the counters before turning back and saying, "How about those shorts?"

He walks up the stairs to the bedroom and I follow. He opens a drawer and throws a pair of black shorts with white stripes down the side. They look like basketball shorts. Like the t-shirt, they are huge.

I look around the room hoping to spot my panties. He knows what I'm doing because I see him grin. Instead of giving him the satisfaction of asking for them, I roll my eyes and turn my back to him slipping the shorts on, guess I'm going commando. They fall below my knees and look like some weird type of capri pants. The waist is not tight enough to stay up. They sag down to my hips and hang there, but at least the t-shirt covers it.

I turn around to let him know I'm ready to go and notice he's studying me. Then he just drops the pajama pants. Okay, crap, I better not look at him. I don't want to think about how he looks without clothes on.

I turn and stare at the wall. I can see him out of the corner of my eye pulling on jeans and a t-shirt. When I think it's safe to look, I turn my head toward him. The neat in his eyes, is a surprise. I thought I would have cured him of that last night.

He turns and heads to the stairs shaking his head. He says, "I'm never washing those shorts again."

Chapter 20

Gunner

Josie is giving me directions to her house as we're riding, but I'm not paying a lot of attention. I already know where her house is located. I'm just enjoying how she has to lean up against me when she wants to yell in my ear. This ride is quite different from last night's ride to my apartment. Josie isn't wrapped around me as tight as she can get, and her hands aren't in my shirt. In fact, I'm pretty sure she doesn't like holding on to me right now, but she doesn't have a choice.

Thinking about her wearing my shorts and nothing else underneath, straddling my bike is driving me a little crazy. I wasn't kidding. I'm not washing them. Hell no.

As we park in her driveway she scrambles off the bike quickly trying to get her helmet off before I try to do it for her. Fuck, she's cute. Now it's like I make her nervous and she doesn't want me close at all. Although, I get the sense that it's not from fear, but from attraction, even if she won't admit it. That's okay, I'm not going anywhere.

I'm going to go so slow with her she's going to beg me to make the moves. I've already got my mind made up. I just need to figure out how to come clean with her about the job so we can put that behind us.

I'm hoping Faith is home. I really want to talk to her alone sometime to see what she'll tell me about Josie. I know she's loyal to Josie, but I'm hoping she'll see the benefit in helping me get closer.

Just as we are walking to the door I hear Josie yell, "Get out of here, you stupid freakin' cat!" Then she takes off running along the little walkway that goes to the back of the house with her arms flailing around.

I follow her wondering why the hell she's yelling at a cat. When I round the corner to the back of the house I see her running to a garden, and a cat running away.

"Ughhhh, I HATE that cat!" she yells. "Every damn day I have to chase it away because it comes over here and poops in my garden. I swear, if I ever catch it I'm going to have fun torturing it!"

Did I mention she's cute? I swear she's practically having a conniption over a cat and a garden. I can barely get her to open up about anything, but she doesn't mind showing her temper about this. It's giving me a hard on.

"Cat's gone babe," I tell her wearing a really big grin that I know is only going to frustrate her further. "Let's head inside."

"Don't laugh at me Gunner, I am a responsible pet owner. I pick up poop from Freddy whenever I have to, but I do not have a cat! I don't want a cat! Yet somehow I have to clean up cat shit every DAY!" She's getting a little more worked up by the minute.

I can't help it, I laugh. Probably a bad idea, but it really is funny.

"Oh, go ahead and laugh. That cat is my nemesis! I swear I will put an end to that cat coming in my garden one day."

"Babe, I hate to bring up the obvious, but you have a German shepherd. Why don't you just let Freddy eat it if it upsets you that much?"

"Freddy doesn't like cats." She says putting her hands on her hips as if she's sticking up for a friend. "He may be a guard dog, but he only attacks humans on my command. Not cats. Believe me, I tried, and Freddy wouldn't have anything to do with it."

Holy shit, she's serious. I turn slightly hoping she won't see how hilarious I think this is. I can't help it, I bend at the waste and let it out. After I'm gasping a bit, I say, "Sorry, but this shit is too good to make up."

"I know, right?" she says, with her eyes all big, like she's wondering why this is happening to her. "I've even tried spreading coffee grounds in the garden every morning, because I read the smell would keep cats away. Oh no, not this cat. This cat probably sits around drinking a cup of coffee in the morning while it plots the best way to shit all over my garden!"

I throw my head back and laugh loudly at that. Funny, sexy, with a little bit of temper mixed in. How the hell did this girl stay untouched for years? I can't figure it out. She had to have a lot of guys come on to her. Or has she just kept herself so hidden away that she doesn't put herself in that position? I'm betting on the latter.

When I look her way, I see she's started laughing too as Faith comes out a back patio door asking us what's so funny.

She's staring at Josie. It's like she's inspecting her trying to figure out what happened last night.

"The cat," Josie says. "He finds it amusing." She gives an eye roll for good measure. Lord help me, I think I might love this girl.

"Well it is pretty funny, thinking about how that cat hates you and Freddy. You know, I bet it sits around plotting ways to poop all over this place just to piss you off," she laughs.

We all laugh at that. I can see Freddy pacing by the back patio door wanting out. He's making a huffing sound while staring at Josie.

"I think someone's mad at you for not coming home last night," Faith tells her. "And it's not me."

Josie walks to the door and opens it. Damn if that dog didn't look like a jealous child. "Awww, I'm sorry Freddy," she coos to him. "I'll make it up to you."

I raise my eyebrows as if in question, and she rolls her eyes again. "He's not used to me being gone. We're always together," she says patting his head.

"Don't worry, I'll win him over," I say confidently.

"Oh really? I'm dying to see this," she says issuing a challenge.

She doesn't think I can do it. However, I have yet to meet a dog that doesn't respond to a treat, and since it's my job to do a lot of lurking around, I keep them handy. I reach in my pocket and pull out a Slim Jim.

"That's cheating!" Josie practically yells.

"Not if it works," I tell her. I rip a piece off the beef stick and say, "Hi Freddy," holding out my hand to him. He gives Josie a look and then comes over and takes the beef out of my hand.

I rip off a second piece and say, "I promise to bring you one of these every time I visit, as long as we can be buds." He takes the second piece and eats it then looks for more.

I give him the third piece and say, "Can we shake on it?" Holding out my hand. Sure enough, he sits on his ass and puts a paw out for me to shake.

"Good boy," I tell him with a smile, then I stand and smile at Josie who's looking at me like she can't believe what she just saw.

"Stop making deals with my dog," she glares at me and spins on her heel, saying, "C'mon Freddy, you traitor." Then she leads him inside and doesn't look back.

I look at Faith wondering why I just earned the look of death. She looks from the door to me, from me to the door and starts smiling really big.

"What?" I ask.

"This is going to be good," she says. "Please tell me you didn't let her blow you off." She looks like she's begging me for the right answer.

Now I understand. This is what Josie does, she runs away when people make her uncomfortable. She's been trying to do it since her panic attack last night.

"She won't get rid of me that easy," I tell Faith, "I can be a stubborn asshole." I say with pride.

She grins back. I think I might have a secret weapon in good ol' Faith.

I look at her seriously and say, "I wanted to set up a time where I could talk to you alone."

"Why?" She looks confused. Then distrustful. Then confused again.

"It's nothing bad, relax. It's just that I want to talk about Josie. I know you're best friends, so I don't expect you to tell her secrets, but I would still like to talk to you in private."

I tell her quietly, "She had a panic attack last night at my place. Scared the living shit out of me. So like I said, I don't want you telling her secrets, but I do need your help."

She's staring at me. I didn't miss the way her eyes got big and scared looking at the mention of one of Josie's panic attacks. My guess is she's seen a lot more of them than me, and she doesn't like them any more than I do.

She nods and gives me her cell phone. "Put in your number, I'll text you." I take it and put in my number then give it back to her. She doesn't say anything else just indicates with a nod of her head that we should go in, so I follow her in.

We walk in the patio doors, through the kitchen. I hear voices as we approach what appears to be the living room. I'm surprised to see the guys from the bar last night in the living room, along with another chick and a little boy.

Josie is sitting next to the one named Eddie and he has his arm around her. I see her leaning into him with her head on her shoulder, and the sight makes me want to spit nails. I've never been a jealous guy, but for some reason the fact that Josie seems to be taking comfort from this guy instead of me hits me right in the gut.

"Well, well, well, he *is* hot, way to go girl! I'm a little jealous." Says the woman I don't know. That gets laughter from the room, except for Josie, she's blushing again and giving the lady big eyes as if to say *shut up* while her foot bounces up and down.

"Mmmhmmm, me too," says Rick. "Go figure, the one with no game gets the hottie." Then he waves his hand around saying, "Whatever."

Josie speaks up and says, "Shut up guys. By the way Gunner, this is Justine. And that," she says pointing to a little boy who's playing with Freddy, "is Levi."

Standing up she goes to the boy and gives him a pat on the head like I've seen her give to Freddy. Damn, I'm now jealous of a toddler and a dog, as well as a gay guy. At least I think he's gay. He better be gay.

146

"Nice to meet ya," Justine says batting her eyelashes at me, which makes everyone laugh again.

"Alright back off you nymphs," Faith says. "Gunner doesn't need to be introduced to all of our craziness on the first visit. We should save some for later."

"That'd be good," I say, "because I'll be back later. Josie and I are going for a run. And Freddy of course."

At the mention of his name Freddy stands up and wanders over to me sniffing my hand that held the Slim Jim. I notice Josie doesn't look very happy about that.

Maybe I should have told her about the beef stick ahead of time. Who knew she'd get mad about a beef stick. Somehow I suspect it has more to do with me working my way into her space, than it does with the actual treat. Fine by me.

I take notice of the looks everyone is giving each other. They aren't used to Josie having male company. Good.

"What time should I be back?" I ask her.

"Well, I have some work to do first, and I'd like to go before dinner. How does four sound?"

"Yeah, you guys can do your run and I'll work on dinner while you're gone, then Gunner can stay for dinner." Faith says smiling.

I see Josie give her a big eyed *what the hell* look again. Faith is going to be my new best friend. I'm lovin' this girl.

"He's just coming for the run," Josie tells her. Faith frowns at her like she's being rude. So Josie says "Well, I mean, that was the plan anyway."

"Well, you do owe me for breakfast," I remind her. That gets more looks from everyone around the room. "So I would love to stay for dinner, thanks."

I see her give a sigh as if she's resigned to the fact that Faith and I have made plans for her. "Fiiinnne," she says stretching the word out, like she isn't happy about it but she's going to agree anyway.

"Well, I'll have him over for dinner if you don't want to," Justine says provocatively. "I can make a mean pot roast." Then she gives me a wink.

"I do like pot roast," I respond in a teasing tone, like I might just take Justine up on the offer. I act like I'm trying to decide, when Josie speaks up.

"That's a great idea. You'd be lucky to…um…have pot roast with Justine."

I give her a scowl. What the fuck? Is she trying to pass me off on her friend? I know she likes me underneath all of that nervousness. I think she's scared we're going to end up where we were last night again, so she'd rather run away than face it.

She doesn't know it yet, but we sure as fuck will end up in bed again, but with a very different ending. I just have to bide my time. Show her I care. Let her get comfortable with me.

"You crazy?" Justine says giving her a look that clearly says, *pull your head out of your ass*. "I was joking, girl. Ooooeeee, you better knock that shit off before you make me mad."

Josie makes her way back to Eddie. It's clear she gets some kind of comfort from him and I'm not sure what to think of it. She doesn't say anything, she just sits next to him and he puts a hand on her back.

"Sooo," Faith says trying to cut the awkwardness. "Dinner it is. I'll make one of Josie's favorites. How about smothered chicken?" Then she goes on to explain that it's a chicken breast covered in all kinds of stuff, like cheese and bacon. I quit listening after that, because it sounds fucking great.

"Sounds excellent." I tell her.

"Josie, you need to make your dip!" Rick yells and claps his hands. "Then give me and Eddie some." He laughs like that's a genius idea. "Or better yet, how about the trifle? Or both. Please?" He begs, while actually poking out his bottom lip.

"I'm not making both! I have work to do. I'll think about the trifle." she says trying to make him happy. I can tell she has a good relationship with these people. I'm glad she has friends. They all seem concerned with her, even though they don't say it.

"I don't know what a trifle is, but I'll try anything once." I tell her with a suggestive tone knowing it will make her blush.

I see Justine slap Rick in the arm, like she's enjoying me flirting with Josie. Josie's cheeks are pink, and I've accomplished my goal. I decide I better go. I don't want to push so hard that she shuts me out.

"Gotta go get some shit done," I tell them. Then I look at Josie and say, "Be back at four." She gives me a nod like that's the end of the conversation, but I'm not letting her off that easy.

I'm not going to push, but I am going to get her used to me, so I walk over to where she's sitting, lean down and kiss her cheek, and whisper, "later babe," in her ear. I notice her pretty little face turning from pink to red as I head out the door.

Chapter 21

Josie

He did *not* just kiss me and say 'later babe' in front of everyone! I'm a little freaked out, and a little turned on at the same time. I don't know what to do with any of this. I'm so overwhelmed. It's been so long since I've had a guy in my home, in my space, interacting with my friends, or touching me. I'm feeling excited, but resentful too. I feel like he's pushed his way into my life and I'm not sure it's safe to have him here.

"Spill it, girlfriend!" Justine practically yells at me when the door shuts. "They told me you were gone *all* night long."

Rick bounces on his chair saying, "OMG! Give me details. Is he as hot underneath the clothes as I'm imagining?"

I put my face in my hands. "C'mon you guys. I didn't have sex with him. I just... I drank too much... I should have never left with him. Now he's being all nice and then annoying and inviting himself to dinner. I mean, I don't think I like any of this!"

"You seemed pretty happy with him last night." Eddie reminds me. "I would have put up an objection to you leaving with him, but you were clearly enjoying yourself and wanted to go with him."

"I know, I know, it's just, I should have known better. I thought I could do it, but I can't." I don't know if I want to laugh or burst into tears when Faith jumps in to save me. She can tell how nervous this is making me. My stupid foot is bouncing like crazy.

"Alright guys, we have to run to the grocery store," Faith says. "Is anyone else coming for dinner tonight?"

I notice they all conveniently have plans for the evening. Right. Any time we offered up smothered chicken and a trifle, they would all be there an hour early just to drool on themselves.

Faith and I hug and kiss them all goodbye and then close the door behind them.

"Okay, you are so going to spill your guts while we get groceries." She says pointing her finger at me with big eyes. She's letting me know I may have dodged the others, but there's no way I'm dodging her.

I watch her walk into the kitchen and come back with my purse and phone, handing it to me. "I charged it for you. You're welcome."

I give her a nudge with my elbow. She succeeds in making me smile. "I need to change, then we can go," I say and head to my room.

"Don't think I didn't notice that what that t-shirt says!" She yells down the hall after me. I shut my door without responding. I mean, what am I going to say? I have to be honest with her, she's my best friend. It's going to suck though.

I know she is going to enccurage me to go after Gunner. She's going to see this as a good thing. She doesn't know that I can't afford to get involved with him.

I quickly change into some shorts, finally putting on some panties. I throw on a bra with a t-shirt that actually fits me anc then head back out.

Things are pretty quiet on the way to the store, Faith is driving us in her red Dodge Charger. As usual, her car is much cooler than mine. I love it though, I think it's an awesome car, especially for someone like Faith, who works hard and loves to have fun.

I know she's waiting for me to talk to her about Gunner. She's giving me a chance to tell her, but I stay quiet. I don't want to tell her about it, even though I know she will always have my back.

Once we park and head into the store, she says, "Times up. Let's have it."

Crap.

I don't know where to start. I shrug, another one of my annoying habits according to her, that

I use to pretend I don't care when I really do care. Whatever.

"Don't give me the shrug or I will run you over with this cart," she threatens. "I know you Josie Black, and this is the first guy you've really liked in a long time. He's the first one you've let get close enough to actually spend some time with. And knowing you like I do, my guess is that you *really* like him, and now you're freaking out."

I hate her sometimes.

"I got carried away okay? I drank too much. I thought I could get back on the horse, as you so eloquently put it, but I can't. I just... couldn't."

"I'm going to need more details than that. Are you saying you tried to... um... get back on the horse... and his equipment failed or what?"

"Oh my God!" I slap her in the arm. "I'm just going to lay it out for you and then I'm done okay? I don't want to spend the day talking about this. There's nothing wrong with his equipment."

"Thank God!" she says throwing her head back like she's so relieved. "I was about to lose faith in humanity."

I giggle at her. At least she can make me laugh when I'm stressed. "I wanted to. I really did. I can't explain the kind of physical reaction I have to him... it's just... "

"I understand completely," she rolls her eyes. "Don't forget I've experienced a Layne brother first hand. They're hot. All of them."

I see the brief look of wistfulness that crosses her face before she hides it behind her smile. I know she and Hunter have a past, but even as best friends, we didn't talk about it.

Faith went out with him once that I know of. Then he was gone and she moped around for months. Anytime I asked her about it she just said it was nothing, but I *know* her. It was not nothing.

"Right." I wasn't touching that subject right now. It was the only thing she had never shared with me, but I knew she would when she was ready. "It's just been so long since I wanted someone." I went on to explain, "I had too many drinks and I just let my body take over. And you know the weird part? In that moment, I didn't care, I didn't need to be in control. I wanted him to take control. I just wanted him and that's all I could focus on, ya know?"

I look at her hoping she understands, and she's nodding her head. She gets it. "Things were really hot and heavy. I mean, we were about to... you know." I whisper hoping nobody is close enough to hear me. "And then... oh my God," I put my hands over my face. "I can't even say it out loud."

She's just staring at me, waiting. She's giving me the big eyes that tell me to spill it or she really will hit me with her cart.

I lean over and whisper to her, "He spanked me!"

I pulled back and saw her mouth hanging open. Then she looks at me and it finally hits her. She throws her head back and laughs so hard I think the whole store hears her.

I'm back to hating her.

This time I slap her on the arm really hard and say, "It's not funny!" Then I push her out of the way and take the cart. I'm walking down the aisles so fast gathering the stuff I need, I don't pay any attention to Faith behind me. I feel stupid enough, I don't need her making it worse.

"Okay, okay, I'm sorry!" she says running up beside me. "It's just the last thing I expected to hear. And then I got a mental picture of Gunner Layne giving you a spanking like a naughty school girl." Then she laughs again.

I roll my eyes and say, "Laugh it up Faith Snyder. I'll have you know... I wasn't expecting it... I was surprised, so I didn't understand what he was doing and it set me off... that sound..." I trail off because it really is mortifying when I think about it.

"I had a full blown panic attack right in front of him. The worst one I've had in quite a while. It was humiliating," I say throwing my hands up in defeat. "I can't be the girl he needs, and this just proves I'm not ready. So I'm going to go for the run, and endure the dinner *you* planned for me without asking my permission, then I'm going to try and forget this ever happened."

As I'm explaining this I see her face fall. She's no longer laughing. She knows what my panic attacks are like.

"I'm sorry for laughing," she says, and I know she is. I can tell by the look on her face. "I can see how you'd be surprised. Hell, look how much it shocked me just hearing about it. Those boys have more in common than I thought..." she says like she's deep in thought.

"Did Hunter do that to you?" I ask incredulously. I know my mouth is hanging open. What is wrong with these men?

"Yep, he sure did." I look over at her and expect to see her smiling, but she's not. She looks angry. I can't tell if it's because she liked it and didn't get more, or because she didn't like it at all.

"I know that most women probably like that stuff, especially with a man like Gunner. Maybe if I knew it was coming I could have enjoyed it or at the very least handled it better. It was horrible. I do not want to get in that situation again. What if he does something else to trigger me again?" I ask feeling nauseous just thinking about it.

"Well, let me give you the perspective of an outsider. I think he genuinely likes you and cares about you. When he saw you last night, he didn't know about anything from your past. He saw a beautiful, hot, birthday girl who was out partying and looking for a good time. I think he got carried away just like you did. It's clear there is some major chemistry between the two of you. If you can open up to him, then I think you would be great together. Maybe he just messed up, the way you think you messed up. Maybe you should just give him another chance." She says logically with hope in her eyes.

I hate to rain on her parade, but it's not going to happen and I tell her so. "It's not going to happen. I can't tell him about my past. He's a detective. He's already asking too many questions." I whisper putting the groceries down on the counter to pay and glance at a magazine while we wait for the clerk to ring us up.

"Josie, I think you can trust him. Think of him being a detective as a good thing, not a bad thing. He can help you..."

I stop her before she keeps listing her reasons. There are too many people around. I don't want to hear anymore. There's nothing I would love more than to feel safe. If I'm honest with myself I hate the thought of never seeing Gunner again, but I know it needs to be that way.

Once we're back in the car heading home Faith says, "Just think about it. He could be really good for You JoJo. He could be, like, the *one*."

She just doesn't get it. I shake my head but don't respond. I'm done talking about it.

"Fine," she says, "be alone, if that's what makes you happy."

I can't tell if she's being snippy, or if she's just stating an observation. I look over at her and I can't tell because her eyes are on the road.

"It doesn't make me happy, but it's not safe to be with him! He doesn't understand what needs to be done, and I can't have him getting so curious that he blows everything." I say, getting annoyed.

"I have no idea what you're talking about," she says as she studies me. "What needs to be done? What is he going to blow?"

Shit, shit, *shit.*

This is exactly why I hate talking so much.

"It's just... it's nothing. I'm just not ready." I tell her hoping that she drops it.

She takes the hint. "Let's just drop it," she says and looks over to study me. "I'm sorry if I was hard on you, I just want to see you happy."

"I am happy," I tell her. I feel like it's true. At least it's as true as it will ever be. I'm as happy as I will ever be. I've known for a long time I would end up alone. I've discussed it with my therapist. I've accepted it. It doesn't mean I can't have a fully functioning, enjoyable life. I even think about adopting a child someday.

She doesn't respond. I know she doesn't believe that I'm happy, but it's a far cry from where I came. "Let's just get home. I've got work to do, and baking to get done, thanks to you. We will get through tonight and then we won't have to worry about this anymore," I tell her. I reach over and squeeze her hand. I know she wants the best for me. I love her for that.

"Whatever," she says with an eye roll, squeezing my hand back so that I know that everything between us is okay.

Chapter 22

Gunner

I knock on Josie's door, and hear Freddy come barreling through the house giving a warning growl.

Good boy. I'm glad Freddy is around watching over our girl.

Our girl? Shit, I'm in deep here and I know it.

I've never met a woman that I don't want to keep a safe distance from. I've been happy playing the field and not getting attached. I've never felt the need to check in with someone, just to know they're okay, except for family of course.

I reach in my pocket and pull out Freddy's beef stick. I want him to know I appreciate the job he's doing. He's at the door with his tongue hanging out, looking like he's in a meat induced trance, when Josie rounds the corner and heads to the door. Damn it, she's wearing spandex.

I notice she unlocks the door to let me in. I'm glad to see that she keeps her door locked, but she could use some more security from what I've seen of the house so far. I haven't noticed an alarm system. I make a mental note to check around more when she's not paying attention.

"Did you get a lot of work done?" I ask trying not to look at the spandex.

"Not bad for a weekend," she tells me. "Normally I don't work much on the weekends, but I don't like to get behind." She's still giving me a reserved look, as if she is trying not to remember that I've seen her naked.

Good luck sweetheart, I think, because I know I'll never forget it.

"I see you're back to spandex," I say giving her my shit eating grin because I know I'm about to make those pretty cheeks get even brighter. "Mind if I get my shorts back from you? I brought you a trade." I say pulling her pink lacy panties out of my pocket from the night before and watch her turn beet red. Holy fuck, why do I find this so hot?

She reaches up and pulls them out of my hand with a jerk and turns to head down the hall. "Wait there!" She sticks a finger out at me, and goes into a doorway. When she comes out her panties are gone and she's giving me my shorts. "I washed them for you," she says, giving me a grin of her own now. Shit. She knew I didn't want to wash them.

"Bad girl," I tell her walking closer. "You knew I wanted to savor these."

She's a little uncomfortable, but I can see the smile she keeps trying to hide. "I know. That's why I did it." Then she gives me a smile while lifting her chin in defiance. On most women it would be annoying. On Josie it just makes me want to kiss that look right off her face and then keep going.

I put my hands at her waist and pull her to me. I bend down into her ear and say, "That just means I'll have to get you naked again." I feel her shiver a little and then stiffen and pull away. Right. I remind myself to stick to the plan. I can't get carried away with her the way I want to.

I let her back up and break contact. Time for a distraction. "How far do you run?" I ask her.

"We usually run to the coffee shop, then walk back."

"That's about 5 miles round trip?" I ask impressed. I don't know many girls that can or would do that. Especially on a daily basis.

"Just under. I go easy on Freddy the last half, but only because I want to drink my coffee."

She goes easy on Freddy the big bad German shepherd? "Freddy doesn't like to run?"

"He tolerates it because he knows if he makes it to the coffee shop Rick will give him treats. Don't let him fool you. He's trained to obey, but on the inside I think he's an old retired guy who lives on the beach. He knows how he's *supposed* to act, but somehow I just don't think 'bodyguard' is his calling in life."

Just as she says this, Freddy gives a loud groan and rolls over onto his back putting all fours in the air.

"See!" She says. I laugh. It's funny because I can see exactly what she's talking about.

"I might start withholding Slim Jims if he's slacking on the job." I see Freddy pop one eye open and give me a look. I think he knows the words Slim Jim already.

Josie walks over to him and bends down to rub his belly. "He's a good boy," she coos. "He's always ready to jump back into protection mode when he needs to. It's funny..." she says trailing off.

"What?" I ask.

"Nothing," she says studying Freddy. "I just was thinking how similar we are, that's all."

I wasn't sure what she meant by that, and she started to get that distant look in her eyes. That doesn't sit well with me. I've noticed that she doesn't see what everybody else sees when she looks at herself.

"Stop scowling," she tells me, interrupting my thoughts. "I just mean that we both kinda do the same thing. You know, act like we're supposed to, but it's not who we really are."

No wonder she was looking a little upset at that. I can't believe she's just now noticing it, because I was willing to bet that Josie had been hiding for a very, very long time.

K. D. Smith

Chapter 23

Josie

Way to psychoanalyze yourself and look like a weirdo, I tell myself.

Comparing myself to my dog. That's so sad I could almost laugh, but then he will really think I'm crazy. So I turn to him and say, "Wow, never mind, that was a dumb thing to say."

"Don't say that," he says. "You are definitely not dumb, Josie. You may keep the real you hidden under a tough act, just like you think Freddy does, but that doesn't mean you're dumb. It means you know how to survive. It's just that at some point we have to do more than survive, babe. We have to really *live*."

His words hit me like a physical blow.

It's true. I know he's right, but it makes me angry. He doesn't know me well enough to know what I've survived or who the 'real me' is. Then he insinuates that I don't really live?

That's the same kind of shit Faith says. Don't they see that I am living? Maybe really living for me is different than it is for them. Not everybody is the same. I don't have to live how they think I should. I just have to live, and I believe that once a little more time passes and I do what I need to do, then things will get even better than they are now.

I turn to get Freddy's leash and put it on him. I'm trying not to show my anger. How can I go from practically having a mini orgasm when he talks in my ear, to anger and shame so quickly?

This is why I need to keep my distance. I need to avoid emotional highs and lows. So far that's all I've had with him. I think for a minute about why I'm feeling this way and decide not to dwell on it. I will bring it up in my next session. God knows Dr. Palmer would agree with Faith and Gunner, even though she is much gentler about expressing those thoughts to me.

He doesn't say anything else until we get outside. Then he says, "I didn't mean to upset you. I just don't like you putting yourself down like that. You're too smart for that. Not to mention beautiful."

Well crap. So much for holding on to my anger. "It's okay," I tell him. "It's not like you're the first person to tell me that. I just don't see it the way you do."

I'm done talking about this now. I want to run, have dinner, and try not to freak out in the meantime. I head down the driveway trying to stretch my muscles, then I break into a jog with Freddy at my side. I don't look to see if Gunner's back there. I know he is. I can almost feel the heat of his stare on my backside.

Freddy looks up at me like he's confused. He's not used to having anyone run with us. He looks from me, then behind me, then back at me again. I give him the *friend* sign so he will know that it's okay for Gunner to run with us.

I get into a rhythm and try to get my breathing in check. Freddy's probably sensing my waning anger. I get lost in thought for a while, the way I normally do when I run then I hear footsteps coming up beside me.

"I don't think I should run back there. That's what got us in trouble in the first place." He says and then speeds up so he's in front of me and I'm staring at his sweaty naked back. His shirt is now off and hanging in the waist band of his basketball shorts.

Breathe. Just breathe. And don't drool for crying out loud, I tell myself. Then I think about what he said.

"What do you mean?" I ask his back. Crap, it's muscular and golden and I can see there is another tattoo. Shit. I never found out what the first one was. I was too busy having my freak out. I try not to think about that.

"What I mean is, from the first moment I met you, I was attracted to you. Standing behind you in line at the coffee shop was torture. Seeing your sexy little ass in spandex... damn baby. I decided then and there I wanted to give it a good smack. Don't get me wrong, I won't do that again, and I shouldn't have, I know that. But the spandex is really at fault when you think about it."

I can't help it, I have to laugh and once I start, I can't stop. I start to get a stitch in my side so I hold it with one hand and Freddy with the other. I have to stop and bend a little trying to breathe again.

"You alright?" he asks me still laughing at himself a little, putting his hand on my shoulder.

"Yes," I choke out. "That was funny though, but I'm going to remember to throw away all my spandex."

"No way." He says looking horrified at the idea.

I'm just kidding anyway, but I love his reaction. Besides, compression shorts are great for running.

"I won't blame the spandex anymore," he promises. "It was all my fault. I got so carried away. Everything leading up to that moment just made it worse. Your smell. Seeing your gorgeous nipples. Tasting them. You have a perfect bare pussy."

"I can't believe you just said that," I whisper.

He chuckles, reaching back he gives my ponytail a tug. "I did. Because it's all true, but please, pretty please keep some spandex."

I shake my head, "Seems like the spandex is to blame for a lot of things. If the wax job impressed you, you have the spandex to thank for that. Pubic hair and compression shorts don't mix well." I inform him. Then I realize I probably should have kept that information to myself, but really, a lot of people in this world need to learn that lesson.

He throws his head back and laughs. It's a beautiful thing. It's a genuine, deep, belly laugh. Wow. I watch him feeling a little embarrassed, but he's too busy laughing to pay attention. I shrug. Well, it's the truth. "Please, never make that mistake," I tease him. "It should be against some sort of law." I start running again with a smile on my face.

We made a brief stop at the coffee shop. Rick wasn't there to embarrass me, so I was a little relieved about that. His employees know the drill. They gave Freddy his water and treat, then we head back. I decided to skip the coffee since it's later in the day and we will be eating dinner soon. We run about half of the way back. I can tell Freddy isn't happy about this by the way he keeps shooting his eyes to the side at me like this is bullshit. I know it sounds crazy, but he really can give dirty looks.

Once we get about half way home we slow to a walk. It's hot, I can't wait to go home and take a shower. I'm afraid of what I look like to Gunner with sweat pouring off of me, but he doesn't seem to notice. At least he's just as sweaty as I am, but it looks hot as hell on him. Figures.

It was nice having a running partner besides Freddy. I thought it would be awkward, but it wasn't. We ran in silence quite often, but I didn't have trouble keeping up with him. I suspect he wasn't going as fast as he would have if I weren't with him though. He's a big guy. His stride is probably double mine. I don't bring it up, but I appreciate it anyway.

I'm not sure how it happened, but a run I was dreading, was turning out to be enjoyable. As we walk and cool down a bit, he says, "Thanks for letting me run with you. I'm impressed that you do this every day."

"Oh, well, it's really more about being able to eat carbs," I tell him. "I'm not one of those women who can eat whatever they want. I run so I don't have to worry about my ass becoming as big as a house." I don't know why it sounds like I'm trying to convince him not to be impressed. I should be proud of myself, but praise makes me uncomfortable. Even though I secretly like his words, I haven't had much of it in my lifetime, only when my dad was around.

"Your ass is perfect," he says giving me a wink. Crap. I'm hoping I look so sweaty right now that he can't tell I'm blushing again. "I hope you don't run so much that it gets smaller."

"I don't think that's an option," I tell him with exasperation, because it's not. I'm just not one of those women who are built to be thin, and I'll never look like that. I'm a bit surprised by his comment. I've heard men complain about women gaining weight, but never about them losing weight.

"Good, it would be a shame to lose all of those gorgeous curves," he says. "I don't like bony women, I don't know why women think it's so attractive."

I look at him, is he for real? "I couldn't be bony if I tried, but it's nice to hear a man say that for a change. I've had a man tell me to lose weight before, but never *not* to lose weight."

My ex, Jim, made comments about my ass being *more than a handful.* Then he had the nerve to say I should tone it up a little more. Asshole.

Gunner is quiet so I look up at him to see his scowl. Uh-oh. I'm not sure what's got him scowling now, but I don't want to find out. So I just keep walking. Freddy is panting beside me. When we turn onto my street I see Mr. Williams walking down the road in his white boxer shorts.

"Hold this a minute," I say handing Gunner the leash. Then I run ahead up the road to Mr. Williams. Edna, his wife, told me that he had the beginnings of dementia. I was genuinely sad to hear this because they are the nicest old couple you could ever meet. I look at their house as I pass and notice her coming out the door as fast as she can. Which is not fast at all. Poor woman has her hands full.

"Sam," she yells down the street. "Get back here honey, you're not wearing any pants!"

Oh dear. "I'll get him," I yell to her. I approach him and try to act like everything is normal. "Hi Mr. Williams," I say, giving him my brightest smile.

He looks at me for a minute. Then I see a light come on. "Hey there Josie girl," he says smiling back. "You been running again? Don't know how you do that shit every day. It's too damn hot."

"Yeah," I say. Not sure what else to do, I just say, "Let's head back to your house. I see Edna outside."

He turns and looks. "What's that crazy lady doing outside carrying a frying pan?" My guess was she was in the kitchen cooking when she noticed her husband went AWOL, but I didn't tell him that.

"I don't know," I look over and see him shaking his head at her. It's a sad situation, but

I can't help but smile at the irony. He just walks back to her not even noticing that he's in his boxers. As we head up his driveway I see Gunner and Freddy approaching.

Mr. Williams just walks right past Edna and says, "You should keep that frying pan in the kitchen, *woman*!" then heads inside.

She looks at me and just shuts her eyes. She says, "Thank you so much Josie. I didn't know if I could catch up to him. Lordy be, what are all the neighbors going to say about this?"

I give her a reassuring pat on the shoulder. "Don't worry about them. There was no harm done. I'm just glad I got here in time to help you."

I see tears start to form in her eyes. "I just don't know what to do with him. Sometimes he's my same old Sam, and sometimes I don't recognize him. It's exhausting."

I take her in my arms and give her a hug. I can tell she's worn out. I can't imagine how sad it would be to have someone you love go through these moments of not remembering the life you'd built together.

"I'm sorry Edna. We're getting ready to have dinner. Would you and Sam like to come? Or maybe we could bring you over some chicken so you don't have to cook?"

"Oh no, that's ok honey," she says pulling away giving my arm a squeeze to let me know she appreciates the offer. "I was about done cooking when he took off on me, and you made that lasagna already," she waves the pan around on a giggle, like she doesn't know whether to laugh or cry.

"Okay then, but please call me if you need anything. I really don't mind helping out."

"You're a saint Josie," she says eyeballing Gunner, who's just standing by holding Freddy's leash. Freddy is plopped down on his butt by Gunner's feet. He's glancing around at everyone with his tongue hanging out wondering what the deal is. "Who's your young man?" she says suddenly sounding a lot more energetic than she did a few minutes ago.

Looking at Gunner, I can't really blame her. I have that reaction to him too, although I hope I hide it better than she does. I expect her to start fanning herself any minute now.

"Gunner Layne," he says coming up and offering his hand.

She takes it and her eyes are sparkling when she says her name in return. Oh my, I almost giggle at her.

"I didn't know Josie had a boyfriend," she states sounding a little breathless and a little surprised.

"I don't," I speak up. "He's... a friend." I don't really know how I should explain him.

"Right dear," she says dropping his hand and giving me a patronizing look and winking at Gunner. I don't argue with her because I don't know what to say. I see Gunner grinning from ear to ear and decide it's time to get out of here.

"I'll be home, Edna, if you need anything." I tell her heading back down the driveway.

I hear Gunner say, "It was nice to meet you ma'am. I'm going to give Josie my business card for you. I'm a private investigator. I hope you never need my help, but if you do, you're welcome to call me."

"Oh, well aren't you a nice young man. Thank you so much," she gushes. "Josie you better hold onto to his one!" she practically yells pointing at him and giving me a thumbs up. Like he can't see her? Oh God.

He's loving this. I just nod and smile and keep going. *If only I could hold on to him*. He's such a contradiction. Sometimes he's scary, sometimes he's funny, and times like this he's truly a nice man. I haven't met very many nice men in my life. I could fall for him so easily.

Look how messed up I am after yesterday and today. I really need to get this dinner over with and send him on his way. There has to be women out there that deserve this guy. It sure isn't me.

Chapter 24

Gunner

When we get back from the run Josie goes and takes a quick shower while Faith is cooking. Now they are both in the kitchen getting dinner ready while I'm sitting in the living room in front of the TV. A guy could get used to this. I was actually hoping to talk to Faith while we were alone, but she ordered me to the couch.

I'm trying to concentrate on the baseball recaps, but my mind is on Josie. I picture the way she ran up to that old man in his underwear and got him home. If I wasn't sure about her before. I am now. Not many people would go out of their way like that to help some old couple who lives down the street. She'd clearly taken time to get to know them and to help them out, she had even made them a lasagna.

There aren't enough people like her in the world, that's for damn sure. I've met my fair share of people and most of them would never make a lasagna for their elderly neighbors, or even consider it. She was someone I wanted to introduce to my family. Someone my mom would actually approve of. I'd never met a woman that I wanted to take home to my parents.

I look into the kitchen and watch her. Her chestnut hair is hanging down and she's put on some type of sun dress. It's long, almost to her ankles but I can see almost every move her body makes underneath. In fact when she turns around I can see that ass of hers sway when she walks. It makes me wonder if she has panties on under there. I can't see any lines. She's barefoot, and I notice how small her feet are. She has pink painted toenails. Shit, I need to get her to trust me. I can't stand the distance she puts between us.

I decide to go into the kitchen, because sitting on the couch is not going to get me any closer to her. I look on the counter and see this big glass bowl that's sitting on a pedestal. It's filled with something that looks like chocolate cake, there's definitely whipped cream in there, and holy shit, I think that's toffee! I go to take a closer look. It's all layered in the glass bowl so you can see the rings of layers from the outside. "What the hell is this?" I ask trying not to drool on myself.

"It's a Kahlua trifle," Josie tells me. As if that explains everything.

"It's one of Josie's famous dishes," Faith tells me on a grin. I notice Josie turn away to do something to some potatoes and see that she's blushing again. Can't this girl take any kind of compliment?

"It looks fuckin' amazing," I say, because it does. I'm ready to skip to dessert. "Can we have dessert first?" I try to give the boyish grin that has been known to work on my mom a time or two.

"No way pal," Faith says. "You can't come in here and just re-write the laws of the universe. Have some of Josie's dip, she decided to make it after all. You will be addicted. Prepare yourself."

She sets a bowl of white looking dip in front of me, then slides a plate over that has crackers, chips, vegetables, and cheese laid out on it. I grab a cracker and dip it. Once I start chewing, I realize she's right, this shit rocks!

"Wow," I say. "Josie, this is like crack." I tell her shoving more into my mouth. She doesn't say anything, just gives me that cute little smile.

"That's why she's required to make it for every mojito night we have at Justine's. Once she forgot to bring it and Rick started crying. For real. Just had a hissy fit in front of everyone," she laughs remembering. I might laugh at the thought too, if my mouth weren't so full.

Josie laughs and that gets my attention. It's not a sound I've heard very often. It's beautiful. She has a soft laugh, just like her voice.

"He's lucky he ever got my dip again after the fit he threw," she says. "Eddie told him to quit being a bitch." The she threw her head back and laughed again at the memory. Fucking precious. I know I'm smiling just watching her, she probably thinks it's because of the story, but it's just because of her.

Faith is laughing too, and says, "Remember when Levi fed it to Freddy? Just dumped it right in his dog bowl." She says laughing even louder.

Josie joins in. Then I see her wipe tears from under her eyes from laughing so hard as she's holding one hand to her belly. Damn it's good to see this side of her.

"Holy crap, I can laugh now, but poor Freddy was miserable all night and he kept looking at *me* like I'm the one that did it to him. Can you believe that?"

"Well, he's probably smart enough to know that you're the one who makes it, so I guess it makes sense if you're a dog."

Josie slaps her on the arm. "You are always taking everyone else's side, even Freddy when he's clearly *wrong*. I swear I'm turning you in for a new best friend."

"I'll stab you, shut up, you'd be lost without me."

Josie laughs again. Okay, they clearly have a weird sense of humor together, but I can see how close they are. Besides, I'm not weighing in. My mouth is full of this kick ass dip.

Finally, they bring dinner over. It's smothered chicken, and I don't know what the hell that chicken is smothered in besides bacon and cheese, but it looks excellent. There's also some kind of garlic mashed potatoes and broccoli. I can't help myself, I dig right in. I haven't ate this good since my last visit home.

I notice that Josie takes the smallest piece of chicken, a very small spoon of potatoes, and a whole lot of broccoli. I remember what she said about hearing men say she needed to lose weight. That shit pisses me off. She's perfect. I hope to God she hasn't let that shit get in her head.

"This is awesome, ladies," I compliment them. "I haven't ate this good since being at my mom's table."

"Well, that's quite a compliment, because I remember how your mom could cook." Faith tells me, "I was only at your house a few times, but she always had something good cooking every time I was there."

"That's mom," I say smiling with fondness. She may be a little crazy, but she's a great mom. She was always thinking up something fun to make for us as kids. "I forgot you were ever at our house."

"I don't think you were there when I visited. I think you boys were grown and out of the house by then. I'm going to have to get ahold of Summer. I miss talking to her."

"Good luck," I tell her. "She keeps to herself these days. Stubborn as shit too."

"Well, that doesn't surprise me. She was always a little emotional," Faith says. She's right, Summer is emotional. She was really sweet growing up. With three over-protective brothers around, she didn't have much of a choice. She had us all wrapped around her finger. She was also a total goofball. I wish I knew why she's stayed away so long.

"She doesn't come home much. She says everything is fine for her, but it makes me wonder," I admit. "She doesn't really appreciate my controlling and nosy ways though, so I try to give her the space she wants."

"Controlling and nosy?" Josie pipes up. "You? Really?" She gives me a fake look of shock.

Whatever. She hasn't seen anything yet.

"Hey, it's what makes me successful," I say grinning at her humor. I'm glad that she feels comfortable joking with me.

We continue eating in silence, until Josie brings over that trifle thing. She gets out a great big spoon and then just starts putting gobs of it on a plate. After my first bite I wonder to myself how long it will take to convince her to marry me.

Chapter 25

Josie

It was a nice evening, even I have to admit that. First we ran together, then had a good dinner with Faith. After that Faith went to her room to use her laptop. I was starting to get a little suspicious of her and that laptop. Gunner suggested we watch a movie, so I begged Faith silently with my eyeballs to watch it with us, but she wouldn't. She had to get online.

Totally getting a new best friend.

Gunner picked the movie *Die Hard*. Go figure. Of course he would pick the macho man movie with bombs and guns. I didn't complain though. I actually love that movie. We sat on the couch and once the movie started he pulled me over to him so he could hold my hand. I didn't really know what to do. It had been a long time since anybody tried to hold my hand. The last time was probably in the fifth grade when my first boyfriend Lenny used to grab my hand with his gross, sweaty one.

Needless to say, I didn't expect this from Gunner. I braced myself for a while, thinking he was going to start making moves, but he didn't.

He just held my hand through the whole movie. When our hands got sweaty or uncomfortable, he would move his hand to my wrist or forearm where he would lightly rub his thumb in circles over my skin. It drove me crazy. As much as I told myself I didn't want this to happen, when he was doing stuff like that it made it hard for me to remember why I felt that way.

When the movie was over, he got up and thanked me for dinner. I walked him to the door, he bent over and pulled me to him. "I enjoyed spending time with you Josie," he said in that low voice of his next to my ear. It always made me shiver when he did that.

I told him it was fun, so he said, "Great, tomorrow night, I'll bring over pizza to re-pay you and Faith for dinner." Then he kissed me on the lips. Not a hot and heavy kiss, but a light brush of the lips that just made me want more. Before I knew it, he was out the door.

I just stood there, feeling a little dazed, and I reached up to touch my lips where his had just been. Then I heard him say from outside the door, "Don't forget to lock the door baby." I jumped, then proceeded to lock it, and then listened to his footsteps walk away. I heard his bike start up and then disappear down the street.

It wasn't until after he was gone and I was lying in bed unable to do anything but think about him, that I realized he had already made sure to invite himself back the next day.

Crap, crap, *crap!*

I picked up my cell next to my bed and typed a text to Faith. Yes we were only a bedroom a part, but we did this stuff all the time.

Me: Gunner says he's coming back tomorrow night and bringing us pizza.

Faith: I love that guy! Pizza sounds so good!

Me: NO! I wasn't supposed to see him again, but he made plans before I could stop him.

Faith: It's just pizza Josie. Relax and go to sleep.

Me: Why? So you can watch internet porn?

Faith: No porn here. Just chatting.

Me: With who?

Faith: Leave me alone mom. I'm busy.

Me: Whatever. Enjoy the porn.

Faith: LOL. GN JoJo

Me: Night

K. D. Smith

Chapter 26

Gunner

It's Monday, I'm sitting at the diner downtown waiting for Faith to show up. I texted her this morning after dinner with her and Josie at their house. She agreed to meet me on her lunch hour. I guess she worked for some publishing company downtown, not too far from my office. I'm not sure what I want to ask her. I just know that I need more information. I feel like I'm always avoiding stepping on a land mine with Josie. I want to understand what she needs.

I made it through the movie last night without putting my hands all over her body, but it was close. So many times I'd feel her pulse speed up when I touched her wrist. I knew she was attracted to me, but I promised myself to move slowly with her. That's why I picked a movie with a lot of explosions and fighting. I knew I only wanted to hold her hand and give her a small kiss at the end of the night. I didn't need to watch people going at it on the screen and then get carried away. Damn if she didn't make me hard no matter what she did. Even sitting there with her little foot bouncing all over the place.

I told her as I was leaving that I would come over tonight and then kissed her before she could argue. I know she wants to avoid me, but that's too fuckin' bad.

I saw her through the little glass on the door when I turned and left last night. She softly reached up and touched her lips like she could still feel me there. She looked so sweet. She had that dazed look on her face that she had that night I took her home. I wanted to walk back through that door so fucking bad, but I made myself stay on the other side. I watched her for a minute and then noticed she hadn't even thought to lock the door, so I reminded her. I had this overwhelming need to know that she was safe.

"I don't have long," Faith said dropping down into the booth opposite me. "I was already late this morning. My boss is chomping at the bit to write me up."

I looked at her and she looked tired. "No sleep?" I asked.

She just waved a dismissive hand and said "Something like that. Anyway, what's this all about? I hope you're not trying to get me to give you top secret information." She raised one eyebrow at me letting me know she wasn't going to sell out her friend.

This is exactly why I liked her. She was loyal to Josie. I knew Josie needed that after she explained her family situation to me.

"I'm not looking for you to betray Josie in any way. I just want to understand some things. The panic attack for instance, that was really fuckin' bad. I need to know how to avoid that ever happening again."

"I can't really tell you much. It's her story to tell." She looks away for a minute with a sad face, as if she's remembering something. "Shit. I can't give you any details, but it was bad," she pauses, then adds, "*Really* bad."

"I thought so," I said wringing the napkin in my hand tighter. Having this confirmed wasn't what I wanted.

"Just be careful with her. Help her avoid small spaces, especially dark ones. If she starts acting like she can't breathe, then get her outside, so she doesn't feel trapped. I don't know what else I can say to help, except what you already know. Don't spank her without warning." She leans over in the booth giving me a knowing grin.

Holy shit. Now I look like Josie, sitting over here with a red face flushed from embarrassment. I can't believe she knows that. I put my head in my hands and shake my head. I guess I can't blame Josie for talking to her best friend about something, especially if she was confused about it. God, I can't believe I did that.

"It's okay, I don't judge. I know your brother is kinky like that, I just didn't know it ran in the family."

Oh shit. Yep, Hunter had done the dirty on her. "Which brother are you talking about?" I asked feigning ignorance. Truth be told, it could have been Walker when it came to being a kinky fuck, but I knew she meant Hunter. I could tell she had some kind of hang up with him.

She pauses for a minute and looks away before saying, "Hunter. Nevermind, I shouldn't have said that, I was just kidding. This is about Josie, so what else can I do to help?"

I decide to ignore that comment about Hunter. Lord knows what he did with Faith. This is news to me. News I'd rather forget. "I'm surprised you're willing to help. It doesn't seem like Josie wants to get involved with anyone."

Faith sighs dramatically. "Well, she doesn't, but it's the fear talking. It holds her back. She gives into it. You can't tell her that though, because in her mind, she is fighting like hell."

"What do you mean?"

She shakes her head and says, "When she first came back here. She was a mess. She lived in sweats and a hoodie on my couch and barely moved. She was like a zombie. We're talking months. She even slept in her running shoes. Only took them off to shower. She said she had to be ready. Then one day, she decided she had to start working her way back, and she has, for the most part. Anyway, I don't want to say much more. It's just that she went from being a zombie who did nothing but cry and stare into

192

space, to this Josie you see now. The one who has everything planned. She runs with Freddy. She works. She does certain things on certain days. Everything is planned, and controlled. Every now and then you see glimpses of the real Josie. The one who laughs like she did last night. The one who's not so uptight and scared of everything."

This was all making sense to me as she was saying it. I could see that she went from one extreme to the other. From being out of control to overly controlled. She was barely living, and now she was living the way she thought she was supposed to.

She slept with running shoes on, just in case. Jesus!

"Listen," Faith says. "I've had guys ask me about Josie before, and I never talked to them, I told them to forget it. But she's never had a reaction to anyone the way she does with you. I can tell she likes you, but she's afraid. Don't let her push you away."

"Not a chance in hell, "I say, and I mean it. "If I weren't serious about her I would back off. I want you to know that. I wouldn't push her if I didn't plan on sticking around."

Faith smiles and says, "You're exactly what she needs."

K. D. Smith

"I just have one more question. Josie came to my office to see about hiring me for something but then changed her mind. Is she in danger?"

"Not that I know of, but there's something she's not telling me, the other day she let it slip out that she was planning something. I don't know what the hell she was talking about, but it scares the shit out of me."

What the fuck?

"I don't know what she means, but I'm afraid she's going to get in over her head. Again."

"I'm assuming that whatever happened, took place in Detroit?" I ask squeezing and twisting my napkin without realizing it.

She doesn't say anything but nods her head that I am correct.

"Listen, I don't want to mess around if she's in danger. She's not going to let me close enough yet to keep her protected. I need time to earn her trust. So I need you to help me keep an eye on her. I'm going to put a security system in your house."

She just looks at me and says, "Um, you should talk to Josie first, she's going to want to know why, and I swear if you tell her that I talked to you I will be pissed. She wouldn't want me here."

"I won't, you have my word. I'll think of something. Just answer me this, does this have anything to do with her old boss Brian Hanson?" I ask watching for her reaction.

I see her eyes get big and she looks a little pale.

Yep, I got my answer.

I knew there was something fishy about that asshole. "She told you that?" she asks me in a whisper?

"No, I'm going to tell you the truth, but I haven't figured out a way to tell Josie yet." I take a deep breath, this could be a total disaster if I don't handle it right. "I was contacted by Brian Hanson. He was looking for Josie. Heard she was back in this area, said she stole money from him. That's when I started looking into Josie."

"Oh God!" Faith cries, "She's going to flip out. Oh shit! So does he know where she is? We need to warn her!"

"Wait, calm down," I tell her. "After I found Josie, there was just something about her that I couldn't let go of. I started trying to figure her out. I didn't believe she was a thief, but I needed to make sure. Anyway, once I got to know her a little, I was satisfied that she was clean. My gut told me there was something off about her boss from the beginning. I had my suspicions, so I told him I couldn't locate her."

"Thank God," Faith says putting her hand to her chest and letting out the huge breath she'd been holding. "But he's looking for her, that's not good. He might not give up." She looks worried.

"I want to put in the security system today. I'm in for the long haul, Faith. I'm serious. I want to keep Josie safe, I just don't know how close she will let me get. That's where you come in. I also need to find a way to put a stop to that asshole, but that's not your concern, I just need you to have her back. Don't leave her alone, unless she's home with the alarm on and Freddy close."

"Okay, but Gunner, she can't know this."

"I'm glad you agree, because I know I have to tell her, but I just need to find the right way and the right time. Right now I just want to make sure she's safe and if I tell her, I have a feeling she'll just run from me."

She nods again. I can see that she's scared for Josie. I decide to try to get to the bottom of it, "What did he do to her?"

"I can't tell you that, but I'll do what you ask, and I'll encourage her to open up with you. God, if she knew about this meeting, and Brian contacting you, she would feel so betrayed. We have to make sure she's safe from him and we have to tell her the truth as soon as we can."

"I agree," I tell her. I don't know what happened with that fucker, but I've heard enough. He's going to pay.

Chapter 27

Josie

"Um... Gunner, I appreciate you bringing over pizza and everything, but what's with all the tools?   And what's up with this?" I ask him holding up a bottle of some sort of liquid he sat on the counter.

"That's an all-natural vapor liquid.   You know, that stuff you use when you have a cold? You pour that around your garden, the cat won't come near it," he said while looking through his tool box trying to find something. As if this was no big deal. He just brings vapor liquid to help me get rid of that stupid cat. Seriously? I can't believe he even remembers, much less cares.

"I'm surprised you remember that cat," I tell him. Because I am. He's hot. He's successful. He has much better things to worry about than my garden. Did he actually spend time trying to figure out how to get rid of the cat?

"How could I forget that? You running into the yard yelling like a loon," he says smiling, like he knows his comment is going to make me object.   Whatever, I'm not giving him the satisfaction.

"Well, thank you, you didn't have to do that."

"It's nothing Josie. From now on we'll pour some around the garden every couple days to keep the cat away," he says.

Did he just say *we'll*? *We'll* pour it around the garden? As in *together*? Uh oh. "Really, don't worry about it. It's nice that you care about my garden, but it's not your problem."

He stopped messing with his tools and came over to me putting his hands on my shoulders. Damn. I can't think when he touches me. I just blink up at him and wait to see what he's going to do.

"Anything that's bothering you is my problem. Even if it's a cat," he says in a low, serious voice. He's staring into my eyes, like he wants me to understand him, but I don't. My problems aren't his problems.

I try to pull back but he keeps hold of me. "I appreciate that Gunner, but you don't need to worry about my problems. I'm fine." Is this guy for real?

"No you're not Josie. That's why I brought these tools. One of my guys will be here soon to help me. We're putting a security system in."

My mouth falls open. He's *what*?

"You're *what*?" I practically screech.

He can't just waltz in here and tell me I'm getting a security system that Faith, nor I can afford.

"If I could afford a security system, I would have one," I inform him.

"No charge, babe. But it's going to be done. Tonight."

"Why are you doing this? I can't pay you for this." I say as my anxiety starts to rise. "I don't want to owe you."

He gives me a gentle smile. "Josie, I saw your panic attack, remember? I see that you have a guard dog. I know you came to hire me, even though you didn't. It doesn't take a rocket scientist to see that you're scared about something. I'm just trying to help. I want you to feel safe, and I want to know you're safe. It'll make me feel better. I agreed not to push for answers, so I'm not asking questions. I'm just doing. You don't owe me for this. I want to do it."

I keep staring at him. I don't know what to say to that. I want to let him do it. I want to feel safe. I want to believe he's just doing this to make sure I do. I'm afraid to believe that. Luckily Faith walks in the door and I don't have to come up with something to say. Faith will not go for this.

"Gunner says he's putting in a security system. Tonight. No charge." I all but tattle on him.

I expect her to tell him we aren't taking handouts. I wait for her to tell him thanks, but no thanks. She doesn't. She just says, "Cool!" Gives me a smile and walks into her bedroom.

Say what?

I watch her walk away in stunned silence. Then I look back at him and he's grinning at me again. I don't know what to say, I guess if it's okay with Faith then it should be okay with me. I just shrug and then call Freddy so I can take him outside.

While we're outside, I decide I'm not going to over-think this. Faith thinks it's okay, so it probably is. I know this sounds nuts, but I don't trust my own judgment anymore.

There have been times when I panic over nothing. Sometimes I have to look to others whose judgment I trust to figure out if I'm overreacting or not. It's pathetic, but sometimes I trust their judgment better than my own.

I notice that Gunner drove a big truck over tonight instead of his bike. I guess it would be hard to carry tools on a motorcycle. I'm checking out his ride when my phone bleeps at me.

Rick: I see hot guy is there AGAIN. I'm peeking out my window.

Me: Why don't you just come over instead of being a weirdo?

Rick: I didn't want to interrupt any hot guy sex you might be getting ;)

Me: No sex. He's putting in a security system.

Rick: Isn't that expensive?

Me: Not when he's doing it for free

Rick: OMG, did you pay him with sex????

Me: NO!!! We are NOT having sex.

Rick: Blowjob? :O

Me: NO!

Rick: Then why free?

Me: Exactly! See, I knew this was wrong, but Faith was all for it.

Rick: Don't be stupid, if he says he's doing it for free, you should take it. But did he say WHY?

Me: He wants me to feel safe.

Rick: Marry him!

Me: Shut up!

Just then I see a truck pulling into the driveway. I'm not sure who it is, but I'm assuming this must be Gunner's 'guy' he referred to.

Freddy comes back to me knowing there's a stranger near. He looks at me waiting for a command. My dog may be a bit lazy sometimes, but he's a good boy.

I watch the man approach and realize he's the man I saw in Gunner's office, the angry looking one and there's someone with him. I tell Freddy to sit and walk towards them just as Gunner comes out of the house.

He comes to me and says, "This is Isaiah and his brother Trey."

I give a slight smile and say hello and, "Come on in." I call Freddy and we all walk into the house.

"I didn't know you were bringing help man, we need more pizza." Gunner says.

"And beer," Trey says giving Gunner one of those strange manly handshakes that includes a slap on the back. I guess it's the equivalent of a hug, only man style.

"I can run out and get some if you want," I offer. I mean after all they're here to put in my free security system.

"That'd be great. Can you grab another pizza too?" He says pulling out his wallet and handing me a couple of twenties. Is he serious?

"I'll get it," I say pushing his hand away.

"You're not buying pizza and beer for us babe, this was supposed to be my treat."

"But you're already putting in a security system. I can handle pizza and beer," I inform him.

"Take it, or I'll run out myself and get it." He says. "Take Faith with you."

What did he just say?

I just look at him and frown. He is *so* bossy. I sigh and head down the hall to find Faith. When I walk in I see her on that damn laptop smiling at the screen like an idiot.

"We need to make a beer and pizza run. Gunner's guys are here."

"Okay," she says typing something and shutting it down.

"You're awful agreeable today, you know that?" I mention to her.

"Sorry, do you want me to be difficult?"

"No, it's just that I was trying to tell Gunner to back off with this security system and you walk in and just say '*cool*'. I mean no questions asked?"

"Josie, I like him, I think he's a good guy. I think he really cares about you and wants to look out for you, so I'm good with that. Just be nice to him. Think about the peace of mind a security system could bring you. You might even sleep better."

She's right. Maybe it will help. I should stop being so distrustful and worried. See what I mean? Sometimes I just can't help myself.

We head to the store in my old Ford Explorer. Freddy is happy about getting a ride out of this deal, he's sitting in the back with his head out the window pretending to bite the air.

After picking up pizza and beer, we head back to the house. I'm not sure what they've done, but they've been busy. I take in the tools and wires all over the place, and just keep going. I have no idea what it takes to put in a security system, but it looks like they know what they're doing. I guess that's why they do this for a living.

I hate to admit it, but I'm starting to really like the idea of having a security system.

I remind myself that I can't allow myself to feel too comfortable though, I still have to be diligent.

I warm up the pizzas that were left sitting on the counter and grab the beer. I set it all on the kitchen table. "Better eat while it's hot, guys," I tell them. Faith grabbed a plate, piled two pieces of pizza on it and disappeared back to her bedroom. She is definitely up to something.

All the guys came and sat around the table eating and talking about security stuff. I wasn't paying much attention to them. They seemed to be comfortable with each other and I felt a little awkward so I just ate my pizza in silence. These boys can eat. Three pizzas were devoured fairly quickly, I wonder where they put all that pizza because all of them looked full of muscle.

"There's some trifle left," I tell Gunner.

"Fuck yeah! Wait 'til you guys taste this," he says as I smile at his excitement. I go to the fridge and bring it back to the table with a big spoon and some plates. I divide the rest of it up between them.

"You make this?" Isaiah asks me.

I nod my head.

"Fuckin' delicious," he says shoving in another spoonful.

Trey finishes his before he speaks. "That stuff is the shit! Can you make some more? Can I watch?" he asks with a playful look on his face.

"She's not making you more, asshole." Gunner says giving him a scowl. I'm not sure what that's about, but to be honest, I like that they want more. I enjoy making stuff for other people if they truly enjoy it. It's easy and I like having something to offer. It's the least I can do.

"I can make more," I offer, "Since you're working here and everything."

"Babe, you don't have to make us anything else. These guys are getting paid. Don't worry about it. If you're making any more of that Kahlua shit, then you make it for me, and I'll *think* about sharing it if these guys are on their best behavior." He frowns, and they almost look amused.

"On our best behavior?" Isaiah asks in his deep baritone voice. "You mean you don't want us to embarrass you in front of your girl?"

Trey has a huge smile on his face. "Maybe you're afraid she'll like me better than you."

His girl? Oh God. I stand there looking like an idiot. I'm not sure if I should clear up the fact that I'm not his girl, or if I should just ignore it. I look over and see Gunner glowering at him. Yikes.

"Back off man," he says. "Don't be gettin' any bright ideas."

Trey holds up his hands in surrender. "Can't blame a dude for noticing a hot chick who can cook," he says. "Don't worry man, you've set your boundaries."

Set his boundaries? Was this like the male pissing match I'd heard about? Was Gunner marking his territory? Shit. Why did that not sound as bad as I thought it should? I need reinforcements.

I say "excuse me" softly, hoping I can disappear and head into the living room. I pull out my phone to type a text.

> **Me:** Get your ass out here. They're calling me his GIRL! Help!!!

Faith: Aw that's sweet. I'm busy.

Me: I can't believe you're ditching me for a date with internet porn.

She didn't even respond to that. I think of something. It will work, I just know it. I take my phone and aim it to where Isaiah and Trey are working and snap a pic. I send it with a message attached.

Me: Hot guys all over my house. Come and get it.

Justine: Holy shitballs! On my way!!

I smile. Justine is not about to miss out on hot men working where she can observe. She made it in less than ten minutes. I grin to myself when she comes waltzing in the door with Levi on her hip. I notice she's wearing an extra tight pair of jeans and a shirt that shows so much cleavage it should be illegal. Somehow she still looks nice. I don't know how she does it. If I dressed that way I'd look like I was dressing up for a Halloween hooker party.

I notice the heads turn as she walks in swaying her hips more than usual. I smile at her. She's going to get all the focus now, which should make everyone happy. It sure makes me happy, I smile at my brilliant idea.

I watch Gunner introduce everyone as I take Levi and Freddy with me into the living room. Next thing I know Justine is following close behind.

"Spill," she demands.

"Well," I take a deep breath let it all out on a whoosh, and as quickly as I can, I fill her in. "Gunner showed and says he's putting in a security system. I told him I couldn't afford one, he said he's doing it for free. I thought Faith would back me up but all she said was *cool*! Can you believe that? What the hell is that about? When does she ever say *cool* and nothing more? Then those guys show up. They work for Gunner. He gave us money, which I tried to refuse also, but he wouldn't hear of it, told us to go grab pizza and beer, so we did. Faith said I should just let him do his thing, but she's hiding in her room on her stupid laptop, and those guys were messing with Gunner calling me his *girl*. I'm not his girl! Then Trey said I might like him better than Gunner or something like that, and Gunner got mad, but he said you can't blame him for noticing a hot chick who can cook. I tried to get Faith to come out here, because I don't know what to do about all of this!" I swing my hands around indicating what's happening in my house. "So I got you over here because you'll know what to do!" I say sounding hysterical as I heave for breath.

Justine started laughing. No, I wouldn't call this laughing, it was more like howling. I don't get what's so funny. "Oh, and he brought me vapor liquid to put in my garden! Says it will keep the cat away. Why does he care about *that*?" I ask her as I bug my eyes out at her like now she will understand how crazy this is.

She didn't catch it. She laughs herself silly while I grow more confused. What the hell? I'm missing the punch line here. Doesn't she see I am freaking *out*?

"Girl, what are you all worked up about? That's just the way men work. At least these kind of men. They find a woman they really want, then they take over. He's claiming you."

I stop her there. "I'm not claimed," I tell her. "We barely know each other. I didn't ask him for anything. How am I claimed? Hell, I didn't even invite him over, he invited himself!"

"Of course he did honey, he wants you. Whether you like it or not, he's claiming you. He keeps showing up. He's giving you things. Having you do beer runs for his boys. He made friends with Freddy and your *awesome* human friends, like *me*," she gives me a patronizing pat on the shoulder. "He even brought fuckin' vapor shit, whatever that is. There is not a man on this planet who would go through the trouble of finding out how to get rid of a cat his woman doesn't like unless he was staking his claim. Men don't do that shit for the hell of it."

Oh God! She's probably right. I watch Levi and Freddy on the floor, Freddy pawing at a squeaky toy and Levi giggling at him like it's hilarious.

K. D. Smith

"Shit!" I whisper loudly hoping nobody is trying to listen. I think we're safe by the amount of tool noise around. "What do I do?"

"You get claimed fool! Ain't no other way. Unless you don't want him. Is that it? Because if it is then you are crazier than I thought. I may have to re-think letting you watch my baby, if you're that crazy."

I sigh and close my eyes. "I'm not crazy, I just don't think I'm ready for this. It could ruin everything."

"Jojo, I don't know your whole story, but as a woman, I understand being hurt and hiding away. But you can't do that forever. You deserve to have a man like Gunner. He's trying to take care of you. Let him. For God's sake look at the man. He belongs on the cover of a smut novel. Shirtless." She tips her head and studies him with a dreamy look in her eye then finishes, "And if you don't take him up on it, somebody else will, and *fast*."

She's giving me the eyebrow. She's right, I know it. The only question is do I want to be with Gunner? I hate the idea of him being with someone else, but I also don't feel ready to be in a relationship. There are a lot of things Justine doesn't know.

"You're right. I need to think about this," I tell her.

"Don't think too long honey," she warns.

I nod my understanding. Women would line up around the block for a shot with Gunner. I don't know why but he seems to want one with *me*.

I change the subject. We sit and talk, playing with Levi and Freddy while the boys finish up their work. Once it's done, Trey and Isaiah go to leave, saying their goodbyes. I thank them for the work and say it was nice to meet them. Justine decides to go too. What a shocker. She walks out with the two men. I can't help but notice how they're checking her out. I wonder if she's going to get a date with one of them. My bet would be yes.

Gunner takes another beer out of the fridge and walks me around showing me how to work the alarm. It seems pretty advanced. I'm surprised at the different features it has. The more he tells me the more I wonder how much something like this costs. I'm afraid to know the answer, so I don't ask.

"I hope I can remember all of that," I say not sounding very confident. I should be writing this down. "Thank you for doing this."

"If you have any questions just call me," he says. "I put my number in your phone and yours in mine."

Oh. My. I don't know what to do with that either. I'd like it better if he'd asked first. I say, "If you wanted to do that you could have just asked."

"It was on the counter babe. No big deal, I want you to be able to get ahold of me if you have any trouble."

Well, how's a girl supposed to be mad about that? Once he's done showing me the alarm he says he wants to watch the game and we sit in the living room much like we did the night before.

He's holding my hand, and I'm trying not to overheat. My foot is bouncing like crazy because I'm nervous again.

"Babe, it's cute that you do that thing with your foot when you're nervous, but there's nothing to be nervous about. Come here."

I don't, I just look at him and make my foot stop moving. When I don't listen he pulls on my hand that he's holding and brings me closer. He lays down on his back taking me with him and then positions me over to the side of him so that I'm lying next to him. Then he puts his leg over my feet so I won't move them.

Once again it seems he's taken over. I try to sit up, but he just pulls me back down. "Relax baby, everything's fine."

I sigh, and lay there wondering if he's going to get up soon. With my feet trapped, I'm not able to move around much so I settle in and end up watching the game with my head on his chest. I think I dozed off because when I wake up he's moving us up off the couch and the game is over. "It's late babe, I should get home."

"Okay," I whisper, still trying to wake up.

He takes my face in his hands. "You're cute when you're sleepy." Then he puts his lips on mine. Once again, my body wakes right up for him. I wish I knew how to shut that shit off. I kiss him back and it's not a soft as the one last night. It's a little more demanding, but still gentle. I want more. I want him to put me to bed and kiss me all night.

I wrap my arms around his neck and press into him. His hard body feels so good. I feel his erection press against me and I shiver. I feel his hands go around my waist and he pulls back a little.

"I better go, or I'm not going to be able to stop."

I want to tell him to stay, I want to beg him not to stop, but I just can't do it. Instead I nod my head trying to focus on those indigo eyes.

"Fucking beautiful," he says pulling me in and kissing me deeper one more time. When he lets me go and I realize I'm breathing heavy. Wow.

"Lock the door behind me and reset the alarm. Do you remember how?"

I nod again, still not trusting my words.

"I'll see you tomorrow, gorgeous," he says then he turns to leave. I almost nod in agreement again when I realize that I'll be gone tomorrow evening. In fact, I'll be gone the next three evenings.

"Um...I won't be home," I tell him. "I have stuff...to do. Tomorrow night." I decide to skip telling him it's three nights. He's starting to get the scowly face.

"I could come with you, or maybe I could come over after."

"It will be late," I tell him. "And this is really something I have to do alone."

"Okay," he says. "Be careful. Remember to set this when I leave. I'll call you tomorrow sometime during the day."

"Okay," I whisper. He's making me feel tingly again. He's looking after me. It feels really good, and even though I'm trying to push him away, there's a part of me that's elated when he wants to see me every day.

He gives me another short kiss and then goes out the door. I can see him waiting, listening for me to lock the door and set the alarm, so I shake myself out of my daze and do it surprising myself that I remember how to work the alarm, and then I watch him walk away.

I tell myself that the next three nights will be good. I can't see Gunner, with time and space, he'll realize what a mistake this is. I should be happy about that because it's the right thing for both of us, but I'm not.

Chapter 28

Gunner

I want to know where she's going tomorrow night. I'm lying in bed thinking about her and wondering why she's going to be gone for a night. It's ridiculous. I've never cared before if a woman was busy for a night. All of these possibilities run through my head. Is she meeting someone? Is she going to be safe? Does she have a friend I don't know about? See what I mean? Totally fuckin' ludicrous.

"Fuck!" I say to myself. She's under my skin. I wanted to rip Trey's face off earlier for mildly flirting with her. Trey is a good friend. If I want to rip my friend to shreds then I know I'm a goner.

I trust Isaiah and Trey with my life. I only have three men working for me right now, as well as Marina. I knew Isaiah from my cop days. Only he wasn't on the force. He was an informant, and a damn good one. He had a military background and although he didn't get involved in illegal activity, he was close enough to it to know what was happening. He wanted nothing more than to keep the streets clean in a town he loved. He could be a mean motherfucker, but he was smart and a good man.

His brother Trey is a few years younger and has a brighter outlook on life. He hadn't seen combat the way his brother had, but he had good contacts, and he was talented with electronics. He's the go to guy for the security systems. Young and cocky, but with the looks and brains to back it up.

Caleb is my other guy. He's the one that handles the more stealthy operations. He can get in and out of a locked place faster than anyone I've ever seen. He's quiet, but loyal and trustworthy. He just doesn't like to share much about his life. He's a big fucker too, and always good to have around when we need more muscle.

Caleb is the only one of my guys that Josie hasn't met yet. I could probably get him to tail her tomorrow night. I let that idea settle in. It made me feel better. At least I would know she's safe.

I don't like the way this Brian fucker is looking for Josie. For some reason he hadn't let go even though she'd been gone from Detroit a long time. He still had her in his sights and that bothered me in more ways than one.

Faith said that Josie was worried about her *plans* getting ruined. She told Faith that she doesn't know everything which means whatever she's planning she's probably doing it alone. Fuck.

I hate how I have to keep going behind her back. Keeping her safe is my first priority, but if she knows I've lied to her then she will run hard and fast. I have no doubt about that.

Life has a way of taking the fucking wind out of your sails. I hate that it happened to Josie. When she laughed it was such a beautiful thing. I hate seeing her eyes filled with fear so often. The glances that I've caught of the *real* Josie are fuckin' amazing.

When she lets that wall down, she's something else. I can't help but thinking back about how she reacted to me at the club, and how she was riding behind me on my bike. Shit, I get hard as a rock every time I think about it. I picture the way she looked naked on my bed. I picture her bare pussy glistening with wetness. Jesus.

I head to the shower to take care of myself. I've jacked off so often the last few days that my dick should be sore. I'm always thinking about how she looked that night. Her dress, those fuck me shoes, her hair. Picturing how she rubbed her body against mine I shut my eyes and lean against the shower wall with one hand and stroked myself with the other. I can see her perfect tits and remember how they taste in my mouth. I can hear her breathy little whimpers begging for more. I think of how wet those pretty pink panties were when I peeled them off of her.

Fuck! I think about that perfect little ass wiggling for me while she held onto the headboard and it does me in. I growl as I cum all over my shower. It's a good thing the cleaning lady will be here tomorrow.

When I dry off and head back to bed, I feel a little more relaxed. I know it won't last long though. I decide that maybe having Caleb follow Josie isn't the way to go.

As long as Faith can stay close, I don't want to overstep too much and risk freaking her out. I'll call tomorrow as planned and check in on her. I don't want to give her a night to herself. Lord knows she will take any space I give her to build those walls up as high as she can. I've just started getting somewhere with her. She might not realize it yet, but I've claimed her as my own, and my woman needs me.

Chapter 29

Josie

Tuesday was a pretty normal day for me. Freddy and I had our run. I got quite a bit of work done. I even cleaned the house a little bit. Around three in the afternoon Gunner called as promised. He asked questions about the alarm system, asked how I was doing, the usual type of conversation I suppose.

His voice soothed me and made me forget about the hang up I received right before his call. I was in the middle of convincing myself that wrong numbers happen all the time when he phoned.

The truth is that it was good to hear his voice. I didn't expect to miss him knowing I wouldn't see him tonight. See? This is the problem! I need to quit giving into these feelings. The more I do the harder it will be in the end when he realizes that he doesn't want me after all.

Yes, he's hot, and nice, and funny, and hot, and everything a girl could ever dream of, but there is just no way he would ever want to end up with someone like me.

I am a mystery to him, and he likes to solve mysteries. I'm a challenge. I'm guessing those alpha types like a challenge. Once he feels like he's conquered me, then what? Then he'll realize I'm not so interesting after all. I'm just fucked up.

It's really too bad, because if I ever was going to have a sex life again, I'd want it to be with Gunner. Now there are all these confusing feelings involved. I wish I could just act on my physical instincts and have hot, wild, sex with him. No complications. God knows I think about it often enough. Last night after he kissed me like that and left, I couldn't sleep. I almost had to touch myself to relieve some of the pressure.

Truth be known, I haven't been able to touch myself in a long time. Not that I hadn't tried, but it never quite worked. I know, pathetic, but even if I used a toy I couldn't get off. I'm betting with thoughts of Gunner naked, it would probably work. I talked myself out of finding out.

Well... maybe later.

It's a good thing I'm on my way to the gym tonight. I train twice a week here. Kai, my trainer, has been teaching me self-defense moves, as well as some fighting techniques, and making sure I have the endurance it may take to win a struggle. He was trained in Judo and Karate. He's impressive, and that's putting it mildly. I like him and he's a total badass.

When I first went into the gym, I wanted to take some sort of self-defense class, but I wasn't sure what to do. Kai had been the one to do my intake and sign me up for a membership. He told me about his fighting background. I explained that I didn't know anything about fighting, but I wanted to learn how to protect myself.

Kai had been nice to me. He started out with some gentle moves, showing me how to use some judo techniques to keep my opponent off balance. The more I learned, the more empowered I felt. It was a good feeling and I enjoyed it, for the most part, even though I was always sore as hell the next day.

I didn't give Kai details, but he knew I was attacked and he was very kind to me. However, I think Kai being Mr. Nice Guy is over. He's been pushing me out of my comfort zone. I understand why he's doing it, I just don't like it very much.

He's been using different ways for me to get my aggression out so that I can focus on the training. He tried to get me to punch a bag over and over again, but honestly, it felt a little silly and I couldn't really do what he wanted, but he wasn't giving up.

I knew this was good for me, so I kept coming twice a week without fail. It was another small step to me getting my life back.

When I got home from the gym, I went straight into a hot bath with lots of bubbles. Just as I started to relax, my cell phone rang. I reached out to grab it and read *Gunner Calling.* I decided to let it go to voice mail. After all, I'm trying to take a bath here.

I lay my head back on the tub and sink down into the bubbles. The warm water feels heavenly on my sore muscles. I start rubbing my calves and thigh muscles, hoping to ease the soreness. As thoughts of Gunner run through my head, I can't help fantasizing about him. About how things would have been that night in his bed if I hadn't freaked out.

I imagine how he would have pushed his cock into me from behind. Maybe he would have wrapped his arms around me and touched my nipples while driving slowly in and out of me. Oh God. Just imagining how it would feel had me squeezing my thighs together trying to ease some of the sensations going on.

Maybe he would have taken me hard and fast. There would have been no sounds except for our bodies slamming into each other, and our heavy breathing. Maybe I would have been moaning his name over and over. He might have moved his hand around to the front of me so he could stimulate my clit at the same time.

Oh my, yes, that was a good idea. I moved my hand down to where I would have wanted him to touch me. I slide my finger through my folds and find myself slick with arousal.

I'd given up on touching myself for pleasure. Maybe this time it will work. My body felt alive again remembering Gunner's touch. I reach one hand up and slide my fingers over my nipple. Mmmm, that's nice. I picture Gunner unzipping his pants for me. I picture him pulling out his hard cock while I watch him. I start rubbing my clit in slow circles. I use the fingers on my other hand to pinch my nipple until it's nice and hard, then I move to the other one. I picture him watching me touch myself while he strokes his cock. Spectacular.

I'm starting to imagine that he's about to come close enough for me to lick the length of him. I start to slide my finger down towards my entrance, I arch my back a little anticipating the feeling of being penetrated but I don't do it yet, I slide them back to my clit.

I think about how Gunner's mouth felt on my clit. I use my fingers on myself thinking about how he made me cum. I imagine his naked body over mine. Oh God, I can feel it building. I'm almost there. This is actually going to work!

I smile to myself as I keep picturing the things Gunner might do to my body. How hot he would look stroking his cock. I start to move my hips slowly rocking against my fingers. I push a little harder on my clit and move my hand a little faster.

Then my phone rings *again*

Damn it all to hell! I snatch up my phone intent on getting rid of whoever is bent on disturbing my first successful masturbation session in a very freakin' long time.

"Hello," I answer and even I realize my voice sounds a little breathy.

"Josie? It's Gunner."

I don't respond. The sound of his voice just makes me want to touch myself even more.

"Josie?"

"Yes?" I practically sigh into the phone.

"You okay?"

"Yes," I repeat.

He waits a few seconds to respond. God help me, I should stop, but I'm so close and hearing his voice in my ear has hurried along the climax that's been just out of reach.

"What are you doing?" He questions.

"Nothing...I'm...just...taking a bath." I struggle to get out words. I think I need to hang up on him so I can finish this, but some naughty little part of me likes the idea of him on the phone with me while I accomplish my mission. All thoughts of breaking it off are long gone, and the only thing on my mind is that I need to mute myself before I come so that he can't hear me.

"Fuck," I hear him whisper. "Baby, I know how you sound when you're turned on, remember?"

Oh. My. God.

"I'm..." I don't even know what to say to finish my sentence. I feel like I'm busted, but there's no way he could know for sure what I'm doing, right?

"Josie, tell me exactly what you're doing," he commands, and go figure, I find myself wanting to follow his orders.

"I did. Taking a...bath," I say trying to sound normal. "With bubbles," I add as if that somehow makes it more legit. Then because I'm a total nerd, I splash water around with my hand that was on my nipple and say, "listen."

"For fucks sake," he mutters. "Baby, I'm not sure why I was calling, but picturing you naked and wet, soaking in bubbles is killing me right now."

Oh no, he's using that deep sexy voice. The one that makes my panties melt. Only I'm not wearing any, but I still feel my clit throb. I can literally feel the liquid heat come out of me at the sound of that voice. I use my fingers to spread it around and circle my clit some more. I don't think I said anything, but I may have sighed, or possibly whimpered a little, I can't be sure.

"I'd give anything to see right now. Are you touching yourself?"

"No!" I lie.

"Don't lie to me Josie." Damn him.

"I...um...maybe a little." Shit. Why does this man make me brain dead?

Silence. Then I hear a rustle of fabric.

"Keep touching baby," he grumbles. "Tell me what you were doing right before you picked up the phone."

Of course he has to skip right to the embarrassing part. I try to think up a lie, but nothing is coming to mind fast enough. I'm torn, but I decide to just tell the truth. What the hell. He already knows he turns me on. I think I proved that much in his bed the other night.

This is all his fault anyway. He's the one who's brought out this side of me, and then he does stuff like lay me on top of his body while he's relaxing on the couch, or kiss me senseless at the door. What does he expect?

He's getting impatient while my thoughts are running around in my head.

"Josie, tell me."

I sigh, maybe I should allow myself some fun before I have to end this. "I was laying back in the bathtub, touching myself," I whisper into the phone feeling embarrassed.

"What were you thinking about?"

"I...was imagining you watching me...and me watching you. And you touching me..."

"I'd love to watch you touch yourself. Tell me where you were touching."

"I was using one hand to rub my nipples," I tell him hesitant to say the rest.

"I bet that's fuckin' beautiful baby. Where was your other hand?" I think he can sense that I'm getting shy so he says, "Was it touching your pussy?"

"Yes."

"Fuck, my cock is so hard just thinking about your pretty wet nipples, and that hot little pussy."

Well, apparently somebody is comfortable with phone sex. I should hang up on him, but I can't, I like what he's saying and it's making me so hot.

"Tell me, were you rubbing your clit?"

"Yes," I say again, and start to rub more circles around it.

"Did you put your finger inside?"

"No," I tell the truth. "You interrupted."

I hear him give a low chuckle. Damn it, even that turns me on.

"I'll make it up to you. How's that? Let me help you finish."

Well what's a girl to do? Say no?

"How are you going to do that?"

"Put your phone on speaker and set it near the tub where we can talk."

Oh, brilliant, why didn't I think of that? I wonder as I comply.

"Okay," I tell him when I'm done.

Then I wonder if he's touching himself too? Or is he just doing this for me? I want to hear him as turned on as I am. I want to know that he comes too.

"You do it too, okay?" I say a little unsure of how this works.

"Don't worry baby, there's no way I could keep my cock in my pants right now. It's too fuckin' hard."

Oh for the love of God. I wanna see it so bad. I whimper escapes my throat at the thought.

"You like thinking about my cock baby?"

"y-yes," I admit.

"Just like I love thinking about that tight little pussy of yours."

Jeez, he's good at this.

"Take your fingers and pinch your nipples for me," he instructs.

I do as he says. "Mmmm," is all that comes out of my mouth. It feels so good.

"Are your nipples nice and hard for me Josie?"

"mmm hmmm."

"Good baby. Now take one hand down and hold those pretty lips open. Then take the other one and dip it in your juices, then rub it all over your clit."

Again, I do what he says. Mostly because it's exactly what I wanted to be doing anyway, and with him saying the words to me, it just makes it that much more exciting.

I never thought I'd like dirty talk, but with Gunner being the one saying those things to me, it just makes me hotter. I let out another whimper as I feel my clit getting harder and more swollen with each caress.

"Let me hear it. I wanna know how good it feels. Does your pussy feel good baby?"

"mmm yes...Gunner, I'm...I need..."

"Is it nice and wet for me?"

"Yes!" I'm breathing harder now, I can feel the orgasm building in me.

"I want you to take two fingers and push them into your pussy and imagine it's my cock."

Oh oh oh oh.

I do it. "Gunner," I breathe. "Please..."

"Come for me baby. Let me hear it."

I'm right on the edge. I can hear his breathing and I know he's right there with me.

"Fuck those two fingers in your pussy and rub your clit at the same time. Think about my cock fucking you. Think about riding it, until you come all over me."

I hear a series of whimpers coming from me as I let his words take over. "Ohhhh, Gunner," I say in a high pitched tone I'm not familiar with. "Mmmmmm," my orgasm slams through me. "Yes!" I feel my back arched as far as it will go and my body is rocked by the tremors coming from my core.

Wave after wave of sensations hit me until I feel it finally start to ebb. I rub myself slower, bringing myself back down and enjoying all of the little aftershocks. I forgot how awesome it was to feel that kind of self-pleasure.

"Fuck yeah baby," I hear him growl, and I know he's just finished too. I hear his heavy breathing slowing down. I think I'm still making a few whimpering sounds as I lay there limp and in between reality and some sort of sex fog.

"God, you're so fuckin' sexy," I hear him say. "You're still purring like a kitten."

That makes me stop and laugh. "I can't help it," I explain, feeling embarrassed. "I haven't been able to make myself come in a long time and you're the one who made it possible, so thank you. I'm feeling a bit like a contented cat I suppose."

"Baby, I've been trying to go slow for you, but after this, I'm not sure I can handle it anymore. I want to see you tomorrow."

Uh-oh.

"Um, about that," I say quickly. "I'm busy the next two nights."

"What the fuck? You said you were busy tonight."

"I was, I'm busy every Tuesday, Wednesday, and Thursday." I'm feeling defensive because he seems angry. I never promised to see him every day. In fact, I want to stop seeing him so much, period. Well, okay, that's kind of a lie, especially after that orgasm, but it doesn't change reality.

"Babe, just let me take you wherever you need to go."

"That's not necessary," I inform him. Besides, I really don't want to tell the hot man who turns me on, not to mention who I just had phone sex with, that I'm going to see my therapist tomorrow. I'm sure he already thinks I'm a whack job after witnessing my panic attack.

"Josie, I promised not to push you for answers, remember? But you also agreed to not push me away."

Shit.

I forgot about that little deal.

"Gunner, I've been taking care of myself a long time. I am capable of going out a few evenings without an escort."

"I know that, it just makes me feel better if you're not alone. Especially at night. If you won't take me, then please take Faith, or even Freddy."

I sigh. I know he means well, but I'm not a child. In fact two of the nights that I'm gone every week, I'm learning to defend myself.

"Gunner, I don't know if I'm ready for whatever it is you want from me," I tell him softly. Because it's true.

"Seriously? Josie, tell me what I've asked you for."

Well, he has a point. He hasn't asked for anything. In fact, he's given quite a bit of himself and not asked for anything in return. It's actually a little surprising when I think about it. Most men would expect something in return.

"You're right. You haven't asked me for anything, but it's not that..." I trail off. I can't tell him what I really think. Can I? Maybe I should just be honest. Maybe that will show him that he's barking up the wrong tree.

"Then what is it? Tell me so I can fix it."

"That's the thing. You can't fix it. You can't fix me," I sigh. I'm just going to have to let him see what he's getting himself involved in. "I get it okay? Men like a challenge. Especially men like you, but that's all this is Gunner. A challenge. But you'll see that it's not worth it."

"You are so messed up," he says sounding exasperated.

My first instinct is to be offended, and tell him he's wrong, but he's not. He's right. This is good.

"Exactly!" I declare. "See? You want to go with me tomorrow? Well, if you did you would see that I really am messed up, because you'd be taking me to see my therapist. Happy now?"

"Babe, you think it matters to me if you see a fuckin' therapist?"

"It should! You said I'm messed up and you're right. You'll see I'm not fixable. You'll see that you deserve something better. And you'll move on when you get bored and realize I'm not what you thought. It's better if it just stops now." I go from sounding exasperated to sounding defeated. "I'm sorry," I whisper, and then I hang up.

I close my eyes. I try not to let tears come. I didn't expect any of what happened on the phone tonight. I knew I would end it sometime, but I didn't know it would be right this minute, and I didn't know it would be after phone sex. Which is the best sex I've ever had, even though it was on the phone. I give myself a few minutes to feel the hurt and then remind myself it's better now than later.

Chapter 30

Gunner

What the fuck? I can't believe she hung up on me last night. She hasn't answered my calls or texts today either. Fuck. I knew she was going to push me away, but I didn't think it was going to be on the phone, last night, after phone sex for Christ sake. One minute she's giving me that sexy little whimper in my ear, the next she says I'm going to get bored with her. So I keep repeating in my head what I've been thinking all day. What the fuck?

Fuck if I can concentrate today for thinking about this shit. I'm pissed. For one thing, I can't protect her very well if she won't talk to me. For another thing, she doesn't understand what's in my head. She thinks she does, but it's like everything else she thinks, it's fucked up. I'm not looking for some casual fling with her.

Does she really think her seeing a therapist should send me running away? True, some men might do that, but from what I've learned about Josie, this is a good thing. I'm glad she's talking to someone. It tells me she's trying to take care of herself.

She thinks I deserve something better? Damn it. I've never met anyone better, or sweeter, or more beautiful than her. She doesn't see herself that way, because she's been through some fucked up shit, I get that. But it's time I give Josie a dose of reality. She needs to know what I really think and not what she thinks I think in her messed up head. Damn if she's not frustrating as fuck!

It's rare I feel my control slipping the way I do today. I know this because I do not like this feeling and it's not one I'm used to. I usually put my mind to something and get the results I want. Josie is making that difficult. The tricky part is knowing when to push. I can't let her run away, but pushing too hard will just make her shut down on me. I close my eyes and sigh. I'd much rather throw something.

I spent the morning with Walker going over some cases, and he could tell I don't have my head on straight. I can't afford being messed up like this. Having a messed up head in this line of work can get you shot. Or worse.

I don't need this shit, but I know she's in my system and I can't get her out. The only option is to make her see that I'm not going anywhere. Damn woman.

I'm lost in thought when Marina comes into my office and says, "You look like shit."

"Nice," I tell her rubbing my hands over my face. "You're fired."

She laughs and sits her ass down in the chair across from me.

"You can't fire me. You'd drown in your own paper work."

She's right. I would.

"What's up boss?" she asks. "Does this have something to do with a little woman named Josie?"

I blow out a breath. Apparently I'm not hiding my feelings as well as I thought.

"Am I that obvious?"

"No, I just know you very well. I also saw her, so I can see why you're hung up. Never thought I'd see it, but it makes sense."

"What the fuck are you talking about?"

"I mean I never thought I'd see you so frustrated over a woman, but after meeting her it makes sense. I can see why you're messed up over her. Just be careful," she warns as she sets more fucking papers on my desk.

"I'm being as careful as I know how to be," I practically snap at her and she just holds up her hands in surrender and walks out.

I lean back in my chair. Shit. This is the first time anyone's ever been worried about my heart getting broken. Maybe I'm getting a taste of my own medicine.

One thing's for sure. I'm not going to leave Josie out there wandering around without protection. I give Faith a call to see if she's going to be with her tonight. She says no, that Josie insists on doing things on her own and she doesn't think it's wise to push it. As it was, Faith checked up on her last night for me without Josie knowing. I tell her I'll handle the next two evenings. I'm going to keep an eye on her whether she likes it or not.

Later that evening I watch from a distance as Josie heads into an office building. I see a sign on the building for a Dr. Judith Palmer at the Women's Counseling Center. While I wait outside I search her name on my phone. Dr. Palmer has a PhD from the University of Michigan, where she started her career at a local rape crisis center. From there she moved to Grand Rapids and opened up this women's counseling center which specializes in women's trauma, including domestic and sexual violence.

I quit reading. Fuck. I was hoping I might be wrong about the kind of trauma Josie was dealing with. I feel my already tense muscles turn to stone and start to feel a rage I am not familiar with.

Jesus, Josie's small for a woman. She's petite. She wouldn't stand a chance against a full grown man intent on hurting her. This asshole was in a position of power with her. He was her employer. I wonder if he used that against her. I wonder a million different things sitting there waiting for her to come out. None of them good.

I finally see her emerge from the building and head to her car. I duck as I watch her look around and take in her surroundings. *Good girl*. I see her keys are ready, and she quickly gets inside the vehicle and locks the door. I hear her engine start, but the car doesn't move yet. I look over and see her resting her arms on top of the steering wheel and then lying her head down on top of them. She looks upset, or tired. Shit. I can't exactly go to her and explain that I'm following her, but I need to do something. I can't just leave her sitting in her car that way.

I get an idea and decide to send her a text to see if she'll answer.

Me: Just wanted to say Hi. Hope you are having a good night.

C'mon Josie, talk to me. Obviously this is not a good night, but she can't know that I know that.

I see her pick up her phone and look at it. Then I see her wipe tears from her cheeks, take a couple of deep breaths, then she looks back to her phone and types

Josie: Thank you. I'm sorry for hanging up on you last night.

Me: I'll forgive you if you let me see you again.

I watch her take a visibly deep breath again, like she's trying to decide what to do.

Josie: Maybe we can talk on Friday?

Me: And by talk, do you mean in person?

I see a small smile on her face and she shakes her head a little as if I'm exasperating her. That's okay. I'll take the smile instead of tears.

Josie: You're persistent.

Me: Always am when there's something I want.

I watch her take that in. She rests her head back down for a minute, like she has to think about how to respond.

Josie: I can't promise you anything.

Me: I didn't ask for anything. Just to spend time with you.

I can see her indecision and she's taking a while to answer. I'm not letting her off the hook.

Me: Pretty please with sugar on top? I promise to be a good boy ;)

I watch her read the message and then laugh. A real laugh. Good. It does something to me to know that I caused her a little bit of happiness. It makes me want to give her more.

Josie: Ok. I'll see you Friday, but only if you're good.

Me: Oh I'm real good baby ;)

I see her laugh again and shake her head like she doesn't know what to do with me.

Josie: Goodbye Gunner :)

Me: Bye baby.

Shit, I almost type a heart. I can't believe I'm thinking this shit. This girl makes me want to get all kinds of mushy. Not that I would ever admit that to anyone. Ever.

I watch her finally pull out and I follow at a distance to make sure she gets home safely.

*****

The following evening I watch again as Josie goes into another building. It's a large brick building. It looks like an old warehouse of some sort. I drive around to the front of the building after Josie is safely inside and see that it's called *Fighting Fitness.*

I can see through the large glass windows in the front of the building, it's a gym. I'm surprised she spends time at a gym considering how she likes to keep to herself. It also doesn't make a lot of sense because she runs every day. Why does she need to work out?

I find a place to park, luckily my years as a detective are serving me well. I'm good at staying invisible and still seeing my subject. I watch through the windows as Josie is talking and smiling with a man who looks to be about the same age. He appears to be Asian and I wonder if he owns the gym because from the looks of him, he is pure muscle.

I watch them talk and start to feel myself get pissed. I don't like her talking and smiling like that with someone else. I want to walk in there and punch him. I don't even know him, but I want to do it anyway.

I see her nodding her head as if she understands and she turns to head into a door. A few minutes later she comes out dressed in workout clothes. She heads straight to a machine and starts warming up. After about ten minutes I see the guy approach her again. They walk over to an area that's covered with mats and he starts working on some self-defense moves with her.

It makes sense now. She's learning self-defense. *Good girl*. I watch as she goes through the moves with the guy, and I can see that she's hesitant in her moves. I can see him talking to her, and then trying again. The more he tries, the more she seems to shy away and withdraw.

Her moves are precise, but she's in her head too much. The thing with self-defense is it only works if you don't freeze when you're confronted with a situation. You have to think fast and use your instincts. She's strong physically for someone her size, but she's allowing fear to guide her actions. I can see it from here.

I watch the guy move away from the mat and put on some padding gear and a helmet that covers most of his face. He approaches Josie and puts his face close to hers telling her something. She seems to back away, but he's not letting her retreat. I see him grab her arm and she wrenches away from him shaking her head.

I see what he's trying to do, he wants to push her. She needs to be confident in the fact that she can defend herself. It's not just knowing the moves.

As much as I understand it, I hate it. I see the fear and uncertainty on her face. She definitely wants to stay in control. She wants to stay in her comfort zone, but he's not allowing it. Part of me is hoping he will break through. Part of me wants to rush in there and stop him from pushing her so hard.

I have no idea how long she's been coming here. If he's any kind of trainer he should know when it's time to push. I could see when she first arrived that she was comfortable with him, so my guess is that she's been coming here for a while.

It would take a while for her to trust someone the way she seems to trust him.

I sit back and watch with my fists clenched on the wheel. I might know in my head that she needs this, but that doesn't mean I have to like it. I don't like watching her struggle. I don't want her to have to defend herself. I want to go in there and carry her out and keep her safe. I want to beat the shit out of anyone that ever comes near her again.

Shit. I sound like a fuckin' caveman.

I wince as she tries a kick that ends up being turned on her. She hits the ground and I can tell he's not going easy on her. She jumps back up and re-engages. I see him move behind her and grab her while she tries to fight him off. She's using the right techniques but she's holding back. Within a minute he has her to the ground and he's in control of her.

Fuck, this sucks.

I watch her get back up. She's sweating and breathing heavily, but she's not giving up. Again and again I watch her hit the ground. I can tell she's frustrated and from the looks of it so is her trainer.

I watch as he seems to yell something at her. I watch Josie look away, but he doesn't let her. He moves back into her line of vision. He says something else, and I can see a look of anger cross her face. He gives her a shove on her left shoulder and I watch her body jerk back and her eyes get wide and then narrow on him.

What the fuck? That's taking it a little bit too fuckin' far.

He does it again, and she goes back on one foot and stares him down. He gets close to her face and I can see him talking, trying to get her to stop him. Then he lifts both arms and shoves her shoulders, so that she almost falls, but catches herself.

Fuck this. That douchebag is about to see what it's like to get pushed around by someone bigger than him. He may have muscles, but I've got at least a foot on that fucker, and I've got muscle of my own. I jump out of my car and start to head to the door when I see her shoot her gaze at him. For once instead of looking terrified, she looks pissec.

I watch as he walks around and tries to get her from behind again, but she uses his momentum against him and breaks away. When he comes for her again, she blocks his advances and tries to take out a knee sending him to the ground, but he comes back at her, and what I see is fucking amazing.

My girl turns into a little warrior. She takes him on and uses the training he's been showing her to block his moves. She grounds him again and then she jumps right on fucking top of him and she doesn't stop.

I can see the smile on the trainers face. He got what he'd been pushing for but Josie is in a world all her own. She didn't let up either. It's a good thing he had on that padding because she was landing some good blows, she used her elbows, knees, hands, and anything she could manage to take out this imaginary attacker.

I watch him get his arms around her to try to snap her out of it but she's still struggling. She's in her head again. She's not in this gym. She doesn't know the training is over and that she's won. She's in survival mode.

He talks to her and slowly I see her come back to herself. I watch her sink into him breathing heavily. Not because of a panic attack, but from exertion. The guy takes off the helmet and padding and I can tell he's praising her the way he's smiling at her. He gives her a hug and she gives him a weak smile. Once he helps her up, he talks a little more, and I see her nod and head off to the locker room to change.

I watch as she comes out and talks to the guy a little longer. He seems to be comforting her now. Putting a hand on her shoulder. I'm starting to get pissed again. I know it's not rational, but I can't seem to control it when Josie is involved. I had decided I liked the trainer, but now I'm back to thinking about punching him.

Once she finally leaves the building and I stop seething, I make sure she's safely in her car, and then safely home once again. Tomorrow she's going to see me and talk to me. Whether she likes it or not we are going to get a few things straight. This protection from afar thing is total bullshit.

K. D. Smith

Chapter 31

Josie

It's been one hell of a week, I think as I get ready to have dinner with Gunner. He called earlier today, to remind me of my promise to talk to him tonight. As if I could forget.

He caught me right when I came out of my appointment with Dr. Palmer. We had just been discussing my relationship (or whatever you call it) with him. Dr. Palmer brought up several good points about why I was pushing him away. Of course they were reasons that only made sense to me, not to anyone else. She advised me to see where it went, to give it a chance, instead of running away because I was uncomfortable and afraid.

I was upset because she was right. She made me see things about myself that I didn't really like. As I sat there in my car upset over my session I received a text from Gunner, as if he knew. Then he made me laugh. I couldn't say no after that.

So here I am again, getting ready to go out with him when I swore I was going to avoid him. I let out a wince as I put my dress over my head. My body is so sore from last night's training session with Kai.

I remembered how he'd pushed me into fighting. How he'd known I had it in me, even when I didn't know. I fought like I'd never fought before since training with him. He was happy about that, I wasn't. I didn't like feeling out of control, and that's exactly what I was.

I will admit, I did kick ass. I was kind of proud about that. Kai says now that I know I can do it, I just have to build my confidence. I have to learn to focus it. I hope to God it doesn't make my body hurt this bad every time, because my muscles are screaming at me.

I don't think that *Ben Gay* will be a very nice perfume for my evening out with Gunner, or I'd be wearing some. Instead I put on my usual scent from Victoria's Secret. I love it. I use the shower gel, the lotion, the body spray and the perfume. The smell is subtle, and it makes my skin super soft.

I don't go out of my way with frilly stuff the way Faith does, but this is one of my guilty pleasures, just like my lip gloss. I look in the mirror and check my appearance. I have on my white sundress. I suppose it looks okay since my skin is tanned from running and gardening outside. It's off the shoulder and flares at the

Finding Air

waist coming down to just above my knees. I put on tan suede wedges and a tan suede belt. I transfer my stuff that I usually carry around in my gym bag to my tan purse. This is stylish for me.

I left my hair down and put some curls in it, and applied some light make-up. I finished up by putting a little extra shimmer lotion on my legs.

I looked at Freddy who's lying on my bed watching me with curiosity. He looked hopeful, as if he was hoping to tag along somewhere. I walked over and sat with him and gave him a good rub on the ears that made him groan like an old man.

When Gunner called earlier to say he wanted to take me to dinner, I agreed. I was still remembering all that Dr. Palmer and I had discussed. Now, I'm re-thinking my decision as I feel the butterflies fluttering around in my stomach.

Freddy startles me by letting out a huff as he jumps up and runs for the door. I know what that means, we have company.

Oh crap. I guess there's no backing out now.

When I open the door, I'm greeted by a smiling Gunner and a bouquet of flowers. I start to feel that tingly sensation again. I can't help but smile at him. He looks hot in his jeans and tight black t-shirt.

251

Why does he have to be so perfect? He didn't even bring me the typical flowers men usually pick. He brought me ones I like. Don't get me wrong, I'm not going to complain if I get red roses, but it's what most men give and there's usually no thought behind it. Instead, Gunner picked a bouquet with different colors of daisies. They are bright and beautiful, they look like summer. Perfect.

Damn.

"Thank you," I say taking them into the kitchen, "They're beautiful."

"They reminded me of you."

"I remind you of daisies?" I ask a little confused. I hope there's not a cheesy pick up line coming.

"Yeah, I thought that bouquet suited you. It's fresh, bright, and pretty. Like you."

Oh I'm in so much trouble.

I'm pretty sure I blush again as I mumble a thank-you. While he slips Freddy a beef stick.

"So where are we going?" I ask, trying to take my mind off the warm feeling that's spreading throughout my body.

"It's a surprise," he says taking my hand.

I give Freddy a goodbye and tell him Faith will be home soon. Gunner sets the alarm and then leads me to his truck. At least he didn't bring the bike.

As if he knows what I'm thinking, he says, "I didn't know if you were wearing a dress, so I thought I'd make it easier on you and bring the truck."

He opens the door and I look up into the truck. I don't know if this is easier. His truck is big. Granted, riding a motorcycle in a dress has its issues, but so does climbing, and that's exactly what I'm going to have to do to get in this thing.

Again, as if he knows what I'm thinking, I hear him chuckle and before I know what's happening he scoops me up and sits my ass in the passenger seat. Holy shit.

"Sorry, I forgot how short you are," he says shutting the door and coming around and easily sliding into the driver's seat.

I would be offended, but it's true. I am considered short compared to a lot of women. I bet all of his previous girlfriends were tall. Probably blondes too. Marina worked for him, she was tall. She was also cool. I wonder if they ever hooked up. I start to frown at the direction of my thoughts.

"Hey," he says, "I like that you're petite, I didn't mean anything bad by it."

That makes me laugh a little because he has no idea what I was really thinking.

"It's okay," I tell him. "I'm used to it."

We start driving and I'm a little confused when we hit the highway. I ask him where we're going again, but he doesn't answer, he just smiles.

Well, if he's going to be mysterious, I'm going to find some tunes. Music helps me relax and I sure could use it right now. I may look fine on the outside but my hands are sweaty, my tummy feels weird and my foot is bouncing like there's no tomorrow.

I take my iPod out of my purse and hook it to his system. I give him a questioning look and he gives me the nod that it's okay. I don't know what kind of music he likes, so I go for my classic rock playlist instead of anything girly. I hit shuffle and the Steve Miller Band fills my ears with some Space Cowboy.

He gives me an inquisitive look with those gorgeous indigo eyes and says, "Nice. I was hoping you weren't going to play me some Britney Spears."

"Hey, there's nothing wrong with a little Brit, but somehow I knew you weren't the type."

The playlist goes on as we ride in comfortable silence. We hear Born to Run by Springsteen, Sweet Child O' Mine by Guns n' Roses, Why Can't This Be Love by Van Halen, and more. I notice when he starts to tap his fingers on the steering wheel, it makes me happy that he's enjoying the music as much as I am.

"So what else is on that thing?" he asks me referring to my iPod.

"You don't want to know," I tell him. "I'm a bit of a music freak. There's not much I don't like. I have a little bit of everything."

"Give me some examples, what's on there that would surprise me."

I hope I'm not about to fall into the nerd category, but he asked, so I might as well be honest.

"George Jones, Mozart, Sugarland, Billie Holiday, Frank Sinatra, Eminem," I could keep going but I stop there when I see his eyes get big.

"Wow, that's a pretty wide range."

"Yep," I say, and look out the window concentrating on Tom Petty's *American Girl*.

I notice we are close to the lakeshore now. I'm secretly hoping that's where he's going to take me. I love the shore. There's nothing like Lake Michigan in the summer. It's like being at the ocean. I haven't been to the lake in so long, and I miss it.

He pulls off of the highway and we head down a strip that has a ton of restaurants. He stops at one, says he'll be back, tells me to lock myself in, and runs inside. What in the world is he up to?

I secretly feel the warmness start spreading again starting somewhere deep in my belly. Nobody has ever cared enough to make sure I lock the doors before. Something that simple is making me feel so wonderful that I know I'm completely screwed.

He comes back carrying two bags, then we're off again. I give him a questioning look but he just smiles and keeps going. We pull into a parking area near the shore and I take a deep breath. We are at the beach. I know I'm smiling from ear to ear, but I can't help it.

"I was hoping this was our destination," I tell him.

"I aim to please," he tells me with a wink.

Sigh. Seriously, could he be any better?

He comes around to my side of the truck and opens the door. As I start to climb down, he grabs me and sets me gently on the ground, then grabs the bags and another bag from the back.

I try to take one from him, but he doesn't let me. He's carrying them all with one arm and then takes my hand with the other and pulls me toward the sand.

Once we hit the sand, I stop and lean on him so I can take off my shoes. Wedges and sand are not a good combo unless you want a broken ankle.

When we get to a spot close to the water he stops and sets down the bags, opening one and laying out a blanket for us to sit on. I'm feeling like a giddy teenager inside. I plop down on the blanket and watch him sit down and start digging through the bags.

He hands me a disposable wine glass, which he must have brought from home and opens a bottle. I'm not much of a wine drinker, so I take a hesitant sip when he fills my glass and find that I really like whatever this is.

He sets out several containers and opens them. We have fried chicken, potato salad, rolls, and fruit salad. It looks delicious.

"This looks amazing," I tell him. "Thank you so much for all of this, I don't even know what to say. I haven't been to the beach in years, God I missed it."

"I love it here. My parents moved over here a few years ago."

"I would love living over here," I tell him honestly. There's just something so peaceful about the beach, even in cold weather, I find it soothing.

We eat and talk a little about his family. He tells me more about his siblings and parents. I listen intently. It seems so odd to hear about a loving family that's close to one another. I only had that with my dad.

I watch him and think it's no wonder he seems so confident. He's strong, he has a great family, he makes a good living, he seems to have a lot of friends, and the thing that impresses me the most, is that he really appreciates all of those things.

He stands up and holds his hand out to me. I take it and he helps me up. It's warm today and I watch as Gunner removes his t-shirt and throws it on the blanket. He kicks off his shoes and socks leaving him in only his jeans.

Gulp.

I try to act casual, as if I'm not overheating underneath my dress. Thank God there's a breeze. I swear, it is not fair for a man look this good.

As we walk along the water I notice the looks women give him. He's probably wishing he was with one of the bikini bombshells that keep giving him eager smiles.

It hits me how glad I am that I'm not wearing a bathing suit because there is no way I can compete with some of these women. I try to pull my hand away, but he doesn't let me, instead he pulls me closer and puts his arm around me while we tell beach stories from our past.

When we get back to the blanket he sits down and pulls me into him so that I'm sitting across his lap and he has his arms around me. I look into those amazing eyes, and I can't help it, my arms go around his neck.

When he kisses me, I kiss him back.

Take that bikini bitches!

His lips touch mine softly and I shiver as I feel tingles starting to spread through my body. I melt into him and he holds me tighter and deepens the kiss, pushing his tongue inside my mouth, caressing my tongue with his. Kissing him makes me feel like I have electricity running through my veins. It defies logic, but my body reacts to him like it's been waiting forever for his touch.

All thoughts of bikinis fly out of my head and I get lost in the kiss as he lays me back onto the blanket so that the lower half of his body is pressed up against my side, but the top half is above me.

I run my hands along his back muscles. He feels so good, I can't help but want more. I run my hands across his shoulders and biceps and then move to his chest. The kiss keeps heating up and we are both breathing a little heavier. I move my hands down his abs. Lord have mercy. This man is hard everywhere, and I haven't even gotten to the good part yet.

I feel his hand run down my leg as he moves one of his legs between mine. I bend my leg that he's not covering and keep it at his hip. I feel his hand going up the back of my dress. I have a brief thought that we are in public and we should stop, but to be honest, I don't really care and I don't want to stop.

I hear him let out a low groan as his hand cups my ass.

"Another lacy thong," he says running his fingers along the edge. "You're killin' me babe."

He moves his mouth to my neck and kisses me there and I shiver again.

He whispers in my ear, "What color?"

"White," I whisper. "I wanted to wear red, but I was afraid it would show through my dress." I don't know why in the hell I'm telling him this. He's making my brain short circuit again.

He gives off another low groan, only this one sounds kind of like a growl. He lifts his head and looks down at me. He kisses me again and trails his finger along the top edge of my dress, across my cleavage.

"What about here?" he wants to know, "I don't see any straps."

I shake my head. This dress is off the shoulder. A bra doesn't work with it, unless it's strapless, but I didn't have one of those. I'm wondering if it was a bad idea, but I thought it looked okay in the mirror. I couldn't see anything through the dress.

I feel his hand trail down over the top of my dress and his thumb rubs across my nipple, and then back again. I draw in a sharp breath at the sensation that runs from my breast right down into my panties.

Gunner looks around to make sure we're not being watched and then dips his head to start kissing my collar bone as his hand squeezes my breast and his thumb goes slowly back and forth over my nipple again.

"Gunner," I whimper.

"Mmmm, yeah baby?" he mumbles with his face still pressed to me.

I don't even know what I was going to say. His name just popped out of my mouth. He moves back a little so his hand can go to my other breast. I whisper his name again.

"Fuck, I love how respond to me. It's like you ignite when I get my hands on you."

I just nod my head between breaths, because it's *so* true. I do feel like I ignite when he touches me. Like I'm combustible.

"Come home with me," he says, and I look up into those eyes. I see the plea in them and even though I don't understand it, I want to go home with him.

"Okay," I say quietly.

He rolls over onto his back and says, "Thank fuck!"

I laugh at him. I'm sure he can't be hard up for women, but for right now, I'm glad that it's me he wants. There are some things a man can't fake, and I can see just how much he wants me as I take in the bulge in his jeans while he's laying back.

I try not to stare, but I can't help it, I never got to see it last time. I'm dying to unzip him right here. I slowly reach over and rub my finger over the length of him. I hear him suck in a breath and he grabs my wrist.

"Baby, you better stop that if you want to make it home to my bed instead of getting fucked in a truck."

With that he gets up and he loads up the bags quickly and we head back to the truck. He lifts me in once again and his hand lingers up high on my thigh for a few seconds. Part of me is hoping he's going to get in the truck and take me right now instead of making me wait until we get back to his place, but he doesn't. He puts on his shoes and shirt and drives back to the highway.

Chapter 32

Gunner

I can't believe I have her in my truck and she's coming home with me. I glance at her out of the corner of my eye to see how she's doing. Her face is flushed and her foot is bouncing again.

I reach over and put my hand on her knee and it stops. She looks at me and gives a shy smile. Damn it, I wish I knew what was going on in her head right now.

I don't want to cause her to panic again. I know I need to be gentle this time and try to control myself. Fuck if she doesn't make it hard to control myself though. My cock could pound nails right now.

I hope it's not a mistake to bring up what happened last time, I don't want her to shut down on me, but I want to make sure before we go ahead. I don't want to do anything to screw this up. She's finally right where I want her. Again. I feel like she's always slipping away, right through my fingers, and it hits me that I have never once cared about letting a woman slip away. Usually I don't even notice.

I take her hand in mine and ask, "Are you sure about this Josie?"

She nods her head yes and says, "Yes, I think so."

"I want you to be sure." I tell her, because I do. As much as I want her, I'll wait if it means she'll feel more secure.

She sighs and looks out the window. Finally she says, "I want to Gunner, and I wanted to last time, it's just sometimes I can't control what triggers me." She looks down into her lap and at our hands. I feel her start to pull hers away, but I hold tight.

"Well, we know I shouldn't spank you," I say a little embarrassed myself. I still can't believe I did that shit. "What else?"

She shrugs those perfect shoulders. "I don't know, I told you it's been a long time. I think as long as there's no hitting, or spanking without warning, or being tied up, I should be okay." Her face gets red again and she looks out the window.

Jesus. That asshole tied her up? I feel my anger at the thought but I quickly mask my expression when she turns back to me. I don't want her thinking I'm pissed at her.

"I want to be with you Gunner, I really do. I can't promise anything... I... I'm sure you're used to more experienced women, and... I know I'm not..."

"Stop it." I say roughly and see her flinch away from me. Damn it. So much for remembering to be gentle.

I sigh, "I don't want to hear you put yourself down. The last thing you need to worry about is if you're going to please me. Fuck, just looking at you gets me hard, there is no way I could be disappointed with you." To prove it to her I place her hand on the bulge that's still in my pants and watch her eyes get big and blink at me.

"I don't give a shit about any of that. I just want to make sure you feel safe with me. I don't want any fear when you're in my bed under me."

She blinks at me again. She's so fuckin' cute.

She gives a small hesitant smile and I leave it at that. I've got the answers I need. No spanking, no binding. I can live with that as long as she's okay. I've been there and done that, it's fun, but it's not a necessity. I don't care about any of that as long as I can be with Josie. I also remind myself that she doesn't like closed, small or dark spaces. I remember her reaction to the elevator.

"I'm not into a lot of kink babe, but I do like control in bed," I tell her the truth. "I don't want to do anything to make you uncomfortable though, so I want you to pick a word. Something you will say if what I'm doing isn't working for you."

"You mean like a safeword?" She asks looking a little freaked. "I mean... I've read the books, but I've never done any of that stuff, I don't know..."

"Like I said, I'm not really into that, I just think it's a good idea, considering last time, that there is a way for you to communicate to me that you're scared. If you say no, I will stop whatever I'm doing, I promise you that, but if I'm doing something that freaks you out, this would be an easy way for you to tell me. I'm hoping it won't be used, I don't plan on pushing you, but it would make me feel better if you had a safeword, and I hope it will make you feel safer too."

I see her mulling this over. Then she nods and says,"Okay, it can't hurt to have one. Just in case..." she looks away, no doubt remembering what happened last time.

"Good," I say giving her hand a reassuring squeeze. "So what's it going to be?"

She thinks for a minute, then says so softly I almost miss it, "Indigo."

I give her a questioning look, but she doesn't explain, she just shrugs.

"Indigo it is then."

It seems like it takes forever to get to my place. When we park, I lift her down from the truck and grab the bags. When we get in the building I head straight for the stairs.

When she realizes I'm not putting her in the elevator again, I see her relax a little and smile at me. Damn, I'd do just about anything to keep those appreciative smiles coming at me.

Once inside I lock up and set the alarm. I see her looking at the alarm questioningly.

"This line of business doesn't always make me popular, better to be safe," I tell her the truth.

"You mean... do people come after you?"

I wince a little trying to decide if I should be honest.

"Let's just say that when you find people's secrets, and sometimes those secrets are not good ones, people can get a little pissed off."

"Have you ever been shot at?"

This whole line of questioning is making me nervous. I don't want to freak her out by telling her the truth, but she's looking at me expectantly so I try to play it off.

"I was a cop too, remember? So yeah, I've been shot at."

She looks concerned, and I'm hoping this isn't going to lead to the next question, which is usually 'have you ever shot anyone?' But she doesn't ask any questions. Maybe she knows she won't like the answer.

She's so quiet sometimes it unnerves me. I want to know what she's thinking when she gets so quiet.

I head into the living room and offer her a drink. She takes more of the wine, and I make a mental note to remember that she likes it as I go put the food away.

We kick off our shoes and sit on the couch. I pull her close to me, which gets me a smile. I love that she's getting used to my touch. I can see that she's trusting me more. It reminds me that I need to come clean with her before this goes too far. I really don't want to bring it up because I don't want to ruin how well things are going, but my conscience is eating away at me.

"There's something we should talk about," I say carefully, watching her reactions.

"Please," she says holding up her hand outward toward me. "Not right now." I get what she means. She doesn't want to anything to ruin this night either.

I go back and forth in my head. I need to tell her, but maybe I should wait until tomorrow. If tonight progresses like I'm hoping, she's going to be mine tomorrow. We will have built more trust and maybe it will be harder for her to run away.

I'm sitting here with her in my arms, battling with indecision. I see she's watching me with questions in her eyes. She lifts one finger and runs it down the center of my forehead where she can see the concentration on my face.

"Stop thinking so much," she tells me. "No more talking." Then she leans into me with those big hazel eyes expectantly, and I know she wants me to kiss her.

Hell. I'm not a fuckin' saint, so I do what she wants, because it's what I want too.

I can tell she's a little hesitant when my lips first touch hers, but like all the times before, she ignites for me within minutes. God, she's so fuckin' perfect.

I do my best to kiss the daylights out of her. I don't want her to ever think about anyone else's mouth on hers but mine. I only want her to be able to remember this kiss, right here, right now.

I carefully put her glass on the coffee table and reach for her. She instantly locks her arms around my neck and presses herself to me. I lift her so that she's straddling my lap while my lips never leave hers.

I hear her give a surprised little gasp when I lift her but she doesn't break the kiss either. I'm dying to get this damn dress off of her, but I remember my plan to go slowly with her. Easier said than done. I don't want to get carried away again, but when I feel her rubbing on me, I about spill my load in my jeans like an amateur.

She grasps at the hem of my t-shirt, so I lift it over my head and get right back to those luscious lips of hers. Fuck. She's running her hands all over my chest and it's driving me wild.

I reach for her belt and undo it, but I don't remove her dress yet. I want to give her time to explore even if it's the death of me. I feel her hands all over my arms, my abs, my chest, then she puts them in my hair and tugs me closer. I take that as a sign that she's ready for more, since she's letting out those breathy little noises and practically dry humping my cock through my jeans. Jesus. Beautiful.

I take my finger and place it at the top of her dress and pull it down to expose her tits. God, she's beautiful, I thought I remembered but I didn't even come close.

I rub my thumbs over her nipples and get a little moan out of her. Oh yeah, that's what I'm after. I give them a little pinch and watch as she moans again only a little louder.

I kiss my way from her mouth down to her neck, saying in her ear, "That's it baby, let me hear what you like. I want you screaming my name by the time I bury my cock in you."

"Oh God," she whimpers in my ear.

"I've been dying to see you like this since listening to you come on the phone the other night."

I put my mouth on one of her nipples and use my tongue on it. She says my name, and I suck it into my mouth and then give it a little nip with my teeth before moving to the other one.

"Gunner," she breathes still rubbing her pussy against me, "I can't wait, I need..."

I decide to help her out, so that I can help her build it up again for me. I'm not anywhere near being done with her. I've waited for this moment, and I'll be damned if it's going to be over this fast.

I put my hand down in between our bodies and lift the hem of her dress that's practically pushed up around her waist anyway. I see those lacy white panties of hers and feel how soaked they are. I don't put my hand inside yet, I just press in with my knuckle a little bit to give her something to ride.

"Gunner," she says my name louder and keeps rocking her hips against me. So fuckin' hot.

I press a little harder and keep sucking on those pretty pink nipples. I see her head fly back and her mouth is open. Oh yeah. She says my name again and comes against my hand. I can feel the heat and wetness coating her panties even more than before.

"That's it baby," I encourage her, "give it to me."

She does. Hot damn. She's got that dazed look on her face again that's so fuckin' sexy.

It's time for a distraction and to get more comfortable, so I say, "Hang on to me."

She puts her arms around my neck and wraps her legs around me as I stand up. I plant my hands on her ass under her dress and carry her that way up the stairs to my room.

I lay her down on the bed, and say "I love watching you come. I hope you're ready to do it again."

She blinks those eyes at me and says, "I don't know if I can..."

"Leave it to me baby, you can, and you will."

"Oh," she whispers, which makes me chuckle a little. She really is inexperienced if she doesn't know she can come more than once. I'm about to rock her world.

I take her mouth again and this time when I get down to her nipples I kiss them and then watch as I roll them between my index finger and my thumb. She starts squirming again and I know she's working her way there.

I pull her dress off and look down at her wearing only those white lacy panties. I put my hand inside and run my fingers through her wetness, which gets me another squirm and a little gasp.

"So wet baby," I tell her. "Is this all for me?"

I watch as she nods her head yes and I take my fingers that are covered in her juices and suck them clean. I see her look become more dazed as she stares at me.

I take one finger and push it into her wet pussy and watch as she lets out a long exhale and closes her eyes. When I start to move it, she starts to move her hips with me.

"I love this tight little pussy," I tell her adding another finger to my ministrations.

"Oh Gunner..."

"That's it baby, just let it happen." I tell her as I settle myself between her legs and push them open. I take in her look, her smell, and reach out my tongue to taste her. Beautiful.

I use my fingers on her. I Lick her clit and suck it into my mouth. I can tell she's going wild. She's trying to grind her pussy onto my face, but I'm holding her hips still. I want to get her there by myself.

"I want to see you come again for me baby, look at me," I tell her.

So far she's had her eyes closed and I want her to see what I'm seeing, I want her to know that it's my mouth on her pussy. My fingers inside of her. Me making her scream and come all over.

She looks down and our eyes lock, just as I bury my fingers in her and start using them against the front wall where her g-spot is, I stick my tongue out and lave at her clit. I watch her eyes catch fire and I know she's there. I put my lips around her clit and suck hard. I watch as she arches her back and comes all over me again.

"Fuckin' beautiful," I whisper working my way back up her body.

If my dick wasn't so hard, I would smile because she's making that purring sound that she made the other night on the phone. I love that I can make her do that and she doesn't even realize she's doing it. I bet if I mentioned it right now, she would stop, so I keep my mouth shut and enjoy the sound.

I kiss her again so that she can taste how amazing her pussy is on my lips. She holds back a little at first, but then she gets caught up and starts kissing me wild again. Damn. I wonder how many times I could make her come in a night. I've had some wild women in bed, but it's more like they were acting out a porn, instead of letting go and honestly feeling it.

I watch her and I know she's feeling it. She's giving me exactly what she feels. She has no idea how special she is. Now I'm going to spend a little bit working her up again and then I'm going to make her mine. Once and for all.

Chapter 33

Josie

Oh.

My.

God.

Holy shit.

I had no idea it was possible to have two orgasms and steadily be working your way to a third in one night.

We didn't even technically have sex yet!

I feel like my body is on fire, and he's right, I do purr. Who knew?

I can't stand waiting anymore. I just want him. Finally and completely. I want him inside of me.

He's taking his time kissing me again, but I can tell he's trying not to rush me. I appreciate the thought, but right now I want him to rush. I want his pants off.

I reach for his belt and he looks down watching me fumbling with it. I must not be doing it fast enough because he gets it unbuckled himself. I go for his button and his zipper and reach my hand inside.

I get my hand on him through his boxers and hear him suck in a breath. I look up and he's closing his eyes. I start pushing at his pants trying to get them down his legs. In one swift move he lifts his hips, pushes them down, underwear and all, then kicks them off.

Wow.

I take him in for a moment.

I swallow. I'm pretty sure I licked my lips too. He's beautiful. Perfect. And very large.

I reach my hand out and wrap it around him and my fingers don't close around him. I wonder if it's going to fit inside me. I give him a tentative stroke and hear him make a low growling noise.

He's given me so much pleasure, I think maybe I should return the favor. I start kissing my way downwards, but he pulls me back up.

"If you put your lips on my cock, I'm going to come, and I want to be in your sweet little pussy when I do that."

"Okay," I whisper. I mean, what else can I say to that?

"Are you on the pill?" he asks.

How the hell did I get this far and never even think about that? He really does make my brain malfunction.

"Yes," I tell him, because I am, it's safer that way.

"I'm clean, I promise you, but I'll use a condom if you want me to until I can get you proof," he says. His voice is low and I can tell he's holding himself back physically because he doesn't want to scare me again.

"I trust you," I whisper. It's true, I do. I didn't think I would be able to have this kind of trust for a man again, but I know I'm safe with Gunner.

"Thank you," he whispers back, rolling himself over me. "You have no idea how much that means to me."

He kisses me hard and deep. It's almost as if his tongue is mimicking what he's about to do to me down below. It's seriously hot. I whimper into his mouth and try to suck on his tongue. I can't help myself.

He trails his mouth to my neck and says in my ear, "Wrap your legs around me baby, I'm gonna try to go slow, but I'm dying to get inside you."

I do as he asks, and I feel him pushing against my entrance. I immediately start moving my hips trying to get him deeper. I look up into his beautiful eyes as he rests his forehead against mine. He's got one elbow down in the mattress and the other arm wrapped around my waist behind me.

I feel him slowly start to push in as his arm tightens on me and starts pushing me down on him. Oh yes. I know he's not all the way in, but I feel it stretching me and it feels divine.

He backs out a little and goes in again a little further this time.

"Gunner..." I whimper. "More. Please..."

Once I ask, I receive, because he pulls back one more time and then gives one hard thrust until he's buried in me as far as he can go.

I gasp loudly and try to breathe.

He holds himself steady. "Did I hurt you?" he asks, his voice sounding tight, searching my face.

"No," I shake my head. Well, it did hurt, but it was getting better. My body was adjusting to his invasion.

He lets out a low growl and starts moving slowly.

"Your pussy feels so good on my cock."

Oh yes. It does feel good. In fact, it feels incredible. I start moving my hips with his and instead of saying *yes* in my head, it starts coming out of my mouth.

He starts pumping into me as he's pulling my body down onto him and I think I'm going to explode. On every downward pull my clit is getting a rub in just the right spot. I feel my inner walls clenching at him and I know this is going to be the biggest orgasm I've ever had in my whole entire life.

"Gunner... yes... please..." I hear myself begging him for it while I try to grind my hips even closer to him.

He takes my invitation and drives into me harder than before. Each thrust is so hard I hear myself letting out surprised gasps at each one as our bodies smack together, but it's so good, I don't want him to stop, I never want him to stop.

"You want more of my cock baby?" he growls at me.

"Yes," I say, because I do, I really, really do.

"I'm making you mine tonight Josie. Do you understand?"

I nod my head, even though I don't. I just want more and I don't want him to stop.

"You're in my bed, and my cock is deep inside you, you're purring for me, and I'm going to come deep inside this tight little pussy. You're mine after this Josie. I'm not giving you up."

He starts pounding faster and that's it. I'm gone. I actually scream his name, just like he said I would. I've never felt anything like this. I know when this orgasm hits me it's going to be huge. I almost try to fight it, that's how huge I know it's going to be. I'm afraid I won't be able to take it. I feel like I'm going to explode into a million pieces.

"Give it to me," he commands, sounding stern and breathing heavily.

"Gunner..." I don't say anything else. I can't think. I'm right there. Right on the edge.

"Come for me, Josie." and that's all it takes. I want to give him what he wants, and my body follows automatically right over the edge. I scream out his name again and feel myself quivering around him while my orgasm goes on and on, I have no sense of time or awareness. It consumes me.

He gives me one more good thrust and I hear him growl as I feel his body stiffen. I can feel his hot come spurting inside me and it makes my orgasm continue for a little longer.

I don't know how long we lay there, with him still deep inside me, and me purring, but I don't care. It feels so good to have his heavy weight on me. His hot breath slowing down against my neck. I'm warm, I'm safe, and I am drained.

After a little bit Gunner gets up saying, "Don't move, I'll be right back." He touches his lips softly to mine before he exits the bed.

I watch him walk into the bathroom and come back with a wet cloth. He comes to the side of the bed and pushes my knees apart.

"Let me clean you up."

What?

"Um, I can do that," I say embarrassed. I start to get up but he doesn't let me.

"Don't get shy on me now," he smiles at me. "I'll take care of you. Besides, I like seeing how you're pussy looks so wet and swollen from my cock, and I really like seeing my come leaking out from inside you. It means that you're mine."

I have no idea how to respond to that, other than I'm sure my face is flaming red. I don't know how in the hell he learned to talk like this, but he's very good at it. I know this because it makes my tummy flutter every time he does it.

He keeps saying I'm his, but I think he means for tonight. That has to be it, but I'm not asking questions. I feel so relaxed right now, all I want to do is stay right here.

I do as he asks and he gently wipes me and then takes the towel back to the bathroom. He climbs into bed and pulls me over to him. He's on his back and he puts his arm around me so that I have no choice but to lay along his side and put my head on his chest and my arm over his abs. Then he kisses my forehead.

I can't believe this is happening. He's everything I've ever wanted. I think back to some of the things we did and a lot of the things he said. I love the way he talks. I love the way he looks. I love the way he's holding me right now, like I'm something special to him. Because he's special to me. Even if this is our only night, he will always be special to me for helping me come back to myself.

I never imagined I could ever feel this good again. I never thought I'd have sex again, especially not the best sex *ever*. I thought I had good sex before, but it was nothing like this. This was off the charts. I don't even know if I could describe it with words. It was *that* good. Yep. Gunner Layne is a sex god.

"Sleep baby," he whispers.

And I do.

*****

I open my eyes and look around. I'm in Gunner's bed and it makes me smile. I feel him give me a squeeze and I know he's awake.

"Good morning," he says and his voice is even deeper in the morning. I can feel it rumbling in his chest against me. Lord help me, I feel myself getting wet again. I stretch and feel how sore I am from the night before, and then I remember. *Everything.* I'm glad my face is buried in his chest because it's probably turning red again.

"How are you feeling?" he asks.

I think about it for a minute and answer honestly, "I feel good. A little sore, but good. I slept." I don't know if he realizes how rare it is for me to actually sleep through the night, but it is. Both times I've been in Gunner's bed I've actually slept through the night.

"I know babe, I was here," he jokes.

I smile at him and remind him, "I didn't have my pills again, but I slept all night. It's like you're magic or something." Speaking of pills, that reminds me that I need to get home and take my birth control pills.

That makes him smile and it makes something inside me feel warm and cozy.

"I guess you should keep me around then."

I don't know how to respond to that. Is he being serious? I want to keep him around, but that's not an option. At least not long term. He has to know that too, and I'm pretty sure he's not going to want me around for long.

The things I'm thinking must make me frown, because he tips my head up to him and says, "What's going on in that head of yours?"

"Nothing," I say, trying to shake it off and sound innocent. I don't want to tell him what I was thinking. He'd probably try to make me feel better, and I don't want his pity. I decide it's best if I just act like it's a normal morning and my whole world hasn't just changed.

"Can I use your shower?" I ask him.

"Babe, I can see those wheels turning. Listen to me. Last night was fuckin' amazing. Don't start doubting it."

It was amazing, I didn't doubt that one little bit. Although, I'm surprised he thinks so. He's obviously very experienced and I'm sure I was not, in any way, amazing for someone like him.

These thoughts start working in my head and I decide it's best to just shower and get home. The night is over, it's time to get back to reality.

I roll to the edge of the bed and grab a throw on the bed. This is the one I wrapped myself in last time. Remembering that night is not helping my worries. I stand and wrap myself in it again and head to the shower.

Cinderella needs to get her ass home. It's way past midnight.

Chapter 34

Gunner

I watch Josie wrap up in the blanket and it's like she's gone back inside her shell. Damn it. She walks to my bathroom and I'm right behind her. When she gets inside I grab her shoulders and turn her to face me.

"Tell me," I demand.

"Tell you what?" she asks looking confused but I can tell she's feigning ignorance.

"Whatever's going on in here," I put my finger to her temple.

"Nothing," she pretty much squeaks at me. She's a shitty liar.

"Babe, quit lying," I call her on it. "I thought we understood each other. Last night was great, and now you're pulling away again."

"I...I just need to get home. I need to check on Freddy, and I need to take my birth control pill."

Fuck, that reminds me we didn't use a condom. Which reminds me how fuckin' good she felt, which starts to make me hard.

"Okay," I say calling her bluff. I know she's running, but I'm not letting her this time. I go and turn the water on in the shower and come back to her removing the throw from her and throwing it out the door into the bedroom.

She stands there gawking at me. She tries to cover herself but I stop her.

"I've seen all of you baby, there's nothing to be shy about," I inform her as I take her hand and lead her into the shower.

"Um, maybe I could have some privacy?" she asks.

"Sorry babe, we're conserving water."

I see her get that fiery look about her and she turns her back on me. Good, I'd rather see her get angry instead of having that withdrawn and lost look that she gets.

I grab some shower gel and lather up my hands, then I start rubbing her back. She can't get away, so she turns to face me.

"Gunner, you don't have to do this. Please, just let me shower and take me home."

"What don't I have to do? Clue me in, because I have no idea what you're thinking right now. Last night when my cock was inside you we were both pretty damn happy. I saw your face when you woke up and you looked pretty damn happy then too, and so was I. But then you started thinking, I could see it, and whatever you started thinking wasn't good. It sure as fuck wasn't about Freddy or pills. Am I right?"

She gives me a heated stare as if she's trying to decide if she should talk or just turn her back on me again. Then she finally says, "You really want to know?"

"Absolutely."

"Fine," she snaps at me. Then she continues to tell me exactly what she'd been thinking as she wets her hair, grabs my shampoo and rubs some in. "You said I should keep you around, and that made me think that you can't be serious, because now that we've..." she waves a hand in the air. "You know... done it... you have to know that there's no way that this can be long term. So you don't need to bother saying that kind of stuff. You also don't have to tell me that it was amazing. Because even if it was amazing for me, I know that it couldn't have been for you. You're obviously very experienced. You're like a phone sex operator or male escort or something. I can't be that exciting for you. I'm sure the women who would like you to spank them and tie them up are much more stimulating." Then she puts her head back rinsing out the shampoo, while I'm still trying to digest this shit she's just thrown at me.

"Please tell me you have conditioner," she mumbles.

I grab the bottle and shove it at her and watch as she squirts it into her hand and starts putting it in her hair. I'm so fuckin' pissed I don't trust myself to talk. This woman is going to drive me fuckin' crazy. I'm pissed and at the same time my dick is hard just watching her.

"Are you serious?" I finally manage to growl at her.

"Yep," she says, and she actually makes the P sound pop as she says it and cocks her head to the side. She's fucking asking for it.

I walk into her and back her up against the wall. She tries to hold her own but I can see that her smugness is receding and she's wondering what the fuck I'm up to.

"FYI babe, I do *not* know this can't be long term. You're the only one who thinks that, and YES, I am experienced. I've done a lot of shit with a lot of women," I watch her look away as I tell her this. "But none of them were you, Josie. None of them made me feel what I feel with you. I was never interested in any of them for more than a night or two. They were scratching my itch, that's it. I'm glad you're not experienced, it makes me want you even more. If you think you don't stimulate me, you better think again baby," I say as I move into her and rub my rock hard cock against her belly.

I see her eyes go wide and she blinks at me. I'm pissed but this is part of why she gets to me so bad. She has no idea how sexy she is. She doesn't flaunt herself around and shove it in everyone's face.

I watch her swallow as she looks down at where my cock is touching her, and then looks back up into my eyes. She still doesn't believe what I'm telling her.

"We went over this last night, but I'm going to give you a refresher," I tell her as I rub my fingers over her nipples and watch them harden for me. I kiss her neck, and then move down to put my mouth around her nipple.

I stand and lather up my hands again and start rubbing them all over her body, paying special attention to those pretty nipples. "You gave yourself to me last night Josie, and I wasn't kidding when I said you were going to be mine." I tell her as I reach down between her legs to wash.

I see her breathing hard and hear her little whimper as I touch her. I know she's sore so I try to be gentle when I push one finger inside her.

"Gunner..." she whispers

"This is mine Josie," I tell her moving my finger inside her again. "Do you understand?"

She doesn't, she shakes her head at me. I take my free hand and reach for the shower head and bring it down to wash away the soap.

"That means, you're with me babe. Long term. For as long as it works for both of us. It means that nobody touches this pretty little pussy but me. Nobody sucks on these juicy nipples but me," I tell her giving them a suck. "Nobody kisses those perfect pink lips but me," I say kissing her hard, "and nobody does this but me," I tell her dropping to my knees in front of her and lifting her leg over my shoulder.

I look at her and see that she's still a little swollen and red, so I go in easy and use my tongue on her clit.

"Oh God..." I hear her whimper and feel her leg that's holding her up start to quiver. I place my hands firmly on her ass and hold her up as I keep going. Within a few minutes she's grinding her pussy on my face and I feel her body tighten. I take one hand and remove it from her ass to put a finger in her, and that's all it takes. She screams my name while grabbing my hair and pulling me as close as she can get me. Oh yeah. I keep giving her gentle licks bringing her back down, and I feel her tremors as the aftershocks hit her. When she's calmed down I kiss my way back up to her lips.

"We clear?" I ask.

She nods and still doesn't speak. Then she grabs the shower gel and starts to wash me. She cleans me all over, having her hands sliding all over me is driving me insane. Just when I can't stand it anymore she starts to rub my cock and balls I put my hands against the tile and hold on. I'm about to come, just seeing her little hands wrapped around me. She sprays me off all over, the same way I did to her, and then she drops to her knees as she keeps her hand around my cock.

She looks up at me and seems a little nervous. "You don't have to do this." I tell her, but holy fuck, I hope she does. I want those pretty lips wrapped around my cock.

I watch as her little pink tongue darts out and touches the head of my cock. I suck in a breath and she does it again. I close my eyes, because the sight of her licking me is going to make me come all over her face and I don't think she's quite ready for that.

I feel her lips close around me and I can't help but look. Holy shit. I look down and she's sucking on me but her eyes are open wide and watching me with the most vulnerable look I've ever seen. She's trying to please me. Fuck. I can't take it.

"That feels so good baby, but I'm about to come in your mouth." I bend and put my hands under her arms and lift her. "Lock your legs around me." She doesn't question me, she just does what I say, she wraps her legs around my hips and her arms around my neck and I lean her back against the wall as I push my cock deep.

"Fuck," I groan. "You feel so good baby."

"mmmm" she's purring for me again.

I try not to be too rough but she's rocking her hips against me begging for more. I don't hold back, I give her a few good hard thrusts and watch her mouth fall open while she pants my name. Oh fuck yeah.

"This is my pussy," I inform her as I give her a hard pump. I need her to understand. I'm not playing. She is fucking mine. I draw back out and say, "Mine," as I pound back in again. "Tell me Josie," I demand as I stay buried deep not moving.

She nods her head, but she gave me that shit last night and didn't mean it.

"I need the words baby. I need to know you're with me."

"Yes..." she gasps, "God yes."

"I need more baby."

"I'm yours!" she says trying to ride my cock and get some movement. "Please..."

There it is. I don't hold back, I go hard until she's squeezing around my cock and coming and I let it go.

"Fuck!" I groan as I come inside her. I pump a few more times emptying myself in her pussy. I know I'm growling like a fucking animal but I can't help it, and she doesn't seem to mind because she's giving me her purr.

Fuck yeah.

I hold her there for a minute while we catch our breath, then I gently set her down and hang on to her as she tries to find her balance.

I lean her against the wall and wash us both off again, then I turn off the water, rub myself with a towel and then dry her off before picking her up and taking her back to my bed. If I could beat my fuckin' chest in victory, I so fuckin' would.

She gets me now. She's mine.

Chapter 35

Josie

After laying in Gunner's arms again for a little bit, I tell him that I really do need to head home and check on Freddy. Not to mention after what we've just done *again*, taking my pill is pretty important too.

We get up and I put my dress back on, along with my underwear this time, and head to the mirror. Oh dear Lord. This is why women don't go to bed with wet hair. I scramble downstairs for my purse and then back to the mirror. I hear Gunner's phone ringing and listen as he answers it.

"Talk," he says in greeting. I hope he knows whoever it is, because he's not using very good manners. I hear him give a couple of yes's and no's and then he says. "Later," and hangs up.

I've noticed this happens quite often when I'm with him. Maybe it's his guys calling to run things past him. He's usually quick about it and I don't ask questions, he must be a pretty busy with cases.

I try not to let my head go to my case, and I run the brush through my hair. Shit. Still not good. I decide to pile it all up on top of my head with some bobby pins that I'm lucky enough to find in my make-up bag I stuck in my purse. I apply my lip gloss. My cheeks are still flushed so I don't bother with anything on my face, I just add some mascara and my perfume before walking out to find Gunner in a pair of basketball shorts that come to his knees, a tight white wife beater that shows off his muscles and his tennis shoes.

Wow.

He makes casual look all kinds of sexy, and here I am with what looks like a birds nest on my head.

He walks over and bends down to kiss my neck, "I like your neck exposed like this, makes me want to kiss it even more. And you smell fuckin' good."

Well then, I guess my hair must not be *that* bad. I give him a smile.

"How about breakfast before we head to your house?" he asks taking my hand and holding it as we go down the stairs. Then he sits me down puts on my wedges for me and takes my hand and leads me out the door. I guess we're going to breakfast.

He heads to the stair well and I can't help smiling. He remembers that I hate elevators and something about that gives me another warm and cozy feeling. Most men would probably want to make me ride in them anyway, because it would be easier for them, but not Gunner, he thinks about what's best for me. My belly flutters again. I am so screwed.

I can't help thinking about the things he said to me in the shower. I can't even argue with him about it. I don't want to fight it anymore. I want what he's offering. I don't know if it will last, but I don't want to think about that.

He takes me to Wolfgang's which has an awesome breakfast. I try not to be embarrassed about wearing a wrinkly dress, and just enjoy it. We talk about everything from my work to the fact that the vapor liquid is still working.

He actually seems pretty interested in my work and mentions finding someone in my line of business to work at his offices. I don't give it much thought but I would imagine he does need someone good with computers in his line of business. It sounds like he's made it by using Marina, but wants someone more specialized.

I try not to drop too many details. I don't want him to know about the illegal stuff I've done in the name of vengeance. I'm sure he would flip his lid about that. Although I could give him some ideas for helping his investigations, but I decide it's better to just leave it alone.

I tell him how I'm worried about Faith. How she's been acting strange and staying on the internet all the time. I tell him I think she's seeing someone but isn't talking. He asks questions wondering if she's being safe, but I really don't know the answers. I don't tell him this, but I'm hoping to get a hold of her laptop and do a little checking of my own. It might be wrong, but I don't want my best friend hooking up with someone dangerous. I never want Faith to deal with being attacked. She will just have to forgive me.

Once we're done eating, we head back to my place. Freddy greets Gunner at the door, but ignores me. "Hey!" I say, pointing to him, but he looks away. "Don't you start! It was only one night."

Gunner looks between us smiling and shaking his head.

"He's mad at me," I inform him.

"Well let's take him for a run, and get him happy again," he suggests giving Freddy a pat. He's being nice to my dog. That makes me tingly too.

I could use a run after that breakfast, so I change and we head out for a run. I hate to admit it, but I love having Freddy on one side of me and Gunner on the other as we run. We wave at Justine as we go by her house and she shouts "mmm hmmm, I knew it!" at us and I just shake my head. I'm glad Gunner doesn't ask what she means.

I see Mrs. Williams in the yard and wave at her, and she gives me a thumbs up, which makes Gunner laugh. Why doesn't the whole neighborhood just act a little more surprised that I have a man with me. Geez.

Once we get back and I make up with Freddy, I shower again and I'm sitting in the living room with Gunner when my phone bleeps. It's plugged into the wall charging, so I go over to check it.

Faith: Soooo???

Me: Why don't you come out of your room and find out.

Faith: Don't want to interrupt all of that cute coupledom you have going on ;)

Me: Shut it. Things are good.

Faith: Yay!!!

I put the phone down and go sit next to Gunner again. "Faith," I tell him who was texting.

"Isn't she down the hall?"

"Yeah, she does that a lot." I tell him giving a shrug.

He shakes his head at that.

We hang out for a while and I make him some lunch using some of the vegetables from my garden. He asks for more of my cucumber dip, so I make him a bowl to take home with him.

We eat outside with Freddy in the yard, and everything seems so normal. I'm happy, for the first time I can remember, vengeance isn't in the forefront of my mind. Gunner is.

Rick and Eddie stop by and say hello. Rick stands behind Gunner and gives me hand signals, making a circle with his fingers on one hand and putting a finger on the other hand into the circle, moving it in and out and raising his eyebrows in question. I bust out laughing because only Rick would do something like that and be dead serious. Eddie tells him to knock it off and gives me a hug saying, "You look happy JoJo," before they leave. I smile, because I am.

"Are you sure that guy's gay?" Gunner asks me.

"Uh, considering the fact that he has sex with Rick, I would say yes, although I've never actually seen it, but I don't really want to," I say wrinkling my nose at the thought.

"You seem pretty tight with him."

Is he jealous of Eddie? The idea seems ridiculous.

"I am," I say cautiously, "But Eddie is very gay, trust me. He just gives great hugs."

"Do you hug him often?"

Seriously?

"Uh... yeah, well, sometimes," I pause and look at him. What the hell, why not give him the truth? I don't think there's anything wrong with it. "We cuddle sometimes," I add shyly, because now I feel kinda weird admitting that.

"What do you mean?"

Oh crap. He's giving me the scowl.

"Wellll…" Hmmm, how do I explain this? "It's nothing like what you're thinking. Eddie is a man, but he's a gay man. So him and Rick are safe zones for me," I try to explain. "We all hang out, but Eddie gives good hugs and there have been times that I needed those hugs, so… um… sometimes I go over there just to get those hugs, although I don't tell him that, I usually make an excuse, like taking them leftovers or something."

I cringe a little at my admission. It probably sounds stupid, but it's the truth. I see him thinking about what I've just said.

"So you take him food, so he'll cuddle with you without you having to tell him you want him to cuddle with you?"

Oh hell. That just sounds weird.

I nod a little and say, "I know it sounds stupid, I can see that. It's just… I don't have family, and these friends right here on my street are all that I have."

"You don't have to explain," he says seeing that I'm uncomfortable.

"No. I want you to understand, but I don't know if you will because you're a man," I sigh a little because I know I'm going to have to let my guard down some so that he can try to understand. So I just spit it out, "Eddie is gay, but he's also a strong man. There are times when a woman, well, maybe I shouldn't speak for all women, but for me, there are times when being held by a strong man... um... kinda makes you feel better?" God this is embarrassing to admit. *Way to be a badass Josie.* "Uh, anyway, there've been times when I needed that, so..." I trail off as I look away and shake my head. I feel really stupid right now.

"Baby, come here," he says pulling me into him. "I'm sorry I questioned it. It's just that I've seen the way you are with him, and I couldn't help but wonder what was between you." He gives me a squeeze and tries to look in my face but I keep it buried in his chest. "I understand, okay?"

I give a short nod into his chest.

"I didn't mean to make you embarrassed. But from now on when you need that, you come to me."

I give another nod. I like the idea of that. Being in his arms is better than anything else I can think of.

*****

Gunner and I get into a routine. Most nights he stays with me, so I don't feel guilty about leaving Freddy with Faith. It also allows me to cook for him, and to spend time with him in my own environment.

He fell in quickly with my crew, hanging out with Faith, Justine, Rick, and Eddie. I even caught Mrs. Williams chatting him up happily the other day. Levi loves him. Justine got called into work on Monday when it was supposed to be her day off and she left him with us. Gunner taught him how to arm wrestle, it was the cutest thing I'd ever seen. Gunner would pretend to try his hardest and then let Levi win.

He even takes Freddy out for me when he's here, which I appreciate but I usually join him anyway. He also fixes stuff. I should have known he would be good with his hands. He fixed the leaky faucet in the bathroom, replaced the water pump, and helped me out in the garden.

He even came over after I went to the gym on Tuesday night. I planned on spending those three days apart from him because we would both be busy working during the day, and my training took up a lot of the evening. He didn't seem to like the idea of spending three days apart. I tried to talk him into it just because I was worried we were rushing things, but he didn't think so. I didn't argue, because if I'm honest, I slept really well with him in my bed. It also helped that he never failed to make me come at least once every night, often times more.

Wednesday, after he went into the office and Faith left for work, I decided to put my own detective skills to work. Faith had been more absent than usual, and it was making me worried. She came home from work and rushed right into her room. She also dodged hanging with us, saying she couldn't, that she was late for her "date".

She had been taking her laptop with her everywhere, and this was the one day that she left it behind. I feel sneaky going into her room to open her laptop, but I need to make sure she's safe. She looked out for me so many times in the past, it was time I return the favor.

It took me a minute to guess her password, but since I knew her better than anyone else, it didn't take long. There it was, her past chats with this guy. Many of them had been deleted, but I saw one of the most recent ones. He went by the name *CooleyB07*. Not very original. It basically told me what I needed to know. My bet was his last name was Cooley or some version of that, and his first name started with a B and his birthday was in July.

Bingo.

I started to shut it down so I could do some research on this guy. Then I realized Faith's screen name was *FSnyder02*. Dear God, didn't I teach her anything?

When I looked at the last chat I saw that she spoke about living in Michigan, and he called her Faith, so he basically knew everything he needed to, in order to find her. She also referred to him as Brandon, and he talked about living in Florida. I shake my head at Faith's carelessness. It's not like her.

I notice that the chat started with him asking her where she'd been, and why she wasn't online at the time they had agreed. She told him about working late, and he was actually pissed off at her. It was like she was being cyber bullied from a man she was cyber dating. I did not like the way this looked. Not at all.

I decide to call it a day and head to Gunner's office. I want to take the guys the trifle I made for them anyway. I would prefer a professional look into this Brandon guy. I might be a good hacker, but I was no private detective. I would pay one of his guys to look into this for Faith. Something about that chat made warning bells go off in my head.

I made my way down to Gunner's office and went inside. Marina greeted me with a smile, wearing her biker attire again. I really want to ask her where she shops.

"Hi Marina," I said giving her a smile and explaining, "I brought this," I said pointing to the trifle, "For the guys, and for you if you want some," I told her. "They were drooling over it at my house, so I made one to bring in as a thank you."

"That looks awesome!" She exclaims standing up to take a look at it. "God bless you, this should put those grouchy fuckers in a better mood."

"Oh..." I said trying not to sound surprised.

"Sorry," she laughed, "But from what I've heard from Gunner you're practically part of the family around here, so I was just letting it fly."

I was? Wow. That felt good. Way good. I'm pretty sure my smile got a lot bigger.

"Part of the family?" As good as it felt, I wasn't sure exactly what she meant.

"Yeah, Gunner says if Josie calls, put her through immediately. If Josie stops by, send her back. If Josie needs anything, take care of it. And between you and me, this is *big*," she exclaims with a hand gesture, "Because usually any women who try to contact Gunner at work are sent away with a very rude message that makes it clear they aren't to try that shit again." She explains giving me a sly smile.

Wow. I feel the warmth spread through me. Part of the family.

"Oh..." I say again because I can't think of anything else to say but she can tell this news makes me happy and so we smile at each other.

"Why are they so grouchy?" I ask thinking now is a good time to change the subject.

"Because they're big alpha men, with big alpha attitudes? Who knows," she says, but then adds, "But there was a problem on one of the cases today, so that's probably why. This will help though." She tells me eyeing the dessert.

"Good. Is Gunner busy?" I ask hesitantly. "If he's busy, I can just talk to him later."

"He had to go pick up Caleb," she tells me. I've never met Caleb but I know he's one of the guys. "He'll be right back. You can wait for him if you want. Whatever Josie needs..." she says with a teasing grin.

I grin back, "Okay, well I'll just catch him later, I'm going to leave this in his office and then I'll head out. If they're having a bad day, I don't think it's a good day to hang." I say wincing a little at the thought of all that testosterone raging in one place. Poor Marina.

"You'll get used to it," she tells me, then goes back to work with a friendly wave.

I take out the paper with the information I'd been able to find on this Brandon character. Leaving it on his desk is probably better anyway. I need to get home and get ready for my appointment with Dr. Palmer.

I go to set it on his desk by the trifle and I notice a picture of myself that makes me stop and stare. I'm confused for a minute because I don't remember him taking a picture of me. The first thing I think is how sweet he is, wanting a picture of me on his desk. Then I realize that it's a picture of me running with Freddy, wearing the shirt I wore the first day I ran into him by the coffee shop.

I get a sick feeling in my stomach. I see there's another picture underneath it of me talking to Rick outside the coffee shop. I pick up the file folder and open it. I don't understand what this is. I didn't hire him that day I came here. Then I see a form, it looks almost like an invoice. When I read it I gasp and cover my mouth to stop from throwing up right on his desk. Under client name it says *Brian Hanson*.

"Oh my god," I say backing away from the file and watching it hit the floor. Just seeing his name is sending me into a panic. I shake my head and try to figure this out. This can't be right. Gunner can't be working for him.

Could he have found out about Brian without me telling him? Maybe he decided to look into Brian on his own without telling me? I keep running through explanations in my head, but there are none that make any sense.

It says Brian is his client. He's working for Brian. He has a picture of me running the day we ran into each other because it wasn't an accident. He planned it all along. The more it starts to sink in, the more I have trouble breathing.

What else did he plan? Why would Brian be paying him? He slept with me to give information to Brian? Oh my God, if he's working for Brian, then Brian knows where I am.

On that realization I start to hyperventilate. There's an exit door a little ways down the hall, I remember making a note of it on my first trip here. I make a run for it. It says emergency exit only, so I know an alarm will probably sound when I open it, but I have to get outside. I don't slow down, slamming straight into the door. I hear a beeping noise behind me, but I keep going.

I stumble over the pavement as I reach my car and try to unlock it. I have to get out of here. He knows where I am. Gunner served me to him on a silver platter. What if he knows about the hack jobs I've done? What if that's the information he was getting from me while pretending to date me. I knew it! I knew he couldn't be for real! God, I'm so stupid! He faked it all. I would almost laugh if I wasn't crying hysterically. Oh God.

I can't breathe, but I have to drive. I roll all the windows down and back out. I hear a horn blow, but I just put it in drive and floor it. I'm about a minute away when I hear my phone ring. I ignore it and it goes to voicemail. A few seconds later, it rings again. I grab my phone and look at it. *Gunner calling*. I turn the phone off and throw it into the seat beside me.

When I hit the driveway I don't even park straight, I just jump out leaving the door open. I run inside and arm the security system. Shit, that's not going to help. Gunner put the stupid thing in, he knows how to bypass it. He probably gave Brian the code. The thought terrifies me, I can't stop all of these horrible scenarios that are running through my head. I quickly run outside and get the spare key before coming back in and locking up again.

The betrayal is like a punch in my face, in fact I would rather him punch me in the face, I know I can handle that better. It took me so long to trust a man, and look what happens. I feel like I'm going crazy, because I start laughing at the thought, even as I'm crying.

I make my way down to my room and grab my suitcase out of my closet. Freddy is following me, looking confused and giving me a whine. I go into the closet to grab some clothes and collapse to my knees. Freddy gives a low howl beside me. He senses my panic but doesn't understand.

I sit back on my ass, bury my face in my knees and wrap my arms tight around my legs. I can't stop the sobs that are coming out of me. I know I need to calm myself, before I pass out.

I start rocking back and forth trying to take deep breaths.

I need to get my shit together and get out of here. Who knows how long ago Gunner told Brian where to find me. The thought wrenches another set of sobs from me.

Oh God. The hang ups. I've had three since that first one. Could it be Brian? That thought sends fear shooting down my spine.

Nothing with Gunner was real. I should have known better than to believe in him. He was so convincing every time I tried to pull away from him, and he would talk me back around. *I should have known*. None of it was real. He played me the whole time. I had sex with him, several times. I wonder if he told Brian that. Was it part of his job? Oh God, I gag just thinking of it.

I can't function yet. I burrow deeper into my closet and give Freddy the *guard* command. He plants his body right in front of me on a low growl. He knows his job. At least there is one male I can count on. I keep checking to make sure the closet door is open. Normally it would be a cold day in hell before you caught me spending any time in a closet, but I can't seem to move yet.

I can't believe I let this happen. I thought I finally found the light at the end of the tunnel. I thought Gunner was the one helping me come out of the darkness. I was truly starting to believe that. Thinking about it, I realize that I loved him. I hadn't let myself acknowledge it, but I had fallen in love with Gunner Layne. What a fool he must think I am. I curl myself into a tighter ball and weep.

Chapter 36

Gunner

I get back to the office from picking up Caleb and see Josie pulling out of the parking lot like a bat out of hell. I wonder what she's doing, so I try to call her cell phone a couple times and get no answer.

I walk in the reception area to find Marina looking freaked when I hear an alarm sounding.

"It was Josie," she tells me quickly. "She brought in this dessert thing, and then she went into your office to leave it. Next thing I know the alarm is going off and she was running from one of the emergency exits out to the parking lot."

She pulls up the security footage and I see Josie running and then tripping next to her car. I zoom in on her and see tears on her face and a look I can't even explain. It looks like pure fear, it's the look she had the night I saw her have a panic attack.

"Fuck!" I say, slamming my fist down on the desk. "Get that alarm taken care of, and stand by." I run to my office and sure enough, I know what caused this, because there is the file for Brian Hanson along with her picture laying on the floor.

Shit!

Fuck!

I have to get to her. I need to explain. I just pray to God she made it home safely so I can make her understand.

I try her cell again as I run to my truck and get sent straight to voicemail. She turned her phone off. I hop in my truck and head out. I dial Faith.

"Dude, I'm working," she whispers into her cell. "Not supposed to be taking personal calls."

"It's an emergency. I'm trying to find Josie."

"What do you mean? She's supposed to be home working."

"She was," I explain, "but then she came to my office. I wasn't there. She saw the file. She knows. I looked at the security footage of her leaving the building by running through an emergency exit and she was losing it. Now her phone is shut off."

"Shit!"

"I'm heading to your house right now."

"On my way," she states hanging up on me.

I pull into the driveway and see her car parked at an angle and her door hanging open.

This does not look good, but at least I know she made it here.

I go to the door and knock. Of course, no answer. I look to where the spare key is usually hidden, and it's no longer there.

Fuck!

If she's having a panic attack I don't have time to wait for Faith before getting inside. She can't breathe if she's panicking. I've seen it, and it's no joke. I'm afraid she will pass out and hurt herself falling, or worse.

I take off my shirt and cover my fist with it, then slam it through the glass. I hear the alarm sound but I make my way in and disarm it.

I follow the sounds I hear coming from Josie's room. The sounds, Jesus the sounds tear me apart. I should have told her sooner, *damn it!* Things were going so well, I was afraid to ruin it, but I knew I had to do it. That's why I pulled the file out this morning. I was going to come clean with her. I should have never let this happen.

When I walk in her room I don't see her, but I hear her, so I follow the sound and see her on the floor of her closet with Freddy sitting right in front of her.

"Josie, baby, please calm down, I can explain," I beg as I walk toward her trying to control my own emotions.

To my surprise Freddy snarls a warning at me. She has him on alert. He's guarding her so nobody can get to her, but Freddy knows me, I try again thinking he'll give me a pass, after all, I always bring him beef sticks. I step forward slowly.

Nope.

He bares his teeth at me. Shit, I should have brought a beef stick, but I doubt he would take it in this situation. The dog is loyal to Josie only, even if he acts like a brat sometimes.

"Josie, call off Freddy so I can come to you."

She doesn't answer she just continues rocking and hiding her face in her arms crying. Her body is curled up into a ball, and it breaks my heart knowing I'm the reason she's like this. I wanted to protect her, and look what I've done. God knows what she's thinking now.

"Call him off Josie," I demand, hoping my tone will get through to her.

"Guard," she commands Freddy on a muffled sob.

Fuck. I guess that's my answer.

I have to try to explain, even if it's with a snarling dog in front me.

"It's not what you think."

She doesn't let me finish, she starts shaking her head back and forth and she moves her hands to cover her ears.

Dear God, what have I done?

"Faith is on her way, okay, please, just breathe, and calm down. I won't say anything else until she gets here."

I sit on the edge of the bed and rest my elbows on my knees watching her.

"Leave!" She shouts at me.

"I'm not leaving until I explain, and I'm not leaving you alone like this."

That gets me a bitter sounding huff. I'll take it.

"Josie, please come out of there."

I rub my hands over my face trying to figure out the best way to handle this. I'm not leaving her alone, but maybe if I leave the room she'll come out. I just need a chance to get to her so I can explain, but I don't want to make her panic any worse.

Faith should be here soon, Josie will listen to her. I stand up, walk out of the room and wait in the hallway. I lean my hands against the wall and try not to punch something. What a fuckin' disaster, and it's all my fault. If I would have told her the truth it wouldn't have been this bad. She may have been pissed, but she wouldn't be hiding in a fuckin' closet. *Fuck*!

I finally start to hear some movement and I look in the door to find her filling a suitcase.

"Baby, what are you doing?"

I see her jump at the sound of my voice and then whirl around to face me. I see that fiery look come across her face and I'm glad for it.

"*Do NOT* call me baby!" she spits at me, "Get out of my house!"

"I told you I'm not leaving until I can explain."

"Too late for that," she proclaims throwing clothes into the suitcase.

"Just talk to me first, then if you still want me to leave, I will."

She hurls a shoe at me. "There's nothing you can say! You work for him!"

"No I don't, Josie, fuck, just listen damn it!" I'm getting frustrated. To be honest, I don't like that she believes the worst about me so easily after everything we've been to each other, but I'm trying to be understanding. I know she's shocked and confused. I take a deep breath.

"He contacted me looking for you," I start to explain.

"Yeah, I get that, so when did you tell him where I am? How much time do I have to get out of here?"

"I didn't tell him where you are."

She gives me one of those sarcastic laughs that means she thinks I'm lying. "Right," she says, "Like I can believe someone who's on his payroll. So did he just pay you to find me and try to get information, or did he pay you to fuck me too?" She says it angrily, but she's wiping tears as she says it.

"Are you fuckin' serious?" I roar at her. I see her step back and Freddy gives me a warning growl. "Call off this fuckin' dog! You want to insult me then do it without hiding behind your damn dog." I'm pissed now.

"You'd like that, wouldn't you? Go ahead, take another step, I'll tell him to tear you apart!" She yells back at me.

How the fuck can I think it's hot for her to be yelling at me. If I wasn't so pissed off at her and worried about her, I'd grab her and fuck her senseless until she understood what I was feeling. Instead I've got a damn dog ready to rip my throat out.

"For all I know he paid you to deliver me to him. Do you charge extra for kidnapping?"

I put my hands on my hips and look up trying to calm myself. "Is that seriously what you believe about me? I get you're hurt and upset babe, and you have every right to be, I should have told you sooner, but do you really think I would kidnap you or fuck you for some part of a job? Are you really going to stand there and accuse me of that shit?"

"How the hell should I know what the truth is about you? You're a liar, I know that for sure. You didn't run into me on accident that day. You planned it. How do I know this whole thing hasn't been part of your plan? How do I know you're not standing there lying to me right now?"

Well shit. I guess she has a point.

"If you work for him then you sure as hell aren't above kidnapping. That's the kind of shit he gets off on. You want to tie me up and rape me too? How about locking me in the trunk of a car while you wait to see if I'm dead or alive? Is that in your job description? Because that's the kind of person you're working for!" She yells, unloading all that shit on me at once and sending another shoe flying at me.

I take a step back, letting all of that sink in. I feel something start burning in my gut. I knew that fucker wasn't on the up and up, and I knew he'd done something to her, but this? This is worse than I ever thought. He tied her, raped her, and locked her in a trunk? I feel like my head is going to explode. I can't even think straight, before I realize what I'm doing I put a fist through her wall. I hear her scream and Freddy start barking at me. This is all happening at the time Faith runs in trying to figure out what's going on.

"What the hell, Gunner?" She asks. I don't answer her, I'm still in a fucking rage. I turn and walk out the door, through the house, outside

320

where I pass a concerned looking Rick, Justine, and Eddie while I hop in my truck and peel the fuck out of there. If I don't get this fuckin' rage under control I'm going to leave a path of destruction from here to fuckin' Detroit.

I do the only thing I can think of, I hit speed dial for Walker.

"What's up bro?" he answers.

"Need to meet. Now."

"What's up? You don't sound so good."

"I'm not. My place. Twenty."

"Roger that."

K. D. Smith

Chapter 37

Josie

I can't believe any of this is happening. I keep throwing stuff in my suitcase. I'm trying not to picture Gunner putting a fist through my wall. That was *not* cool. I hear Freddy give Faith a growl as she approaches. I take a deep breath and call him off as I bend to pet him. I know he likes Gunner and must have been confused by my command, but he still did what I said. He's a good boy. I give him a hug of appreciation. Who knew the most reliable thing in my life would be a dog?

"Tell me what's going on," Faith demands.

I put a few more clothes in the suitcase and watch in exasperation as she takes them out.

"Knock it off Faith, I need to get out of here."

"No. You need to listen to me," she says sounding exasperated.

"You don't understand. Brian Hanson hired Gunner. He's working for him. None of this was real Faith." I tell her while I feel the tears start again. Shit. I don't have time for another break-down. I swipe at my cheeks and grab my clothes back from her. "He's found me. I need to get out of here, at least until I can figure out what's happening."

I hear a horrified gasp in the doorway and turn to see Rick, Eddie, and Justine. Rick is covering his mouth.

"What do you mean none of this was real? Who's Brian whatshisname?" Rick asks with his eyes wide with concern.

Great.

"Gunner's not working for him JoJo."

"Yes! He is! I went to his office, I saw the file myself. That day we *ran into each other,*" I explain using air quotes with my fingers, "It wasn't real. He planned it. He had pictures of me."

I hear Rick gasp again and see Justine cross her arms over her chest, narrowing her eyes. Eddie is just standing there watching me closely.

"I know," Faith whispers and plops down on my bed.

My gaze flies back to her. She *knows*? I can't be hearing this right. My ears are buzzing, my face feels all swollen, and I'm a complete mess. I shake my head as if that will help clear things up.

"What do you mean, you *know*?" I hear Eddie ask on my behalf. Thank you Eddie.

Faith lets out a loud breath. "Gunner told me." She spits it out fast as if it will lessen the blow. "Listen, JoJo, I can explain all of this, just please sit down and stop freaking out. Gunner told me you were having a panic attack."

I watch all eyes come back to me. They know about these, but they don't ask me questions. I can see the questions in their eyes now. Even Freddy is looking at me like he wonders if I've lost it.

"Faith, spill it, because I'm wondering how you knew Brian Hanson hired Gunner and I didn't. And how could you encourage me to be with him if you knew. Talk. I'm holding it together by a thread here, and if he knows…" I trail off not wanting to think about what might happen if Brian knows how to find me.

All eyes go back to Faith. God, I don't even care right now. I don't care if we have an audience. I don't care if they know my past. I know they're here out of concern, and I just want some answers. Like *now* would be nice. I look at her and try to communicate this by putting my hands on my hips and tilting my head to the side. She knows that look.

"Okay, okay," she holds up her hands palms out, "I talked to Gunner. Brian did try to hire him to find you. Said you stole money from him or some crap. Gunner found you, didn't believe him, liked you, and turned him away." She rushes to get it all out before I interrupt to start asking questions. "I talked to him at lunch one day. I'm sorry for that, but he was concerned after the first panic attack, and wanted to talk to me about it. I did *not* give him details though, I swear. We were both worried how you'd react if you knew, so he wanted to wait to tell you and I agreed. That's when he put in the alarm system. He was trying to keep you safe. We both were."

I try to take all of this in. So that's why she agreed so quickly about the security system. I don't like the idea of them talking behind my back and making decisions about *my* situation.

"Does somebody want to tell me who this Brian motherfucker is?" Justine demands.

I look at her, and she might sound pissy, but I see concern on her face.

"We all know you're running from something Josie, we've never asked questions, but I for one, would like to know what's happening here. For shit sakes, we're your friends, we share everything with you." This is coming from Rick who, for once, is looking very serious.

"Jesus, Josie, we saw you drive up to the house. You didn't even bother to park it, you just jumped out leaving the door open and then ran, stumbling inside, like there's a ghost chasing you. And the panic attacks? I mean, c'mon, I think it's time you clue us in," Eddie says looking frustrated.

Great. Now I'm getting pressure from all sides. I can see they're hurt by this. Damn it. I can't worry about that right now, I need to know what Gunner told Brian. I need to know if I'm safe.

I put my hands on my head and turn away pacing to the window. It's all too much. I turn back and look at Faith. She looks afraid. I don't like that. I don't like that all of my friends look upset with me. I close my eyes for a minute. There's too much to take in.

First things first, "Are you sure that Brian doesn't know where I am?" I ask Faith.

"Gunner had a bad feeling about him, he told him he didn't find you. He said that doesn't mean that Brian's not still looking, but he didn't learn anything from Gunner. He must suspect you're still in the area though, or else he wouldn't have called him in the first place."

Okay, so he's looking for me, but he hasn't found me. I take a deep breath and let that settle. I sit on the bed and bury my face in my hands. I suspected he might try to find me, but having confirmation is unsettling, to say the least, but at least I know. I can prepare.

I'm so tired of all the secrets, and my mind is consumed with Gunner. I have a sinking feeling in my stomach.

I look around at my friends, they've been my family and support since I moved here. I know it's not fair that I don't share my past with them.

"Guys, I will explain everything, I promise, but can I please have a little time?" I start to feel my eyes burning again. "I love you all, you've always been there for me and I owe you so much, but I just need to figure out exactly what's happening first."

"You don't owe us shit, girl. This is what friends *do*, it's time you learn that," Justine says pointing her finger at me and then coming to give me a hug. "I'm holding you to your promise too, don't *think* I will forget."

I just nod. I know she won't. None of them will. I give them all hugs and say goodbye. I know I'm lucky to have them in my life, and I appreciate them so much.

I turn to Faith who's lying back on the bed watching me closely, like she doesn't know if I'm going to blow up or burst into tears. I lay down with her and stare at the ceiling.

"Um, we need to get our door fixed. I think Gunner punched a hole in it trying to get to you. Before he punched a hole in the wall I mean..." I think she's trying to tell me that I owe him an apology, but I can't think about that yet.

"He should have told me," I whisper. "And you should have told me too."

328

"I'm sorry JoJo, but I knew how scared you'd be, and you were finally..." she sighs, "I just didn't want to see you go back to that dark place. I thought letting Gunner handle it would be best for you." I see tears in her eyes when I look at her, and I realize just what I've put her through. She was there for me when I couldn't function. She should have told me the truth but I can understand why she was afraid to.

We lay there for a little bit, then she says, "You know Gunner was on your side the whole time, right?"

Shit. I almost had my dog attack him. I accused him of horrible stuff. He should have told me the truth from the beginning, I'm still pissed about that, but I can see now that I was unfair.

"What would you have done? Finding that file..."

"I know, it had to look really bad. I'm not blaming you for freaking out."

I close my eyes. It did look bad. Really, *really* bad. At the same time I think of the things I said to him and about how he had been trying to protect me and I just don't know. I don't know if I should be mad. Or if I should be sorry.

"I'm going to go take care of the door, why don't you rest a little?"

I sigh in agreement and watch as she moves my suitcase off the bed. At least I don't have to run. He may be looking for me, but he hasn't found me, not yet anyway.

Chapter 38

Gunner

Walker is staring at me like I've lost my damn mind. I think maybe I have. I've been pacing back and forth since I got home and Walker showed up. I wouldn't be surprised if there was steam coming out of my ears.

"What the fuck, bro? Sit down."

I stop, look at him, and then continue to pace.

Finally, I just decide to lay it all out. I have so much rage right now. Walker has always been more level headed than the rest of us. He's usually the one we all go to when we don't know what to do. He's tough, but he has a tendency to think before he acts, and even though it's annoying, I've learned that he's usually right about things.

"It's Josie," I tell him.

"I knew it," he says leaning back on the couch with a big smirk. "You never get this worked up. Had to be over a woman."

"Fuck off Walk, this is serious."

He drops the grin and leans forward, "Okay, then quit the pacing and tell me."

"You knew I was checking her out, and I was checking into Brian Hanson. What you don't know is that I've gotten to know her. She's..." I trail off, because I don't even know how to describe Josie.

"She's what?"

I finally sit down, "She's beautiful, sexy, but it's more than that. She's the kind of person people love because she's not full of herself. She bakes lasagna for her elderly neighbors for fucks sake." I look at him not knowing if this is making any sense.

"Oh shit, you've got it bad," he tells me with his smirk back in place. I immediately give him a scowl, I don't need his jokes. This is serious shit. At my look he holds up a hand to me, "Okay, so what's got you so pissed? I get you like her. Girls like that don't come around often. So what's the problem? You fuck her?"

You can always count on Walker to shoot straight and get right to the heart of the matter. He notices my non-response and nods. He gets it. You don't find a girl like Josie and not claim her for yourself. We're brothers. We understand each other, sometimes without needing explanation.

"You know her former boss, Brian, had me looking for her. I told you something didn't feel right about that guy. When I got close to Josie, I knew there was more to the story. The first night... well... let's just say she has panic attacks. She's scared. And I don't just mean a little. She's got the kind of fear in her that is palpable. You can feel it. It runs that deep"

I see his scowl and know that he's starting to get it.

"I didn't tell her that he tried to hire me."

"Oh fuck. So let me guess, she found out and freaked."

I give a quick nod. "When I found her she was having a panic attack again, she wouldn't listen. She was packing a bag, ready to run because she thinks he'll find her. Said some shit about being kidnapped, tied up, raped, and locked in the trunk of a car. Asked if that's what he hired me for." As I say it I stand back up to pace. She didn't come right out and say that Brian Hanson did those things to her, but in my gut, I can feel it. I know that's what's happened to her and the thought has me right back to wanting to punch shit.

"Are you saying those things happened to her?"

"It would sure as fuck explain the panic attacks. It would explain why she has a fuckin' guard dog. Why she needs a therapist that

specializes in women's trauma. Why she trains
in self-defense twice a week at a gym downtown.
Why she can't take dark enclosed spaces or even
ride in an elevator. Fuck. It makes sense. And
now she's scared of me."

"Maybe you should explain yourself to her
when she's calmed down, and then back off man.
This sounds like a lot to handle. Do you really
want to be involved with a woman that has that
many issues?"

"What the Fuck Walker? You think I should
walk away because she has trauma in her past?
That's bullshit and you know it."

"It just sounds like a lot of baggage bro, and
I'm trying to look out for my little brother here."

"It's not like that. You should see her when
something isn't scaring her. She's smart, she's
funny, and she's just a good girl. Something
messed her up, but she's solid underneath all
that fear. Shit, she doesn't even have a good
family like we do, but she's made it through all
of this shit and she's still fighting to get her life
back. She doesn't know it, but she's tough.
She's got a fire about her."

"Oh hell, you really do have it bad," Walker
says as he stands and gives me a slap on the
shoulder shaking his head. He checks his phone
and then says. "If you have feelings that deep,
you need to go back and explain. You need to
help her get and stay safe. Don't let her push
you away, but be sure about what you want.

Don't get in there if you're not sure. You'll only hurt her more."

I nod again, he's right and I know it. My phone alerts me that I have a text and I check it.

Faith: She's sleeping.

I feel myself relax a little. I'd been worried that she would take off.

"She's calmed down enough to fall asleep," I tell him. "I'll talk to her when she wakes up."

"Good luck man, I gotta get back to the station. Call me if you need me." Simple as that and Walker is gone. It's easy to take him for granted and forget that he's always there when someone needs him. Walker Layne is like a rock for our family.

I wish Josie knew that kind of stability. I can't imagine not having it and I vow to myself that I will give that to her. I grab some things to take with me, because she's not pushing me away again. I'm getting answers even if I have to camp on her couch. I'm not leaving her house again without them.

I grab my keys to hit the road, time to go buy some fuckin' beef sticks.

Chapter 39

Josie

I could feel the dream sucking me back under. It was the same as always. Dark. No air. Pain.

I jerk awake with a gasp. It's a familiar feeling. Those first few seconds of trying to suck in air, knowing I can breathe, reminding myself that I am free.

I sit up a little and scoot back to the headboard running my hands through my hair to get it out of my face. For a minute I forgot the pain of finding that file at Gunner's office, but then it all comes back to me. I lean my head back to the headboard and see movement out of the corner of my eye. I stifle a scream when I see Gunner sitting in my room wearing his familiar scowl with his eyes locked on me.

"What are you doing here?"

He doesn't answer right away, he just continues to scowl.

I swallow. I'm not sure if I'm ready for this talk.

"Came back when I knew we had both calmed down," he says glancing at the hole in my wall.

I take a breath. I guess it's time to get this over with.

"I realize I jumped to the wrong conclusion. But you should have told me the truth." I whisper and close my eyes. I still feel betrayed.

"Yes, I should have. I was wrong."

What? I'm not sure what to say to that. I've never known a man who admits he's wrong and doesn't try to make excuses. I open my mouth to say something and then shut it again.

"I should have told you. I get that. I think it's time we both stop holding back information."

Oh crap.

Again I find myself being quiet. So once again he keeps going.

"I know a lot babe. I know you see a therapist once a week. I know you don't like small spaces. Know you have panic attacks. Know you take self-defense. I know you're planning something. And I know you're scared shitless of Brian Hanson. What I want to know is if the things you accused me of, are things that he did to you in Detroit."

What? He seriously had to quit blowing my mind so I could say something that sounded semi intelligent. I shake my head. How does he know all of this?

"How do you know all of this?" I go ahead and ask.

"Babe," he gives me a look that says I need to wake up, "it's what I do."

"Have you been following me this whole time?"

"Yes."

This is starting to make me angry.

"I realize that's what you do, Gunner, but you can't just follow me around and talk to my friends behind my back."

"It was necessary. You wouldn't open up and I needed to make sure you were safe."

"I'm not your case!" I yell at him. I swing back the covers and stand.

"In the beginning you were, then I turned down the case, but by then you were something else to me." He says standing from the chair and stalking his way over to me.

"It's not fair that you've been digging around in my past behind my back."

The truth is there's part of me that likes that he wants to protect me. But I don't like feeling as if I'm being investigated.

He sits on the edge of my bed and pulls me in front of him. His hands are holding mine, I'm standing between his legs and he's looking up at me, but he doesn't have to look up very far.

"Okay then," he says softly. "Let's just be open with each other."

Oh crap. His soft voice always gets me in trouble. I can already feel my anger melting.

"Fine," I say, even though I really don't feel fine about it. "What did you mean when you said you know I have plans?"

I notice he's watching my face and damn it, I know I sound nervous asking that question. I try to look around anywhere but his eyes.

"You told Faith you were worried about us ruining your plans."

Shit! Faith and her big mouth! I am *so* going to kick her ass. I don't say anything and I continue not making eye contact.

"You wanna share what these plans of yours are babe?" he asks softly.

I shake my head back and forth.

He moves his hands to my hips and mine automatically move to his shoulders. God I wish he didn't feel so good.

"Okay, if you don't want to answer that, then how about my other question."

"What question?" I whisper, trying not to think of how I feel when he's touching me while still trying to avoid his eyes.

"The one where I asked if the accusations you threw at me were things he really did to you."

I stiffen instantly and drop my hands, but he doesn't let go of my hips. I feel him give me a squeeze urging me to answer.

I cross my arms in front of me, as if that will protect me from the memories I have to share. I just close my eyes and nod quickly. There. He knows.

"Look at me Josie," he whispers.

I shake my head and keep them closed. I can't bear the look I will see in his eyes now that he knows the truth about me.

"Please look at me. You have nothing to be ashamed of."

I take a breath and open my eyes slowly sliding them to him then away quickly.

"Tell me," he urges softly.

I walk to the chair and sit down facing him. I can't be that close if he wants to hear this. I need space. My hands start fidgeting in my lap and I direct my gaze there. I take a breath, keep watching my hands and then tell him what he wants to know. It comes out so quietly I wonder if he can even hear me.

"I worked for him. He asked me out constantly. I said no constantly. I can't explain it, I just had a very bad feeling about him." I trudge forward. Maybe if I get it all out quickly, it will be less painful.

"After a while it was making me very uncomfortable. I noticed him watching me. Staring at me… In a sexual way. I thought after a while he would give up, but he didn't. The computer system was a mess, I was designing and implementing a new program. I found some things that didn't add up. A lot of business transactions that were false. A lot of discrepancies in funds." I swallow and look up to see if he's following me.

"He was embezzling?"

I nod. "Nobody would notice it except for me, because I was going through every piece of information in the old program. I kept digging trying to find proof. The thing is, he's really not that smart, there was evidence, it was just hard to link it directly to him. So I found everything I could and saved the information, then transferred everything in to the new program."

I pause to collect myself because the bad part is just beginning. "I wanted to get rid of him. He made my job uncomfortable. To the point where I would be nervous going to work, and stay nervous all day. I decided I would find the proof I needed to get him out. I needed the link. Just the discrepancies weren't enough because he could have blamed it on someone else. So I accepted his invitation to dinner one night and took my recorder to see if I could get him to open up."

"Jesus, Josie!" He seems exasperated, as if I had done something incredibly stupid. Which I had. I know that now. I didn't know that then.

"I know, but I thought I was being safe. I didn't ride with him, I met him at the restaurant, but things were bad from the beginning. He had us in a little booth in the back corner, his hands were all over me, and he wouldn't let up enough for me to even try to get the conversation started. Finally, I had to do something, so I decided to just tell him about the discrepancies and gage his reaction. I tried to play it like I was impressed. Like some sort of genius had stolen money. I could tell it was working, he was smiling, like he was really proud of himself and he said he had something to tell me, but there were too many people around. He wanted me to go for a ride with him."

"Like I said, he's not that smart, but the thing is, he has money and he's dangerous. I shouldn't have gotten in that car, but I did. I was so close to a confession, I couldn't give up! I liked my job. I wanted to keep it. I wanted to get him away from the company and from me. When we got in the car and drove away he told me it was true and I had it recorded. I had him." I look at him hoping he understands. He's watching me closely. "I just had to get all of the information together and into the right hands. I had him!" I whisper, needing him to understand that I was trying to do the right thing.

"Okay, baby, so you had him, but then what happened."

I sigh and look away. "It all went very wrong. He drove to a rural area, pulled the car into a field and parked it." I look back at Gunner to see his muscle in his jaw clenching.

"Tell me what he did."

I look down and my hands trembling in my lap and my foot bouncing as fast as it will go.

"I told him that I wanted to go back to my car. He said he'd been waiting a long time to get me alone. After all, I acted impressed that he pulled off embezzling from the company. So he seemed surprised that I wanted to get away from him. Then he started to get suspicious. Asking if I had been lying. Asking if I was setting him up. He started to get angry and I was scared, I didn't know how to answer him. He ripped open my shirt looking for a wire, then went through my purse and found the recorder."

"I got out of the car and ran, but he caught me and dragged me back. I fought him..." I whisper. This is the hardest part to admit, but I just want to finish it. "He was strong and he was a lot bigger than me. I tried to punch, kick, bite, anything I could, but the more I fought him the angrier he became. He was hitting me, telling me to stop fighting, but I didn't, so he got rope out of the trunk and tied my hands up. Then he raped me. After the first time..."

"The first time?" He hisses.

I decide to ignore that and carry on. "I tried begging him to let me go. I promised I would never tell anyone anything. But he was so angry, not just that I tricked him, but that I hadn't wanted anything to do with him. He wanted me to pay for every time I rejected him. His anger... there was just something seriously wrong with him, it was like he turned into a psycho right in front of me. He... raped me more than once, and after the blows to my head I kept losing consciousness. At some point I think my brain just drifted off somewhere else. I was waiting to die." I say softly and swallow the bile creeping up my throat. *Finish, Josie, just finish*.

"He locked me in the trunk when I was out cold. When I woke up it took me a minute to figure out where I was, then I started kicking and screaming because I couldn't see, I couldn't move much, I didn't feel like I could breath, and I remember him opening the trunk and looking at me like he was surprised. I think he thought he'd killed me, it was so strange, and I only remember bits and pieces, but I think he was relieved I wasn't dead. I think he lost control and didn't know what to do. I begged him again to let me go, I swore to him I would quit my job and disappear. He took the recording from me and swore to me that if he ever saw me again, or if I ever told anyone what he did, he would kill me and he was serious Gunner. He meant it and I believed him, one hundred percent. He left me there to find my way back and I was lucky enough that some woman saw me walking and gave me a ride without calling the police, when I got home I packed my stuff and that's when I came back here."

I took a shaky breath. God, it was exhausting every time I had to tell someone. Dr. Palmer said the more I told my story, the easier it would be and that it would lose some of its power over me. I really hope that is the truth because even as I'm sitting here, I'm realizing that I still have to tell Justine, Eddie, and Rick. I look to Gunner and see him bent forward, elbows on his knees and his head down. I'm done talking, so I just wait for his reaction. I wait for his judgment to come.

He looks me in the eye and I can't gage what he's feeling. I wipe my cheeks and stand. I'm not sure what I expected, but I'm nervous waiting for him to say something. I don't want his pity, I don't want him to think of me as a victim, I don't want him to tell me how stupid I was for getting in that situation. I don't know what I do want, but I know I don't want that.

"Why is he looking for you now?" he asks. His voice sounding low and dangerous.

I shrug and look away.

"Josie, I swear to God. After what that fucker did to you, you better tell me everything. I want to hear it, right now! Does he have reason to be looking for you?" His anger is palpable and makes me flinch.

"Maybe," I say softly while I walk to the suitcase I'd thrown clothes into earlier so I can put them away. I need a diversion.

"Maybe?"

I shrug again.

Oh crap.

"You didn't turn him in, because there's no record. Walker would have found it. So what reason does he have to come after you?"

"I'm not sure." I say lightly, and that's the truth. I don't know if he's found out what I've done, or if he's just looking for me because he's a psycho.

"Josie." The way he says my name has my gaze snapping over to him.

Uh-oh

"I don't know, okay?" I say a little exasperated. "I'm not sure what he knows. I might have done some things to make him angry," I look away and go back to the clothes, "but he could also be looking for me just because he's crazy, or because he wants reassurance that I kept my promise. That's why I was going to hire you. I just wanted to look into him and see

347

what he was up to. I wanted to find out if I was safe. Maybe he's doing the same thing. Maybe he's afraid I will turn him in eventually. I don't know what he wants. I didn't turn him in. I did what I promised and disappeared. He never saw me again. That's what he said to do." I ramble on nervously.

"Babe, stop. Come here."

I freeze and look at him.

He walks over and takes my hand leading me back to the bed. He lays down and pulls me down beside him and wraps his arms around me. I wish it didn't feel so good. I know he's trying to get me to settle and give him a straight answer, but I'm not sure I should share the rest.

"Josie, I'm going to keep you safe. If that fucker comes near you I'll kill him. I fuckin' hate what he did to you, and it's taking everything I have not to drive my ass to Detroit right now and take him out of commission."

Oh. Well. That's not what I expected to hear. I feel like I should tell him not to get upset, but the truth is I like what he said. I like it a lot. I wasn't sure if Gunner had taken people out of commission before, I wasn't even sure what that meant, but whatever it was, I liked it.

"But please baby, don't give him a reason to come after you. Whatever you're planning, you put a stop to it."

I start to argue and he puts his nose right to mine and stares me down.

Yikes.

"It's not worth your life Josie. You let me take care of him."

"This isn't your problem, Gunner," I protest as I feel the familiar bitterness creeping in. "You don't understand. You don't know how it feels to have your power taken away like that. You don't know what it's like to live in fear. To know someone can take something away from you or hurt you just because they're bigger and stronger than you. He got away with what he did to me. Do you understand? He didn't pay. It was like it never happened for him, while I've lived with it every day and while I've had to fight every day just to live a normal life." I feel angry tears sliding down my face.

It's easy for him to tell me to drop it. It wasn't him who was beaten and raped repeatedly and made to stay quiet. A guy like Gunner would never know what that felt like.

"Baby, I'm so sorry," he whispers to me and brushes at my tears with his thumbs as he holds my head in his hands. "You're right, I don't know how that feels, but your life is more important than revenge. I want you safe."

"This is about justice, Gunner." I tell him honestly. I understand what he's saying. That doesn't mean I will give up my plans for justice though.

Freddy picked that moment to hop up on the bed with us and put his nose next to our faces.

"Why does he smell like beef sticks?" I ask narrowing my eyes on Gunner.

"Wasn't taking any chances." He says smiling down at me.

I look over and watch Freddy lick his chops and I don't know why but it makes me laugh out loud.

It feels so good to laugh after everything that has happened today.

"Can we please stop talking about this for now?" I ask him feeling exhausted once again.

"I need to fix your door and your wall."

"Yes you do, it would be nice if you quit putting holes in stuff." I tell him with mock indignation.

He laughs. "Quit giving me reasons."

I guess he has a point, so I just wrinkle my nose at him and try to slide out of bed, but he grabs me and holds on. When I look back at him he leans in for a kiss. It's a kiss that starts slow and tender, and when it starts to heat up and I start to go limp with desire he pulls back. I give a little whine of protest.

"Don't worry baby, later I'm going to make you whine and whimper for me *real* good." He says giving me another peck.

I give his shoulder a slap.

"Promises, promises." I tease.

"I keep my promises," he says in my ear using the low voice that makes me shiver and my nipples instantly turn hard.

This day has been total shit, but I hope he ends it by making good on those promises because there's nothing I want more than to get lost in him and forget.

K. D. Smith

Chapter 40

Gunner

I spent the rest of the evening fixing Josie's wall and boarding up the door until I could get someone there to fix it tomorrow. It felt good to take a hammer to something.

You don't know what it's like to live in fear.

He got away with what he did to me.

Fuck!

Josie seemed content to sit and talk to me while I worked, which I liked even though in my mind I really wanted to break more shit. Now that she told me what happened to her it seemed that she was a little more relaxed with me. I was glad for that. What I was not glad for was the fact that Brian Hanson was looking for her again.

The thought of what he did to her makes me want to find that piece of shit and pound his fuckin' head in with this hammer. Any man who uses his strength against a woman like that deserves no mercy, and I don't plan on showing him any. I don't know when, and I don't know how, but I will get that motherfucker.

I'm trying to put that out of my mind until I'm alone. I don't want her to see my anger and misinterpret it. Instead I'm going to focus on her and making her feel safe with me. I'm relieved that I finally know the truth, but I know she's still hiding things. I'm not sure what, but my gut is telling me she's putting herself in danger.

"I'm going to go make something to eat," Josie tells me as she stands to head towards the refrigerator.

"Got any of your dip?"

She smiles at me, and damn it feels good to see her smile.

"Yes," she says getting out a container. She sets it on the table and pulls out all kinds of things for dipping. Carrots, celery, crackers, cheese, chips, pieces of bread.

"Babe, I know it's good with everything, but you don't have to give me everything." I say with wide eyes as she keeps bringing me stuff to the table. Finally, she hands me a beer and sits down with me snagging the carrots.

"Variety is essential," she tells me seriously.

I watch as she chews on a piece of carrot. That foot of hers is bouncing up and down and she's looking across the room, but I don't think she's really seeing anything. She looks lost in thought.

"What's going on in that head of yours?" I ask, hoping she will tell me the answer.

She sighs and looks into her lap nervously. "I need to call a meeting."

"Huh?" I say, not following. "What do you mean, a meeting?"

"I need to explain things to Rick, Eddie, and Justine," she pauses and looks at me. "They don't know, but after what happened today, they have a lot of questions. I need to be honest with them."

I take that in. I'm surprised that she hasn't told her friends about her past. They seem so close, I thought she would have told some, if not all of them.

"Call them if you're ready," I tell her. "I want to be with you when you do it."

She looks at me and I'm not sure what emotion I see cross her face. Relief maybe? But she quickly hides it before I can figure it out.

"Thank you," she whispers. "It's not going to be easy."

We continue to eat in comfortable silence, sometimes making light conversation, until her phone beeps with an incoming text. I watch her look at the screen and take a deep breath.

"Justine says it's time for mojitos. I guess there's no time like the present."

"Mojitos?" I ask a little confused.

"Yeah, it's a tradition, you'll see," she says simply and stands. I watch as she packs up food.

*****

I guess mojito night is a regular thing. I notice they have a routine as the Mojitos are made and the food is arranged. I see each of them watching Josie closely without trying to be obvious. I know how hard this is for her, but her friends should know about her past. They are close, and I know they care. It will also give me extra sets of eyes to watch over her when I'm not around. I glance around noticing the only person who's not in attendance is Faith.

I expected Josie to avoid the subject for as long as possible, but the woman is full of surprises, and again I'm amazed at her strength.

"I love you guys," she says taking a sip of her drink and then taking a deep breath and moving ahead like a trooper. "I only want to say this one time and then I really don't want to talk about it anymore, at least not tonight. I know I should have done this sooner, but, well, it's just not easy to do." Then she continues softly but quickly explaining everything that she told me earlier.

I see tears in Justine's eyes. Rick gasps and holds his hand over his mouth. Eddie is staring with a mixed expression of anger and understanding.

When Josie is finished she says, "Now that that's over with, can we please proceed with Mojito night?" She takes a long drink and heads to the kitchen. I watch as Rick goes to her and hugs her closely whispering in her ear and making tears fill her eyes as he pulls away wiping his own.

Then Justine who says, "Girl, I knew it was bad, but I didn't know it was *that* bad!" Then proceeds to give Josie a tight hug without saying anything else.

Eddie waits for the others to leave and then leans on the counter and looks at me asking, "You taking care of this?"

"Yep." I give him a nod. He returns it then looks at Josie.

"I knew you weren't just bringing us food for the hell of it."

She surprises me again by giggling and declaring, "Guilty!"

"We're here for whatever you need. Anytime. Always." He promises.

This starts to make her teary again, and she whispers a thank you, and it's obvious how much that means to her.

Then the evening progresses into what I'm told is a true mojito night. There's music, food, laughing, a lot of joking, and it ends with them arguing over who is the true champion of *Taboo*. Apparently they play this game often and take it very seriously.

Half way through the evening, Faith shows up and looks a little off until she gets a drink then sits down to participate in the argument. Looking around the room I think what an odd group of people Josie has attracted into her life.

They are offbeat, that is a fact, but they are good friends and I like that she has that. I like it a lot. My girl needs people who will look out for her, although I plan on keeping a very close eye on her myself.

My gut clenches just remembering the reason for this little meeting. I haven't forgotten that she didn't answer all of my questions, but she has gone through enough for one day. Hell, she's gone through enough for a lifetime.

On that thought, I sit down beside her and put my arm around her as I join in the conversation and laughter with her and her

friends. I notice the easy expression she's
wearing on her face. She looks tired, but
relaxed now that the worst is over. It gives me
a very good feeling seeing that look, right here
and now I'm making a vow to keep that look on
her face as much as possible.

K. D. Smith

Chapter 41

Josie

I've just finished my morning run with Freddy, as we enter the house I now automatically turn to put in the alarm code. I shake my head at Freddy who groans and drops on the cool kitchen tile with his tongue hanging out the side of his mouth.

"Summer gettin' to you big guy?" I ask him, bending to give his big head a scratch. He gives another groan but his tail starts smacking the floor with a heavy thud. As soon as I stand from him he drops his head to the floor laying out on his side panting.

God, I love my dog, that's what I think as I head to the shower. In fact, I've been loving life for the last few weeks in general. Freddy is just a bonus to my newfound exuberance.

I know it can't stay this way forever, but let me tell you, I have enjoyed it to the fullest extent possible. After that horrible day when I found the file in Gunner's office and admitted to him and my friends the truth about my past, I felt as if the weight of the world had been lifted from my shoulders.

I've realized that the people in my life are not just great friends, but they are supportive, and loyal to a fault. Between them and Gunner I have felt more like my old self than I ever thought possible.

Just the other day, I found myself having so much fun at Mojito night that when Isaiah came up behind me and grabbed me unexpectedly, I didn't even freak out. I felt not one ounce of panic. I saw Gunner sitting right in front of me, smiling his handsome smile, and I just knew that everything was safe.

You heard me right. Justine invited Isaiah to mojito night, and so far he has been there *twice!* Gunner has been there more than twice. In fact ever since the first night, he hasn't missed one. I think he enjoys my eccentric friends as much as I do. Not that he would admit it.

Of course he could just be tagging along to keep an eye on me, which he also does often, but he should know that I'm safe with my friends. This is another reason to be happy. If he wanted time away from me, leaving me with a group of friends would be a perfect opportunity, but he doesn't do it. Which means he's with me because he wants to be, not because he feels he has to be. I can hardly believe it.

Gunner has been staying most nights at our house. I've had innumerable orgasms at his hands. Or mouth. Or, well, any way possible. I've learned things about my body I didn't know.

I've become so accustomed to his control in the bedroom that there is nothing left for me to worry about. I don't have to worry. Gunner takes what he wants and makes sure I get what I need. I never dreamed my sex life would be so good, and the word 'good' is a huge understatement. It's phenomenal. Exceptional. Explosive!

He's been going on runs with Freddy and I. He's been spreading that vapor liquid around my garden (which is still working!). We've gone to the beach twice, once riding his motorcycle, which was completely *awesome*! We even went grocery shopping together. Which oddly enough, is one of my favorite things we've done together. It's just so *normal*, and for a girl who hasn't felt normal in a very long time, that is a feeling that I tucked away somewhere deep inside to carry around with me for the rest of my life.

Things have changed for me so quickly that I sometimes forget that I have a mission to complete. In fact every time my plans have come to mind, I shut them out. Life with Gunner, and with friends who I don't have to hide things from, has been so calm and peaceful. I've been afraid to taint it.

Gunner hasn't asked me about my plans again, and I'm grateful for that because the last thing I want to do is lie to him. I could just accept my past and move on, but when I think of doing that I get that familiar churning in my stomach. The one that drives me. The one that seeks justice. I know I need to finish it so that I can keep finding that normal feeling that gives me peace.

The problem is that I've completely fallen for Gunner. I've been walking around with my head in the clouds like a teenager with her first crush. I haven't been able to focus. I just have to tie up these loose ends and I will be free.

With this in mind, I finish my shower, dress and go sit at my computer to start working on the final phase of my plan. I take a deep breath, *I'm so close*. I've almost gathered all of the proof I need and I'm feeling anxious about getting the data into the right hands.

To my surprise there is a new security measure in place when I try to hack my way into Brian's computer. Interesting. I guess I should have expected this after the havoc I've wreaked in the past. For once he made a smart move, but not smart enough to hinder me. It takes some time, but then I'm in.

Over time I've gathered evidence against Brian Hanson and his dirty business deeds. Of course I'm not going about it the legal way, so it's going to take some finesse to make sure I bring him down in a way that's going to stick. But I also have a backup plan. Every smart girl knows she needs a plan B and believe me, I have prepared myself for just about any scenario.

After finding what I need I set my sights on Brian's personal information. Funny how he has been looking for information on me, and here I am looking at his own personal bank statements. If I weren't so anxious about pulling this off, I would have a good laugh at his expense.

Just as I'm saving all the information I need onto several flash drives (just to be safe), Faith walks in the door. I watch as she throws down her messenger bag, kicks off her heels, and plops down on the couch.

Freddy gets up from his spot at my side and heads straight to her. He sits and leans his whole body against her legs and puts his head in her lap.

"Hey Freddy boy!" She greets and gives him some head pats. His tongue falls out and he blinks with every pat to the head looking like he's in doggy heaven.

"What's up?" I ask feigning shock. "Do you actually have time to talk to me instead of your cyber stud?"

"Shut up. Not all of us can be lucky enough to have a Layne boy in our bed every night." She says rolling her eyes to the ceiling. "Seriously, you two are driving me crazy."

I giggle knowing that she's heard us going at it, but I'm not about to apologize. If it weren't for Freddy, I would stay at Gunner's apartment more often, but I've felt guilty about leaving him too often.

"Don't worry, tonight I'm staying with Gunner after I go to the gym." I inform. Gunner says I can bring Freddy, but I worry about Faith home alone. "Is it ok for Freddy to stay home with you?"

"Of course! Freddy and I can hang. Right boy?"

He gives her a *woof* and then sneezes on her.

"Just don't be doing internet porn around him. He's sensitive." I warn her.

"Har har, you're hilarious." She says in a deadpan voice that cracks me up.

"Seriously though, please be careful with this guy. You don't know anything about him. He could be a complete psycho."

Although I found information on him weeks ago, I hadn't followed through with asking Gunner to check him out yet. Another thing I got sidetracked from while having my head in the clouds. I reminded myself to do that soon. Faith hadn't been her normal happy self lately and I was getting worried.

"He's not psycho. Intense, but not psycho. And he really likes me."

"Do you really like him back?" I inquire.

She blows out a long breath and says, "I don't know. It's just nice to have someone so interested in me."

"Faith, anyone with a brain would be interested in you. Just don't sell yourself short."

She doesn't go any further with the discussion. Like usual she's guarded about this guy, which only makes me worry more.

We say our goodbyes as she heads to change and I get ready for the gym. My training with Kai is going so well. The changes in my life spilled over to my performance in the gym and he's been very pleased with my progress.

I contemplate cancelling for a night so I can get to Gunner's place earlier, but I decide that's not a good idea. This is part of my preparation, I have to be diligent until my plan is complete.

K. D. Smith

Chapter 42

Gunner

"That's it baby, give it to me." I whisper in Josie's ear as she's straddling my lap. My hand is down her yoga pants and my fingers inside working her.

She throws her head back and whimpers as she's moving her hips and riding my fingers. She's close, I can feel it by the way she's squeezing my fingers with her hot, wet pussy.

Damn she feels good. She looks good. Her face flushed with excitement. She's only been here about five minutes, but I swear, I can't keep my hands off her. A good man would sit her down to relax after coming from the gym, maybe give her a glass of wine, but not me, here I am making her come for me on my lap before I've even said hello.

I'm a bastard.

I'm also not sorry. I move my thumb to rub over her clit and bite her earlobe saying, "I want it Josie. Give it to me." And she does. Fucking beautiful. I watch as her orgasm rolls through her. Her body shaking. I feel how wet my hand is and it's all I can do not to throw her down and fuck her fast and hard.

Not yet.

She puts her head down on my shoulder purring and shuddering from the aftershocks of her orgasm. It's amazing how much she's opened up in the short time we've been together. It does something to me every time I see that bright smile on her face. It makes me feel like the luckiest man in the world.

"Well hello there." She says finally coming back to herself and lifting up her head to smile at me shyly. It kills me how she can come for me like that and then look shy about it.

"Hey baby." I grin and give her a kiss full of promise. She doesn't know it yet, but tonight we are going to get to the bottom of things. She's going to tell me her plans, and I'm going to tell her I love her.

I've tried not to, but there's just no way around it. This woman is everything I've ever wanted and I'm keeping her. Always.

"Now, how about I feed you and then we soak in the tub, because I plan on licking every single part of your body later.

"Okay," she whispers and I feel her shiver.

I pat her ass and lift her off my lap so I can get us the take-out pasta I brought home. As we eat I ask her about her time at the gym. I'm glad to hear that it's going better. We talk about my work, and her work. I ask after Freddy, who has more than won me over at this point.

"I thought about bringing him over, but I don't like Faith being home alone. I feel better if he's with her," she admits.

Then she starts fidgeting, which I've learned means that she has something she wants to say.

"What is it?" I ask worried that something has happened with the Brian situation. I haven't told Josie that I've had Caleb keeping track of him, or that as of yesterday Brian Hanson hasn't been at work or at his home.

"I... Well..." She takes a moment and then finishes. "I'm worried about Faith and this internet guy she's spending all her time with."

"Why are you worried?" I ask watching her eyes move away to avoid my gaze.

"I might have done some snooping," she spits out. "And I might have noticed some things I don't like. He seems like a bully and I did some digging..." She's still not looking at me. I'm not sure why she's not comfortable discussing this.

"What do you mean digging?"

"Well, I found out who he is and I was hoping... maybe... you know... maybe you could look into him?"

She finally looks at me quickly then looks away again.

"Babe, I can look into him, but why are you afraid to ask me that?"

She looks down at her foot which is bouncing away. "I know you're busy, and I really hate to ask you for a favor after all you've done. I mean, I can pay you if you want..."

Jesus.

"Are you kidding me?"

"Um... no?"

"Josie, you don't get it. You don't have to pay me. You're with me. You need something, you ask me. I handle it. Simple as that. No feeling weird or guilty about it."

She stares at me and I see so many emotions cross her face that I'm having trouble following. Finally, she gives her smile to me, and reaches over to squeeze my hand.

That smile cuts me open every damn time. I think I could spend my whole life making her smile and enjoy every fucking minute of it.

"Can we take a bath now? Because I'd really like to get to that licking part of the evening you mentioned. And since I'm allowed to ask for anything, I have another request for you." She starts to blush even as she's still smiling.

"Really? What request might that be?" I ask grinning back, because I hope to God it's a sexual one. I'm dying to hear what is working in that brain of hers.

"I'm not telling until we're surrounded by bubbles."

She doesn't have to say any more, with her hand still attached to mine I pull her up the stairs into my bathroom and turn on the water. Then I realize I don't have bubbles.

Shit.

"Babe, I hate to tell you this, but I don't have any bubbles," I say honestly. Out of everything I can give her, she wants bubbles and I don't have any.

"We can use some shampoo to make bubbles," she suggests and then giggles. Yes, she's giggling so much her shoulders shake and I see her cover her mouth trying to hide her laughter.

"What's so funny?"

At this she finally lets out a full belt of laughter and I don't know what the hell she's laughing about but I don't want her to stop. I'm smirking just looking at her face.

"You... Gunner Layne... bubbles!" She practically squeals.

"What, you don't think tough guys can take bubble baths?" I ask pretending to be offended.

At that she wipes a tear from her eye trying to calm herself.

"I was just picturing you hear all alone enjoying a bubble bath...and...and...oh God! I don't know why that's so funny, but it is!" she declares.

When she gets herself under control she grabs the shampoo bottle and puts some in the running water, and sure enough, bubbles start forming. I make a mental note to buy some bubble bath for her, but not before I set her straight.

"I'll make sure to buy bubble bath for you, but just so we're clear, I won't be using them by myself. The only way my ass is sittin' in a tub full of bubbles is if you're naked and sliding around against me in that tub. If I have to sit in some bubbles to enjoy that, then I'm a willing participant."

She blinks at me and then I see her eyes warm and I know my words are taking effect. Slowly she starts peeling off her clothes with her eyes on me the whole time.

I stare as she pulls her top over her head, then her bra hits the floor, then she shimmies out of those yoga pants taking her panties down with them and as she does this her breasts sway enticingly and I swear to God I must be the luckiest man on Earth.

Fuck!

She walks past me, her hips swaying as she moves. She lifts one gorgeous leg into the tub, then the other and bends to sit not saying a word the entire time.

The thing about Josie is, she isn't putting on a show. I've seen plenty of women strip and they know what they're doing. They know how to work it. With Josie, it's like she doesn't even know what she's doing or how fucking beautiful she is.

"Are you getting in or what?" She asks genuinely curious.

"You bet your sweet ass I am." Then I strip and join her as quickly as possible.

Once I'm settled behind her with my legs stretched out in front of me and her ass nestled between them, her back leaning into my chest, I see her legs propped up on the other end of the tub showing her pink toenails, her nipples are peeking out of the water, and I realize that bubbles definitely have benefits.

I take some soap and leisurely wash her and then myself swiftly.

"So," I say as I glide my hands over her hips and stomach, "What was it you wanted to ask?"

She wiggles back against me and leans her head back onto my shoulder. I take the opportunity to swirl my fingers around her nipples and watch them harden.

Her breathing quickens as I continue, but she doesn't say anything. I pinch her nipples a little bit and say, "Tell me."

"Gunner..." she sighs my name.

Fuck yeah, I love that.

I continue by squeezing her tits together with my palms and then watching them bob in the water as I let go and carry on with her nipples. I bend down to nuzzle her neck at the same time and whisper, "Tell me."

She turns her head slowly to me with that hazy look in her eyes. I know what that means. My girl is wet. She wants to come. I feel my cock at full attention and nudge her with it as I take her mouth and she moans.

When I pull away she still doesn't answer, so I pinch her nipples again and pull them outward from her body and her back arches telling me she likes it. I do it again and roll them in my fingers roughly. She gasps.

"Tell me and I'll reward you. Don't tell me, and I won't make you come."

She groans and finally whispers between pants as I'm continuing my assault on her pretty nipples, "I want to try something... again."

"And what's that, baby?" I ask sliding one hand beneath the water all the way to her smooth pussy. I stroke and squeeze her lips and feel her shiver and her nipple harden further.

"Remember..." Then I slide my finger lightly across her clit. "Oh God. Remember when... the first time..."

"I remember everything Josie, but you're going to have to be more specific," I say with another swipe across her engorged clit.

"You spanked me."

I freeze. She wiggles trying to get my hands moving again and then turns to me when they don't.

"I want to try it again," she whispers.

I don't know what to do with this. I'd love to spank her round little ass, but after last time I'm afraid of what it will do to her.

She turns in my arms and starts kissing my neck, rubbing her hands over my chest.

"I wasn't expecting t last time. This time I'm asking for it. I think .. I think I might like it and I trust you."

"Are you sure? I don't want to do anything to..."

She puts her fingers to my lips and I stop talking looking deep into her eyes. I see the heat in them. I don't see any fear.

I've noticed that as much as Josie loves being cuddled, when it comes to sex, she seems to enjoy it most when I dominate her. Well, she's enjoyed everything, I've made sure of that, but when I've let out my more aggressive side during sex, that's when she has gone absolutely wild for me.

I let out a groan remembering how it's been and realizing that she wants more. "We'll try anything you want baby, but you remember your word if you don't like it?"

"Indigo," she says softly and holding my eyes communicating to me that she's ready.

I kiss her again and then pull back saying, "Towel off. I want you in the middle of the bed on all fours when I get there."

Her eyes round and then she blinks and nods and I see her blush before she grins and turns her head away from me to climb out of the tub with her round, wet ass pointed right at my face.

Oh fuck yeah. I know exactly what to do with her.

Chapter 43

Josie

I crawl onto the bed trying not to allow myself time to be nervous. I can't believe I just asked him to spank me! Am I crazy?

I think of all the times Gunner has taken control of me in bed, and I realize that I need that. I've come to crave it. There are times when I've been so far gone enjoying what he's doing to my body that afterwards I've wondered if he's holding back trying to be careful with me.

I don't want him to hold back. I want all of him, and I know there's more. I can feel it. The more I've seen of that side of him and the more I've felt it, the more I've wanted it. I want pure, unadulterated Gunner. I wouldn't have asked him if I didn't think I could handle it.

I remember every time he's dominated my body, making me come when I didn't think it was possible. Making my body quiver and shake until I'm begging for more. Yes. That is what I want. I love how he can get me to a place where my mind no longer works and all that matters is satisfying my hunger for him.

I feel the bed shift as he comes up behind me covering my back with his torso. Wrapping one arm underneath me to toy with my nipples as he kisses my neck, moving his kisses slowly down to my shoulder as I shiver.

"You sure about this baby?"

"Yes," I say shakily, but not because I'm scared, because I've been in the middle of Gunner's bed, on all fours, thinking of the times I've been begging him to make me come, and I want more.

He kisses slowly down my spine, down to the cheeks of my ass, giving me a couple of gentle bites along the way. I don't know what I was expecting, but I wasn't expecting to feel his face shove into me as he uses his tongue on my pussy.

Oh *yes*!

"Mmmmm, you're wet for me waiting here like this," he growls and then dives back in.

His tongue finds my clit and then circling it over and over. Before I know what I'm doing, I find myself moving my hips and pushing back onto his face whimpering for more while I tilt my hips giving him better access.

I feel his tongue penetrate me as he squeezes my ass spreading my cheeks apart. This is what I mean. If I were thinking straight, I would be embarrassed right now. Instead, I'm trying to ride the man's face while he's licking and sucking at me.

I gasp and my body jerks as I feel his teeth nibble lightly on my clit. Oh dear God in heaven that feels good, almost too good. I think I'm going to come right then and there.

"Yes!" I wail.

Smack.

Smack.

He pulled back enough to deliver one to each cheek and then sucks on my clit. He repeats the process until I can't stand it anymore, but only in a good way. Each smack sends heat right to my core and I can feel more wetness seeping out every time.

"Oooh! Yes!" I pant right on the verge of orgasm as he lifts up behind me and shoves his cock deep inside me. My ass feels warm and tingly and it spreads throughout my whole body.

At this point I'm so far gone, all I can do is moan and rear back onto his big, hard cock with every thrust.

"Fuck yeah baby," he says in a gruff voice. "You gonna come all over me?"

"Yes! Please!"

I feel him powering into me as he wraps my hair around his hand and I feel a pull. It doesn't hurt, it feels fucking fantastic! Then I feel another slap across my ass.

"Come for me." He demands.

I do. Oh God do I *ever*!

I cry out as it hits me hard. Gunner has made me come hard plenty of times now, but this is different. My body shudders as I spasm around him. I feel his torso cover me again and his breath in my neck as he takes two more long, hard strokes and then growls his release in my ear. I feel his cock pulsing and his come filling me and he keeps coming.

Even though my body is trembling and I've fallen down to my elbows, I smile in awe that I just did that for Gunner. *That* was what he was holding back because he was being careful with me. *That* is what I asked for, and *that* is what I wanted to keep getting.

I collapsed in bed, Gunner pulling back the covers and quickly walking to the bathroom, returning with a warm cloth he used on me, then himself and threw aside. He covered us and pulled me to him, as we both still tried to breathe evenly.

I sighed a contented sigh and snuggled in.

"You okay?" he asks squeezing me tighter.

"Mmmmhmmmm."

"You sure?"

"I'm more than sure. Can we do that again?" I ask dreamily.

Gunner lets out a loud laugh and blurts, "God I love you," and then laughs some more.

I'm not laughing, I've gone straight from my sex fog to shock, confusion, and finally complete terror in about twenty seconds flat.

Okay, surely he's just using that like a figure of speech. He can't mean that. He couldn't love me, and even if he thought he did, he would change his mind. I couldn't handle it if he gave me that and took it away. It would kill me.

All the sudden I wasn't so fond of him using this figure of speech so lightly. He shouldn't just say things like that so flippantly. I mean who just says that? Seriously! Now here I am after getting my very first, very enjoyable spanking, and now I'm freaking out. *Again*! At least this time I could speak, so I did.

"I should go home and check on Freddy."

This is total bullshit of course. Faith is taking care of Freddy. Gunner knows that, but it's the best excuse I can think of since he's freaking me out.

I start to roll over and his arms tighten on me like a vice.

"Freddy's fine," he states with his eyes searching my face.

"You don't know that. I better check," I say softly while avoiding his eyes. I try harder to roll but he won't let me.

Shit!

Instead he rolls pushing me back and looms over me searching some more.

I fixate on his chin and say, "Let me up."

"No."

"Gunner, let me up."

"No."

Shit, shit, *shit*!

This isn't good. I'm freaking out because he said the L word as a joke. Why didn't I just laugh and then pretend he didn't say it?

"Look at me Josie."

"I am looking at you," I whispered while staring at his chin.

He sighed as if he needed patience.

"Tell me what happened."

"Nothing."

"Nothing? One minute you're purring for me and asking for another spanking the next minute you look freaked and you want to go home. Was it the spanking?"

"No."

"Because of what I said?"

384

I kept looking at his chin. I couldn't think of any good way to avoid this conversation so I said, "You shouldn't joke about things like that."

"Joke?" he asked sounding like he was getting angry.

I didn't want to make him angry. I suddenly felt very stupid for making a big deal out of it. *Ugh. Why can't I just be normal for once?*

"Uh..."

I decided to slowly move my eyes upward to sneak a peek at his eyes and when I saw them I immediately moved them back down. He was definitely angry.

Oh no.

"Well... I mean..." Finally I let out a frustrated groan and said, "Let's just forget it."

"Forget it?" he asked in a dangerously low voice while moving his face closer to mine.

I swallowed.

"Can we go to sleep?" I asked sounding hopeful.

"Josie, I don't know where your head is at, but I am not messing around. I thought you were clear about that. We've been in bed with each other almost every night for weeks now."

Okay, shit, he wasn't making a joke. That's even worse!

385

Well, this is true, we have been together almost every night, but I know what I know, and that is that even though I've fallen head over heels in love with Gunner, there is no way he could feel the same way. I know this because he is him (and that is a lot of things, all of them good), and I am... well... *me*. I am a lot of things too. Most of them are not good. Soon he'll see this.

I decided the plan of action was to just nod, because he wasn't messing around and he wasn't going to listen to me. So I just had to move past this. When he figured it out, I could remind him of this conversation. Then I could nurse my broken heart, because I knew no matter how hard I tried, there was no way to protect myself from that. I just had to keep reminding myself that it wasn't true. If I let myself believe it I would be broken when he's gone. I don't want to be broken any more than I already am.

"We on the same page?"

"Yes." I whispered.

"Well thank fuck," he breathed and then positioned us so he was on his back again and I had my head on his chest.

I close my eyes willing myself not to think about it.

Think positive.

At least we made it through the spanking and sex part before I freaked out and ruined everything this time. That's progress. My ass still felt a little tingly from the smacks and if I weren't concentrating so hard on thinking positive, I would have grinned. As soon as I felt Gunner's breathing change and I knew he was sleeping, I thought myself right to sleep. And once again, I had another good night's sleep without medicine and without dreams.

K. D. Smith

Chapter 44

Josie

This morning Gunner brought me home and we took Freddy for his run, he went to work and now I'm sitting at my desk the next day trying to do some work when my phone chirps.

Gunner: Can you come to the office for lunch?

I glanced at the clock noticing that I had about an hour if he meant at noon. I still needed to shower and time to get ready.

Me: What time?

Gunner: 12. Caleb is picking you up.

Me: That's ok, I'll drive.

Gunner: Caleb will be there. See you then.

Me: Ok, see you soon <3

Then I thought that was too much after the strange night we had so I deleted the heart and put a smiley instead.

God, I'm such a dork.

Why is Caleb picking me up? I haven't met Caleb yet. I'm getting accustomed to Gunner's overprotective ways, but this seems like a bit much.

This isn't the first time Gunner's asked me to lunch at his office, we've done it a few times. I planned to stop by there anyway, because I wanted to leave one of the flash drives there. The thing is, I'm not sure how to do this without Gunner knowing. I stashed one at his apartment, but only in a place I would look for it. It was in the box of tampons I left under the bathroom sink.

I also stashed one in my gym locker and one in Eddie's garage. It's overkill, I know, but I don't want to lose my evidence. I went over every outcome in my head. The best being I'd never need them. Worse being that Brian would figure me out and somehow get to my copy. Even worse being that he would try to find the back-ups. And worst of all being that he would do something to me making it so I couldn't use them myself. By spreading the evidence, I knew he would never find them all, I also knew that if he did find me and follow through on his threat, somebody would come across the evidence and avenge me. Eventually. I hoped.

This is not a line of thought I like to have, but I've promised myself that I would be smart this time. I would be prepared for anything.

After my shower, I don my black shorts, a mint green silky spaghetti strap tank that fits loose and airy, black strappy sandals and leave my hair down. After lotion and minimal make up I'm ready to go. I make sure the flash drive is in my purse. At the last minute decide to take the guys some of my dip with all the trimmings.

When Freddy warns me we have company I look out the window. There is a dark SUV with a very large man inside. This must be Caleb, and he doesn't look very happy, so I decide it's a good idea to head out and not make him wait.

"Um, hi." I say approaching his window with a tentative smile.

He looks at me through sunglasses and jerks his head to the side saying, "Get in."

Thinking it's probably best to do as he says, I walk around and climb in. Once I'm sitting next to him and he turns putting an arm around my seat to back out I can't help but stare. He's *huge*! Then a thought comes to me. I've never met Caleb. What if this isn't Caleb?

"You're Caleb right?" I ask trying not to sound like a dumbass all while being nervous that he might not be Caleb.

"Yeah."

Whew. Okay. That's good to know. We drive in silence since he's not making any conversation and I assume he wants it that way.

Oddly, when we get there, he pulls up to the door instead of parking. I figure that's my queue and I climb out mumbling a "Thanks for the lift."

"Next time find out a name before you get into the vehicle," he says with a straight face.

Right.

I still can't see his eyes, but he's being very serious.

"Sure thing!" I say smiling brightly and shutting the door on him.

Sure thing? Nice one Josie.

Once I walk in still feeling like a dork I'm greeted by Marina who I have learned does not have a biker husband and biker babies. Instead she has a girlfriend and a pet bearded dragon named Flame. I knew she was the shit!

"Meeting the family, ey? Must be love!" She said winking at me.

Seriously, why do people need to keep using the L word?

"Family?" I ask hesitantly.

"Yeah, Walk's in the back. Thought you were having lunch with them."

"Oh." Well, Gunner hadn't mentioned his brother Walker coming to lunch. Of course I knew of him but I had never officially met him. I know he's a cop. I've thought about trying to get information from him, but I could never think of way to do it, especially since I hadn't been introduced and I didn't want to ask Gunner. This could be good. I have no idea how to broach the subject, but I need a trustworthy source at the department in Detroit. I've never tried to find one in fear of trusting the wrong person. Then again the thought of sitting in a room with a man who is probably like Gunner, is a little nerve wracking. One Gunner is plenty for me to handle.

"Gunner asked me to lunch, but he didn't say it was with his brother."

Since Marina has always been super friendly to me, and she also tries to look out for me in her own way, always being a calming influence, as if she'd known I needed that sometimes.

She says, "Don't worry, Walker's a teddy bear."

Okay. I can handle a Teddy Bear.

"Good," I breathe. "Not sure I could take two of them. Seriously, I have no idea how you can work here."

She laughs, "Sometimes I don't either honey."

I start back to Gunner's office and look back telling her, "I brought dip, if you want some feel free to come and get it."

"Now I know why he loves you," she says offhandedly without looking back.

Really people? *Enough*!

I walk down the hall shaking those thoughts from my head. I've got other shit to worry about. After I bury Brian Hanson once and for all (not literally of course, although a girl can dream), I will worry about the L word business. I can't freak out about two things at once!

Focus!

My hands are full so I can't knock, I balance holding a bag in each arm and lift up one foot tapping my sandal on the door. It immediately opens and I almost fall over before getting my foot back to the ground.

Holy shit!

Teddy bear my ass!

I stare at a man who is about the same size as Gunner, with about as much muscle as Gunner, but who has brown hair. Instead of my beloved indigo eyes, he has intense brown eyes. He smiles and there it is, I see the resemblance immediately.

"Let me help," he says grabbing both bags out of my arms and holding the door. Finally I quit staring and move forward. Gunner rounds his desk and comes straight for me, kissing me on the mouth. I try to give a peck and pull back, but he pulls me closer and takes more. By the end of the kiss I practically sigh and look up at those eyes and see him smirking, then I remember why I tried to give him the peck.

"I guess you're Josie," I hear in an amused voice behind me. Immediately I jerk up straight and turn around embarrassed that I forgot.

"Yes. Sorry," I say knowing my blush is spreading.

He chuckles and says, "Now I get it."

I crinkle my forehead in confusion. "Get what?" I ask because I have no idea what he means.

"Nevermind," Gunner says, "Josie, this is Walker, my brother."

"Hi," I say softly, still embarrassed. I give him a little wave.

"Hi," he grins.

Why is he grinning?

"Let's eat," this coming from Gunner, who has a big bag sitting on his desk that looks like it's got sandwiches in it.

"I brought dip!" I say a little too excitedly, trying to change the subject.

"Oh fuck," Gunner rolls his eyes.

"Did you just roll your eyes at my dip? I thought you loved my dip."

"Babe, I do love your dip, and so does everyone else. Now Walker's going to love your dip, so that's one more person I have to share with."

I giggled at him. He really didn't like to share.

"I can always make more," I assured him.

We settled around the desk to eat, and Gunner was right, Walker did love my dip. He called it *fan-fucking-tastic* and I noticed Gunner sigh and shake his head a little.

After eating and talking a little bit I can say that I like Walker Layne a lot. He's similar to Gunner. A little scary and intense, but a good man. When the subject turned to Detroit I bided my time hoping for an opening to ask Walker if he ever worked in Detroit.

Finally it came.

"Nope, but I've got some buddies there."

"Cops like you?" I ask trying to feign moderate interest when I was really hanging on every word.

"Yeah, can't say I'm a fan of the D though. Too much shit. I visit for the occasional game, but that's it."

I smile hoping he will get back on the subject of his cop friends.

"Heard you had some trouble there."

My head jerks up.

What?

"I had Walker look into that asshole's record when he tried to hire me."

I swallowed. Well, I knew that much but now I didn't know what to say. I didn't like Walker knowing these things about me. It made me uncomfortable and ashamed.

"I didn't tell him every detail Josie."

Whew. That made me feel better. But now Walker was looking between us strangely.

"What didn't you tell me?"

I see Gunner give him the eye and I decide it's time to change the subject to see if I can get back around to finding a contact.

"So can you do that? I mean look into his record? Or did you have to talk to someone local?"

"I can do it, but sometimes talking to someone local helps when digging needs to be done."

"So did you have to dig?"

"I did, so did my buddy Jack," he says slowing eyeing me. I don't know if he's on to me, or if he's just wary about this conversation. Gunner's probably told him of my tendency to freak out.

Jack. Bingo. Now I need a last name.

"Seemed to me, when I was there, that the cops were almost as hard to trust as the citizens." Then I realized how that sounded and added, "Uh... no offense."

He smiled. "None taken. Unfortunately that can be true, but there are some good ones."

"Like Jack?" I ask looking down innocently at my bouncing foot.

"Yep."

"I know someone on the force named Jack, wonder if it's the same guy," I decided to lie. I felt guilty doing it, and hoped it wasn't written all over my face.

"Jack's name is not Jack, it's Kyle. Kyle Jackson."

"Oh," I say trying not to sound relieved, "not the same one then."

I realize Gunner has been quiet through all of this and I glance at him to see he's eyeing me suspiciously.

Uh oh.

"Well..." I look between them, "Uh, if the guys are in the surveillance room, I can take them the rest of the dip."

"That's my dip," Gunner claims.

Walker laughs, "You always were selfish. Thought you might outgrow it."

"Why the fuck would I do that?"

I grin knowing that Gunner is half joking and half not, he *really* does not like to share.

"I'll make you more," I say softly going to kiss his cheek and gather up the food. "Thanks for lunch."

"Anytime baby."

"Nice meeting you Jo..." Walker starts, but then his phone rings.

"Scuse me," he says walking over to the other end of the room with his back to us while putting his phone to his ear and saying, "Layne."

Then Marina walks in telling Gunner she needs a signature and starts to explain something while he's staring at a piece of paper. I can't believe my luck. I thought I would have to come back with the flash drive, but I might have my chance right now.

I casually walk over to the book shelf and pretend to be waiting for everyone to finish their business. I pick up a book and pretend to glance through it before sliding the book back in with the drive going first, then the book covering it.

Hot damn!

Once everyone's done and I have the food packed up, I say goodbye to Gunner. Walker accompanies me down to the surveillance room on his way out helping me with the bags.

"Thanks," I say, "It was nice to meet you."

"You too Josie, and I mean that. My brother is crazy for you, and honestly, now I can see why."

Ohhh. So *that's* what he meant.

"Uh... Thanks?" I whisper because I'm at a loss. How does one tactfully respond to that?

He chuckles and opens the door to the room taking the bags to the table, then he turns to me and surprises me with what he says.

"I know Gunner can handle things, but if you ever need something, you just give me a call."

Wow. That was sweet. Walker Layne was a teddy bear after all. Only a big one with a lot of intensity.

"Thanks," I said genuinely grateful for his offer.

"Hey Josie, is that the Kahlua shit?" Trey asks spotting the bags.

I turn to see him and Isaiah sitting in front of some monitors.

"What's up Walk?" Isaiah rumbles in his deep voice.

I watch as they do that weird version of a man hug. Trey on the other hand is still looking at the bags longingly.

I take pity on him, "No, I brought dip though."

"Seriously?" He asks happily.

"Yes." I take the stuff out of the bag and start arranging it on the table. Trey grabs a paper plate and starts loading up.

"I love this shit," he mumbles while shoving a whole cracker full of dip into his mouth.

"It's dip. Not shit." I correct while I watch him shove a carrot with dip on it in his mouth next.

"Good shit." He smiles with a mouth full of food.

I can't help but be amused. He really is a charming guy even though he's a bit obnoxious. Then again, I guess that could be said about all of these guys.

Isaiah fills a plate while talking to Walker, then Marina walks in stating, "You assholes better leave me some dip." Then as if she doesn't trust them she grabs a plate and loads up some for herself just in case.

It makes me happy to see everyone enjoying my dip so I smile and look up to see Caleb enter and walk to the table.

"You gotta try Josie's dip man, it's the shit." Walker tells him. He doesn't have a plate but he already ate.

Caleb looks at me with a piercing turquoise gaze that I have to admit, is very nice, but I still think he's scary. He doesn't say anything but loads up a plate as well.

He takes a bite and gives no reaction, but then puts more on his plate, so I think that's a good sign.

As I'm watching everyone enjoying my dip and chatting amongst themselves, I feel a change in the room. Whatever it is, it's firing warning signals right up my spine. I see eyes shoot towards the door and I turn to see Gunner standing there and he looks furious. Not just furious, he looks *livid*.

Yikes!

"You have something you want to tell me?" He booms with his eyes directed right at me.

"Oh fuck," I hear Walker say under his breath.

Caleb looks between Gunner and me and then walks out the door carrying his plate.

Can't say I blame him. I kinda wish he would take me with him. This is because I don't know how to answer Gunner's question. Could he have seen the flash drive? Did he look at it? I wanted to give the correct answer so he would wipe that look off his face, but I couldn't say that answer because if he didn't see it then I would be telling on myself.

Oh no. *Shit!*

So with everyone staring at me waiting for my answer, I say, "Uh... I..."

"What the fuck is this shit?" He blares, his face getting angrier as he pulls the flash drive out of his pocket and holds it up.

I immediately deflate. *Fuck*! This is bad, bad, *bad*.

He advances toward where I'm standing and I take a step back, then another.

I'm fairly certain he must have looked at what was on the flash drive in order to be this angry, then it was confirmed he yelled, "I thought I told you to drop this shit!"

Okay, well now he is starting to make me mad and scaring the shit out of me at the same time.

"I told you I would handle it."

"Gunner, I told you..."

"And I told you I would handle it!"

"Stop yelling at me!" I yelled at him.

"You don't want me to yell? You're going out of your way to piss off a psychopath and you don't want me to yell?"

"Can we talk about this later?" I hiss, putting my hands on my hips.

He doesn't pay attention to any of the people in the room and yells, "No! We are not talking about this shit later, we're talking about it *now*!"

At this Walker says, "Calm down Gunner."

"Calm down? I told her to drop this. I told her I'd take care of it. Do you know what is on this?"

Alright, this did not need to be public knowledge but since he was yelling in front of everyone, and even if he wasn't they would still probably hear him down the hall, I decided to cut to the chase.

"It's evidence Gunner. Evidence that I need and I was trying to keep it safe, you weren't supposed to see that."

That was the wrong thing to say. He narrowed his eyes on me and stalked closer. "I get that since you were hiding it *in my office*!"

I let out a frustrated huff and unwisely shared, "Just forget about it then, I have plenty of others."

The already tense room got thicker as everyone's eyes moved between me and Gunner.

"You don't need the others. I will handle it from here."

"No, you won't, you have to let me handle this my way."

"You're done with this!"

"Gunner if you do something with that evidence then you are going to ruin *everything*!"

"What am I going to ruin?"

"My *plan*!"

"Well, gotta get back to the station," Walker blurts then walks out the door.

As we all stand there silent for a second and Gunners eyes drill holes into me, I hear the phone start ringing.

"Better get that!" Marina says all too quickly and escapes out the door.

Then I see Isaiah is turned looking at the monitors again and Trey is still staring at us while he chews.

I glare at him for no reason other than I am just plain annoyed and then I turn my glare on Gunner.

He starts to get closer and I back up further until I hit the wall behind me.

He gets in my space putting his hands on each side of me to the wall.

"You are not going anywhere until you tell me about your plan," he whispers dangerously low.

"I'm going home," I announce.

"You can't, you don't have a car here," he whispers close to my lips.

Shit. I forgot about that.

I glance hopefully at Trey who decides at that moment to swivel in his chair and mind his own business. Right. Guess they weren't going to help me out.

"Do you want to tell me here, or in my office?"

Well that isn't much of a choice. I don't want to tell him at all.

"Neither."

"Josie, I'm about to lose my patience. Take your pick, but you *will* tell me. Or I'll be forced to use drastic measures."

That didn't sound good.

"What?" I whispered losing my false bravado.

"I know I can get you to talk, but I don't think you want me doin' it in front of them." He jerked his head in the direction of Isaiah and Trey.

I glanced to see Trey watching again with a grin on his face, still chewing. Isaiah turned to him and slapped the back of his head then turned back to the screen, Trey's grin got even bigger.

If I wouldn't have been freaking out again I would have rolled my eyes. Men. Sex and food. Seriously. Trey was a walking cliché.

"Fine!" I huffed and tried to push Gunner out of the way so I could stomp to the door but he didn't budge. Instead he grabbed my hand in his, turned and pulled me out of the room. I glanced at Marina who was bugging her eyes out at me as if to say *oh shit* and I returned the look.

Gunner pulled me all the way to his office slamming the door behind us, then pushing me down into a chair while he stood leaning against the desk behind him and crossing his arms over his chest.

It would have looked hot if I wasn't freaking out, and even then, it still looked pretty hot.

"You've got to let me take care of this Gunner. I *need* to." I stressed the one word hoping he would comprehend what I meant.

He looked up and let out a long breath and then tilted his head back down to me. I know I look desperate, because I am. If he does something with the information on that drive my plan to make Brian Hanson pay in every possible way I can think of will be toast.

"Tell me your plan."

Well, at least he's not yelling anymore.

"My plan is sensitive," I tell him, pleading with my eyes for him to understand. "There are two parts. If you do something with that," I say pointing at the drive. "Then he might go down, but not as hard as he should. The timing has to be right."

He's staring at me with those eyes, making me fidget. I really shouldn't have tried hiding that drive with him in the room. I got sloppy in hopes of putting an end to this once and for all.

"Okay, let's talk this through," he sighs, finally calm.

He moves from the desk and sits in the chair beside me, then pulls my arm so I'm no longer in my chair but on his lap. This annoys me, because he tries to keep me close and I want distance if we have to discuss this. It's hard to be strong and rational when you're sitting on someone's lap. Especially Gunner's lap. When I'm near him I want to lean on him and not think of anything other than how good it feels to be close to him.

"You should let me go," I whisper. "I don't want to taint what we have with this."

"There is nothing you could say or do that would taint this."

That was nice. Sweet even, but I didn't believe it. I tried to move from his lap but he kept a firm grip on me and didn't allow it.

"Josie, I know what happened. I also know you're planning to bring him down. What I don't understand is why you feel like you have to do it alone."

"I am alone, Gunner," I tell him the truth.

I feel his body tense underneath me and he turns my face to his and asks, "Didn't you hear what I said to you last night? Did it sink in at all?"

Now it's my turn to tense up. Here we go again. I don't know what else to do, so I'm just going to have to lay it out for him.

"I heard you Gunner, and maybe you believe that right now, but you will change your mind. I know you will. Someone like me is not meant for someone like you. You're smart, and hot, and successful, and you're a good guy. You don't see it now, but I *am* tainted.   You should have someone who is beautiful, and normal, and smart, and..."

"Jesus, you are so fucked by the things that have happened to you, you can't even see that you *are* all of those things. You aren't what was done to you, Josie, you are *you*. And I love *you*," he professed in a strong steady voice giving me a gentle shake with each emphasized word. "And babe, you do not make my decisions. I decide who I want to be with, and what I want in my life. Don't tell me I don't know what I'm doing."

God. Every time he used the word love it was like a knife slashing through my chest. I had to make him understand.

I looked him dead in the eye and told him the honest to God truth. "Please stop saying that! You can't say that and then change your mind later. You can't offer everything I've ever wanted, to feel loved and safe, and to feel that I *belong* somewhere." I shook my head making the tears finally fall, "You don't understand. You say I'm a survivor, and I am, but I won't survive this. I won't survive believing I have it and then having it taken away from me when this doesn't work."

I was desperate to make him understand. I took his face in my hands and said, "Look in my eyes and know that I am telling you the absolute truth when I tell you I will not survive that."

"Josie..."

"No. Please. Stop." I begged. Couldn't he see this was killing me?

He stood abruptly and set me on my feet with a thud, then he started pacing. His hands were on his head as he did this, and I thought this was a bad sign.

"I should go..."

I started to turn when I heard him mutter, "I bought you bubble bath." Then he walked behind his desk and opened a drawer and smacked a bottle down on top of it.

"I swear to God I don't know how to get through to you. I'm trying my damnedest to keep you safe. I've been watching you struggle, and I fuckin' hate it, but I try not to step in. Try to give you your space. I've tried to go slow and be gentle and not push, but *fuck* woman! You won't believe my words, and they say actions speak louder than words, so believe my actions. What do my actions tell you?"

This was a good question. Surely I could make him see the light. I start thinking over the past several weeks with Gunner. Let's see, so it started as a job for Gunner. A job he turned down to help keep me safe. This was before I even knew about the job. He put in the alarm system to help keep me safe. He took care of my garden. He took me to the beach. He took care of Freddy. He followed me to watch out for me. Okay, well that was still kind of weird, but I know he meant well. He didn't push me to ride in elevators. He gave me many, many, many amazing orgasms. He gave me a safeword to use in bed in case I freaked out. He was there for me when I had to share my past with my friends. I kept going over everything. I couldn't find anything that disproved him.

Not.

One.

Thing.

Then my eyes moved to the bottle of bubble bath. It was just last night when I wanted to soak in bubbles and he didn't have any. Today he went out to buy me bubbles. On this my eyes filled again and I looked at him watching me as I worked through all of this in my head.

"Light dawns. Thank fuck!" he muttered going back to the chair and putting me in his lap again.

Now that I started I couldn't stop crying as I thought of all the things Gunner had done for me in such a short time. I was wrong about him, and that hurt me, because I knew the way I acted probably hurt him.

"I'm sorry..." I said with my head on his shoulder as he held me close.

"It's okay, baby."

"No. It's not!" I bawled. "I haven't been very nice, and you have been nothing but nice to me. I mean, you're bossy, but you've always been so nice to me."

He gave me a squeeze and assured, "Baby, it's *okay*. I get where you're coming from. But you've got to get where I'm coming from, and now I think you do."

I nodded and sniveled against his neck as he squeezed me even tighter.

God, I love him. I do. Totally and completely, and he loves me back! Part of me wanted to laugh and dance and shout even as I was making a mess of his shirt with my tears.

"Now, I'm going to take the rest of the day and work from home so we can discuss some shit."

Uh oh. I know what *that* means.

Instead of arguing, I nodded and leaned over to grab the bubbles, "Alright, but I'm taking the bubbles with us."

Gunner threw back his head and laughed and it made me smile, even with a wet face, because I loved that laugh, and he looked seriously hot normally, but especially when I could make him laugh.

Chapter 45

Gunner

I took Josie back to my apartment. I told the guys (and Marina) to call my cell if anything important came up, otherwise I made it known that we were not to be disturbed. It was time that Josie and I were straight with each other. I was holding back information from her, and apparently she was doing the same.

I still can't believe she tried to hide that fuckin' flash drive in my office while I was sitting right there. Honestly, I almost missed it, and thank God I didn't. The thought of her going after that motherfucker by herself makes my blood freeze.

First things first though. She finally got it. She understands I am not messing around when I say that I love her. Last night when it slipped out I knew she was going to freak out. I just didn't understand how deep her fear was.

I kept thinking about when she looked me dead in the eye while sitting on my lap in my office, and told me what was holding her back.

I won't survive believing I have it and then having it taken away from me.

Fuck.

Fuck.

Fuck.

That made my gut hurt.

I know she's just starting to see it, and she will probably freak out again, but I swear to God I will do everything in my power to make her feel safe and loved.

When I got her to my apartment, I laid her down and for once, I didn't lose myself and fuck her as hard as I always wanted to. I gave her slow and sweet and gentle. Something I have never been good with, and something I've never wanted, but Josie needed that, and I wanted to give it to her. I needed to show her that.

With Josie, seeing the look in her eyes and her reaction to me, I knew it was the right move. That doesn't mean that I won't fuck her brains out later, because I will, but now we have got to get some shit straight.

"Alright baby," I said as I sat in a stool at the bar and watched her looking through my cupboards for something to make for dinner. She was wearing my t-shirt again and I don't think there was a sight I liked any better in the world. "We've got to come clean. I've got info to share, and so do you. I think we've made it clear today that we are in this together, so I want you to lay it out for me and I will do the same."

"You've got info?" She turned to ask, her eyes curious.

"Yeah babe. You didn't think I would sit idly by after the shit you told me did you? You do realize my line of work, right?"

"Well, yes, but..."

"Been checking things out. I've got markers called in Josie. I told you that I would deal with that motherfucker and I meant it."

Her eyes get round. Sweet. I love that look.

"So what did you find?" she asks still looking surprised.

"I'll tell you, but first you're going to tell me about this plan."

At this she turns and starts going through the cabinets again, but I know she isn't paying attention to what she's seeing.

"Stop looking Josie, we'll order in."

I get some menus, we decide to order Chinese food, then after it's called in I take her out to the balcony. I sit her in a lounge with her legs pulled over my lap so we can talk.

"Tell me how you got what's on that drive."

I watch as she purses her lips.

"We're in this together. You are not alone. You have to trust me with this plan so I can help."

"I... well... I kind of hacked into his computer, and the company's computer system. And some of it is from when I worked in the company, but I've gotten a lot more since then."

Holy fuck.

"You can hack?"

"I'm good at it," she smiles.

That's my girl. Smart, but also too innocent for her own good.

"That stuff is going to be inadmissible in court." I inform.

"I know. That's why I need to contact Kyle Jackson and see if he will work with me."

There it is. I knew she was digging for something in that conversation with Walk. She might be on to something.

"So you think he will twist things and make it admissible? That's a big risk babe, you don't know him."

"I know, but Walker trusts him. I avoided contacting anyone in the Detroit police department because I didn't know who could be trusted or how they would treat the evidence. Now I know of someone. I figure if there are that many cops who are willing to bend the law to help the bad guys for a price, there have to be some good ones who will bend it to help the good guys."

She had a point. From what I knew of Jack, she may be right. Then again, she may not be. He would have to put his ass on the line. It's worth exploring, but after my experience on the force I felt it was a long shot. Most of the good guys didn't like the idea of bending rules. Even if it was for the greater good.

"So if we have someone who agrees to help make this evidence admissible, then what? You turn him in and that's that?"

"No. There's more." She says looking nervous as her foot starts bouncing in my lap.

I grab it and hold it.

"Tell me."

"He has a lot of money," she whispers.

"I know that."

"So at the very least he can afford the best defense possible. Or worse, with that kind of money he can still have power behind bars. Or worst of all, he buys his way out of trouble."

"And?"

"And I'm going to make it so he can't do that."

"How?"

"It's probably best you don't know this part," she says looking away.

"Josie don't clam up now. We're getting somewhere and I'm willing to help and make sure you stay safe, but I need to know what you're talking about here."

"Gunner, I can handle the money part. The first part of the plan is legal. Well, actually it's not considering how we'll have to go about getting the evidence to be admissible, but it will *appear* legal. The second part isn't legal, but it's necessary. The important part is the timing. The money can't be handled after he's in custody or it will be known he didn't handle it himself, as I plan to make it seem. It also can't be taken care of too soon or else he will be on a rampage. It's nothing more than some computer transactions that can't be traced anywhere except right back to Brian. Now it's your turn."

"Josie, do you really think you can handle having a man sent down for stealing when you're about to do the same damn thing?"

Her hesitant eyes turn fiery. Okay, maybe she can, but I know my girl. She's good right down to her core.

"That's bullshit and you know it. He may be going down for stealing because that's the only thing I can prove, but that is *not* why he has to pay. He's going to pay for what he did to me, even if I'm the only one who knows it. And besides, it's only stealing if I keep the money. I don't want his money, but I know exactly where to put it." She folds her arms across her chest and says, "Now I'm done sharing, it's your turn."

I have to admit, this is a side to her that I did not know existed. I'd seen her fiery before, but not like this. She was determined. She'd planned and prepared. As much as I wanted to be able to discount her plan, I saw the way her mind was going, and I have to admit, with proper handling it could work. It wasn't what I expected, and it certainly wasn't the route I'd have taken.

"We could just make him disappear."

I felt her body jerk in surprise and her horrified gaze swung up to meet mine.

"I'm just sayin', if I had my choice, I'd make sure the fucker was no longer able to use up good air."

"Gunner..."

"Seriously babe. Your plan has merit. And being who you are, it makes sense. It's just not how I'd handle it."

"You mean..."

"What I mean is he hurt you. He almost killed you. You've been living it for a long time. The fear, the fuckin' panic attacks, barely living your life. He's been strutting around town like a big man. I know this because I've checked. He's skated through trouble his whole life, not once seeing a consequence. He's a total piece of shit. Not anything good about him. Not one fuckin' thing."

419

"You've checked?" she breathes.

"Yes."

"And?"

"And like I said, he's a piece of shit who's up to no good. Has a history of violence, and not just with you, he's had legal issues before, but nothing that hurt him badly enough to make him see the error of his ways. Obviously, because now he also deals in the drug trade."

"What?" She sounds surprised.

"After what he did to you, do you think he's above running drugs?"

"Well… no. I just never knew he was into drugs."

"I had Caleb on him for a while. Then he went off the grid."

"Off the grid?"

"Yes, disappeared, so I brought Caleb back, but I'm watching for him. My guess is he figured out he's being looked into, especially since it's coming from multiple sources. He's not bright, like you said, but he's not completely stupid either or he never would have skated this far."

"Oh my God!" she half shrieks grabbing my arm. "He's looking for me! I've messed with him before and now he's looking for me. He could be here!"

"Baby, calm down. He can't get near you. Since he's been missing you haven't been alone anywhere and you won't be. We have to stay smart, which means I need you to listen and do what I say. That's why Caeb brought you to the office today."

"Oh my God!"

"Josie, you're safe."

"But what if he finds me? I thought I was safe doing this from across the state, behind a computer, but what if he knows?"

"Is there any way he can trace it to you?"

"No. But I think he would suspect me because he knows my computer skills. He upgraded his security not long ago. It was still shit, but he did it. Trying to prevent any more trouble and I bet he knows where that trouble is coming from. Me!"

"Josie, even if he does know it's you, he doesn't know where you're at, remember?"

"Right." She whispers putting her face in her hands. "But if he suspects, he will hunt me down. He already promised me that."

"We can end this," I share casually, trying not to freak her out anymore. "I'm not kidding. I know you don't want to clue me in on anything illegal, but let me ease your mind. I quit being a cop because I am perfectly fine with crossing that line. In my world, the end justifies the means, and I'm good with that. I am *not* good at letting a bunch of red tape stop justice from prevailing. I've done a lot of shit that isn't exactly within the confines of the law. Shit that includes making the decision on whether or not someone needs to disappear. Shit that ends with someone having two broken legs that never quite heal right. And after what he's done. I'm more than willing to make either of those happen."

I watched her swallow and try to think through what I just said. With someone like Josie, this option wouldn't even cross her mind. She's sitting behind a computer fighting him because that's the only way she can fight him and win. I understand that. I admire it too. I just want this shit to end for her and I don't like the idea of Brian Hanson having a state funded vacation for several years before he gets out and commences with being a drain on society.

I rub my hand over her legs, "Not trying to freak you out baby, I just want you to know, that I am more than willing to make this end."

"By disappear… do you mean… what I think you mean?"

"It's probably best if you don't know this part," I grinned throwing her own words back at her.

She stared.

I stared back.

"I have to think about this," she whispered.

422

"Okay," I said back, "just know if you want to stick to your plan, I'll help you, even if it wouldn't be my plan."

I want her to understand this. I want her to have the choice and feel like she's got the power in this situation. It isn't lost on me what this plan of hers symbolizes. I could also always have him taken out once Josie got her justice. I decided not to share this.

At my words she crawls into my lap and wraps her arms around me. "Thank you," she whispers in my ear.

"I'd do anything for you, babe."

She smiles, which I think is a good sign, considering I just offered to have someone whacked for her and she still crawled into my lap and curled up to me. I have to admit, I was a little worried about her reaction to me after that.

I smiled back and pulled her tight.

Yeah, my girl is getting it.

K. D. Smith

Chapter 46

Josie

I must admit, it's been a strange couple of weeks since the conversation with Gunner after he found the drive.

First of all, I wasn't quite sure how to handle all of the information that came out that day. Not only did Gunner Layne say he loved me, but he also told me that he can make people disappear.

I knew he was a little scary, and I suspected that he didn't really follow any kind of rules. I got this from knowing that he quit being a police officer for the reasons he did. I also saw the employees and friends he surrounded himself with, and those were not people who were afraid of breaking rules. I also sensed he could handle getting physical if those circumstances came about, but I didn't know he could take someone out! I mean... who actually knew someone who could do *that*?

It didn't change my feelings for him one single bit, and I think he was worried that it might. As far as I am concerned, I know what I need to know about Gunner. He may be dangerous, but he's a good man. I suspected any of the times he's gone to extreme measures were exactly what he said. The end justifying the means. I know he isn't the kind of person who would take that lightly.

It was tempting to take him up on his offer. If that makes me a bad person, then I guess I am a bad person. The idea of never having to worry about Brian again was very appealing. There would be no worrying about if and when he would be released. There would be no trial to worry through. There would be no anticipation of retribution. It would be over. Once and for all. I was surprised by how much I liked the idea.

It's not like I hadn't plotted his murder in my mind a million times. Each time being more painful than the last. I imagined it often. I even dreamed of it. That didn't mean I could go through with it.

Having his blood on my hands would be something I'd have to live with every day. Knowing that, I just couldn't do it. I struggle enough with anxiety and shame, I didn't think adding a murder to that would be wise for my own well-being.

Brian still hadn't resurfaced and this made me uneasy. Yes, Gunner was keeping me safe, but I wanted to put an end to this. I'd waited a long time to be able to execute my plan, and now that I had everything lined up, the asshole had disappeared.

I broached the subject with Gunner of going ahead with the plan. If anything, it would make

Brian a wanted man, which meant he would probably be found sooner rather than later. In other words, I was ready to move forward in hopes of flushing the bastard out.

The good news is that Gunner had recruited Walker and his friend Jack to help. I also learned that Gunner and Walker had additional evidence about the drugs. Evidence that led to Jack to being able to get a warrant when the time came. Once jack had the warrant, nobody would question the evidence that he 'found'. It would all be admissible.

A few days ago Gunner had Trey pick me up and take me to his office and when I arrived Walker and Jack were already deep in conversation with him. I wasn't sure what was shared, but I got the sense that Jack was more than willing to help.

I knew this because when I walked into the office all of their faces turned to me and they all had that familiar scowl that Gunner had when he was hearing something he didn't like.

This made me pause in the doorway wondering if I should leave and come back in when they finished. But Gunner being Gunner, wiped the scowl off his face and introduced me to a still scowling Jack.

Jack shook my hand and said, "I'm in."

Yep, that's all he said.

That was enough for me, so I smiled at him and breathed, "Really?"

Then for some strange reason he turned to Gunner, shook his head and said, "I get it. Pure sunshine."

I ignored that because I had no idea what he meant, but I was so pleased that I could have done a happy dance right there. I knew it was a lot to ask of him, he was a nice guy and a good cop and even though he wanted to help us, it was a risk for him, but he also got to take all the credit for bringing Brian down. I suspect he would have helped anyway though, even if he didn't get the credit.

After some details were discussed Walker and Jack left the office and I told Gunner that I was going to make them both a trifle, to which Gunner said, "Fuck."

So I quickly assured him that I'd make him one as well. Then he asked if he could use me as a plate and eat it off of me. This made me feel tingly all over, especially somewhere private, so I agreed. After that, I had my first sexual experience on a desk, and let me tell you. I highly recommend it.

That brings me to now, and it's all about to come to an end and I can't describe my feelings. I'm excited to end it. I'm also nervous as can be that something will go wrong.

Jack was in the process of the getting the warrant. That means my plan to strip Brian of his power, which all came from money, was next because Jack told us that once he had the warrant things would move quickly.

With shaking fingers I logged into my computer to access Brian Hanson's accounts. I looked at Gunner nervously and said, "This is it."

"It's about time Josie. You've been dealing with this shit long enough. Let's take him down."

I gave him a nod and forged ahead. Gunner watched me work as I accessed information.

"Jesus, babe. You've got serious skills. I think you should work for me."

My fingers instantly stopped moving on the keyboard as I threw him a look. "Could you please not freak me out while I'm trying to deal with millions of dollars?"

He grinned, but didn't apologize.

I decided to ignore that and keep working.

"Where did you learn how to do this?"

"College. Being a techie nerd pays off at last, now shhhhh."

I needed to concentrate. I also didn't want Gunner thinking about me as a techie nerd.

I moved funds, I made donations, I covered my tracks, and an hour later I logged out and let out a long breath that felt like it'd been locked away for years. Maybe it had.

I looked at Gunner.

He looked at me.

I smiled.

He smiled back.

"How do you feel?" he asked.

"Great!" I yelled, jumping up from my chair and shouting, "Take that sucka!" with my hands in the air.

Freddy looked at me and barked.

Gunner laughed and came closer putting his hands around my waist.

"You did it, I'm proud of you."

I wrapped my arms around his neck and leaned into him. God, how did I get so lucky?

"Thanks," I whispered. "You think Walker and Jack are going to figure out what I did?"

"I'm sure they will suspect, but it's best they have no knowledge."

I knew what I just did was completely illegal and I didn't want them to get in any trouble, even though I didn't think anyone could trace it, I wanted to shield them from that part of it. They already put their neck on the line for me, and they did that because of Gunner. I knew that. If

I wasn't Gunner's girl, I wouldn't have gotten the help.

"Thank you," I whispered, kissing him.

He kissed me back whispering, "Anything for my girl."

Then he took me to bed so we could celebrate.

K. D. Smith

Chapter 47

Josie

It's been a month since I transferred Brian's funds. Not long after that, there was a warrant put out for his arrest. He still hasn't surfaced. Although I'm not exactly happy about this, I'm not letting it paralyze me. For the first time in my life I feel safe. I feel vindicated. Of course it doesn't erase what he did to me, that's always going to be there, but I no longer feel like a victim, and it shows in almost every aspect of my life.

My workouts with Kai have been awesome. My visits with Dr. Palmer have been progressive instead of upsetting. Obviously she has noticed the change, but she doesn't know all of the reasons behind it.

Not only that, things have been easier with my friends now that I'm not hiding anything from them. Eddie has taken time to stay with me when Gunner can't, because it's very rare that I am left alone these days. Gunner is still making sure I'm protected until Brian is found.

Isaiah has been to almost every mojito night at Justine's house unless he's working. He's really taken to Levi. Justine hasn't shared details, but I suspect she's got it *bad* for Isaiah. I know Justine, and if he weren't important to her she'd be talking up a storm, as usual. The fact that she's not saying much at all tells me that she cares for him more than she intended. I don't know how Isaiah feels, but I like the way he is with her. He's sweet and protective the way Gunner is with me. This led to some knowing smiles passing between me and Justine while drinking mojitos.

Faith is still being secretive, but she's always around to be supportive. With everything that's been going on I haven't had time to find out more about what she's up to. Gunner hadn't mentioned anything about it, but since he had his normal case load on top of the search for Brian, I figure he'll get around to it when he's able. That's one of the first things I plan to handle after everything has been cleared up.

So many things changed since Gunner first barged into my life. Even though I fought it, looking back, I can't imagine where I would be now without him. Life feels serene for the first time since I can remember. That's the only reason I can do what I'm about to do.

I took the package I ordered online from my bedside drawer. I open it and stare at a pair of handcuffs. The old Josie would *never* do this. I toy with the cuffs and get familiar with the feel of them. I try the key in them to make sure they work. Then I set the key on the night stand beside the bed.

I look in the mirror again taking in my appearance and try to mentally prep myself for what I'm about to do. This is something the old Josie would *never* wear. I have on a sheer, red lace nightie that is tight *everywhere,* and conceals nothing. And I do mean *nothing*. You can see straight through it. The only other thing I have on is red stilettos w th a sexy ankle strap.

All I need to add is my wrist accessories.

Holy shit! I can't believe I'm doing this.

I've overcome a lot of fears since being with Gunner. Many of them sexual. The one thing I hadn't done was let him tie me up. Not that he asked. He never mentioned it, but knowing Gunner and how he likes control, I know that it's something he'll like.

I have to admit, in the place I'm at now, where I trust him completely, the idea turns me on. Like, *a lot*. I know he would never do anything to hurt me, but I know he will dominate me beyond comprehension.

Yippee!

Since this is a surprise for Gunner, and I had to be able to prepare myself, I opted for the cuffs instead of rope. I had no idea how I would go about tying myself, but I thought I could handle cuffs on my own.

This is something I've been thinking of for a while, obviously, since I ordered the hand cuffs a while ago. But once they arrived, I couldn't find the right time or opportunity. I needed time alone to get ready, and Gunner *never* left me alone, but tonight he got called away and I immediately started planning when the opportunity presented itself.

I opened one cuff and put it over my wrist listening as it made a *click, click, click, click* noise when I closed it over my wrist.

At this juncture I start contemplating everything that could go wrong. Freddy is sitting beside the bed looking at me with his head cocked to the side as if he's already anticipating problems.

What if Gunner doesn't show up on time?

What if Faith comes home early?

What if we lose the key and I'm stuck in handcuffs forever?

Then I realize I'm thinking like the old Josie. This is the new Josie, the one who doesn't live in fear.

With that thought, I laid back on the bed, slid the other cuff around one of the wrought iron panels in the headboard and put my wrist inside the other cuff.

Okay, maybe I'll just wait until I actually hear Gunner before I slide it closed and trap myself.

Should I text Faith, just in case? What would I say? 'Hey! I'm cuffing myself to the bed for some kinky sex, when you get home make sure I'm free.'

Right. I would never live that one down. Then I secretly smile to myself thinking about how fun this surprise is going to be.

As I'm lying there in mental limbo trying to decide what to do, to wait or not to wait, Freddy made a huffing noise and quit staring at me to turn his head toward the door. Gunner!

Here goes nothin'!

Click, click, click.

Freddy takes off with a warning growl, then I hear the door open and the alarm start beeping.

I can't wait until Gunner walks in here and I can see his face when he notices I'm cuffed to the bed. He's going to be so surprised!

I heard Freddy growl again and it didn't sound right. That is not how Freddy would greet Gunner, or Faith, or Rick, or anyone he's familiar with.

I froze listening for any sign about what was happening. I feel like ice water is running through my veins.

A few more seconds and the alarm went from beeping to blaring. Nobody punched in the code. Freddy snarled and I heard a man's voice.

"Shut the fuck up, mutt!"

Oh my God!

Oh my God!

Oh my God!

I know that voice and all of the hairs on my body stand up when I hear it again. I would never forget it in a million years.

Brian!

I have to get out of here!

I did the only thing I could, I yelled the command for Freddy to attack as I tried to pull my hands out of the cuffs.

Freddy understood, because his snarl went vicious and I heard Brian scream.

Completely in panic mode, I just keep yelling the command and Freddy kept at it, until all the sudden he stopped and I heard a high pitched whine.

No no NO!

I manage to get one hand through the last cuff I had started clicking but hadn't finished and I pulled my hands free, the handcuffs still dangling from one wrist. Then I saw him appear in the doorway.

Oh my God!

It's him! Only he looks like haggard. He doesn't look anything like I remember. He's bleeding from Freddy's attack, but it isn't only that. His hair is long and dirty. His clothes are dirty. He looks like a homeless person, and worst of all, he looks *insane*. And he has a knife in his hand.

"Turn off that fuckin' alarm!" he screeches at me.

This is it, my opportunity to get away, so I immediately nod, pretending to agree, and push past him running for the alarm. I stumble a bit and choke back a sob when I see Freddy on the floor with blood all over his fur, but I know I can't stop.

Oh God, I'm so sorry Freddy!

Brian is behind me but I know he's hurt. Instead of putting the code into the alarm, I hit the panic button, just like Gunner taught me and I run out the door.

I'd give anything for my running shoes right now.

Damn it!

I'm so stupid! How did I let this happen? I've prepared myself for his violence for years, and now here I am in stilettos!

I've gotten a little ways up the street and he's not moving very fast. I duck behind a car and start unbuckling these motherfucking ridiculous shoes.

Shit, shit, *shit!*

Why didn't I wear the kind without buckles? Why did I wear them at *all*?

I hear someone approaching and I finally get my feet free of the shoes, crouching as I circle the car trying my damnedest not to breathe too loud.

I hear a shuffle past the car and I raise myself up enough to peer through the car to the other side and my heart stops.

Brian is there and Mr. Williams is heading this way wearing his bathrobe.

He spots me before Brian does and shouts, "There's my girl!" Until he gets a better look at me and barks, "What the hell are you doing out here in your nightgown?"

Under normal circumstances I would find his question ironic, but I don't have time to worry about that, I start running back towards the house leading Brian away from Mr. Williams.

I hear his labored breathing behind me. He grunts, "Get back here you little bitch!"

I feel his hand grab the ends of my hair and I falter but pull free. I feel gravel grinding into the bottom of my feet but I ignore it and go as fast as I can. I swear I can feel him closing in and I take a sharp turn into the street. I can go to Ricks! The idea gives me a burst of energy and I run full out for the house screaming my head off.

I see the lights are off, but I hope Rick is asleep and not gone. I make it to the door looking behind me to see Brian is still not far behind. I bang on the door and keep yelling for someone to open it, but nobody does.

I run around the side of the house to try the back door and just as I reach it Brian comes barreling around the other side of the house. I turn and head through the yard but I stepped on something sharp and as soon as I start to hobble I feel an arm close around my neck and wrench me backward.

No!

My mind is screaming and I start to put my self-defense moves to use by stomping on his foot, but without shoes it doesn't faze him. I go for an elbow to the ribs and hear him groan with contact so I try pulling away but he pulls me back with one arm and shoves the blade of the knife into my face.

I stop fighting.

"I always knew you were a fucking slut!" he murmurs in my ear.

Then he raises the knife and brings the end of the handle down smashing it in the side of my face.

Once.

Twice.

I saw it coming a third time and everything went black.

Chapter 48

Gunner

I'm in a hurry to get back to Josie's house knowing that she's alone. I'm also in a hurry because she told me she had a surprise for me tonight. If I know my girl, it's gonna be something kinky. I can always tell by the look on her face when she's got her mind in the gutter. I love it.

When my phone rings I figure it's her, but it's an unknown number.

"Layne."

"Mr. Layne? This is Edna Williams. Josie's neighbor."

She sounds upset and I start hoping that her husband isn't out wandering around somewhere right now because I really want to get to Josie.

"You gave me your card, and well, Sam was out and he said he saw Josie running down the sidewalk in her nightie and that someone was chasing her."

My heart hammers at her words.

No!

"I didn't know whether or not to believe him, because...well, you know... So I, oh Goodness, I came down here to see if she was alright, and the door was wide open and Freddy... Freddy's hurt."

Motherfucker!

"Have you called the police?"

"They just got here. They said someone pushed a panic button?"

"I'm almost there," I told her and hung up trying not to break my phone by throwing it or squeezing the hell out of it.

I can't believe I let her stay by herself!

If anything happens to her I'm never going to forgive myself.

When I pull up I see a squad car with lights flashing and people milling around. I swing out of the truck and don't even bother to shut the door. I go inside and see things in disarray as if there has been a struggle. I don't stop to let myself think about that. There's blood on the door and on the floor. My heart sinks and I feel a rage building inside of me that I'm not familiar with.

Please God, don't let that be Josie's blood.

I see Mrs. Williams sitting on the floor talking softly to Freddy and I feel a heavy weight settle

444

in my gut. I can't even stop to check on Freddy. The only thing I can do is find Josie. My mind won't process anything else.

I walk through the house, and don't see any other signs of trouble and I don't see Josie anywhere. There's a candle burning in her bedroom and I blow it out. It reminds me of the surprise she had planned for me because my girl always likes candles when we're in bed.

Jesus, now she's out there running.

In a fuckin' nightie!

I can't even think that she's not still running. She can't be caught. I remind myself that my girl knows how to run, and she knows how to fight. Suddenly I'm grateful for all of those sessions at the gym.

I take in her phone that's still sitting on her dresser and feel that rage build even further. Whatever happened didn't even allow her the time to grab her phone.

Walker arrives as I walk into the living room. Mr. Williams follows wearing a bathrobe and holding a pair of red heels.

"Don't know why that girl had on these shoes with a nightie, but she left them in the street."

"Christ! She's out there running from that asshole barefoot!" I roar at Walker.

"You need to keep calm Gunner, we're not sure this is Brian."

"Bullshit! You know it's him just as well as I do."

Walker knows. I can see it in his eyes, but he's trying keep me calm.

Mr. Williams goes to sit by his wife who is now talking to Freddy as an EMT is looking at him.

Walker talks to the EMT and then joins me outside.

"Freddy has a stab wound, but he'll make it."

My eyes burn into his and I don't respond.

"By the looks of the blood around his mouth, he gave worse than he got."

Thank fuck! That's the best news I've heard so far. If he's injured Josie has a much better chance of getting away.

"Listen Gunner, I know how much you care about her, but we gotta play this smart. You can't bulldoze everybody and go off half-cocked."

"You see those shoes she was wearing? She was wearing those for *me*. Waiting in bed for *me* to get here. *I* left her here alone, and now she's out there somewhere *barefoot, in a fucking nightgown, running from a psycho*!" I shout at him getting louder with each word.

"We'll get her back Gunner," he says placing a hand on my shoulder, trying to calm me.

I turn my back on him and pace away.

"Walker, one of the neighbors said they saw a man carrying a woman and putting her in a car," I hear a young officer saying. I get a rundown of the car, a silver Lexus, no plates, and I dial my phone to wake up Trey. His computer skills aren't as good as Josie's, but I need them right now or I'm going to be stuck here all night trying to cut through this police bullshit.

I assemble my team and put them to work. Trey is searching electronically for anything he can find and calling out hits to us. Caleb and Isaiah are out searching, and now so am I. Walker is keeping me updated from his end.

Every silver Lexus in the county has been searched out one way or another tonight. Still, no signs of Josie, but I know I'm ahead of the game, the police are probably still searching out the vehicle reports. I've covered almost all of them between me and my men.

With each dead end, we widen the search to a new area, avoiding any areas Walker reports in so we don't waste time. I can only assume Brian's heading East towards Detroit, but I have to cover all the bases.

It's now been 3 hours since Josie was last seen and with each passing minute I get more worried. I can't allow myself to think about what he might have done to her. I knew I should have put a hit on that fucker. *Fuck*!

I'm heading to a hotel on the east side of town to check out another silver Lexus being reported when my phone rings. I'm expecting Trey so I keep my eyes on the road and put it to my ear.

"Talk."

At first I don't hear anything, and then I hear the softest whisper, "Gunner?"

Jesus, I feel relief flood every ounce of me.

"Josie? Tell me where you are." I don't mean to shout at her but I'm so fucking relieved to hear her voice.

"I... I..." she keeps whispering sounding confused. "I don't know."

"It's ok baby, you keep this phone on and we'll track you. Okay?"

"Okay," she whispers so softly I can barely hear her.

"Hold on for me Josie, I need to get this number," I quickly pull the phone from my ear, get the number and relay it to Trey.

When I get back to her line I ask, "Are you alone?"

"No."

"Brian?"

"Y... yes," she starts to cry and I can hear her voice shaking."

"I'm coming for you baby, you stay with me, okay?"

"I think I might be in a ho... hotel. I'm on a bed"

Fuck, fuck, *Fuck!*

I take a deep breath and try not to think about what that means.

"Okay Josie, can you look around, tell me what you see?"

"It's dark," she whispers, and the fear in her voice cuts through me. I can sense how afraid she is, and I can tell the she's probably hurting but I don't ask about any injuries yet. I just need to get to her so I can take care of her.

"Do you remember where he was driving?"

"No."

I ignore that too, because I know what that means.

"My arm is tied. Oh God Gunner, please hurry!"

"Okay baby, I'm coming, you just hang in there."

"Freddy..." she says in a pained voice.

"He's going to be okay," I offer her the little bit of comfort I can.

She lets out a broken sob and it fucking kills me. I swear that Brian Hanson is about to be a dead man. I'm going to finish the job that Freddy started, if it's the last thing I do.

"Shhh baby, don't cry he might hear you if he's close."

"He... he..." she stops and I hear a man in the background.

"Give me that fuckin' phone!" he spits at her and I hear a scream and a thud, and then dead air.

I let out a roar and hit the steering wheel.

God damn it!

Chapter 49

Josie

I cringe away from him with a scream as he throws the phone across the room. I can see now, he turned on a light. Well, at least I can see out of one eye. It is a hotel. Or a motel. It's smells terrible and looks even worse.

I don't know how he got me here. The last thing I remember is being in Rick's yard. The pain in my face reminds me of the blows.

When I woke up I had one armed tied to a headboard and Brian was stretched out beside me. I could smell his blood and filth invading my senses. Fighting the urge to vomit, I tried to focus on the outlines of what I could see.

I moved and the bed creaked so I stopped instantly. Brian didn't move. As I started to remember more, his injuries came back to me. He managed to get me here, but I knew he was bleeding a lot. I could smell it.

I risked another movement, and he didn't stir.

I hope you're dead! I screamed in my head.

Okay, think Josie. *Think!*

He wasn't moving, but he was breathing. I leaned a little closer, trying to make out the knife in hopes of getting my hands on it, but I couldn't see a damn thing.

I took a shaky breath and risked a touch.

Oh God, please don't wake up!

With a shaky hand, I lightly felt for his pocket nearest to me, running my fingers over it to see if the knife was there. Nothing. I inched closer to try the other one. Slowly, barely breathing, I reached over him and I traced my shaking fingers over the other side until I found the pocket.

Bingo!

Please don't wake up, please don't wake up, please don't wake up!

I pushed my fingers into his pocket as softly as I could when he jerked and mumbled, I stifled a scream and pulled my hand back. My heart was beating like a sledge hammer as I tried to pretend I wasn't conscious.

He moved a little, but then settled again and I waited. I wanted to make sure he was out before I tried again.

It seemed like an eternity, but in reality it was probably ten minutes. Then I tried again. I tried to control my shaking as I slowly reached across his body, holding my breath.

I got my fingers into the pocket, thinking it was the knife, but it wasn't. I felt hard plastic. I slowly pulled it centimeter by centimeter up and out of his pocket as carefully and slowly as I could with my shaking hand.

A phone!

Yes!

I turned to my side, facing away from him as far as my arm would allow and waited again. When he didn't move, I shoved my head under the pillow with the phone and waited another few beats, then I dialed Gunner.

That was how he caught me on the phone and ended up throwing it across the room.

"You stupid little bitch," he spits at me. Then he goes crazy, picking up the phone and hurling it again.

"God damn it! Now we have to leave!"

I don't say anything, I just watch and try not to be terrified.

I can tell by the way he's moving that he's hurt badly, but he doesn't stop. He yanks out the knife.

Shit. Back pocket. I shove that into my memory.

He stalks towards me and I crawl back into the bed as far as I can. I see my arm is tied to the headboard. The same wrist that is still adorned with a set of handcuffs. My wrist is sore from trying to pull free when I first woke. He yanks my arm outward painfully and then slices through the rope dragging me out of bed.

"You're going to put back every dime, do you understand me?" He snarls at me an inch from my face. He looks like a demon. I remember what Gunner said about the drugs, and it's obvious he's on something.

I nod my head to appease him. Seeing his evil eyes, and having him near me made me want to vomit. The memories of what this man is capable of are flooding my mind. My breath is coming too fast and I fight to control it knowing what will happen if I don't.

"Did you think I wouldn't know it was you? All of my money donated to those women's bullshit crisis centers!"

Again, I didn't think it was wise to answer that question. I mean, yes, I figured he would know it was me. I also thought he would be behind bars before he could do anything about it. I thought it was the perfect way to take everything from him. His money would help thousands of rape and abuse victims while he was rotting away. To me, *that* was justice. That's why he's not getting a dime of it back. Even if I could do it, which I can't, I wouldn't.

"You're going to give me back my money, and if you do, I'll consider letting you live." He leans in menacingly grabbing me by the back of the hair and pushing me around until I'm headed to the door.

"Do you understand me?" he yanks my hair as he asks, before opening in the door.

I try nodding again, which isn't easy when you feel like your hair is being pulled out by the roots. My voice failed me, I couldn't speak. Of course, I don't mean it. He's not getting his money back, but I'm not telling him that. I'm buying time for Gunner to find me. Besides, I know Brian's lying. There is no way he's going to let me live. He already did that once. It came back to bite him in the ass.

"If you want to live, you're going to walk out this door and straight to the car without giving me any problems."

He pushes me out the door. I'm still barefoot and the bottoms of my feet are screaming at me. I know I have cuts on them and they burn as I walk, not to mention the pounding in my head. I hope somebody will see me. Surely a beaten up woman in a red nightie that shows *everything* will draw some attention. Then I realize the type of place we're in. People will probably think I'm a hooker with her pimp.

Oh God!

Taking in my surroundings, I see that we haven't gone far, we are still close to home. A surge of hopefulness settles into me. I assumed we were close to Detroit because I figured that's where he would take me. He really must be hurt if he stopped so close in order to rest. I feel another slice of hope settle as I realize the damage the Freddy inflicted.

Freddy...

He shoves me into the car and the only thing I can think is that he left the phone in the room, which means that when Gunner traces it, he's going to come here and I'm going to be gone. There's no way to track me from here.

In a split second decision, as he rounds the car I jump back out and run. I just have to buy time. Gunner will find me here. I know it. He's searching for me, and I know Gunner won't give up. I feel another piece of hope settle. I run across the front of the hotel, passing door after door as I hear Brian shout and then start to come after me.

There's no way he can outrun me. I know I can win, and again I feel it settle. I've prepared for this. I've learned how to run, I've learned how to fight, I've learned how to survive.

I pick up speed ignoring the pain searing through my feet. I'm almost to the side of the building, I just hope there's somewhere to go once I get out of his sight.

I turn the corner and start to pass the first door when it swings open, someone grabs me around the waist, pulls me through the door and shuts it. I let out a shriek before a hand settles over my mouth and I freeze. I can't figure out what's happening, my eyes are wide swinging from side to side trying to figure it out as I watch a hand lock the door in front of me.

I hear, "Don't scream, you need to stay quiet."

I don't recognize this man's voice. Without much of a choice I give a shaky nod and he releases my mouth. I turn to look at him. He looks a little familiar but I don't think I know him. He's tall, as in *really* tall. Taller than Gunner. He has sandy blond hair and a beard. There's a small scar across his eyebrow that makes him look even more menacing. He's wearing camouflage pants and a tight army green wife beater. His muscles are pronounced, as in *big time*.

I take all of this in as I think that I don't stand a chance against this guy. I'd rather take my chances with Brian any day. At least Brian is injured, he's strong, but nothing like this guy.

I start backing away to the door and he barks, "Don't move."

I freeze. I mean, what else am I going to do?

He moves to the window and looks out before turning back to me and moving again. I start to back away again, going the other way.

"I said don't move. You're safe in here."

I'm safe? Did he just say I'm safe?

"Um... I'm not safe," I inform him. "There's a crazy guy out there who kidnapped me and who's chasing me." I point at the window with a shaking finger. I think I've done pretty well at staying calm, but now I'm starting to lose it, I can feel it.

"I know, that's why I came to get you. Stay put. Lock this door behind me. Do *not* under any circumstances open that door unless it's me or Gunner. Got me?"

My breath hitches at the mention of Gunner. He must be one of Gunner's guys!

"You work for Gunner?" I whisper hopefully.

"No. Now tell me you understand."

"I understand," I whisper.

"Good girl," his voice rumbles at me, then he's out the door.

I run to it and lock it like he told me to.

I peek out the window but don't see anything. It's probably a bad idea to turn on a light, so I back up and sit on the bed. My feet are killing me, but I don't want to get occupied with trying to clean them up. Just in case I need to be able to run again.

On that thought I decide it's probably not best to sit right in front of the door, so I scoot between the bed and the wall. I curl my knees up into my chest and rest the side of my face that isn't pounding on them.

Then I wait.

And wait some more.

This isn't good. My adrenaline is crashing. I'm shaking and getting visions of Brian in my head. I see Freddy on my floor bleeding. I see Gunner's smiling face the last time I saw him.

Just keep it together a little bit longer Josie.

I start to rock back and forth while I hum. I focus on a song, repeating the words in my head, keeping my mind busy.

It's rainin' but there ain't a cloud in the sky

Must've been a tear from your eye

Everything'll be okay...

Waitin' on a sunny day...

I whisper the lyrics over and over, I don't know how long I do it, but I do it until I hear, "Fuck!"

I know his voice. I slowly lift my head and look at Gunner.

He crouches in front of me and looks at my face, and then says, "Fuck!" again.

"You should stop saying Fuck so much," I tell him softly.

His face warms at my words.

459

"It's a really bad habit," I continue.

"Fuck," he repeats as he looks over my body and sees my nightie. Which I really hate now, by the way.

"See?" I whisper. "You can't stop saying it."

Then he looks at my feet and growls, "motherfucker!"

I find that funny. Gunner doesn't. He scowls and I start to giggle because I'm thinking about making a swear jar for Gunner. Every time he says the F word he has to add a quarter. He could afford it, and I'd make a serious *load!* On that thought I giggle again.

I know it's crazy, but I can't help it.

He stands and then bends to pick me up. I think this is very nice of him considering how bad my feet hurt.

He sits on the bed, resting me on his lap. I continue to giggle hysterically and he just watches me with guarded eyes.

I hear sirens in the background and that totally brings me back to reality. Gunner feels it because my whole body tenses up in his lap.

"It's okay baby, you're safe now."

I don't know what to feel. The emotions swirling in me are extreme and I can't begin to process them. I wrap my arms around Gunner's neck and put my face down into his neck so he can't see me and I burst into tears.

K. D. Smith

Chapter 50

Josie

Turns out the man who rescued me at the hotel was Gunner's brother, Hunter. Gunner didn't even know he was back in town until he got to the hotel. Apparently Hunter has connections, and by that, I mean *connections*. At least that's how Gunner explained it when I asked him how Hunter knew about the kidnapping. It's also important to note that these connections aren't something they want to talk about. I figured it was best to let this go.

I also learned that Hunter stopped Gunner from killing Brian, by pulling him off of Brian's beaten body when the police showed up. I owed Hunter a big thank-you for that one. I really didn't want to survive only to spend the rest of my life visiting Gunner in prison.

After the police came and took Brian away, I was taken to the hospital to be checked out. They kept me overnight for observation because I had a concussion. Other than that, I only had a lot of cuts, bruises, and some stitches in my feet.

Gunner stayed the night in the hospital room with me. I knew Brian was being checked out in the same hospital, but was under guard. Just knowing Brian was in the same building freaked me out, but Gunner never left my side. Even when the Doctor examined me, he refused to leave the room.

He laid next to me that night and told me, "God baby, my heart stopped when I walked in your house and you were nowhere to be found. I saw that blood..." he cuts off clenching his jaw.

"It wasn't mine honey," I whisper trying to make him feel better.

"I know that now, but I didn't then, and I swear to God Josie, I almost lost my fuckin' mind."

I don't say anything I just scoot closer and rub my hand over his chest.

"Should have never left you alone..."

"Gunner," I whisper, "you couldn't have known. Don't blame yourself for this. I was the one who handcuffed myself to the bed while wearing stilettos. I mean seriously, how stupid was *that*?"

"Wait. You handcuffed yourself to the bed?"

"That was your surprise," I mumble. Geez, I can't even talk about it without turning red. Luckily the handcuffs had been removed, however, when I was talking to the police, I left out the part about using handcuffs on myself. Can you blame me? How embarrassing! "Luckily, I didn't get the second cuff closed all the way before I heard Freddy and knew something was wrong. That's how I got my hand out."

He doesn't say anything for a few minutes, and I can tell he's processing this new information.

"You handcuffed yourself to the bed?" He repeats.

"Yes, but if anyone else asks. I did *not*."

"You handcuffed yourself to the bed to surprise me?"

"See, I totally would have surprised you. Well, you know, if I didn't get kidnapped."

He's quiet again. Then he finally shares, "I don't know whether I should laugh, or spank your ass for doing that while you were home alone. Babe, you can't do that stuff without me around. What if you couldn't get loose?"

I ignore that question because I may be in the hospital, my head may feel like it's going to explode, and my feet hurt so bad I can't even put the sheet over them, but the instant Gunner mentions a spanking, my body turns liquid and I get tingly.

He recognizes that look and smirks at me. "Hold that thought," he whispers. "Once you're healed up, I'll take care of you. And next time handcuffs are used, I'll be doing the cuffing. Because I'm really pissed that I missed out on that."

That gives me another tingle. One that shoots right to my nipples and my clit.

Wow.

You'd think the idea of using cuffs again would repulse me, but with Gunner, I know I'm safe. However, I would never *ever* do it myself again.

Like, *EVER*.

"I owe you one." I tell him with a smile. "But next time you can do the cuffing."

"That's one I'm going to collect," he smiles back.

Our quiet time together didn't last long. Grand Rapids is a fairly large city, but it's also a small town in many ways. Word travels fast, especially when those words include things like abduction, psychopath, or kidnapping.

Faith made it to the hospital first busting through the door while the nurse loudly called after her, "Excuse me! It's past visiting hours!"

"Oh God!" She exclaimed ignoring the nurse. She came to the side of the bed I was on and sank down in a chair grabbing onto my hand tightly. "Oh God!" She repeated.

"I'm okay," I squeezed her hand in reassurance as tears once again hit my eyes. Seriously, I was all over the place. One minute I would crack a joke or get turned on and the next minute I would burst into tears.

"You're face!"

I winced. I hadn't seen my face yet. I knew by the way it felt that it was probably a good idea not to look yet.

"Are you really okay?" She half sobs the words. "I got home and saw the mess and the blood, and when I found out you were gone..." She breaks off shaking her head.

"Just a concussion and some stitches. I'm going to be fine." Oddly, I realized how much I meant those words. I can't tell you the amount of times I've been asked if I'm okay, or the amount of times I've said I was fine. It was never true. I never felt fine. You just say *fine* because that's what you're supposed to say, whether you mean it or not. But now I actually meant it. I *knew* that finally, I would be fine.

Brian would be put away for a long time, because now on top of everything else, he would be charged with kidnapping and assault. I would never have to worry about him coming after me again.

There's also the fact that Gunner loves me. I can have a normal relationship with a man I love. He knows everything and he still loves me. He would even help me go about committing a crime (technically), to ensure that I received justice. Some people might not see that as a positive, but I did.

In the next few hours I realized that my friends were not just any friends, they were the best friends *ever*. Every single one of them ignored visiting hours and barged into my hospital room.

Rick came in crying and swearing that he would never forgive me if I ever got kidnapped again.

Eddie was quiet and strong as usual, but I didn't miss the fact that after he told me he was glad I was okay he gave me a kiss on the forehead and then he disappeared with Gunner. No doubt to have some sort of manly conversation that resulted in talking about kicking someone's ass.

Mr. and Mrs. Williams came in and Mr. Williams finally had pants on. It almost seemed odd that he was dressed normally. They told me that Freddy was going to be okay. Brian stabbed him, but not fatally. He had been stitched up and given a sedative. I breathed a sigh of relief, even though Gunner told me earlier that he was going to make it, I was afraid to ask again. I thought

Gunner may have been protecting me from the truth at the time.

I knew that I had Freddy to thank for my escape just as much as Hunter and Gunner. If Brian hadn't been badly wounded by Freddy, I would most likely be in a very different situation right now.

Justine and Isaiah showed up after talking Trey into staying with a sleeping Levi. Isaiah went to join the ass kicking conversation with Gunner and Eddie while Justine informed me that, *that motherfucker is motherfucking cracked!*

This made me laugh, to which Justine said, "Girl, this shit is *NOT* funny!"

I don't know why, but looking around the room at my friends and hearing Justine swearing like a sailor made me feel good. The kind of good that made me feel comfortable. The kind of good that made me give in to my exhaustion and medication, and fall asleep while they were all still standing around.

Little did I know that when I fell asleep I was also visited by Walker and Jack. Then I missed it when Hunter came in, took one look at Faith, and walked right back out leaving her sitting there staring at the door while all the color drained out of her face.

Chapter 51

Gunner

When Josie was released from the hospital I tried to get her to come home with me. She wouldn't have it. I gave in mostly because she's been through enough and I don't want to upset her. My girl wanted to see her dog, so that's what we did.

Even I have to admit that it was a touching reunion. Josie stroked Freddy softly and talked to him and even through his sedated haze he responded to her. His only movement was to lift up his head and lick her wounded cheek. Josie fought tears while telling him what a good boy he was and promising him a lavish retirement if only he healed up quickly. Somehow I think Freddy understood this because I swear I saw him open one eye and shut it again.

After seeing Freddy and learning that he had a good prognosis and could likely come home in a few days, Josie seemed in a good mood. Although I must say, her mood since the whole ordeal took place was surprising to me. She had her moments when it all came rushing back, but for the most part she seemed to be doing great.

I'm suspicious of this and erring on the side of caution with her. Don't get me wrong, I'm glad she's bouncing back quickly, I just don't trust it. This is the same woman who was sent into a panic just from hearing the sound of a smack against her skin. I'm having trouble buying that she is as fine as she says.

Since she refused to come home with me, I'm going to have to talk her into it as soon as she's ready. I want her with me. Permanently. I need to know she's safe. Even with Brian contained, I still can't get the picture of her huddled behind a nasty motel bed while singing softly to herself, out of my head. That image will be burned into my memory for a long time, along with her bruised face.

Fuck, I can't think about that.

I decide to check my phone to see if there's a message from Hunter.

Nothing.

Unfortunately, if Hunter wants to go off the grid, there is no way to track him down.

I was surprised to see him at the motel when I got there looking for Josie. Apparently he's been home for a few weeks, but wasn't ready to see anyone yet. At least until he heard about the trouble with Josie. Hunter may be gone all the time, but he always keeps up on the pulse of the family.

He'll be in contact when he's ready, I just hope he's planning to stay awhile and I know Walker feels the same way. I didn't miss the strange vibe between him and Faith when he came to the hospital. Whatever happened between them must have been serious because Hunter isn't someone who gives much of a reaction to anything, but there was definitely a reaction there.

"You look deep in thought," Josie says from her spot on the bed, her eyes still sleepy from the nap I insisted she take.

"Just thinking about Hunter."

"Oh."

She knows that I can't share much information about Hunter so she doesn't ask. It's not so much that his work is highly questionable, dangerous, and confidential, which is all true, but it's more about the fact that I can't tell her what I don't know. Hunter's life since he joined the Army has been like an impenetrable vault.

"How're you feeling?" I ask brushing her hair off her face.

"I'll be better when my feet heal and I can walk like a normal person again."

On that statement she rolls and starts to push out of bed.

"What are you doing?"

"Going to the bathroom."

"Here. I'll take you."

She looks at me as if she's horrified by the thought.

"You're not taking me to the bathroom," she says incredulously.

"Babe, your feet are hurt."

"I am still capable of going to the bathroom by myself."

My stubborn girl. She's cute when she gets like this.

Instead of arguing with her I go over and pick her up.

"Gunner! Put me down!"

I walk her into the bathroom and put her down.

She glares up at me and I smile at her.

"Are you going to watch me pee, or are you going to leave?"

"You mean I have an option?"

"Get out!" she yells, slapping my arm.

I go outside and shut the door, laughing at how cute she is when I frustrate her. I make a note to do it more often. Might as well start now.

"You ready to come home with me?" I ask through the door.

"Gunner, I just got home," her muffled voice comes through the door.

"I know, but you had some rest. If you're ready I can start moving your stuff while you take it easy."

The door swings open, "What do you mean moving my stuff?"

"Well, you'll need your stuff if you're going to live with me."

Her eyes get big and round and she blinks at me in that sweet way of hers.

"I'm not living with you!"

"If you have to wait a couple days, then I'll stay here, but then you and Freddy are moving in with me where I can keep an eye on you."

"Keep an eye on me?"

"Yes."

"Uh... no."

"Yes."

"Uh Gunner? We are not living together."

"Babe, we are, so it's either you're ready now, or you want to wait a few days. But it's gonna happen."

"You can't just order me to move in with you."

"Just did."

She makes a frustrated noise and slams the door again.

I wait patiently for her to finish and when she opens the door again I pick her up and carry her back to bed.

"I wish you'd quit carrying me everywhere!"

"Shut up Josie, you're feet are hurt, let me help."

She sighs and then mumbles, "Fine, but I'm not moving."

"Do you love me?"

That question stuns her for a second and then she says softly, "You know I do."

"Okay, then it's settled."

"It most certainly is *not!*"

I can tell I'm going to have to bring her around to my way of thinking. On that thought I kiss her, which always makes her go quiet.

When I pull back I decide to lay it out for her.

"Josie, I almost lost you, and I cannot explain to you how that felt and I won't try, but I can tell you that it's something I *never* want to feel again. I protect what's mine, which means you and Freddy live with me so I can do that. The only other option is for me to live here. If you are set on staying here, I will, but baby, I gotta say, I like the idea of my place better. There's a lot more space and we won't have a roommate. We're going to need our privacy." I give her a grin when I see she's thinking about having privacy with me and she looks as if she likes the idea.

"Gunner..." she whispers.

"I'm not leaving you alone Josie, so what's it going to be?"

"But... What about Faith?"

"Faith will be fine, we'll make sure of that."

She doesn't say anything else, I can tell she's deep in thought so I stay quiet while she thinks. I know I can't force her to move, but I am prepared to move in here if I have to, that was no lie. I never thought I'd be doing this with a woman, but with Josie there's just no other options. She's mine and I need her close.

"This is so fast..." she whispers. "Maybe we should give it more time."

"I don't need any time Josie. You're with me, and I'm with you. We're together. That means we don't live separate because I can't take care of you that way."

"I don't need to be taken care of, I can take care of myself."

"I know you can, but what I mean is I need to take care of you the way a man takes care of a woman that he loves. I need to cherish you, watch over you, protect you, pleasure you, enjoy you..."

I know my voice is husky with feeling because I mean every single word, and so much more. I don't know how else to convey it, especially when she's recuperating, I just need her to... Well, I need her. Period.

I guess that's what I should have said to begin with.

"I need you with me Josie. I need you close."

She searches my eyes with her own teary ones. "Okay," she whispers.

I close my eyes in relief and ask, "How about today?"

"No! I need at least a week, Gunner, I just got home, and I can't pack yet because I can't stand that long. Besides, I want Freddy home and doing better first."

Well, I guess I can't have everything.

"Okay, a week, but I'll be staying here during the week."

She gives me a wobbly smile, "Okay Mr. Bossy."

Then as an afterthought she says, "I can't believe you just ordered me to move in with you and I agreed! Seriously, how do you *do* that?"

I laugh at her. She's back to her exasperated, adorable look.

"I can be very persuasive."

"Ya think?"

"I might be hard to live with, I obviously like to do things my way, but I promise you that I'll always be there for you, whatever you need."

"I know," she says quietly.

"I mean that Josie. After what you just went through..."

"I'm okay."

"Baby nobody would be okay after that."

"Well, call me weird then, but after you found me, and everything with Brian was finally over, I just knew everything was going to be okay for once in my life. I can't explain it, but it's like..."

"Like what?"

She looks away and I can tell whatever she's feeling is profound.

"Like I can finally breathe again. Like I finally have clean, fresh air surrounding me wherever I go. I'm not always struggling to find air, I'm surrounded with it, and it feels so good."

I guess she's not pretending.

"I can't tell you how happy I am to hear that." I say placing a kiss on her forehead.

"I can't tell you how happy I am that you quit being bossy."

There she is. The real Josie. Making me laugh, and standing steady in the aftermath of the storm.

Epilogue

Josie

I leaned into the mirror inspecting my make-up. I have more on than I would normally wear, but this is a special occasion. I moved in with Gunner a month ago and since then my life has turned inside out.

First, it took Freddy longer to heal than I hoped. I spent a lot of time with him, nursing him back to health. Gunner said Freddy was milking it, but I didn't care. Freddy risked his life for mine, and in the end, he helped save me. So I didn't listen to Gunner when he told me Freddy would adjust faster if I quit babying him. Instead I babied him so much that I now have the most spoiled pet on the planet. Seriously, if there were a spoiled rotten dog contest, Freddy would win. I'm good with that.

Second, now that my plotting and planning is finished, I realized I didn't have enough clients lined up to keep me busy. What's more, I haven't been able to spend much time at the gym with Kai since my injuries took a while to heal completely. This all resulted in Gunner bringing me work from his office after I pouted about not being able to do things. Let me tell you, I was good at this private investigator stuff. Marina and Trey were happy to have the help, so I kept doing more and more. Gunner liked that I was helping him, and I suspect he also liked that I was sitting behind my computer safe and sound in his apartment and not complaining anymore.

Third, moving is never easy. It takes a while to unpack and organize things the way you want them.

Fourth, my friends have been wanting to have a party to celebrate the end of my nightmare, and the beginning of me and Gunner, as well as Freddy's heroic act, not to mention Gunner and Hunter saving the day. Justine was all over it. However, I've been keeping her at bay, because of all of the aforementioned things, and the fact that Justine was *serious* about this party. When I mentioned having a get together at one of our homes, she about flipped her lid. So I told her if she was planning something fancy, she would have to wait until I could comfortably walk in heels again.

I graduated from slippers to sneakers, it was a slow process, but finally, I could wear cute shoes again. Funny how I never cared about shoes before Gunner. Once he took notice of me in sexy shoes, I had a whole new interest in them. Therefore, I had on a pair of black, glittery, strappy, four inch heels.

I had a moment when I first put them on, remembering when I tried to run in the red ones.

My thoughts automatically set on the fact that heels hindered running and that was a bad idea. Then I shook it off. I was going to be with Gunner, and he would appreciate these shoes. *A lot.*

Yippee!

After shaking it off I continued to put on my dress. Since Faith couldn't take me shopping, we sat at my computer and ordered a dress online. When it came, I was so excited that I wouldn't let Gunner see it.

I was also ecstatic that it fit well, because you just never know when you order things online. Honestly, if I could have tried it on in a store first I probably wouldn't have bought it. It hugs every curve I have, even the ones I don't like! It hits me at mid-thigh and travels up over the curve of my hips, showcasing my waist, and my ass, then it fits like a halter, only it twists over my chest so there is a keyhole giving a peek at my cleavage (okay, maybe a little more than a peek).

I take another look at myself. My hair is pulled up into curls on top of my head which is showing off my shoulders. There are some pieces escaping that give it a sexy look look. I have on pearl earrings and matching bracelet. I'm even wearing lip liner! Faith insisted.

I decide it's best to just walk out quickly, tell Gunner I'm ready so we can leave, kind of like pulling off a band aid. I have no idea how he will react to this outfit, and I'm feeling kind of shy about it.

I don't know where this party is going to be, but I insisted that it had to be somewhere Freddy could come. After all, he is a guest of honor. It would be rude to celebrate without him.

I open the bathroom door and walk into the bedroom. Gunner is buttoning up his blue slim fitting dress shirt over his black pants and I about trip over myself.

Good Lord!

My man looks good in blue any time, but he doesn't normally wear dress shirts. The one fits him so well, it makes his chest and arms look even bigger than normal. The fact that he rolls up the sleeves on his forearms and leaves it untucked with the top couple buttons undone... *wow!*

He freezes mid button and looks me over. Kind of how I'm looking him over, only I hope I don't look that hungry while I'm doing it. Even though I totally am.

He starts walking towards me, and I know that look in his eye.

Uh-oh.

When he gets close he runs his finger over the cleavage peeking out of my keyhole dress, then he traces my shoulder sending shivers through my body. This is not a good thing. I can't wear a bra with this dress and he's making my nipples hard. Of course, he doesn't miss that. His finger traces a path right back down my dress and right over one of my now pointy nipples.

"Turn around," he orders gruffly.

I don't know if that's such a good idea, because if he likes the front of the dress, he's definitely going to like the back. I turn slowly and I can see him behind me. The dresser and mirror are right in front of me. I keep turning so that I can make a full circle, but he stops me so that I'm still facing away from him. He makes a low throaty noise. Yep, he likes the back.

"Put your hands on the dresser."

"Um... but we're going to be late..."

"Hands on the dresser."

Alllrighty then.

I put my hands on the dresser which leaves me bending over slightly. I feel the back of my dress slide up over my bottom and there's no way it's sliding back down unless I pull it down. Next he pulls down my black lacy thong so that they're gathered around my ankles. I watch him crouch behind me and disappear, and then I feel one foot being lifted, then the other, and suddenly I'm pantiless. When he rises I can feel his breath across my back and I close my eyes in anticipation, but he moves away, sitting on the bed behind me.

"Spread your legs."

I comply, I mean, what's a girl to do?

"Now don't move."

I stand there with my ass out and my legs spread, instead of worrying about being late, I wonder if we can cancel.

Then I wonder what Gunner's doing back there, so I meet his eyes in the mirror.

Then I lower my eyes because I can see the bulge straining through his dress pants.

Yippee!

My body responds instantly. I can feel parts of me heating and swelling. I feel moisture gathering between my legs and suddenly it's hard to stand still.

Another glance tells me he's still looking. His hand has moved to the bulge and I see him rub his hand over it.

"Gunner..."

I was going to beg him to move, to touch me, to fuck me, anything but this torture.

"I'm going to be seeing this image in my head for a long time," he murmurs.

Well, I'm glad he's enjoying the view, but I want him to touch me. I contemplate giving him an even better image in hopes that he will. I bend over further wresting my elbows on the dresser and shift my legs a little wider, and just

486

for good measure, I slowly move my hips side to side while I turn and smile at him wantonly.

"Fuck."

Suddenly, he's off the bed and undoing his pants as he walks up behind me. Then within an instant, he's driving inside me. I can see the look on his face. It's feral and hungry and just watching it while feeling him pumping into me already has me on the edge.

I moan and whimper in pleasure, "Feels so good," I tell him.

He gives a growl and pulls me up and back against him, he literally has me off my feet but he's still inside me and before I can comprehend what he's doing he's sitting on the bed again, me on his lap, still facing away from him, his cock buried deep.

"Look," he says in my ear.

I look up to the mirror and almost can't believe what I see. It looks too naughty. Too sexy. It should probably be wrong, but I can't help it. The sight I see drives me wild.

Gunner has my legs spread wide and his knees are holding my legs open. I see his big hard cock disappearing as he pushes it inside me and I can see how wet it is when it slides back out. My dress is up around my waist. I can't help but stare. God, it looks *hot*.

Gunners face is beside mine and I see that look on his face that I knew was there, and I see him staring down at where we're connected and I know he likes the view as much as I do.

I start to move my hips slowly, savoring it. He undoes the halter of my dress behind my neck and it falls down below my breasts and he instantly starts tugging my nipples and rolling them with his fingers as we watch ourselves.

When his hand slides down the front of me and his big finger circles my clit and then presses harder, still circling, I can't take it anymore. I throw my head back to his shoulder and close my eyes.

"Gunner..."

"Fuck yeah baby, come all over me."

I let out a long shuddering moan as I do just that while he starts pounding into me using his hips. I look just in time to see it, and then feel his come fill me. God, it looks and feels so good that I have another orgasm washing over me before the first one finishes.

I stay there snuggled on his lap for a few minutes as we catch our breath. When reality has made its way back to me, I say, "So I guess you like my new dress?"

I feel his low rumble of laughter as he says, "You can say that again."

Gunner made me get off of his lap so I could get fixed up. *Again*. This time when I walked back out of the bathroom I said, "Behave!" and walked straight downstairs.

When we arrived at our destination, I couldn't believe it. I knew Justine was serious about this party, but I didn't know she was *that* serious.

She threw the party in the courtyard of an old manor house that wasn't far from town. I'd heard of it. It was rented for weddings and private parties, but I never imagined I would be attending a party there. The place felt decadent.

There was a fountain in the middle of the courtyard, around the upper patio were tables all burning with oil lamps. There was a gazebo decked out with fairy lights, and a huge sprawling green lawn that was adorned with topiaries. It was gorgeous!

It was enclosed, so I didn't mind when Freddy took off to start sniffing everything, I just hoped he wouldn't start peeing on all the beautiful landscaping.

Freddy looked pretty handsome, if I did say so myself. I'd put one of Gunner's bowties on him.

The night air was cool so I was glad I'd brought a pashmina to wrap up in. I just couldn't believe Justine had done this. I headed for a chair to sit down by where she was drinking a glass of champagne and talking with Isaiah.

"The guest of honor!" she yelled, then she said, "You're late!"

I know I turned red but I was hoping she didn't notice since it was getting dark and the lighting was dim.

Justine didn't miss much though, she murmured, "Mmmhmmm."

I decided to skip over that discussion altogether.

"I can't believe you rented this place," I told her.

"Well, I have to admit, I planned the party, but I didn't rent it by myself. We all pitched in."

"Really?" I breathed.

I couldn't believe that these people had thrown a party for *me*. Especially at a place like *this*.

Looking around, I was surprised by some of the attendants. Of course, Faith was there, along with Rick and Eddie. But Trey, Caleb, Mr. and Mrs. Williams, Marina (and what looked like her very attractive girlfriend) were there. Then I turned and saw Walker, Jack, and Kai huddled over on the other side of the patio, and Gunner was talking to an older couple that I knew right away were his parents. Tom and Lena.

I was so overwhelmed that I knew soon I would burst into tears if I didn't get myself under control.

"None of that," Justine said taking my hand and squeezing it.

"It's just so nice." I whispered.

"That's right, so don't forget who put this shindig together! Now let's go get some food, because let me tell you, we had this mother catered, and the spread is to die for!"

Apparently I had worked up an appetite earlier, because I couldn't wait to eat. I headed in the direction of Gunner because I figured he would want to eat too. When I approached his Dad gave me a warm smile and patted my shoulder, saying "There she is. Glad to see you looking so well, Josie."

I smiled up at him. I could see where Gunner got his stunning looks. I tried not to stare too long, looking at him made me miss my own dad something terrible.

I turned my gaze away and was caught in a tight hug and rocked back and forth while I tried not to fall off my shoes.

"Oh Josie, I know this has been hard on you, and we don't really know you, but if you ever need anything, we're here for you. Isn't that right Gunner?" Lena said turning an expectant look on him.

"Right mom, but Josie has me if she needs anything." He said.

"Well of course honey, but I mean if she needs something *not* from you."

"I'll take care of her, don't worry."

"I'm not worried, I just want Josie to know she can come to us."

Gunner opened his mouth to say something else, but I cut in and said, "Thank you, that means so much to me."

She wrapped me in another hug. I saw Gunner shake his head and look at his father who just shrugged as if to say *you know your mother*.

I got the impression that Lena was an emotional woman who took care of a lot of things and a lot of people, and she was the type of parent who would never stop being a parent just because her children were grown. I don't know if her children appreciated this, but they should. I would have to remember to share that with Gunner. I knew what it felt like to have a mom who didn't care, so I was elated that Lena was so lovely.

Before I got a chance to make it to the food, Faith, Justine, Rick and Eddie stood up on the patio and clinked their glasses to get everyone's attention.

"Oh no." I whispered. I was already on the verge of tears and I didn't want to cry in front of everyone. Gunner put his arm around my shoulders and squeezed my front to his side obviously knowing what I was afraid of. I wrapped my arms around him and put my head on his chest.

Justine started, "I want to thank everyone for coming and making this a special night."

I'd never heard Justine sound so serious and formal. I didn't know what to make of this.

"I especially want to thank our boy Freddy for protecting his mama." Tears stung my eyes and I looked down to see Freddy, who never got very far from me, lift his head in a regal pose like he knew he was being praised. "And for trying to tear that fu..." She stopped and cleared her throat and I saw Faith stifle a giggle.

"Anyway," she went on. "I also want to thank Gunner for walking into our lives and taking care of our girl. You're both heroes in my book."

There were hoots and clapping and I smiled up at Gunner to see him looking down at his feet with his jaw set. Okay, so apparently he didn't like public praise.

Justine stepped back and I thought of Hunter. He should be here celebrating too. He was another hero, but nobody had heard from him.

Faith stepped up and I saw her take a shaky breath. I swallowed because I knew she was going to say something to make me cry more. I knew this because if our roles were reversed I would be feeling what she's feeling right now.

She spoke, "I want to thank everyone who helped Josie, including Walker and Jack, and anyone who might not be present tonight." Then she paused.

I personally thought she should be included on that list. They all should but I had a feeling she was thinking of Hunter.

The she continued, "But mostly I want to thank Josie, for being my best friend for as long as I remember." I could hear the lump clogging her throat. She raised her glass and simply said, "I couldn't bear it if you were taken away," on a choked sob. Then she stepped back swiping away at her tears. I gave her a shaky smile through my own tears and blew her a kiss. She blew one back.

Rick stepped forward wiping his own tears and said, "JoJo, not only do you make the most awesome dip in the universe, but you're special to all of us. We're beyond happy that you're not only okay, but thriving, and can be here with us so we can celebrate the ending of a bad chapter in your life," at this he paused and raised his champagne glass and grandly stated, "and by the way, may he *rot!*" This got loud laughter and clapping. Then he continued saying, "Now it's time to celebrate the beginning of your fairytale."

I laughed through my tears as they all dispersed and Gunner held me tight. Eddie followed Rick towards the food and gave me a wink. He didn't make a speech but he didn't have to.

I was relieved they kept it short, and partially humorous because I was afraid I would end up with mascara smeared all over my face if they didn't. A girl could only take so much. And really, what more was there to say?

We finally got to eat, and Justine was right, the food was to *die* for. Lena came and sat next to me at one point asking for my dip recipe. This led to Gunner telling her about the trifle.

"Oh, I hope you'll be able to come for Thanksgiving this year. We can swap recipes!"

I told her I would love that, which made Gunner smile. Call me crazy, but swapping recipes with Gunner's mom sounded awesome.

The night wore on, and it was one I would never forget. I danced with Gunner and then his dad. Walker swept me away next, and then Kai, who I thanked personally for everything he taught me. He patted my shoulder and told me he was proud of me. Honestly, I wanted to cry at hearing those words, so instead I hugged him tight and finished the dance.

I danced so much that my feet were killing me (in a good way). And I had to take off my pashmina because I was feeling warm all over.

However, I think this might have been a mistake, because when I looked at Gunner he was staring at me in a way that made me even hotter. I could tell by the look that he was remembering the visions from earlier. This made me think about the things I'd watched us do in the mirror earlier too. Then I started wondering what it would be like to have sex behind a topiary. Gunner recognized my look too, because I heard him mumble, "Fuck."

I grinned at him.

He walked to me with a straight face.

I grinned some more.

He ran his hands down my arms and I shivered even as I kept grinning and whispered, "Ever played Lord of the manor?"

He shook his head, "No, but I'm game."

"You think we can hide behind a topiary?"

"We can do better than that. We have a room upstairs."

"Seriously?" I whispered my grin getting even bigger.

He nodded. "You know, if I'm the Lord of the manor, then you have to obey my wishes."

"Okay." I sighed dreamily.

He chuckled and murmured, "Fuck yeah."

I giggled and said, "I need to talk to Faith though, before she leaves." I'd been looking for her since her speech and was getting worried.

"She's staying here too, everyone is."

Wow! I seriously had the best friends in the world!

"Maybe she's in her room, I've been trying to find her."

"We'll find her in the morning." He said dragging me towards the doors.

"What about Freddy?"

Gunner turned and let out a whistle and Freddy mosied our way.

"Freddy gets to sleep in the manor too?"

"Baby, Freddy stays where we stay."

I loved that. Gunner and Freddy were bonded now and that pleased me greatly. The man I loved, loved my dog, and that made me love him even more. Besides, if your man didn't love your dog, then he was not the man for you. I firmly believed this.

"I should really thank Justine again and..."

Gunner kissed me, effectively shutting me up.

"We'll see everyone at breakfast. Right now, we're done talking to people. We're going to do other things."

"Like what?" I asked, even though I totally knew what.

"Baby, quit messing around unless you want me to lift that dress up and fuck you again right here."

Gulp!

"Um... that wouldn't be good."

He grinned this time. "Oh yes it would."

I smacked his arm and rolled my eyes as he dragged me by my hand through the manor and up the stairs to a lovely room with a great big bed.

Once he got me there, he did things to me that made me think that he might really be a Lord after all. At least he was the Lord of my manor, if you know what I mean.

When we were curled around each other about ready to drift off to sleep, I whispered, "This is the best night of my life."

He gave me a squeeze and whispered back, "They're only going to get better from here."

I sighed thinking about that happy thought.

"Go to sleep," he whispered in my ear and then touched his lips to mine before settling in a comfortable position.

"Yes, M'Lord," I tried to say in an English accent with a straight face, but totally failed and giggled. In fact I thought that was so funny I couldn't stop giggling.

I only stopped when Gunner pushed me to my back and rose over me putting his mouth on mine.

K. D. Smith

<u>Stay tuned...</u>

Hunter and Faith's story, will be told in *Finding Faith* the second book of *The Layne Series*.

For more information connect with K. D. Smith online: www.KDSmithAuthor.com

Facebook: Like the **K. D. Smith** fan page, or send a friend request to:
www.facebook.com/K.D.Smith.Author

Twitter: @KDSmithAuthor

Email: KDSmith.Author@yahoo.com

K. D. Smith